# a
# song
# for
# summer

# Eva
# Ibbotson

## WITH AN INTRODUCTION BY ELLA RISBRIDGER

**MACMILLAN**

*For my family, with love and gratitude*

First published in Great Britain 1997 by Arrow Books
Published 2006 by Young Picador

This edition published 2019 by Pan Books
an imprint of Pan Macmillan
20 New Wharf Road, London N1 9RR
Associated companies throughout the world
www.panmacmillan.com

ISBN 978-1-5290-1224-8

1 3 5 7 9 8 6 4 2

A CIP catalogue record for this book is available from
the British Library.

Typeset by Intype Libra Limited and Nigel Hazle
Printed and bound by CPI Group (UK) Ltd, Croydon CR0 4YY

# INTRODUCTION

I object to introductions as a point of principle – I think they are impossible to write or read without spoiling the story. So why did I write this? Because – when you get right down to it – there is almost nothing better in the world than getting to really explain why you love something you love and have loved for a long time.

We don't spend enough time talking about Eva Ibbotson and not nearly enough time talking about her adult novels. And I love them *so* much. I love all of Eva Ibbotson's books, but especially these – her romance novels – her grown-up books.

Everything about the romantic novels she once described as having written 'for old ladies, and people with flu', ought to be sentimental, ought to be slush. They aren't. They are perfectly observed worlds full of people doing the most human of things in the most human of ways, written with care and consideration and practical talent, deftly and diligently applied.

Nobody writes like Eva Ibbotson – literally. An Eva Ibbotson sentence is obviously and clearly an Eva Ibbotson sentence. 'Person' is an Eva Ibbotson word, 'particular' is an Eva Ibbotson word, 'one' is an Eva Ibbotson word. The drift of an ellipsis, the emphatic twist of italics, the faintest hint of a tidy German sentence structure underneath the fluid and lovely prose. There is a secret precision to writing like this that stops it from ever being purely sentimental. There is of course an acknowledgement that sentiment should have its place in our lives, but that it also deserves to be afforded a little dignity.

Ibbotson's writing *always* has dignity to it: dignity, and courtesy, and a common sense that doesn't relinquish (and never steamrolls) the romantic. I mean the romantic in its broadest sense: that these are romantic novels, as well as romance novels. The word 'romance' comes from the old French *roumant*, a tale of courtly love. And there is something fundamentally courtly about Eva Ibbotson's stories – some sense of fair play, goodness, manners, and trying to do the right thing. Almost always someone is longing for someone else from afar, but held back by their sense of what is *right*.

Both Quin and Ruth in *The Morning Gift* are so terrified of taking advantage of the other that they manage to avoid each other for two thirds of the novel; Anna in *The Secret Countess* knows that she can't break up the engagement between the Earl of Westerholme and Muriel Hardwicke, the repulsive heiress who will save his home. And here, in *A Song for Summer*, Marek will not do anything to disrupt Ellen's 'relationship' with the infinitely pathetic Kendrick Frobisher.

And yet, Kendrick acquires a happy ending of a kind and so too does the abhorrent Muriel. In fact, so do nearly all of the antagonists in Ibbotson's grown-up novels. They might not be the happy endings you'd wish for yourself, or for your heroines – they are strange and a little bit awkward and often very funny. But they are happiness of a sort. Muriel for example pursues a glorious future in eugenics and seems wholly satisfied with the arrangement. (Kendrick, by the way, is last seen in a cheerful sex scene involving a stuffed osprey.)

Because, somehow, this is the kind of ending that is *fair*. And I think Eva Ibbotson cared a great deal about fairness. Ellen's 'morality, though fervent, was her own' and the same is true in many ways of Ibbotson's writing. These are mostly very moral books, although never preachy – there is a pragmatic, practical goodness to them that relies not on what people say, so much as what people *do*.

The structure beneath the trappings of Eva's depiction of romance is goodness and practicality, sound and true and solid. 'Your beautiful state of mind is totally irrelevant,' Marek says, in a speech that ought to be required reading for anybody who wants to make things. 'Write something – then it's there. If it's what you wanted to write, if it exists, then leave it. If it doesn't, throw it away.' For Marek, and for Ibbotson, it's no good thinking noble thoughts if you don't try to live up to them.

This doesn't mean you have to be perfect, or indeed that notions of 'perfection' are in any way desirable. You just have to try your best with what you've got: a talent for dancing, perhaps, or an outdated manual for housework, or an inexplicable desire to go to Austria just as Europe begins to fall apart, as in *A Song for Summer*. People are complicated and they try really hard. Sometimes it works and sometimes terrible things happen anyway. Ibbotson somehow manages to effortlessly fit those complicated, vivid characters into what might otherwise so easily have been paint-by-numbers cardboard cut-outs.

What, for instance, could be more 'romance novel hero' than a secret aristocrat? A secret aristocrat who is also the greatest composer of his time. Oh, *and* a hero of the Resistance, the son of a revolutionary and an English rose, brought up speaking many languages and tending to wild creatures with his elegant, capable hands. He makes wheels for paralyzed tortoises and throws Nazis out of windows. He has had many glamorous lovers, none of whom he loves as much as our heroine. He is the most fanciable man *of all time*, and yet, somehow, in Ibbotson's hands, he is also a *person*.

He is flawed in big ways and in small: he throws a small boy into a lake and leaves Ellen for no good reason other than that he is unhappy about something unrelated. He has the quick temper of so many Ibbotson heroes – frequently stubborn, irritatingly hopeful and occasionally wildly impulsive. Marek 'is a person much addicted to abundance' we learn, which should make him awful but just makes him more himself; just as Ellen's desire to leave behind the protofeminism of her aunts ought to make her seem small or weak to us today, but does exactly the opposite.

Ibbotson delights in showing us the depth and richness of human experience and character. There's a real joy in the way she pulls the rug out from under any assumptions you might be tempted to make about her characters. She isn't perfect, of course (there's sometimes an unnuanced sense of class and money here that belongs in a fairy tale) but she, like her best characters, *tries*.

In the hands of a less gifted writer, Ellen's colleague Chomsky's scar *might* have come from the camps (as she assumes), misunderstood pupil Leon's oppression *might* be cause for his horrible behaviour towards the other children, and the hypocritical big chat about the 'proletariat' might be left to stand unchallenged. For even these background characters are complicated: clingy Sophie who wants to wear clean white socks and go to bed on time, cross lonely Bruno, pretentious Hermine Ritter, PhD, with her natural daughter Andromeda kept tucked down the front of her practical sacking smock. Idealistic, in-love, broken Bennet, FitzAllan who just wants his awful, awful musical to be performed as he wants it to be performed, even Tamara with her terror of being found out. We *understand* all of these people. We understand why her aunts, suffragettes to their bones, are so afraid of their niece's desire to scrub floors and bake Kipferl and we understand why that same desire must be acknowledged.

We understand why all these small things are important. Why, in fact, the small things are the *only* things that really matter. All sweeping ideologies fall down before the small things of really living. Ellen is afraid of 'not being able to see . . . not seeing because you're obsessed by something that blots out the world'. It is this dedication to really *seeing* the things of the world that I love most about Eva Ibbotson, about this book, and really about being alive at all. Eva Ibbotson taught me to see eternity in a scrubbing brush, in a bowl of fruit – and I hope she does the same for you.

*Ella Risbridger, May 2019*

# PART 1

# 1

In a way they were born to be aunts. Emancipated, eccentric and brave, the Norchester sisters lived in a tall grey house in Bloomsbury, within a stone's throw of the British Museum.

It is a district known for its intellectuals. Blue plaques adorn many of the houses, paying tributes to the dead dons and scholars who once inhabited them and even the professors and librarians who were still alive walked through the quiet London squares with the abstracted look of those whose minds are on higher things.

No. Three Gowan Terrace, the home of Charlotte, Phyllis and Annie Norchester, belonged firmly in this tradition. It was a three-storey house of amazing discomfort. The furniture was dark and disregarded; the bedrooms contained only narrow beds, desks and outsize typewriters; in the drawing room the chairs were arranged in rows to face a large table and a notice board. Yet in its own way the house was a shrine. For the sisters, now middle-aged, had belonged to that stalwart band of women who had turned their back on feminine frippery, and devoted their whole beings to the securing of votes for women.

Charlotte, the oldest, had been for six weeks on hunger strike in Holloway Prison; Phyllis had spent more time chained to the railing of the hated women's gallery in the Houses of Parliament than any other suffragette; and Annie, the youngest, had knocked off the helmets of no less than seven policemen before being dragged away, kicking and protesting, to join her sister in prison.

It had been a glorious time. Victory had come in 1918 when the heroic work of women in the Great War could no longer be gainsaid. But though women had had the vote now for some twenty years, the sisters were faithful to the cause. The curtains – in the suffragette colours of purple, green and white – might be frayed and dusty but they would never be removed. The picture of their leader, Mrs Emmeline Pankhurst, still hung in the dining room, though she herself had been dead for many years and was now a statue on Victoria Embankment. Rubbing themselves down with the frayed, rough towels in the bathroom with its cake of carbolic soap and rusty geyser reminded them of those heady days being hosed down by brutal wardresses in prison; the boiled fish served to them by the elderly cook general scarcely differed from the food they had thrown out of the windows of their cells as they began their hunger strike. And the suffragette motto, *They Must Give Us Freedom Or They Must Give Us Death* was still written in large letters on a poster in the hall.

But if they played the 'Do you remember?' game as they sat in their Jaeger dressing gowns drinking their cocoa, Charlotte and Phyllis and Annie never forgot how much was still owed to women even though the vote was won.

Charlotte had qualified as a doctor and was now Senior Registrar at the Bloomsbury Hospital for Women – a brisk and busy person who wore her stethoscope as society women wore their pearls. Phyllis was the principal of a teacher training college and Annie was the only female professor of Applied Mycology, not only in the University of London, but in the whole of Britain.

They might thus have rested on their laurels, but they did not. Every week there were meetings in the ice-cold drawing room: meetings to proclaim the need for more women in Parliament, in the universities, on the committee of the League of Nations. Lecturers came to discourse on the evils of female circumcision in Bechuanaland, on the shamefully low intake of women in the legal profession, on the scandalous discrimination against girls in Higher Mathematics. Leaflets were circulated, articles written, meetings addressed and as the Twenties moved into the Thirties and the canker of Fascism arose in Germany and Italy and Spain, women were urged to declare themselves against Hitler with his dread doctrine of *Kinder, Kirche und Kuche* which threatened to put them back into the Middle Ages.

But it was during this decade that something disquieting began to be felt in Gowan Terrace, a development as unexpected as it was difficult to deal with, and it concerned Charlotte's only daughter, Ellen.

None of the Norchester sisters had intended to marry but in the year 1913 a brave and beautiful women named Emily Davison threw herself under the King's horse in the Derby to draw attention to the suffragette cause, and was killed. It was at her funeral that Charlotte found herself standing next to a good-looking gentleman who, when she faltered (for she had loved Emily), took her arm and led her from the open grave. His name was Alan Carr, he was a solicitor and sympathetic to the movement. They married and a year later their child was born.

It was, fortunately, a girl, whom they named Ellen, and Alan had time to dote on her and spoil her before he was killed at Ypres. The baby was enchanting: plump and dimpled with blonde curls and big brown eyes – the kind of person found in paintings leaning out of heaven and bestowing laurel leaves or garlands on deserving mortals down below.

What mattered, however, was that she was clever. Every possible kind of intelligence test proclaimed that all was very well and her mother, Dr Carr, and her aunts, Phyllis and Annie, spared no effort to stimulate the little creature's mind. This girl at least should not struggle for her opportunities. Oxford or Cambridge were a certainty, followed by a higher degree and then who knew . . . an ambassadorship, a seat in the cabinet – nothing was out of Ellen's reach.

So they did not, at first, feel in the least alarmed. All little girls picked daisies and arranged them in paste jars, usually in inconvenient places, and Dr Carr, bidden imperiously by her daughter to smell them, duly did so though the scent of daisies is not easily perceived by someone accustomed to the strong odours of lysol and chloroform. It was natural for little girls to bake buns and Ellen, perched on a stool beside the usually morose cook general with her curls tied in a handkerchief, was a sight that her mother and her aunts could appreciate. Children made little gardens and planted love-in-a-mist and forget-me-nots, and for Ellen to claim a patch of earth in the sooty square of ground behind the house which all the sisters were far too busy to cultivate, was natural. But children's gardens are generally outgrown and Ellen's little patch extended until she had cultivated a whole flower bed and then she found cuttings of honeysuckle and clematis and trained them to climb up to the first-floor windows.

Then again there was the question of the maids. It was of course all right for children to help servants: servants after all were a kind of underclass and should have been liberated except that it wasn't easy to see how to run a house without them. But it soon became clear that Ellen *enjoyed* making beds and polishing the grate and setting fires. They would find her folding sheets and putting her nose voluptuously against the starched linen. Once when the maid was ill they came across her with her school uniform hitched up, scrubbing the floor, and she said: 'Look, isn't it beautiful, the way the light catches the soap bubbles!'

Did she perhaps do altogether too much looking? The sisters had read their Blake; they knew it was desirable to see the world in a grain of sand and eternity in an hour. But the world in a scrubbing brush? The world in a bowl of fruit?

'Perhaps she's going to be a painter?' suggested Aunt Phyllis.

A great woman painter, the first female president of the Royal Academy? It was a possibility.

But Ellen didn't want to paint apples. She wanted to smell them, turn them in her hands and eat them.

Other members of the sisterhood were called in, honorary aunts to the child, and consulted: Aunt Delia, an inky lady who ran the Left Book Club Shop in Gower Street, and the headmistress of Ellen's school, a full-bosomed and confident person whose bottle-green girls were the most academically motivated in London.

'She *is* clever, isn't she?' Dr Carr demanded. 'You wouldn't lie to me, Lydia, after all we've been through together.'

And Lydia, who had shared a cell with Charlotte after they threw a brick through the windows of No. 10 Downing Street, said:

'I tell you she is very bright indeed. Her last exam results were excellent.'

But at the end of the following term Ellen came to

her and asked if she could take cookery lessons in the Sixth Form.

'Cookery! But my dear, that's just for the girls who aren't going to university.'

'I don't want to go to university,' said Ellen. 'I want to go to a domestic science college. A proper one where they teach you to sew and to cook and clean. I want,' she said, opening her soft brown eyes in a look of entreaty, 'to use my hands.' And she spread them in the air, as pianists spread their fingers over an invisible keyboard, as if cooking was equivalent to the playing of a Chopin étude.

In facing this crisis, Ellen's mother and her aunts knew whom to blame. A woman who was the embodiment of everything they disliked in their sex: an abject doormat, a domestic slave, a person without a mind or will of her own – an Austrian peasant who kept house for Ellen's grandfather and whom Ellen, since the age of six, had inexplicably adored.

The grandfather in question did not come from the Norchester side of the family. He was Alan Carr's father; a scholar engaged in a great work, the compilation of a glossary of Greek fishes, which seemed unlikely to be completed before he died. He had travelled to Vienna shortly after the end of the war to consult some manuscripts in the Hofburg library and had taken lodgings in an inn in Nussdorf, where Henny, the landlady's daughter, had looked after him. She was a quiet, fair girl, gentle and deft, who both admired and pitied the serious Professor, for he had lost a son in the war and a wife soon afterwards with cancer.

When he returned to Britain he asked her if she would come and keep house for him and she agreed.

No house was ever so 'kept' as Walnut Tree Cottage in Wimbledon. Henny cooked the Professor's meals and washed his clothes and polished his furniture but she did much, much more. She found the pieces of paper with their Greek hieroglyphics which he had dropped on to the floor; she warmed his slippers; she cultivated the little London garden in which, inexplicably, there was no sign of a walnut tree.

'Well, you see, he is a very clever man and I like to make him comfortable,' was the only defence she could put up against the shocked comments of Ellen's family.

After she had been with him for three years the Professor said he thought they should be married.

Henny refused. She was not of his world, she said; it would not be suitable. She had shared his bed from the start, understanding that this was as important to gentlemen as the proper preparation of their food and the certainty of hot water for their baths, but when visitors came she retreated to the kitchen which alone she had claimed for herself and turned into a replica of the country kitchen in the Austrian mountains where she had grown up.

Ellen was six years old when she was first taken to Wimbledon. Wandering away from the drawing room, where literature was being discussed, she found Henny with a cullender in front of her, shelling peas.

Afterwards Henny always remembered the child's first words. She did not say 'I want to help,' or 'Can I help?' She said: 'I *have* to help.'

So it began. In Henny's kitchen with its scrubbed table and red and white checked curtains, its potted geranium and cuckoo clock, she spent the hours of her greatest happiness. Together she and Henny tended the little garden with its rockery of alpine flowers; they baked *Krapfen* and *Buchteln* and embroidered cross-stitch borders on the towels. Ellen learnt to hang up muslin to make *Topfen* and that cucumber salad could have a smell – and she learnt that it was all right to be pretty. Being pretty had worried her because she had noticed that when visitors came and praised her silky curls or big brown eyes, her mother and her aunts had not been pleased. But Henny laughed and said being pretty came from God and gave people pleasure and it meant one had to brush one's hair and buff one's nails just as one had to scour out the saucepans to keep them shining.

Henny held coloured stuffs against her face and said, look how it brings out the gold of your eyes, and without her saying a word about love, Ellen knew that Henny loved her, and loved the selfish old Professor with his Greek fishes, and learnt that this much discussed emotion could be about doing and serving and not about what one said.

One day they were making *Apfel Strudel*. The white cloth was spread on the table and they were lifting the paper-thin dough from below . . . lifting it with spread

11

fingers so slowly, so gently, making it thin and ever thinner without once letting it go into holes, and Henny stopped for a moment and said more seriously than she usually spoke: 'You have a real talent, *Hascherl*. A proper one.'

Even so, when the time came to choose her career, Ellen didn't have the heart to rebel; she took her Higher Certificate and went to Cambridge to read Modern Languages because she spoke German already and was extremely fond of chatting. As it happened, not much chatting went on during her tutorials and her supervisor found the Austrian dialect in which she recited Schiller's poetry singular in the extreme. But she liked Cambridge well enough – the river and the Backs, and the friendly young men who paid her compliments and took her punting and asked her to dances. She learnt to deflect their proposals of marriage and made good friends among her fellow students, the shopkeepers and the ducks.

With Kendrick Frobisher she was less adroit. He was a blond, serious, painfully thin young man of twenty-eight with pale blue eyes, and belonged to her life in London, where he assiduously attended the meetings at Gowan Terrace, addressed envelopes and showed a proper concern for the Higher Education of Women.

Kendrick was the youngest son of a domineering mother who lived in Cumberland and had, when she was a young woman, personally delivered a camel on the way to church. This had happened in India, where

12

she grew up, the daughter of an army colonel stationed in Poona. The camel was pregnant and in difficulties and though she was only nineteen years old, Kendrick's mother had unhesitatingly plunged an arm into its interior and done what was necessary before passing on, indifferent to her blood-stained dress and ruined parasol, to worship God.

Returning to Britain to marry a landowner, this redoubtable woman had produced two sons, young men who hunted, shot, fished and would presently marry. Then came Kendrick, who was a disappointment from the start – an unsporting, pale, nervous boy who was bullied at school and read books.

In the London Library, researching the minor metaphysical poets on whom he was planning a monograph, or at the many lectures, art exhibitions and concerts he attended, Kendrick was happy enough, but real people terrified him. It was causes that he espoused, and what more worthy cause than the education of women and the emancipation from slavery of the female sex?

So he started to attend the meetings in Gowan Terrace and there found Ellen handing round sandwiches.

'The egg and cress ones are nice,' she said – and that was that.

Because he was so obviously a person that one did not marry, Ellen was not careful as she was with the young men who kissed her in punts. It seemed to her sad to have a mother who had delivered a camel on the way to church, and Kendrick had other problems.

'What is your house like?' she asked him once, for he lived in a small bachelor flat in Pimlico and seldom went home. 'Wet,' he had answered sadly.

'Wetter than other houses?' she wanted to know.

Kendrick said yes. His home was in the Lake District, in Borrowdale, which had the highest rainfall in England. He went on to explain that as well as being wet, it was red, being built of a particular kind of sandstone which became crimsoned in the rain.

Realising that it could not be easy to live in a wet red house with two successful older brothers and a mother who had delivered a camel on the way to church, Ellen was kind to him. She accompanied him to concerts and to art galleries and to plays without scenery, and smiled at him, her mind on other things, when he paid her compliments.

These were not the ordinary kind: they involved Kendrick in hours of pleasurable research in libraries and museums. Ellen's hair had darkened to an unsensational light brown and she had, to her great relief, largely outgrown her dimples, but in finding painters and poets who had caught the way her curls fell across her brow, or the curve of her generous mouth, he was on fertile ground.

'Look, Ellen,' he would say, 'here's a portrait of Sophronia Ebenezer by Raphael. Or it may only be by the School of Raphael,' he would add conscientiously.

'The attribution isn't certain. But she's tilting her head just like you tilt yours when you listen.'

In the delectable Nell Gwyn Kendrick discerned the curve of Ellen's throat and her bestowing glance, and Wordsworth's lines: 'She was a phantom of delight' might have been penned with her in mind. Even music yielded its images: the Scherzo of Beethoven's Fifth Symphony seemed to him to mirror precisely her effervescent capacity for joy.

Aware that he was enjoying himself, Ellen was caught quite unawares when he followed her into the kitchen one day as she was making coffee and forgetting Sophronia Ebenezer and Nell Gwyn and even Beethoven, seized one of her hands and said in a voice choked with emotion: 'Oh Ellen, I love you so much. Won't you please, please marry me?'

Too late did Ellen reproach herself and assure him that she did not love him, could not marry him, did not intend to marry anyone for a very long time. It would have been as well to try to deprive Sir Perceval of his quest for the Grail as persuade Kendrick that all was lost. He would wait, if need be for years, he would not trouble her, all he asked was to serve her family, address even more envelopes, attend even more meetings – and be allowed to glimpse her as she went about her work.

Ellen could hardly forbid him her mother's house; there was nothing to do except hope that he would grow out of so one-sided a passion. And during her last year at university something happened which put the erudite young man entirely out of her mind.

Henny fell ill. She had terminal cancer and Professor Carr, whom she had served with her life, proposed to send her to the geriatric ward of the local hospital to die.

Like many peasants, Henny was terrified of hospitals. Ellen now stopped trying to please her relatives. She left college three months before her finals and told her grandfather that Henny would die in her own bed and she would nurse her.

She had help, of course, excellent local nurses who came by day, but most of the time they spent together, she and Henny, and they made their own world. Herr Hitler was eliminated, as was Mussolini, strutting and braying in Rome. Even the clamour of King George's Silver Jubilee scarcely reached them.

During this time which, strangely, was not unhappy, Henny went back to her own childhood in the lovely Austrian countryside in which she had grown up. She spoke of the wind in the pine trees, the cows with their great bells, about her brothers and sisters, and the *Alpenglühen* when in the hour of sunset the high peaks turned to flame.

And again and again she spoke about the flowers. She spoke about the gentians and the edelweiss and the tiny saxifrages clinging to the rocks, but there was one flower she spoke of in a special voice. She called it a *Kohlröserl* – a little coal rose – but it was not a rose. It was a small black orchid with a tightly furled head.

'It didn't look much, but oh Ellie, the scent! You could smell it long before you found the flowers. In the books they tell you it smells like vanilla, but if so, it's like vanilla must smell in heaven. You must go, *Liebling*. You must go and put your face to them.'

'I will, Henny. I'll bring back a root and –'

But she didn't finish and Henny patted her hand and smiled, for they both knew that she was not a person who wanted things dug up and planted on her grave.

'Just find them and tell them . . . thank you,' said Henny.

A few days later she spoke of them again: 'Ah yes, *Kohlröserl*,' she said – and soon afterwards she died.

Ellen didn't go back to finish her degree. She enrolled at the Lucy Hatton School of Cookery and Household Management and Henny was right, she did have talent. She graduated *summa cum laude* and her mother and her aunts and Kendrick Frobisher watched her receive her diploma. As she came off the platform with her prizes, grace touched Dr Charlotte Carr, who was a good woman, and she threw her arms round her daughter and said: 'We're all so proud of you, my darling. Really so very proud.'

And three months later, in the spring of 1937, answering an advertisement in the *Lady*, Ellen set off for Austria to take up a domestic post in a school run by an Englishman and specialising in Music, Drama and the Dance.

# 2

It was listed in the guide books as an important castle and definitely worth a detour, but Schloss Hallendorf had nothing to do with drawbridges or slits for boiling oil. Built by a Habsburg count for his mistress, its towers housed bedrooms and boudoirs, not emplacements for guns; pale blue shutters lay folded against pink walls, roses climbed towards the first-floor windows.

Carinthia is Austria's most southern province; anything and everything grows there. In the count's pleasure gardens, morning glory wreathed itself round oleander bushes, jasmine tumbled from pillars, stone urns frothed with geraniums and heliotrope. Behind the house, peaches and apricots ripened in the orchards and the rich flower-studded meadows sloped gently upwards towards forests of larch and pine. And to the front, where stone steps descended to the water and black swans came to be fed, was a view which no one who saw it ever forgot: over the lake to the village and up . . . up . . . to the snowy zigzag of the high peaks.

But the Habsburg counts fell on hard times. The castle stood empty, housed wounded soldiers in the Great War . . . fell empty again. Then in the year 1928, an Englishman named Lucas Bennet took over the lease and started his school.

Ellen stood by the rails of the little steamer and looked back at the village with its wooden houses, the inn with its terrace and chestnut trees, the church on a small promontory. It was a serious church; not onion-domed but with a tall, straight spire.

In the fields above the village she could see piebald cows as distinct as wooden toys. Were they feasting on Henny's *Kohlröserl*, those fortunate Austrian cows?

There was still snow on the summits, but down on the lake the breeze was warm. It had been a moment of sheer magic, coming through the Mallnitz tunnel and finding herself suddenly in the south. She had left London in fog and drizzle; here it was spring. The hanging baskets in the stations were filled with hyacinths and narcissi, candles unfurled on the chestnut trees; she had seen lemon trees and mimosa.

The steamer which rounded the lake three times a day was steeped in self-importance. The maximum amount of bustle accompanied the loading and unloading of passengers, of crates, of chickens in hampers – and the captain was magnificently covered in gold braid.

They stopped at a convent where two nuns came out with wheelbarrows to fetch their provisions, passed a small wooded island and stopped again by a group of holiday houses.

'That's where Professor Steiner lives,' said an old peasant woman in a black kerchief, pointing to a small house with green shutters standing alone by the water's edge. 'He didn't get on with the Nazis so he lives here now.' The boat drew away again and she moved closer to Ellen. 'You're bound for the school then?' she asked.

Ellen turned and smiled. 'Yes.'

'Visiting someone?'

'No. I'm going to work there.'

A rustle of consternation spread from the old woman to her neighbours. They drew closer.

'You don't want to go there. It's a bad place. It's evil. Godless.'

'Devilish,' agreed another crone. 'It's the devil that rules there.'

Ellen did not answer. They had rounded the point and suddenly Schloss Hallendorf lay before her, its windows bathed in afternoon light, and it seemed to her that she had never seen a place so beautiful. The sun caressed the rose walls, the faded shutters . . . greening willows trailed their tendrils at the water's edge; a magnificent cypress sheltered the lower terrace.

But oh so neglected, so shabby! A tangle of creepers seemed to be all that held up the boathouse; a shutter flapped on its hinges on an upstairs window; the yew hedges were fuzzy and overgrown. And this of course only made it lovelier, for who could help thinking of the Sleeping Beauty and a castle in a fairy tale? Except that, as they came in to land, Ellen saw the words EURYTHMICS IS CRAP painted on the walls of a small Greek temple by the water's edge.

'The children are wild,' hissed the old woman into her ear. 'They're like wild animals.'

The steamer gave an imperious hoot. A boy came forward with a rope.

'You can always come back,' called a youth in lederhosen. 'They'll find room for you at the inn.'

Ellen made her way down the gangway, left her suitcase and walked slowly along the wooden jetty. There was a scent of heliotrope. Two house martins darted in and out of the broken roof of the boathouse with its tangle of clematis and ivy – and in the water beside it she saw, among the bulrushes, a round black head.

An otter? An inland seal?

The head rose, emerged and turned out to be attached to the somewhat undernourished body of a small and naked man.

It was too late to look away. Ellen stared and found unexpected feelings rise in her breast. She could feed him up, whoever he was; help him, perhaps to cut his hair – but nothing now could be done about the manic zigzag which ran like disordered lightning across his lower abdomen.

'Chomsky,' said the dripping figure suddenly. 'Laszlo Chomsky. Metalwork,' – and with extreme formality, he clicked his heels together and bowed.

Which at least explained what had happened. A Hungarian, born perhaps in the wildness of the *puszta*; a place abundantly supplied with horses, geese and windmills, but lacking entirely the skilled doctors who could deal competently with an inflamed appendix.

Moving up the shallow stone steps which lifted themselves in tiers between the terraces towards the house, she saw a girl of about twelve come running down towards her.

'I'm late,' said the child anxiously. 'We forgot the steamer's on the summer schedule now. I'm supposed to be meeting the new matron but she hasn't come.'

Ellen smiled at the first of the 'wild' children to come her way. She had long dark hair worn in pigtails which were coming unfurled, and a sensitive, narrow face with big grey eyes. Her white ankle socks were not a pair and she looked tired.

Ellen put out her hand. 'Yes she has; I'm her,' she said. 'I'm Ellen Carr.'

The wild child shook it. 'I'm Sophie,' she said, and put one foot behind the other and bobbed a curtsy. The next minute she blushed a fiery red. 'Oh I'm sorry. I shouldn't have done that.'

'Done what?'

'Curtsied. No one does it here like they don't go to bed much and they don't wear white socks, but I haven't been here very long and in Vienna in my convent it was all different.'

'I liked it,' said Ellen, 'but I won't give you away. However I have to tell you that now I'm here people *will* go to bed and if they want to wear white socks they will wear them *and* they'll match and be clean.'

The child turned to her, transfigured. 'Will you do that? Can you really?' Then her face fell; the look of anxiety returned. For Ellen Carr had shoulder-length tumbled hair and gentle eyes; she wore a green jacket the colour of moss and a skirt that made you want to touch it, it looked so soft. And that meant lovers – lots of lovers – as it had meant with Sophie's mother, who was beautiful too and had left Vienna for Paris and Paris for London because of lovers and was now in Ireland making a film and did not write. 'No,' she said. 'You'll fall in love and go away.'

'No I won't,' said Ellen.

She put her arm round Sophie's shoulders but their progress towards the house was slow. A pink camellia detained Ellen and a white snail, fragile as a snowflake, swaying on a blade of grass.

Then suddenly she stopped. 'Sophie, what on earth is that?'

They had reached the first of the level terraces. Coming across a patch of grass towards them at an amazing speed was a tortoise. It looked much as tortoises do, its neck extended, its demeanour purposeful – but fastened to its back end was a small platform with two wheels on which it scooted as if on roller skates.

'It's Achilles,' said Sophie. 'His back legs were paralysed and he was dragging himself along. We thought we'd have to have him destroyed and then Marek came and made him those wheels.'

Ellen bent down to the tortoise and picked him up. Retreating only briefly into his shell, Achilles submitted to being turned upside down. The contraption supporting his withered legs was unbelievably ingenious: a little trolley screwed to his shell and supporting two highly oiled metal wheels.

She put him down again and the tortoise scooted away over the grass like greased lightning.

'It took Marek hours to do. He shut himself up in the workshop and wouldn't let anyone come near.'

'Who's Marek?' Ellen asked – but before Sophie could answer, a stentorian and guttural voice somewhere to their right cried: 'No, no, *no*! You are not being rigid, you are not being steel. You are not being pronged. You must feel it in your spine, the metal, or you cannot become a fork!'

Deeply curious, Ellen crossed the terrace. A second, smaller set of steps led down on to an old bowling green surrounded by a yew hedge. On it stood a large woman with cropped hair wearing a hessian tabard and a pair of men's flannel trousers, shouting instructions to a dozen or so children lying on their backs on the lawn.

'Now open the fingers . . . open them but not with softness. With these fingers you will spear . . . you will jab . . . you will pierce into the meat.'

'That's Hermine. Dr Ritter,' whispered Sophie. 'She's terribly clever – she's got a PhD in Dramatic

24

Movement from Berlin University. She makes us be bunches of keys and forks and sometimes we have to give birth to ourselves.'

But before the children could exhibit proper forkdom there was a fierce, mewing cry from what seemed to be a kind of herring box under the yew hedge and Dr Ritter strode over to it, extracted a small pink baby, and inserted it under her tabard.

'That's her Natural Daughter. She's called Andromeda. Hermine got her at a conference but no one knows who the father is.'

'Perhaps we should show her how to make an opening down the front of her smock,' said Ellen, for the baby had vanished without trace into the hessian folds. 'And I didn't see any nappies?'

'She doesn't wear any,' Sophie explained. 'She's a self-regulating baby.'

'What a good thing I like to be busy,' said Ellen, 'for I can see that there's going to be a lot to do.'

She followed Sophie into the castle. The rooms, with their high ceilings, gilded cornices and white tiled stoves, were as beautiful and neglected as the grounds. But when she reached the top floor and Sophie said: 'This is your room,' Ellen could only draw in her breath and say: 'Oh Sophie, how absolutely wonderful!'

The child looked round, her brow furrowed. The room contained a broken spinning wheel, a rolled up scroll painting of the Buddha (partly eaten by mice) and a pile of mouldering Left Book Club paperbacks –

all left behind by various housemothers who had not felt equal to the job.

But Ellen had gone straight to the window.

She was part of the sky, inhabiting it. One could ride these not very serious clouds, touch angels or birds, meet witches. White ones, of course, with functional broomsticks, who felt as she did about the world.

Lost in the light, the infinity of space that would be hers each day, she lowered her eyes only gradually to the famous view: the serrated snow peaks on the other shore, the climbing fir trees above the village, the blue oblong of water, with its solitary island, across which the steamer was chugging, returning to its base.

Sophie waited. Her own view was the same – the room she shared with two other girls was only just down the corridor – but when she looked out of the window something always got in the way: images of her warring parents, the terror of abandonment, the letters that did not come. Now for a moment she saw what Ellen saw.

When Ellen spoke again it was to ask a question. 'Are there storks here, Sophie? Do you have them at Hallendorf?'

'I don't think so.'

'We must get some,' said Ellen decidedly. 'We must make them come. Storks are lovely; they bless a house, did you know?'

Sophie considered this. 'It could be difficult about the blessing,' she said, 'because we don't have anybody to do it here. We don't have God.'

'Ah well,' said Ellen, turning back into the room. 'One thing at a time. What we need now is a bonfire. Can you find me two boys with strong muscles? Big ones.'

Sophie puckered her forehead. 'The biggest are Bruno and Frank but they're awful. Bruno wrote "Eurythmics is . . .", he wrote that thing about Eurythmics on the temple and Frank is always thumping about and banging into people.'

'They sound just what I want. Could you go and get them for me please?'

Lucas Bennet sat in his study with its book-lined walls, sagging leather armchairs and the bust of William Shakespeare which held down the sea of papers on his desk. He was waiting to interview his new house-mother and had prepared himself for the worst. Ellen Carr had only been in the building for an hour and he himself had not set eyes on her, but he already knew that she was very pretty and very young and this could only mean disaster. She would want to produce a ballet based on Book Three of the *Odyssey*, which she would not actually have read, or write a play in which she would take the lead while the children filled in as woodland spirits or doomed souls in hell. Chomsky would fall in love with her, Jean-Pierre would flirt with her, the children would run wild in their dormitories and after a term she would leave.

Which was unfair, because this time he had taken the advice of his sensible secretary and advertised not in the *Socialist Gazette* or the *Progressive Educator*, but in the *Lady*, a magazine in which employers sought old-fashioned nannies and housekeepers and cooks. Visions of an ample widow with bulging biceps had sustained him ever since Conchita's need to join a Marxist flamenco troupe could no longer be gainsaid and she had removed herself, two weeks into the term, leaving the children with no one to care for their domestic needs.

And now it was all going to start again.

Ten years had passed since he took over the lease of the castle and started his school. A small, plump and balding visionary, he came from a wealthy and eccentric family of merchant bankers, diplomats and scholars. His time at Oxford (where he read Classics) was cut short in 1916 by the Great War, which left him with a troubling leg injury and a loathing for nationalism, flag-waving and cant. Obsessed by the idea of art as the key to Paradise – as the thing that would make men equal and set them free – he decided to start a school in which children from all nations would come together in a common endeavour. A school without the rules and taboos that had made his own schooling so wretched, which would offer the usual subjects but specialise in those things that were his passion: Music, Drama and the Dance.

The time was ripe for such a venture. The League of Nations gave hope of peace for the world; in Germany the Weimar Republic had become a byword for all that was exciting in the arts; the poverty and hardship of the post-war years seemed to be over. And at first the castle at Hallendorf did indeed attract idealists and enthusiasts from all over the world: followers of Isadora Duncan came and taught Greek dancing; Russian counts explained the doctrines of Stanislavsky; disciples of Brecht came from Germany to run summer schools and put on plays. True, the villagers continued to stand aloof, not pleased to find naked Harmony professors entangled in their fishing nets, but in those first years it seemed that Bennet's vision would largely be realised.

Now, nearly ten years later, he had to face the fact that Hallendorf's early promise had not really been fulfilled. The intelligentsia of Europe and America continued to send him their children, but it was becoming clear that his idealistic progressive school was being used by the parents as . . . well, as a dump. The children might come from wealthy homes, and certainly he extracted the maximum in fees so that he could give scholarships to those with talent, but many of them were so unhappy and disturbed that it took more than experimental productions of the Russian classics or eurythmics in the water meadows to calm them. And the staff too were . . . mixed. But here his mind sheared away, for how could he dismiss incompetent teachers when he allowed Tamara to inflict her dreadful ploys on his defenceless children?

It had to be admitted too that Hallendorf's annual performance in the theatre the count had built for his mistress had not, as Bennet had hoped, brought eminent producers and musicians to Hallendorf. Toscanini had not come from Milan (and a lady rumoured to be the great conductor's aunt had turned out to be someone quite different), nor Max Rheinhardt from Berlin, to recognise the work of a new generation, and the villagers continued to stay away.

And now of course Max Rheinhardt couldn't come because he had fled to America along with half the theatrical talent of the German-speaking countries. It had happened so quickly, the march from the last war to the possibility of the next. Bennet did not think that the insanity that was Hitler's Germany could last, nor did he think that Austria would allow itself to be swallowed by the Third Reich, but fascism was on the move everywhere, darkening his world.

Furthermore, the money was running out. Bennet's fortune had been considerable, but short of standing on a bridge and throwing banknotes into the water, there is no faster way to lose money than the financing of a school.

A knock at the door made him look up. The new matron entered.

She was all that he had feared yet it was hard to be disappointed. True, she was very young and very pretty, but she had a smile that was funny as well as sweet, and there was intelligence in the soft brown eyes. What held him though, what surprised him, for he had found it to be rare, was something else. His new housemistress looked . . . happy.

'You're very much younger than we expected,' he

said when he had asked about her journey and received an enthusiastic reply about the beauty of the landscape and the kindness of her fellow travellers.

She acknowledged the possibility of this, tilting her head slightly in what seemed to be her considering mode.

'Might that be an advantage? I mean, there's a lot to do.'

'Yes. But some of the older children are not easy.' He thought of Bruno, who that morning had defiled the Greek temple with his opinion of Eurythmics, and Frank, who was on his fifth psychoanalyst and had seizures in unsuitable places when his will was crossed.

'I'm not afraid of children,' she said.

'What are you afraid of then?'

She pondered. He had already noticed that it was her hands which indicated what she was thinking quite as much as her face and now he watched as she cupped them, making them ready to receive her thoughts.

'Not being able to see, I think,' she said.

'Being blind, you mean?'

'No, not that. That would be terribly hard but Homer managed it and our blind piano tuner is one of the serenest people I know. I mean . . . not seeing because you're obsessed by something that blots out the world. Some sort of mania or belief. Or passion. That awful kind of love that makes leaves and birds and cherry blossom invisible because it's not the face of some man.'

For a moment he allowed hope to rise in him. Might she see how important it was, this job he was asking her to do? Might she have the humility to stay? Then he forced himself on to the denouement.

'I'm afraid I didn't have the chance to lay out your duties completely in my letter. My secretary, Margaret Sinclair, will tell you anything you want to know, but briefly it's a question of seeing that the children's rooms are clean and tidy, that they get to bed on time, of collecting their laundry and so on. We try to see that everyone speaks English during the day. I suppose the English language is the single most important thing we have to offer now. Not because it is the language of Shakespeare,' he said wistfully, touching the bust of the man who made the whole vexed question of being British into a source of pride, 'but because increasingly parents look to England and America to save them from the scourge of Nazism. But at night you can let them chatter in their own tongue.'

'Yes,' she said. 'Of course I will do all that, but I was wondering how much time I should spend –'

Ah, here it comes, he thought, and his weariness was the greater because for a moment he had believed in her integrity.

'Ellen, I have to make one thing absolutely clear,' he said, not letting her explain to him that she was an experienced producer of operas for the Fabian Society or had understudied Ariel in Regent's Park. 'Your job is an arduous one and absolutely full time. Of course you could watch rehearsals at the weekend – last year we did *The Lower Depths* by Gorky – and if you wish it you could join the choir, although our music teacher has gone to fight in Spain. And the weekly meetings in which the productions are discussed are open to everyone, but –'

Ellen's eyes widened. She half rose from her chair.

'Oh please, I can't sing at all. And I'm not very good at meetings. I was brought up with meetings and they always make me fall asleep. Surely –' She drew breath and tried again. 'Of course I'll do anything I have to do . . . but what I wanted to know is how much time I'm entitled to spend in the kitchen.'

'Entitled?'

'Yes. Obviously the welfare of the children comes first, but it's not easy to separate children from what they eat and I can't supervise the kitchen staff without doing some of the cooking myself, it wouldn't be fair on them. And quite honestly, Mr Bennet –'

'Bennet. We're very informal here.'

Ellen, remembering the appendix scar, nodded. 'Well, Bennet, I just think it would be rather unfair if I had to watch rehearsals and listen to meetings about *The Lower Depths* when I could be cooking.'

Bennet closed his mouth, which had been very slightly open.

'You mean you have no desire at all to act? To be an actress?'

'Good heavens no! I can't think of anything worse – always in the dark and getting up at midday and worrying what people think about you.'

33

'Or to produce?'

She leant back and clasped her hands behind her back. She looked thoughtful and – there was the word again – happy. 'Oh yes, I'd like to *produce*. I'd like to produce a perfect crêpe suzette for everyone in the school. It's easy for one person – but for a hundred and ten . . . That's what interests me very much. How to quantify good food.' She broke off and looked out of the window. 'Oh good, how very nice of them! What kind and helpful boys!'

Bennet followed her gaze. There were a lot of ways of describing Bruno and Frank, his two most objectionable seniors, but this was not one of them. Bruno was trundling a wheelbarrow on which were piled a broken spinning wheel, a shattered wooden chair and a pair of ancient bongo drums towards the kitchen gardens. Behind him followed Frank, dragging a sack from which various scrolls protruded and a battered guitar case.

'I asked them to make a bonfire. No one seemed to want the stuff in my room and they said they'd be very careful and only light it in the incinerator.' And, as Bennet was silent, 'You don't mind?'

'No,' said Bennet. 'I don't mind at all.'

At the door, leaving to go, she paused. 'There's something I think we should have here.'

Bennet glanced at the letter from his stockbroker lying on his desk. 'Is it expensive?'

She smiled. 'I don't think so. I'd like us to have

storks. Only I don't know how to make them come. One needs a wheel, I think.'

'You must ask Marek, he'd know. He'll be back in a few days.'

She nodded, thinking of the tortoise. 'Yes,' she said, 'he'd know. I see that.'

After she had gone, Bennet limped over to the window and looked out over the lake. Was it possible that something could go right? That she would stay and work – that in her care his children would be *seen*?

And Tamara is away, he thought. She had not, as he had asked her, organised the turning out of Ellen's room, but when had Tamara done anything he had asked her? But he would not go down that road. Tonight he would not work late on the accounts. He would go to bed with a large whisky and golden Nausicaa in Homer's tensile, homely, heart-stopping Greek.

'She won't last a week,' said Ursula, sitting in her hideous striped pyjamas on the edge of her bed.

Sophie sniffed back her tears and agreed. With the advent of darkness the hope she had felt when she met Ellen had died. Ellen would barricade herself into her room like the others had done, Frank and Bruno would go on sliding up and down the corridor and crashing into doors – and her father would go further and further away, past America where he was giving lectures, and disappear over the rim of the world for ever.

'I get so tired,' she said.

Ursula shrugged. She didn't mind Sophie as much as she minded most people, but she was soppy. Ursula got by on hatred – for her ancient grandparents in their horrible house in Bath, for Frank who teased her because she wore braces on her teeth, for Dr Hermine who breastfed her revolting baby during Movement classes and expected Ursula to give birth to herself or be a fork. Above Ursula's bed was a row of the only human beings for whom she felt concern: a series of Indian braves in full regalia.

The door opened and the new matron entered.

'I came to say goodnight and see if you needed anything.'

She came over to Ursula's bed, smiled down at her, put the bedclothes straight. For a dreadful moment Ursula thought she was going to kiss her, but she didn't. She stood looking carefully at the labelled portraits Ursula had put up: Little Crow, Chief of the Santees, Geronimo, last of the Apaches and Ursula's favourite, Big Foot, dying in the snow at Wounded Knee.

'Isn't that where the massacre was?' asked Ellen.

'Yes. I'm going to go there when I'm grown up. To Wounded Knee.'

'That seems sensible,' said Ellen. Then she went over to Sophie. 'What is it? What's the matter?'

'She's lost her parents. I can't think it's anything to make a fuss about – I lost my parents years ago. I killed my mother because my arm stuck out when I was born and I killed my father because he went off to shoot tigers to cure his grief and died of a fever. But Sophie gets in a state,' Ursula explained.

Ellen sat down on the bed and smoothed Sophie's long dark hair. 'When you say "lost", Sophie, what exactly do you mean?'

But what Sophie meant was not something she could put into words. She had been shunted backwards and forwards between her warring parents since she was two years old, never knowing who would meet her or where she belonged. Her homesickness was of that devastating kind experienced by children who have no home.

'I've lost my father's address. He's not in Vienna, he's lecturing in America and I don't know where he is. And my mother's making a film somewhere in Ireland and I don't know where she is either.'

Ellen considered the problem. 'Is there someone who's connected with your father's work in Vienna? Has he got a secretary?'

'He's got Czernowitz.' Sophie was sitting up now. 'He's my father's lab assistant. He looks after the rats. He gave me a rat once for myself. It was beautiful with a brown ear but it died.'

'It died of old age,' Ursula put in. 'So there's nothing to make a fuss about.'

'Well look, have you got Czernowitz's address?'

'Yes, I have.'

'Then it's perfectly simple. We'll ask Bennet if you

can telephone to Vienna and then he'll tell you about your father.'

Sophie's sobs grew less. 'Would that be all right? Could I do that?'

'Of course you could. Now, where's Janey, because I'm going to put the lights out.'

'She doesn't come to bed. She sleeps in the bathroom.'

'What?'

'She wets her bed though she's quite old. Older than us. And the Coucoushka said she wouldn't deal with her sheets any longer. She was supposed to look after us when the last housemother left, till you came. Bennet doesn't know she said it – he'd be furious, because Janey's mother keeps trying to commit suicide and –'

Ellen interrupted them. 'Who is this Coucoushka person?'

'She's a ballet dancer. Her name's Tamara. She pretends to be Russian and she likes people to call her Coucoushka because it means Little Cabbage, at least we think it does, and the Russians call people that. It's an endear—, it's something you call people when you like them, like the French calling people *petit choux*. But it doesn't work in English.'

'No, it certainly doesn't,' said Ellen.

She found Janey, a pale girl with wistful blue eyes, sitting beside the bath, wrapped in a blanket and reading a book.

'Come to bed, Janey, the others are ready to go to sleep.'

'I don't go to bed. I sleep here at the minute.'

'No you don't. You sleep in your bed and if you wet it I shall wash the sheets in the morning because that is my job.'

Janey shook her head. 'The Coucoushka said –'

'Janey, I am not interested in what the cabbage person said. I am now your housemother and you will sleep warmly and comfortably in your bed. Eventually you will grow out of the whole business, because people do, and till then it's not of the slightest consequence. Now hurry up, you're getting cold.'

'Yes, but –'

Ellen glanced at the cover of Janey's book, which showed a jolly girl in jodhpurs taking her pony over a jump. 'Did you know that Fenella Finch-Delderton used to wet her bed when she was young?'

Janey stared at her. 'The one that got second prize in the Olympics? Honestly?'

'Honestly,' said Ellen, whose morality, though fervent, was her own. 'I was at school with her sister.'

Which left Bruno and Frank. She found them crashing about in the corridor but not, had she known it, with quite their usual energy.

'Ah good,' she said. 'I'm glad you're not in bed yet. I thought you might be kind enough to roll up the rug in my room and take it down to the cellar; I shall do better with bare boards. And there's the footstool; it seems to have a leg missing, so that can go down too.'

She kept them at work, going up and down the three flights of stairs to the cellar till Frank stopped, looking mulish. 'It's past our bed time,' he said. 'We're supposed to be in bed by nine-thirty.'

'Oh dear,' said Ellen innocently. 'That's what comes of being new. Hurry along then.'

Ten minutes later the west wing was bathed in silence and Ellen could go to her room. It was almost empty of furniture now; she would pull the bed under the window so that she could see the stars.

'You were right, Henny,' she said, leaning out to listen to the slow slurp of the water against the shore. 'This is a lovely land.'

Images crowded in on her. The first sight of Sophie running down the steps towards her; Bennet's hand cupping the head of his beloved Shakespeare . . . the house martins skimming in and out of the boathouse roof. But the image that stayed with her longest was that of the tortoise, rollerskating with abandonment across the grass.

There was so much to do here – so terrifyingly much – but she knew that Marek, when he came, would help her. Which made Bennet's words when she had asked him who Marek was seem all the stranger.

'That's a good question, Ellen,' the headmaster had said. 'You could say that he works here as a grounds-man, and that would be true. Or that he teaches fencing to the older boys, and that would be true also, and that at the moment he is acting as chauffeur to Professor Steiner across the lake. But when you have said that, I don't know that you have said very much. I think,' and he had turned to her with his friendly smile, 'you will have to find out for yourself – and when you do I would be very interested to hear what you discover.'

# 3

They had driven for the best part of the day, leaving Hallendorf by the road over the pass and turning north east along the river. The mountains became foothills with vineyards clinging to their slopes; the well-kept fields and quiet villages were tended by people who asked only to be left alone.

Now the forest began. In an hour they would be at the border.

The forest suited Marek; he settled into it as into a familiar overcoat – a large man, broad-shouldered with thick, straight hair, blunt, irregular features and reflective eyes. The road was straight here, a woodcutters' road; his hands lay on the wheel almost without movement. The scents he had grown up with – resin, sawdust, leaf mould – came in through the open windows of the van.

'The wind's from the south,' he said.

He'd always known where the wind came from: in Vienna, in Berlin, in New York in the narrow tunnels between the skyscrapers. Women had teased him about it, thought of it as a parlour trick.

'Are you missing the beautiful Tamara?' asked the man sitting beside him.

The uncharacteristic banter came with an effort from Professor Steiner. He was twice Marek's age: a scholarly man with a face from a Dürer etching – the full grey beard, the wise, short-sighted blue eyes, the features worn by time and, in recent years, by grievous sorrow.

Marek smiled. The relief of being away from the crazy school in which he had taken refuge made him feel almost light-hearted yet no emotion could be less appropriate. He had allowed an old man of delicate health and considerable eminence to accompany him on an adventure which was more than likely to end in disaster. What they faced was not the danger risked by those who pit themselves against mountains or the sea. There was no evil on the rock face or in a tempest, but the force within the men they were confronting in the hell that Nazi Germany had become was something other.

'Could I once again ask you to wait for me this side of the checkpoint?' Marek began. 'I promise you –'

'No.'

The old man spoke quietly and with total authority. If anyone knew the risks they were taking it was this high-born Prussian whose family had been at the heart of German affairs for generations. Steiner had spent most of his life in Weimar, a town which seemed to stand for all that was finest in the country's history. Schiller had lived there, and Goethe – the squares and statues resounded with the names of the great. The shopkeepers could set their clocks by Professor Steiner's progress each day, his walking stick aloft behind his back, as he made his way to the university. Steiner's work on the folk music of Eastern Europe was renowned; scholars and disciples came from all over the world to learn from him; his lectures were packed.

In 1929 he had moved to Berlin as Head of the Institute of Musical Studies and continued to live the life of every decent German academic: lectures, concerts, music-making in his home and the constant care and support of his students.

So why was it that when Hitler came to power it was he and not any of his colleagues – left-wingers and political activists – who had refused to dismiss his Jewish students? Why was it he and not Heinz Kestler, who had addressed so many meetings of the Left, who stood up for the social democrats on his staff? Why was it impossible to silence this elderly man who fell silent so easily during the interminable meetings of his faculty?

The Nazis had not wanted to dismiss Professor Steiner. His family was eminent; he was exactly the kind of German, Aryan to his fingertips, they needed to endorse their cause. They gave him chance after chance, cautioned him, arrested him, let him go.

In the end they lost patience. He was stripped of his post and his medals and told to leave the country.

Others in his position went to France or America or Britain. Steiner only went over the border to Austria, still independent and free. His family had long owned a small wooden summer house on the Hallendorfer See. He had lived there for the past three years with his books and his manuscripts, needing almost nothing, looking with gentle irony across the lake at the antics of the strange school which now occupied the castle.

Then, two months earlier, Marek had suddenly appeared. He had known Marek's parents, but it was not the family connection which years ago had drawn Steiner to the boy. Even before Marek's special gifts had become apparent there was something about him: a wholeness, a strength allied with gentleness which is sometimes found in those who as children have been given much.

'I only want to borrow the van, Professor,' Marek had said. 'And the equipment. There's no question of involving you. If I'm known to be one of your students and authorised to carry on your work, that's quite enough.'

'You can have the van, but I shall come too. I have to say you don't look like the popular image of a folk-song collector. You will do better as my driver and assistant.'

They had argued and in the end Marek had agreed. It had cost him dear, allowing this frail and saintly man to risk his life, but he knew why Steiner had refused the posts he had been offered abroad and was still in

Austria. He too had hostages to fortune in what had been his native land.

They drew to a halt in a clearing. Marek got out and opened the door of the van. It was painted black with the letters INTERNATIONAL ETHNOLOGICAL FOLK SONG PROJECT written on it in white paint. Inside were the microphones, the turntables and wax discs, the piles of manuscript paper which they needed to record the ancient music of the countryside. And other things – food and blankets, because folk-song collectors frequently have to venture far off the beaten track, and a loaded rifle, for these woods were part of the great primeval forest which stretched across Eastern Europe as far as Poland and Russia. Bears had been seen here not long ago, and wolves; guns were a necessity, as were spades and sacking for getting the van out of a rut, and a torch . . .

'We'd better find something nice for Anton,' said Marek. It was not the first time they had crossed the border and the guards were becoming interested in their work.

He put a needle on the turntable and an eerie, querulous wail broke the stillness.

'Why are the wedding songs always so sad?' asked Marek, remembering the tears streaming down the face of the old man, almost insensible on slivovitz, who had sung to them in a smoke-filled Ruthenian hut.

'I don't know why, but they always are. On the other hand, the funeral songs are always jolly – and the curses too.'

'Well, one can understand that,' said Marek. 'We'd better get on then.'

He shoved a driver's cap on to his head and the van moved forward in the gathering dusk.

Both men were silent as they drove towards the place where the map makers, confused by the rise and fall of empires, had allowed the boundaries of Austria, Germany and the Czech Republic to converge. A hundred miles to the east was Marek's home. The men would be coming in from the forest now and from the farm, unhitching the great horses from the wagons, and the westering sun would turn the long windows of the ochre house to gold. The storks on Pettovice's roofs fell silent at this time, weary of their domestic clatter, and the snub-nosed little maid would be lighting the candles in the drawing room.

But it was best not to think of Pettovice, which had once been Pettelsdorf. Marek's home was out of bounds. Czechoslovakia was free still but there was dissent there too, Nazi sympathisers stirring up trouble, and he would not risk harm to those he loved.

Professor Steiner too was thinking of the past: of his formidable grandfather, the Prussian *Freiherr* in his doeskin breeches and lynx cape, who had turned Jewish pedlars from the gates of his home with a string of curses. That they had plucked von Einigen and his friends from their guards and led them to safety might have amused him: highborn hotheads who had tried to blow up Hitler might have been to his taste. Even the man they were hoping to meet today might have passed muster; a former Reichstag councillor, impeccably Aryan, who had spoken out against the Nazis. But what would the old bigot have thought if he'd known that his grandson was plunging into a Bohemian forest on account of a small man with sideburns named Meierwitz? It was Marek's determination to rescue his friend that had made them throw in their lot with the partisans who helped to lead victims of the Nazis across the border. There had been no news yet of Isaac Meierwitz, who had escaped from a camp and was in hiding, but till he was out of Germany there would be no safety for Marek, and no rest.

The old often welcome adventure, having little to lose. But Marek, thought the Professor, had everything to lose. He took the greatest risk, leading the fugitives east along the hidden pilgrim routes he had known since childhood while Steiner waited with the van. And it was wrong. The world needed what Marek had to offer; needed it desperately.

Yet how could I have stopped him? thought Steiner – and he remembered what Marek's mother had told him once as they walked back from a concert.

'When Marek was three years old I took him to the sea,' she'd said. 'He'd never been out of the forest before but friends lent us a villa near Trieste. He just stood there looking at all that water and then he said: "Mama, is that the sea?" And when I said yes he turned to me very seriously and he said: "Mama, I'm going to drink it all up. I'm going to drink up every single drop!"'

Well, he had not done badly in his twenty-nine years, thought Steiner, looking at Marek's face, set and absorbed now that they were coming close to their destination. He had drunk his fill – but what he was doing now was madness. This man more than any he had known had no right to throw away his life.

Perhaps I'm wrong, thought Steiner. Perhaps he is not what I think he is.

But he knew he was not wrong.

# 4

By the end of the first week, Ellen had settled into her work. She had begun with her own room, for she wanted the children to feel that they could come to her whenever they wanted, and this had involved her in some creative 'borrowing', for by the time she had disposed of the archaeological remains of previous housemothers she was left with bare boards and a bed.

In refurnishing the room, she called on the help of Margaret Sinclair, the school secretary, to whom she had taken an instant liking. Margaret trotted round the picturesque confusion of Hallendorf in a neat two-piece, lace-up shoes and a crisp white blouse. She had been perfectly happy as a secretary in Sunny Hill School, Brighton, where the girls wore plum-coloured gym slips, addressed the teachers as 'Ma'am' and charged round frozen hockey fields shouting, 'Well played, Daphne!' – and she was perfectly happy at Hallendorf. Chomsky's sun-dappled appendix scar troubled her not at all, nor the oaths of the noisier children, and for Lucas Bennet, who had founded, and now carried selflessly the burden of running, this idealistic madhouse, she had a respect which bordered on veneration. That she would have carried the portly little headmaster between her teeth to safety if the school ever caught fire, was the opinion of most members of staff. Certainly Hallendorf would have run into the ground pretty soon without her.

'I should just take anything you find, dear,' she'd said to Ellen, in whom she recognised a kindred spirit. 'If anyone comes looking for it, I'll give you warning.'

So Ellen borrowed two beaten-down mattresses from the gym and made them into floor cushions, which she covered with an Indian cotton tablecloth she had found scrunched up in a dressing-up trunk. She took an armchair which had suffered enough from a common room, stripped the covers and polished the arms. She 'borrowed' a kitchen trolley and painted it . . . and decided that a small lime tree in an earthenware pot would be in less danger with her than in the courtyard.

But what Sophie saw, after she knocked timidly on the door, was mostly light.

'Oh!' she said. 'How did it get like that? What did you do?'

'It was like that already. So is your room. Rooms tell you what they want, you just have to listen!'

Sophie's life had so far been devoid of certainties. The marriage of her beautiful English mother to an austere scientist in the University of Vienna was a mistake both partners quickly put right. Carla wanted to be an actress, have parties, have fun; Professor Rakassy needed routine, silence and respect for his work. The only thing they had in common was an ego the size of a house and an apparent indifference to the happiness of their little daughter.

They separated and Sophie began her travels across the continent of Europe: on the Train Bleu to Paris, on the Nordwest Express to Berlin when Carla got a walk-on part at the UFA studios . . . on the Golden Arrow to London and back again . . . always trying to please, to change identities as she arrived . . . To be charming and prettily dressed and witty for her mother; to be serious and enquiring with securely plaited pigtails for her father . . .

Then suddenly the tug of war stopped. Both parents dropped the rope and she was packed off to a school that was unlike any she had known. That it was the beginning of a permanent abandonment, Sophie was sure.

But now there was Ellen. Ellen had kept her promise about ringing Czernowitz and she kept other promises. Sophie attended lessons assiduously; she endured eurythmics and did her stint being a bunch of keys or a fork, but when there was a spare moment in her day she came back to her base, trotting behind Ellen with laundry baskets or piles of blankets and curling up in the evening on the floor of Ellen's room.

And with Sophie came Ursula, bringing the red exercise book in which she was chronicling the brutalities the American Army had inflicted on the Red Indians, still scowling, still committed to hatred – but sometimes turning over what Ellen had said that first night. She had said it was *sensible* to go to Wounded Knee, and the calm word dropped into Ursula's turbulent soul like a benison.

Others came, of course: Janey, and Ellen's bodyguard, Bruno and Frank, and a long-legged American girl called Flix who was said to be a brilliant actress but wanted only to be a vet and kept a plaster of Paris ant nest under her bed.

And a dark, irritating, handsome boy called Leon who used his origins to secure sympathy.

'You have to be nice to me because I'm Jewish,' he would say, which drove Ursula into one of her frequent rages.

'You're only half Jewish,' she said. 'And I bet it's the bottom half so I'll be nice to that but not to your horrible top.'

Leon was a committed Marxist and filled his room with posters of Lenin rallying the proletariat, but the carefully unravelled jerseys he wore were made of purest cashmere and his underclothes were silk. Leon's father (whom he referred to as a 'fascist beast') was a wealthy industrialist who had transferred his business interests from Berlin to London when Hitler came to power, and his devoted mother and sisters sent him innumerable parcels of chocolate and delicatessen from Harrods which he despised, but ate. But if it was

53

difficult to like the boy, no one could dispute his gift; he was intensely and unmistakably musical.

Ellen had expected the children to come, but she hadn't quite bargained for the staff, abandoning their cluttered bedsitting rooms to eat her Bath Oliver biscuits and drink her Lapsang Souchong tea. Hermine Ritter came with her love child in its herring box and sat with her grey-flannelled legs apart and spoke of the historic conference in Hinterbruhl where she had been overcome, virtually in her sleep, by a professor of Vocal Rehabilitation who had drunk too much gentian brandy and left her with Andromeda, who was being brought up to be self-regulating but always seemed to be in a temper.

'I will be glad to mind her for you sometimes,' Ellen said. 'But you must get her some proper nappies.'

'Oh surely not? In the book by Natalie Goldberger –'

But Ellen, watching the puce, distempered baby flaying about inside Hermine's tabard like Donald Duck in a tent, said she thought nappies would be *nice* for Andromeda.

Jean-Pierre came, with his boudoir eyes and practised cynicism; a brilliant mathematician who professed to loathe children and could send them out of his classes reeling with excitement about the calculus, and Freya, a sweet-natured Norwegian who taught History and PE and was in love with a hard-hearted Swede called Mats who lived in a hut in Lapland and did not write.

David Langley came, the bony-kneed Biology teacher who was busy identifying the entire frit fly population of Carinthia, and Chomsky of course, fixing his congenitally despairing eyes on Ellen, and eating a quite remarkable number of biscuits.

There was one member of staff, however, who was conspicuous by her absence. The Little Cabbage did not come and when Ellen met her, two days after her return, the encounter was unfortunate.

Ellen during those first days worked as she had not worked before. She scrubbed, she sewed on name tapes, she set up her ironing board in the laundry room, she brought pots of flowers upstairs and emptied washing baskets and mended curtains.

Soon the words 'Where's Ellen?' could be heard with increasing frequency as children came in with grazed knees, bruised foreheads or more complex bruising of the soul. They learnt by the state of her hair how much time she could give them: when it was screwed up on top of her head it was best to fall in behind her with a cloth; when it was in a plait over one shoulder she was bound for the garden; when it was loose she had time to talk. Her clean, starched aprons, pink or white or blue, became a kind of beacon. On the days that they were blue, Chomsky would make an excuse to leave the metalwork shop and tell her that she reminded him of his nursemaid, Katya, whom he had deeply loved.

During that time, when she took almost no time off and did not even allow herself to think of *Kohlröserl*, Ellen began to feel that she was some way to accomplishing her task.

But pride goes before a fall. Ellen's fall came at the end of the first week when she was cleaning out a strange collection of debris she found in a small round room in the East Tower.

She had noticed a painting hanging on a dark wall above a table full of unsavoury litter: an old tin of Cerebos salt, rusty round the rim, a candle-end burnt dangerously low, a dead bunch of marigolds with slimy stalks and a piece of bread covered in mouse droppings.

Appalled by this health and safety hazard, Ellen got to work. She tipped the bread and salt into her dustpan, threw the dead flowers away, gathered up the frayed cloth with its mouse droppings and soaked it in disinfectant. Half an hour later the room was clean, the blinds rolled up to let in the light and the painting – which was of a number of little men in conical hats and underpants adrift on an ice floe – was left in possession of the field.

Ellen had gathered up her dustpan and bucket and was turning to go when her way was blocked by a tall, thin woman with long strings of hennaed hair, a pinched nose and wild, navy-blue eyes. She wore a muslin dress with an uneven hem, her long feet with their prehensile-looking toes were bare and slightly yellow, and she was in a towering rage.

'How *dare* you!' she shrieked in a strange accent which Ellen could not place. 'How dare you destroy my sanctuary – the only place where I can refresh my soul.'

'Sanctuary?' stammered Ellen, looking at the mouldy bread, the rusty salt tin in the waste bucket.

'You ignorant English peasant!' the woman shrieked. 'Of course you know nothing of how the Russians worship. You have never *heard* of the icon corner which in every Russian household is the heart of the home.'

Ellen could find no words. The woman's wrath flowed out of her; her narrow nose was white with anger and to her own annoyance, tears came to Ellen's eyes.

'I didn't realise . . . the bread was mouldy and –'

'Oh yes, of course; that is all you care for, you little bourgeois housekeeper. I have heard how you have scrubbed everything . . . This picture,' she pointed to the little men cowering in their shifts on the ice, 'was given to me by Toussia Alexandrovna, the prima ballerina of the Diaghilev Ballet. These men are the martyred bishops of Tula – they died on an ice floe rather than renounce the Old Faith. Every day I light a candle here in this corner – the *Krasny Ugol* – and now you come here in one hour and destroy the atmosphere with your lower-class hygiene.'

'I'm sorry; I really am. I didn't know. But the flowers were dead and –'

'Enough!' The woman raised a hand as long and yellow as her feet. 'Go! I shall speak to Bennet of this. It is possible you will be dismissed.'

Though she could see the absurdity of the encounter, Ellen found it difficult to shake off the misery and embarrassment of having upset a fellow member of staff, and instead of going to the common room at tea time, she went to find Margaret Sinclair in her little office.

'Oh there you are, dear,' said the secretary. 'I was meaning to have a word with you.'

'Margaret, I have done this awful thing – but I didn't know. I just thought it was . . . well, you know there are so many things lying around that have been forgotten and I'd simply never heard of the martyred bishops of –'

'No, of course you hadn't. It's a disgusting place and we're all absolutely delighted that you got rid of it.'

'Yes, but she . . . Tamara was furious. She's going to tell Bennet and she said she'd get me dismissed.'

'Oh my dear . . . Come, I'll make you a cup of tea. What nonsense! Bennet knows all about the work you're doing; he wouldn't dismiss you in a thousand years and he never takes the slightest notice of what Tamara says.'

But Ellen was not so easily comforted. 'Do you think I should go and explain to him and apologise all the same?'

'Well, he'll be happy to see you – he's going through a bit of trouble with the new play at the minute. But it's best not to talk to him about Tamara; it's not easy for him. He never speaks against her, but of course she is a deeply unpleasant woman, and what he goes through –'

She broke off her words and busied herself with the teapot. 'But if she's so awful . . . and I must say what she did to Janey . . . I mean, why doesn't he get rid of her?'

Margaret spun round, her kind, plain face amazed. 'Good heavens – did no one tell you? I suppose they thought you knew, and it's true we don't mention her if we can help it. We're all fond of Bennet – and the children too.' She handed Ellen her cup. 'She's his wife, you see, Tamara is. He's married to Tamara, only that isn't her real name, of course.'

'Oh!' It seemed incredible and also unutterably sad. In the short time she had been here, Ellen had conceived a great admiration for the hardworking, scholarly little man who powered the whole place with his vision. 'But how? I suppose one shouldn't ask or pry, but –'

'It happened in Paris. Bennet was there looking up some texts in the Sorbonne – he's a fine classical scholar, as you may know. This was twelve years ago when he was still at Oxford. He was walking across the Pont Neuf; it was night time. Do you know Paris?'

'Yes. I was there for a term learning French.' Ellen could see it: the Seine, the lamps lit, the moonlight, the boats sliding under the bridge.

'And he saw this girl, huddled under a lamp-post and weeping. She had long hair and a thin face . . . and all that,' said Margaret, and paused, noting the bitterness in her voice. 'You can imagine. He's a chivalrous man. It turned out that she was a dancer from the Diaghilev Ballet who'd been dismissed because she was pregnant. Her lover had deserted her, her mother wouldn't have her back, she had nowhere to go.'

'Yes, I see. It would be difficult to resist that kind of despair. And she was Russian?'

'Well, no – that's what's so ridiculous. She isn't Russian at all. Her name is Beryl Smith and she comes from a mining village somewhere in the north of England. She had one of those ballet mums who pushed her through exams and she got taken on by Diaghilev for the Ballet Russe. They all had to have Russian names, so she became Tamara Tatriatova. I suppose it was her happiest time, being part of the troupe, all the warmth and the chatter and people lighting samovars and calling each other Little Pigeon and Little Cabbage and so on.'

Margaret's effort to be fair to Tamara was taking its toll. She had decided to give up sugar in her tea but now she reached for the bowl and spooned in a generous helping.

'Actually I wondered about the cabbage thing,' said Ellen. 'Doesn't Coucoushka mean Little Cuckoo? We read a lot of Chekhov at school and –'

'Yes it does; you're quite right. But the children are convinced it means cabbage, and I must say, I myself –'

She broke off, not wanting to admit that being fond of birds she also preferred to think of Tamara as a vegetable. 'Anyway, Bennet married her,' she went on. 'The baby was stillborn – apparently her grief was terrible. Bennet said he'd never seen anyone so distraught. He brought her here soon afterwards to regain her strength and she saw the castle and wanted to live in it and it was then that Bennet thought of the school. She said she'd like to be a mother to other children if she couldn't have any of her own, but of course it hasn't worked out like that. Not that one can blame her entirely,' said Margaret, 'for it is an unfortunate fact that the needier a child is the less attractive it is. I think she thought they would be smaller, like fairies in a ballet. Since then she has got sillier and sillier and clings more and more to the Russian fantasy. No one believes it; I don't think she believes it herself. I suppose she is a little mad but that makes no difference. Bennet will never leave her; he is not that kind of man. He stops her teaching as much as possible but she's convinced she has a mission about the Dance.'

'Is it she who teaches Eurythmics?' asked Ellen.

'Yes it is.'

Ellen nodded. 'You've been extremely kind to tell me all this.'

She sent Ellen away comforted, but Margaret had not comforted herself. Why did I leave my peaceful plum-coloured girls? she wondered, rinsing the teacups. What am I doing here, eating my heart out for a small, bald man who's shackled to a cabbage?

The morning after Margaret's revelations, Ellen got up early and went down to the store rooms and fetched a tin of white paint, two large paintbrushes and a bottle of turpentine.

She had told Bruno what she was going to do and

had left it to him whether he accompanied her or not. She did not really expect him to – Bruno liked his sleep. She had been determined to make Bruno undo his handiwork – her vision for Hallendorf did not include the defacement of Greek temples; but now that she had met Tamara, Ellen felt different. Tamara had stood over an empty cradle and wept, and whenever Ellen wanted to hit her, which she suspected would be often, she would think of this and refrain.

But however careful she intended to be about Tamara, Ellen considered that any lesson she gave, whether it was Eurythmics (about which Ellen was still hazy) or anything else, would be hard for anyone to bear, and certainly for a boy like Bruno who had set himself up as a muscle man destined for the army. So she was prepared to paint out what he had written on her own account.

But when she reached the little temple, set so romantically on the edge of the lake, she found Bruno waiting on the steps.

'What have you got?' he said, coming over to inspect the paint pot and brushes. 'Seems OK. I'll have the bigger one.'

He took the bigger brush, added a small amount of turps to the paint in the tin, nodded. He seemed to have forgotten about the punitive aspects of the expedition and to be interested technically in the job in hand. As he began to sweep the paint across the letters on the wall, Ellen stood for a moment, watching. He was handling the paint easily, in sweeping broad brushstrokes but covering evenly. She had expected to do the bulk of the work herself, but soon found herself in the role of assistant. It occurred to her also that the letters they were eliminating were not scrawled on in the usual way of graffiti; they were stylishly painted and with a considerable panache.

'It's a mess,' said Bruno when they'd finished. 'The rest of it will have to be done over. You leave the paint here, I'll see to it.'

Ellen, about to argue, decided to obey. It was Sunday – Bruno would not miss any lessons. 'I'll bring you some breakfast,' she said.

But later that afternoon she went to find Rollo, the Art and Design master, who was making frames in the studio.

'I wanted to ask you about Bruno.' She told him about the morning's work. 'He seems so good at painting, so assured.'

'Don't talk to me about that blasted child,' said Rollo, a red-haired Welshman with a wide grin and a beer paunch. 'I could kill him.' He walked over to his cluttered bench, opened a drawer. 'Look at this!'

He pulled out a tattered exercise book, filled with sums, most of which had been marked wrong by Jean-Pierre in red ink. 'Look at the cover.'

Ellen looked. Scrawled in pencil were kittens that leapt from baskets, were folded hands, were Jean-Pierre's head in profile and the unfurled ends of Sophie's pigtails as she leant over her desk.

'He can draw anything but he won't. If you catch

him unaware he'll doodle like this but I can't make him do anything in the classes. Just glares and acts dumb sullen. When we're doing designs for the plays he'll put on glue or hammer the flats, but if you try and make him create something original he just pushes off.'

'But why?'

'Have you ever heard of Klaus Feuermann?'

Ellen screwed up her forehead. 'Is he a painter?'

'Yes. A fashionable one; quite talented but an idiot: goes round in a cape and a great hat pretending to be Augustus John. Bruno's his son and the poor little brat spent the first six years of his life being a putto. You know, those fat things with dimpled bums they have on painted ceilings. All Feuermann's kids were used as models, and he had plenty, by plenty of women. You can see Bruno on the ceiling of the Zurich Odeon and in the Guildhall in Rotterdam and God knows where else. When he wasn't a putto he was slapped on the knee of some woman, having to be the Baby Jesus, or hung from the top of a four-poster being Cupid shooting his arrows. By the time he was ten he wouldn't go near a picture and all he did when the kids teased him was to fight them. That's why he wants to be a soldier and acts the tough. But I can tell you, Ellen, it's bloody frustrating. This place needs talent.'

'Yes,' said Ellen. 'I see.'

'For God's sake don't tell him I told you. Don't tell anyone. I only found out because I'm in the business. Bennet knows, but no one else. He's run away from

64

three schools because the kids found out and teased him.'

'I promise I won't. Thanks, Rollo.' At the door she turned. 'You know, I sort of pledged myself when I came here to love the children – all of them, however awful they seemed – and I think I might manage it. But to love the parents . . . that's going to be the problem.' She gave a shake of the head and was gone.

If no one had spoken of Tamara before her return, both children and staff spoke frequently and willingly of Marek Tarnowsky.

'He's got this amazing trick,' said Frank. 'If you blindfold him – really properly with layers and layers of stuff – and make him sit with his back to you and then you get a lot of twigs and swish them through the air he can tell you what they are.'

'It's true,' agreed Janey. 'He'll just say "oak" or "ash" or "birch" – he doesn't make a mistake once. He says they just *sound* different.'

'And he dredged up the duck punt – it was a complete wreck – and sawed some new planks and caulked it –'

'He didn't do it by himself,' one of the other boys put in. 'We helped him.'

'Yes, but he really knew what to do and it's afloat now and it's much the best boat.'

Sophie said that Marek was a person who *found* things.

'What sort of things?' asked Ellen.

'Oh . . . mouse's nests and fireflies . . . and stars with their proper names. And when he shows you it's like getting a present.'

A shy French boy, who spoke little English, said Marek had made him understand what fencing was about. 'It is not . . . that one only tries to hit others. It is a system of the body.'

Ellen herself had seen Marek's spoor everywhere. In the prop he had made for the aged catalpa tree in the courtyard, in the rim of the fountain he had repaired, in the newly built frames in the kitchen garden.

So she was surprised that one child seemed to hate him. Leon did not only criticise Marek; he spoke of him with an anger which startled Ellen and alarmed her.

'He's not honest. He's a liar and a cheat.'

'What on earth do you mean?'

'He just is,' said Leon. He had come from the practice rooms where she had heard him wrestling with a Beethoven sonata. 'He absolutely hates music – he rushes away when the recorder group plays or they're rehearsing the choir. So what is he doing driving about the country collecting folk songs; just tell me that?'

'He's only acting as Professor Steiner's chauffeur.' And as Leon continued to glare and mutter: 'No one could be a liar and do what he did for Achilles,' said Ellen, for whom the tortoise had become a kind of talisman. 'You'd have to practically *become* a tortoise to do that.'

'Well, that's lying, isn't it? Pretending to be a tortoise,' said Leon, and stalked off, swinging the monogrammed leather music case which he had not yet managed to reduce to the wrecked state he regarded as suitable for the proletariat.

By the end of Ellen's second week the weather became properly warm and not only Chomsky but others began to take to the lake. Ellen thus found herself acquainted not only with the Hungarian's appendix scar but with the thin white legs of the Biology teacher, David Langley, whose pursuit of the Carinthian frit fly did not seem to have affected his musculature, and the brilliantly orange curls covering both Rollo's chest and his stomach.

Beyond reflecting on the sad difference between the Naked and the Nude, Ellen was untroubled, confining herself to seeing that the children brought in their towels and did not drip water on to the freshly polished corridors.

Others were not so insouciant. Sophie said she couldn't swim because she had a mole on her shoulder, and Ursula said she wouldn't because swimming was silly. An Indian girl called Nandi also retired indoors, though what was supposed to be wrong with her perfect body was hard to imagine.

Ellen listened to these dissidents without comment. Then on a particularly fine afternoon she invited the girls to come to her room to admire her bathing costume. 'It's nice, isn't it? It was terribly expensive.'

'It's lovely,' said Sophie. 'But are you going to wear it?'

'Yes, I am. It was a present from my mother.'

'But is it all right? I mean, *could* one wear a bathing costume? Wouldn't people mind?'

'Now Sophie, don't be absurd. What could freedom and self-expression possibly mean except that you can wear something to swim in or not exactly as you please? I'm going to try it out tomorrow afternoon.'

# 5

Marek sat on the wooden seat in front of Professor Steiner's little house drinking a glass of beer. His face was relaxed; the eyes quiet. Above the reeds on the edge of the lake, the swallows skimmed and swooped; the afternoon sun held the warmth of summer, not the uncertain promise of spring. Soon now he must row himself back to the castle; he had been away longer than he intended, but he was in no hurry to return to Hallendorf's fishbone risotto, the racket of the children and Tamara's embarrassing advances.

The journey had gone well. They had reached the border without mishap and found the man they had come for. A year in a concentration camp had not broken Heller. Beneath the emaciated body, the spirit of the debonair Reichstag delegate with his eyeglass and his bons mots was undimmed.

'It won't go on,' he'd said, as they drove east through the Bohemian forest. 'The rest of the world will wake up to what is going on. God forbid that I should hope for a war, but what else is there to hope for?'

But he was angry with Marek, whom he had recognised at once, having known him in Berlin. 'You shouldn't be doing this; you've other things to do. I was at –'

Marek hushed him. He didn't want to hear what he heard continually from Steiner. Ten miles from the Polish border they left Steiner with the van and prepared for the last part of the journey on foot. As they crouched in the undergrowth waiting for the darkest part of the night, Marek asked if he had heard anything about Meierwitz.

'He's still alive,' Heller had said. 'At least he was a month ago. A woman on a farm was hiding him. He's got guts, that little chap. He could have got out in '34, only –'

'Don't,' said Marek. 'It's because of me that he stayed.'

'Now that is nonsense,' said Heller. 'I heard all about that and it was his choice to remain behind. He wanted the glory of –'

The barking of a distant dog put an end to all further speech, even in the lowest of whispers. At three a.m. the moon went in and they took off their clothes and waded across the river, and a man rose silently from a field of rye and beckoned them to follow. Heller would be all right, thought Marek now. He had a forged residential permit allowing him to stay in Poland; his sister had married a Pole and would give him shelter. He had been a flyer in the war and intended to offer himself as an instructor in the Polish Air Force. They would take him; he had the Iron Cross.

From Steiner's living room came the cracked voice of the old crone he had found in the hamlet in which he had waited for Marek to return. He had led her into the van with the highest hopes: she was poor and toothless, her brown face seamed with dirt. If there was anyone who should have been a repository of ancient music it was Olga Czernova, from whose black clothes there had come the smell of decay and leaf mould as if she had been dug up from the forest floor.

But the tune which now drifted out towards Marek was not a work song from a bygone age, not a funeral dirge. It was 'Take a Pair of Sparkling Eyes' from *The Pirates of Penzance* and it was followed by 'Lippen Schweiget' from *The Merry Widow*. For in the bosom of this old witch there dwelt a girl who had been to the city, escorted by a young man who swore he would marry her. The city was not Prague or Vienna, though Olga knew of them both: it was Olomouc, where once a Hapsburg emperor had been crowned. And in Olomouc there had been music! And what music! Not the boring dirges she had been brought up with, but lovely, lilting tunes played by the town band and sung in the operettas by hussars in silver and blue, and gypsies in layers and layers of twirling skirts . . . And in the cafes too there had been music!

The young man had left her – he was a wastrel – but the tunes of that magical time had stayed with her

71

always. To the increasingly desperate Steiner she had sung the Champagne Aria from *Fledermaus*, Offenbach's Can Can and a duet – taking both parts – from a musical comedy called *Prater Spring*.

'Put it in,' she kept saying, while Steiner begged uselessly for the old songs she had learnt in the forest. 'Go on. This is the part where he finds out she's really a princess.'

And Steiner had done so, meaning to erase the disc later, for it was hardly suitable for despatch to Bartok's Ethnographical Music Collection in Budapest. But now he decided to leave it, for he too had been young and sat in cafes, and Olga's final screechings reminded him of the moment when he had seen Marek return from the phalanx of trees and knew that he was safe. It got worse and worse, the waiting for the boy.

Marek, sitting sleepily in the sunshine, heard Steiner moving about in his kitchen, preparing the evening meal. He made no attempt to help him: Steiner's kitchen, like his house, was tiny – it was this which had made Marek refuse the Professor's offer of hospitality and go to work in the school. Then he heard himself called.

'Marek, come here a minute!'

Steiner's only luxury in his exile was a large and very powerful telescope through which he watched the stars. But not only the stars . . . He was the least voyeuristic of men but it amused him to watch the people on the steamer, the animals wandering on the high pastures, the holiday-makers picnicking on the island.

Now though the telescope was trained on the castle and as Marek put his eye to it he could see, as if to touch it, the grass at the foot of the steps, the punt drawn up beside the boathouse . . . and the wooden jetty along which there walked, with a purposeful grace, a young woman whose shoulders were draped in a snowy towel.

And behind her, in single file like a brood of intent ducklings, came four . . . no . . . five little girls. They too moved with a look of purpose, they too were draped in snowy towels. Marek could make out Sophie with her long plaits and the bad-tempered English girl with a passion for Red Indians.

But it was the woman who led them who held his gaze. Ellen now had dropped her towel, and brought one arm up to gather in the masses of her light brown hair and skewer it on to her head – and what Steiner had suspected was correct. She wore a blue one-piece bathing costume which entirely covered all those places that such a garment is structured to conceal.

As if on a string, the little girls dropped their towels also and copied her movements, trying to scoop up and tether their hair as best they could – and, yes, they too were wearing bathing suits.

'I've never seen that before,' said Steiner.

'Nor I,' said Marek, thinking of the hollows and sinews of Tamara's body as she lay splayed across his path, the white limbs of the Biology teacher and Chomsky's notorious appendix scar.

Still watching the young woman, he saw her nod to

the little girls, and then she dived neatly into the lake and one by one the children followed her: some jumping in, some diving, and the cross English girl going down the wooden steps.

In the water she turned to see that all of them were safe and then she struck out into the lake, swimming strongly, but several times looking back to see that all was well – and behind her came her brood, fanned out in a V exactly like the ducklings that nested in the reeds.

He stood aside to let Steiner have another look.

'How seemly,' said the old man, and Marek nodded.

It was the right word for the behaviour of this concerned and purposeful young woman. For a moment Marek let his mind dwell on Nausicaa, the golden girl at the heart of the *Odyssey*, who had left her maidens to bring help and succour to the weary Ulysses as he came from the sea. But the high-minded analogy was replaced by a different thought: that it was a little bizarre that the first person he had come across in that strange place whom he would have enjoyed seeing naked, was so resolutely clothed.

Ellen had not expected that there would be morning assemblies at Hallendorf, but there were. Three times a week the whole school met in the Great Hall which ran along most of the first floor of the castle. Instead of pictures of school governors, the Royal Family and shields embossed with the names of prize winners, the hall was decorated with posters bearing rallying slogans and a frieze painted by Rollo's art class showing workers getting in the harvest, for the proletariat, of whom most of the children at Hallendorf knew remarkably little, were very dear to their hearts.

On the platform at the far end of the hall was a piano and a large radiogram attached to an amplification system which had been about to be renewed when yet another letter came from Bennet's stockbroker. There was also a screen and a magic lantern.

In the absence of prayers and hymns – and indeed of God – the assemblies, taken by members of staff in rotation and by any children who volunteered, were hard work, but Ellen found them genuinely moving, for in their own way they concerned themselves with the struggles of transcendence, uplift and the soul. There was one in which Bennet read from *The Freeman's Worship* by Bertrand Russell, a philosopher whose unsavoury private life did not prevent him from penning some discerning thoughts about the human condition. Rollo gave one about Goya, who had emerged from illness and despair to become one of the most compassionate painters of human suffering the world had ever known. Jean-Pierre, abandoning his cynicism, told them what the early manifestos of the French Revolution had meant to the huddled poor of Paris – and an American boy projected slides of Thoreau's *Walden*, that unassuming segment of Massachusetts which for so many became a touchstone for what is good and gentle on this earth.

But when Leon gave an assembly, Ellen found herself homesick for the boring, familiar routine of hymn singing and gabbled prayers she had known in England, for there was something disquieting about his performance.

She had come in at the last minute and stood at the back. The hall was full and silent, but Leon, seated at the piano, did not begin.

He was looking anxiously in Ellen's direction – not at her but at the door. Then it opened and a man entered quietly and stood beside Ellen. She had not met him yet but there could be no doubt about who he was – indeed it was strange how correctly she had imagined him: the size, the strength, the relaxed way he leant against the wall with folded arms. The warm greenish-blue eyes fitted too, as did the thick light hair falling over his forehead. Only the large horn-rim spectacles covering part of his face surprised her. She had expected him to be keen-sighted, a forester out of a fable, and thought how absurd she had been.

As though Marek's entrance was a signal, Leon began to play. He played a movement from a Beethoven sonata and he played it well. Both staff and children were silent, for if Leon was difficult to like, his talent was undoubted.

When he finished, he rose and went to the front of the platform, commanding the hall as all these stage-trained children had learnt to do. He was very pale and surprisingly nervous for such an extroverted and bumptious boy.

'That was Beethoven's Opus 26 – the one with the funeral march – and it's Beethoven I'm going to talk about. Only not all of his life – the part of it that happened in Heiligenstadt when he was thirty years old.'

He cleared his throat, and once again he looked at the back of the hall, his gaze, which had something frantic about it, fixed on the man who stood unmoving beside Ellen.

'Heiligenstadt is a village outside Vienna. It's pretty with linden trees and brooks and all that, but that wasn't why Beethoven went there. He went because he didn't want to be seen; he wanted to hide. He was terrified and wretched and trying to escape from the world. He was going deaf, you see, and it was there that he finally gave up hope that the doctors would be able to cure him.

'It's awful to read about the things he did to try and heal himself,' Leon went on. 'He poured yellow goo into his ears, he syringed them, he swallowed every kind of patent medicine, he stuck in hearing aids like torture instruments, but nothing made any difference. So he decided to die.'

Leon paused and rubbed his nose with the back of his hand. No handkerchief, thought Ellen, blaming herself, and her heart smote her at the emotion generated by this unprepossessing boy.

'But he didn't,' said Leon. 'He didn't kill himself,' and he threw that too intense, slightly hysterical look towards the place where Marek stood. 'He wrote a thing called *The Heiligenstadt Testament*, which is famous. He started by telling people to be good and love one another and all that, but the part that matters is what he wrote about art. He said if you have a talent you had to use it to go further into life and not escape from it. I'll read that bit to you.'

He took a book from the top of the piano and first in English, then in German, read the words with which the unhappy composer had reconsecrated himself to music and to life.

'So you see,' said Leon fiercely. 'You see . . .' and Ellen saw Bennet turn his head, frowning, to follow Leon's gaze as it travelled yet again to Marek, still standing with folded arms beside the door. 'You have to go on. Beethoven went back to Vienna and he wrote another seven symphonies and the violin concerto and *Fidelio*. He wrote dozens more string quartets and the *Missa Solemnis* and the *Hammerklavier* . . . All right he was grumpy and bad-tempered, he hammered pianos to death and the people who came to see him fell over his unemptied chamber pots, but he *never gave up*. And when he died, all the schools in Vienna were closed. Every single school was closed so that the children could go to the funeral. *Our* school would have been closed,' said Leon, as if that clinched the matter.

He had finished his speech. Sniffing once more, pushing back his hair, he walked over to the radiogram. 'I'm going to play a bit of the Ninth Symphony to end up with. At least I am if the blasted gramophone works,' he said, descending from the heights.

But as the triumphant strains of *The Ode to Joy*

rang out across the hall, Ellen felt a momentary draught beside her.

The man at whom this strange assembly had been directed, was gone.

It was Ellen's habit to get up early and make her way round the grounds before anyone else was up. The lake was at its loveliest then; the mist rising from the water; the birds beginning to stir.

But as she wandered, she *garnered*. Into a trug she kept for the purpose, she put the yo-yos she found tangled in fuchsia bushes, the roller skates left dangerously on the steps, the dew-sodden exercise books and half-knitted khaki balaclavas which (had they ever been finished) would have much reduced the chances of the International Brigade in their fight against Franco.

On the morning after Leon's disquieting assembly, having collected a broken kite, a pair of braces and a damaged banana, she made her way towards the well in the cobbled courtyard behind the castle, to dredge up a gym shoe which she had noticed the night before.

But there was someone else who valued the peace of the early morning. Marek did not sleep in the castle itself. He had a room in the stable block reached by an outside staircase. It was furnished as simply as a monk's cell – a bed, a table, a chair – and visitors were not encouraged.

Now he made his way down the steps, carefully locking the door behind him, and strode off across the cobbled courtyard on his way to the shed where the tools were kept.

The girl bent over the well did not at first see him, and he would have gone past, but at that moment she lifted her head and smiled and said 'Hello'.

'Not a frog, I hope?' he asked, fishing his spectacles out of his pocket and going across to her, for her sleeve was wet and a small tuft of moss had caught in her hair.

She shook her head. 'No. And if it was I wouldn't kiss it, I promise you. I might kiss a prince if I could be sure he'd turn into a frog but not the other way round. What it is is a gym shoe, but I can't get at it. It's stuck on a ledge.'

'Let me have a look.'

She had the idea that if it was necessary he would have torn up the iron grille screwed into the ground, so marked was the impression he gave of power and strength. But he merely rolled up his shirt sleeve and presently he fished out the shoe which he laid on the rim beside her.

'I spend so much time picking gym shoes out of wells and yo-yos out of trees and sodden towels from the grass,' she said when she had thanked him. 'I wanted to teach them to be tidy by *showing*, but there's so many of them and there's only one of me. I suppose some of them will never see.'

'But some will.'

He had sat down on the stone rim beside her and as she looked up at him, grateful for his encouragement, he found it necessary to correct the impression he had formed of her. As she swam out with her brood, she had seemed strong-willed and purposeful. Since then, Chomsky's besotted ravings, Bennet's praise and the legend of the icon corner had led him to expect a kind of St Joan wielding a bucket and mop. But she looked gentle and funny . . . and perhaps vulnerable with that wide mouth, those thoughtful eyes.

Ellen too found herself surprised. If Marek's broad forehead and shaggy hair, his sojourn in the stable block, accorded well enough with the image of a solitary woodsman, his voice did not. He had spoken in English, in deference to the custom of the school, and his voice, nuanced and light, was that of a man very much at home in the world.

'There was something I wanted to ask you,' she said. 'Bennet said you'd help me. I want us to have storks at Hallendorf. I want to know how to make them come.'

His face had changed; he was silent, withdrawn.

'Perhaps it's silly,' she went on, 'but I think the children here *need* storks.'

The silence continued. Then: 'With storks it isn't necessarily a question of needing them. It's a question of deserving them.'

But she would not be snubbed.

'Sophie deserves them. And others too. Storks mate for life.'

'It's too late this year, you know that.'

'Yes. But there's next year.'

'Ah, next year.' She had not deceived herself;

somehow she had made him angry. 'Of course. What a little islander you are, with your English Channel which makes everyone so seasick and you so safe. You think we shall still be here next year? You think the world will stay still for you?'

'No,' she said, putting up her chin. 'I don't think that as a matter of fact. I came here because I wanted to find *Kohlröserl* and thought maybe I didn't have very long, but it doesn't matter; the storks would still –'

'*Kohlröserl*? Those small black orchids?'

'Yes, my grandmother spoke of them before she died, but never mind about that. I want storks because –' and she repeated the words she had spoken to Sophie, 'because they bless a house.'

He had withdrawn again but she no longer felt his anger. 'What exactly do you intend for this place?' he said presently.

It was her turn now to fall silent. She had tucked her feet under her skirt, still perched on the rim of the well.

'I can't put it into words . . . not properly. It's to do with those paintings of places where the lion lies down with the lamb . . . you know, those primitive painters who see things very simply: birds of Paradise and great leaves and everything blending with everything else. Or the Forest of Fontainebleau – I've never been there, but I saw a picture once where the stags had crucifixes between their antlers and even the animals who are probably going to be shot look happy. When I saw the castle from the lake that first time, I imagined it all. The rooms clean and clear and smelling of beeswax and flowers, and the roses still free and tangly but not choked . . . a sort of secret husbandry that made them flourish. I thought there might be hammocks under the trees where the children could lie and I imagined them running out when it rained so as to turn their faces to the sky – but not before they'd shut the windows so that the shutters wouldn't bang. I thought there could be a place where everything was received with . . . hospitality: the lessons and the ideas . . . and the food that comes up from the kitchens. Of course the food wouldn't be like it is now,' she said, smiling up at him. 'There'd be the smell of fresh rolls in the morning and pats of yellow butter . . . and somewhere in the theatre which the count must have built with so much affection for his mistress, there'd be a marvellous play full of magic and laughter and great words to which people would come from everywhere . . . Even the villagers would come, setting sail for the castle in their boats – even the man who found Chomsky in his fishing nets would come.' She looked up, flushing. 'I know there can't be such a place, but –'

'Yes, there can,' he said abruptly. 'I could take you to a place that . . . feels like that. If times were different I would do so.'

'And it has storks?'

'Yes, it has storks.'

He rose, dropped the gym shoe into her trug. Then he stood looking down at her – not smiling . . . considering . . . and she caught her breath, for she felt that she had been, in that moment, completely understood.

'I'll look for a wheel,' he said – and walked away across the courtyard to begin his work.

But later, tending to the bonfire of lopped branches and hedge clippings, Marek wondered what had made him liken his home to this mad place. Pettelsdorf owed its existence – its wealth – to the forest which surrounded it, and those who are custodians of trees lead a life of rigorous discipline. To his father, and his father's father before him, the two thousand hectares of his domain were wholly known. An architect coming to bespeak oak planks for the belfry of a church was led to one tree and one tree only in the seemingly limitless woods. There were trees of course which were sacrosanct: a five-hundred-year-old lime, with its squirrel nests and secret hollows, which Marek as a boy had claimed as his own, would never be cut, nor the elm by the house beneath which he'd lain on summer nights watching the stars tossed back and forth between branches. But in general there was no room for sentiment at Pettelsdorf; a forest of sweet chestnuts and pine, of walnut and alder and birch, is not something that looks after itself. Only a meticulous daily husbandry ensures the balance between new growth and ancient hallowed trees, between sun-filled clearings and dense planta-tions.

But Ellen had used the same word: husbandry. She saw the children (he had realised this at once) as his father, and he himself, had learnt to see their trees: those that needed pruning, those that grew aslant, those that required only light and air. She was like those girls one sees in genre paintings: girls labelled *Lacemaker* or *Water Carrier* or *Seamstress*. Quiet girls to whom the artists had not bothered to give names, for it was clear that without them the essentials of life would cease.

Oh damn, he thought, having promised storks, having opened the door to a place he had never meant to leave and that was lost to him until his wearisome task was done. For it was strange how easily, had things been different, he could have taken her to Pettelsdorf. She would precede him up the verandah steps; the wolfhound would nuzzle her skirt; his mother would give the little nod she gave when she found the right word for one of her translations and his father would put down the gun he was cleaning and take out the 1904 Imperial Tokay he kept for special guests. While in the brook behind the house, the storks she craved would solemnly perambulate, searching for frogs . . .

Which was nonsense, of course, for the work he had to do must involve no one, and even if he did what he set out to do he would still not be free, for incredible as it seemed, it looked as though there was going to be another war.

It was not till the beginning of her second week that Ellen was able to devote herself to the kitchen and its staff.

The kitchens, which had once supplied the Hapsburg counts with roast venison and casseroles of grouse, and had sent sucking pigs and flagons of Napoleon Brandy upstairs, had not changed substantially since the days when the last of Hallendorf's owners had feted Franz Joseph after a week of hunting. An electric cooker had replaced the huge bread ovens and the range, and there was a frigidaire stuck with revolutionary slogans proclaiming the need for the overthrow of the Costa Rican government. But the vast wooden kitchen table was the same, the long passages which separated kitchen and larder and the stone steps down to the cellars.

Nevertheless, Ellen, entering to begin her supervisory duties, looked at the room with pleasure. It was not dark; the windows at the back looked on to the courtyard and the catalpa tree, and everything was solid and clean.

The cleanliness surprised her because the food which had hitherto been served up was dire. Lumpy brown rice risottos to which spikes of bony fish adhered; strange salads devoid of dressing but rich in small pieces of gravel and slimy tropical fruits which had come from far away in tins.

Ellen's arrival, in her crispest apron, was not greeted with enthusiasm either by the persecuted Costa Rican, Juan, or by Fräulein Waaltraut Nussbaum-Eisenberg, an impoverished aristocrat whose nephew was Mayor of Klagenfurt.

Juan cooked for his keep and a vestigial salary and expected any day, he said, to hear a knock at the door and to be taken away by the secret police of his country, and Fräulein Waaltraut disapproved of meat, eggs and fish and would have fed the school entirely on borage and bilberries if Bennet had let her.

'Well, of course we must have salads,' said Ellen, 'but not with gravel, and stinging nettles *must* be picked young. Also these children are growing so we must make sure that there is plenty of protein.'

She laid her cookery books on the table and asked if she could see the larder. This went down badly, Fräulein Waaltraut pointing out that she wasn't used to being inspected and Juan waving his arms and declaring that it was a Thursday, and it was on Friday that the boat came with fresh supplies.

Since it was obvious that both Juan and Fräulein Waaltraut, like the tinned mango shards from impoverished African countries, belonged to Hallendorf's tradition of succouring the needy irrespective of worth, Ellen continued to be surprised by the wooden table scrubbed to whiteness and the pots and pans scoured and neatly stacked. Clearly there was someone else working down here and presently she found her; not in the kitchen itself but in the scullery, washing up the breakfast things.

Ellen came on her unobserved and as she watched, her spirits rose. The girl was very young – not more than eighteen – and dressed in a spotless dirndl: a blue sprigged skirt, a pink bodice, a white blouse. Her blonde hair was pinned neatly round her head, she was small and sturdy and she worked with a steady rhythm and concentration, as though what she was doing was . . . what she was doing, and nothing else.

'*Grüss Gott*,' said Ellen, holding out her hand. 'I'm the new supervisor – my name is Ellen.'

The girl turned, wiped her hands. 'I'm Lieselotte,' she said – but as she dropped a curtsy Ellen had to restrain herself from rushing forward and taking the girl into her arms. For this might have been Henny, come back from the dead: Henny as she had been in her own country, wholesome, giving and good.

'Tell me, Lieselotte, was it you who boiled the eggs and made the poppy seed rolls on Sunday?'

Lieselotte nodded. 'Yes. I am not supposed to cook, I'm just here to clean and wash up, but on Sundays Fräulein Waaltraut isn't here and –' She flushed. 'It's difficult. I am thinking of giving in my notice.'

'Oh no!' Ellen shook her head with vehemence. 'You can't possibly do that. Don't even think of it. From now on it is you and I who are going to do the cooking.'

The girl's face lit up. 'Oh, I love to cook. Everyone thinks Austrian food is heavy and greasy, but that's only *bad* Austrian cooking. My mother's omelettes are like feathers and her buttermilk is so fresh and good.'

'Your mother taught you to cook, then?'

'Yes.'

'And do you have any brothers and sisters? We shall need some help because I have to work upstairs as well.'

'I have two sisters. They wanted to come but my

mother thought it wouldn't be good . . . they're young – and sometimes the children behave so badly.'

'Well, anyone would behave badly if they had to eat fishbone risotto,' said Ellen. 'I tell you, Lieselotte, we're going to transform this place.'

'But,' the girl looked towards the kitchens where an altercation was beginning between Juan and Fräulein Waaltraut, 'how will you . . . ? He has nowhere to go and she is related to the Mayor.'

'I think perhaps Juan could teach pottery. And – well, I shall think of something. Now, here are the menus I thought of for next week – but I'd like to use as much local produce as possible. I expect you know people who would supply us?'

'Oh yes. Yes.' She smiled. 'But they do not live in Abyssinia.'

# 6

In Gowan Terrace, Ellen's mother and her aunts missed her more than they could possibly have believed. The house without her seemed empty, silent and cold. If Dr Carr had scarcely noticed, in her busy life, the flowers Ellen had brought in and arranged, she noticed their absence. Below stairs, the cook reverted to boiled fish and virulently coloured table jellies, and the man who came to help in the garden dug up Ellen's peonies and destroyed the clematis.

Not that the sisters didn't keep busy. There were more meetings than ever: meetings about the disenfranchised women of Mesopotamia, about mathematics teaching in communes and free contraception for prostitutes. But even the meetings were not quite what they had been – they were briefer, there were fewer young men, and the sandwiches sent up by the cook were so unappetising that they abandoned them and settled for digestive biscuits.

It was different, however, when one of Ellen's letters

arrived from Hallendorf. Then Dr Carr and her sisters allowed special people to stay behind after the chairs were cleared and the lantern slides put away, and the letter was read not only to initiates like the 'aunt' who ran the Left Book Club Shop or the former head-mistress of Ellen's school, but to others – even men – who had a record of good work for the causes. And among these was Kendrick Frobisher.

Kendrick had made himself so useful in Gowan Terrace, addressing envelopes, sorting slides and fetch-ing leaflets from the printers, that he could not really be left out of anything as enjoyable as reading the next instalment of life at Hallendorf. It was true that Annie (the one who was a professor of Mycology and there-fore saw things dispassionately) had voiced her doubts about the advisability of this.

'He's very much in love with Ellen; don't you think it might encourage him to hope if we invite him to what are, in a sense, family occasions?'

But advisable or not, no one had the heart to exclude Kendrick, who had been compelled to visit the wet house in Cumberland for a family reunion in which his oldest brother, a major in the Indian Army, had told him about pig sticking, and his other brother, a stock-broker who was learning to fly his own plane, had given an account of looping the loop.

So Kendrick sat with Charlotte and Phyllis and Annie and heard about the strange behaviour of the Little Cabbage (for whose Eurythmics classes the chil-dren drew lots) and the play chosen for the end of the year performance, which was set in a slaughterhouse and was politically sound but sad. They heard about the discovery of Lieselotte in the kitchen, about Ellen's rage with parents who did not write to their children, and her triumph in weaning Andromeda from sphagnum moss to Turkish towelling. And they heard – though briefly – about someone called Marek who had put a tortoise on wheels and was going to help her find storks. Sometimes Ellen would add: 'Please give my love to Kendrick and tell him I'll write properly soon,' and this would send the young man out into the night walking on air, and more determined than ever to fulfil what he saw as his mission.

And his mission was no less than to bring to Ellen, through his letters, all the cultural activities of her native city. Now, when Kendrick went to an exhibition of Mexican funeral urns, or saw a Greek play in a basement in Pimlico, he went not only for Ellen, but in a mystical sense *with* her. He invariably bought two programmes and made careful notes throughout the performance so that he could share his experiences, and these he added with his comments and impressions to the weekly letter.

Thus it was that when he attended a concert of contemporary music at the Wigmore Hall, Ellen was treated to a complete breakdown of the music played, an annotated copy of the programme and two sheets of comments stapled to the back in Kendrick's handwriting.

'Curiously enough, I think I know the man who

wrote the songs I have marked, the ones which were encored. As you see, his name is Altenburg. He was becoming well known in Germany before Hitler came to power but now he has withdrawn all his music from performance in the Third Reich – he won't even allow his compositions to be printed there. There was a boy at school with the same name – he had a German father, or maybe it was Austrian – and he stood out from the others because he was so good at music but also because he was so strong and unafraid. He was expelled after a year for hanging one of the housemasters out of a first-floor window. He didn't drop him but he held him out over the shrubbery by his ankles. It was a big scandal, because the master could have fallen and been killed, but we were all glad because the master was a sadist and he'd been beating small boys in the most appalling way, so Altenburg was a hero, but he left straight away. The school said they expelled him but we thought he just went. He didn't seem at all bothered about what he'd done. He just said defenestration was quite common in Prague where his mother came from.'

Kendrick paused, wondering whether to explain about the defenestration of Prague, which was a famous event in the history of Czechoslovakia. He was a person who could spell Czechoslovakia without recourse to a dictionary and was quite conversant with the religious disputations of the Bohemian capital which had resulted in two Catholics being thrown out of the window by irate Protestants who believed themselves betrayed. But there was no more room on the programme, and Ellen sometimes looked tired when he explained things at length, so he put the notes to one side and returned to his letter, telling her once more that he would always love her and that if she could ever bear to think of him as a husband he would be unutterably happy.

He then signed the letter, put in the theatre programme of the Greek play, the reviews cut out of *The Times*, two exhibition catalogues and the annotated programme of the Altenburg concert, and took them to the letter box.

These all arrived safely, delivered on the yellow post bus with its Schubertian horn which careered round the lake at dawn. Ellen read the letter, for she continued to feel sorry for Kendrick, but she left the catalogues and the concert programme on her work table to look at later, for she was planning a complete refurbishment of Hallendorf's dining room and the cultural life of the metropolis would have to wait.

# 7

On the same morning as Ellen heard from Kendrick, and Sophie once again turned away empty-handed from her pigeonhole, Marek received a postcard which he pocketed with satisfaction. The picture showed a pretty Polish village complete with smiling peasants and the text read simply: 'Tante Tilda's operation a success. She sends her love.'

Heller was safe then. Marek could imagine him, his monocle restored, holding forth in the officers' mess of the Flying Corps. So now there was nothing to do till he got news of Meierwitz: the enquiries he had set in train as the result of Heller's disclosures would take time. And this rescue would be the last. He had promised Steiner, and he himself was aware that the time for lone adventures was past. Hitler's defeat now could only come from the other countries waking up to their responsibilities, not, as he had once hoped, from within.

Marek therefore turned his attention once more to

Hallendorf's neglected grounds, spraying the trees in the orchard, repairing the frames in the kitchen garden, staking the roses. Wherever he worked, boys congregated to watch but they did not watch for long. One either left Marek alone, or one helped, and the 'helping' was not of the kind that involved self-expression or ceased when the novelty of the task had worn off.

Most of the children were genuinely useful, but Leon's desire to 'help' was different. This quicksilver, twitchy child wanted something from Marek; his apparent affection was a kind of persecution. Marek was aware of this. He sent him to work as far away as possible: hoeing a path on the lower terrace, or wheelbarrowing logs from a distant wood pile, but it was impossible for the boy to stay away for long.

Ellen, busy with her plans for redesigning the dining room, found Marek unobtrusively helpful. She would be dragging trestle tables out of doors so that she could feed the children in the courtyard till the job was done, and he would appear at her side unexpectedly to lift and carry or – with a few words – show her an easier way to do something.

He was helpful in other ways too, explaining things she had not completely understood.

'Chomsky does swim a *lot*, doesn't he?' she said, as the metalwork teacher splashed past them once again. 'I mean, three times a day.'

'It's because of the exceptional weight of his liver,' said Marek. 'Bartok swims a lot too.'

'Bartok?'

'A Hungarian composer. Probably the best one alive.'

'Yes, I know. But is it something about Hungarians? That they have heavy livers and have their appendices taken out in the *puszta*?'

'Chomsky's appendix was taken out in the most expensive clinic in Budapest,' said Marek, looking mildly offended, as though she had taken the name of Central Europe in vain. 'His father is a high-ranking diplomat.'

It was not only the children who followed Marek about as he worked.

Tamara was creating a ballet called *The Inner is the Outer*, based on a poem by Rilke she had found in the library but perhaps not completely understood. It was a solo ballet, since the children had proved uncooperative, and its rehearsal, involving the kind of contortions to be expected of someone whose inside was outside, usually took place as close as possible to where Marek was.

The way Marek coped with this was impressive. This man who noticed the smallest beetle on the trunk of a tree or picked the emerging, thumb-nail sized frogs from the path of his scythe, dealt with Tamara as if she did not exist. Once, finding her splayed sunbathing across his path as he was going to the village, he tipped his hat to her as to an acquaintance encountered on the Champs Elysées, and walked on. Only when she picked up her balalaika and began to sing did he instantly disappear, showing the same unexpected skill in flight that he showed when teaching fencing.

Ellen's own troubles with Tamara were horticultural. For it seemed that the girls of the Russian Ballet had gone about with flowers in their hair – large, mostly red flowers – and it was flowers such as these that Tamara plucked or tore up with her bony fingers and stuck into her hennaed locks.

'I feel as though it's me she's picked and hung over her ear,' Ellen admitted to Marek as the Little Cabbage yanked a perfect, double-petalled peony from its stem.

Aware that she needed comfort, he said: 'I think I've found a wheel. A farmer in the next valley's got one in his shed. He isn't sure yet whether he'll let me have it but I'm working on him.'

'Oh!'

Ellen realised that her belief in storks was excessive. Storks would not necessarily make Sophie's parents write to her or stop Janey wetting her bed. It was probably beyond their powers, too, to turn Tamara into a decent wife who would help Bennet run his school. But she felt so hopeful that Marek, seeing her face, was compelled to add: 'A wheel doesn't make storks come, necessarily.'

'No,' she said happily. 'But it's a beginning.' And success going to her head she added: 'Maybe we could have doves too – white ones? Fantails. There's a dovecot up in the fields. They'd look beautiful.'

'*No!*'

'Why not?'

'Because they breed and breed and people who own them are compelled to collect the fledglings in washing baskets and try to give them to their friends,' said Marek bitterly, recalling his mother's early and unsuccessful efforts to bestow her surplus on the landlords of Bohemia. 'They are permanently in season,' he said, making his point clear.

'Like Tamara,' said Ellen – and put her hand to her mouth, for she had sworn not to speak ill of the Little Cabbage who had suffered so much.

The reopening of Hallendorf's dining room turned out to be unexpectedly dramatic, indeed there were children who remembered it long after they had forgotten the expressionist plays and dance dramas in which they had taken part.

For two days before, the dining room had been closed and they were served alfresco meals. Then on the third day a notice appeared in the hall asking everyone to assemble outside the dining room five minutes before the evening meal.

Needless to say this created considerable anticipation and even Rollo, who preferred to go to the village for beer and pretzels, and Chomsky, whose constitution was delicate, were waiting.

At six-thirty, Bruno, who had been guarding the door, threw it open and everyone flocked in to find a transformation scene. Gone was the oil cloth with its institutional smell, gone the uncurtained windows, the crockery jumbled up in metal baskets. The pine tables shone with beeswax; on the centre of each was a posy of wild flowers in a blue and white pottery jar; the places were carefully set.

And the serving hatch, in which Fräulein Waaltraut usually stood with her ladle, was shut. Next to it stood four children with napkins on their arms, ready to serve their peers.

When everyone was seated, Sophie, standing at a side table, picked up a bell and rang it. It was a cow bell, sweet-toned and mellow, and reminded those children whose parents had managed to get together long enough to celebrate Christmas, of reindeers and presents and candles on a tree.

At this signal the door of the hatch opened. There, instead of Fräulein Waaltraut looking harassed, stood Ellen. She wore a white overall, and a white coif concealed her hair so that she looked like a devout and dedicated nun.

But when she spoke, her words were not nun-like in the least.

'As you see,' said Ellen – and her voice carried without difficulty to all corners of the hall, 'we have tried to make the dining room more inviting – and we hope and intend to serve up more inviting food. You all know that the school is on a budget so we can't perform miracles, but we will do everything we can to see that what you get to eat is fresh and well cooked, even if sometimes it has to be plain. But there is one thing I want to make absolutely clear and it concerns the proletariat.' She paused, surveying her audience, who seemed to be suitably cowed. 'I have heard a lot about the proletariat and the downtrodden workers of the world since I came here, and I think that to care about them is right and honourable and good. But I want to make it absolutely clear that the proletariat doesn't only happen in far-off places. Not only in the sweatshops of Hong Kong or the factories of the American Midwest. The proletariat is also here in this kitchen. Lieselotte, who got up at five in the morning to bake the rolls you are about to eat, is the proletariat. Frau Tauber, who washes up for you, is the proletariat when she stands by the sink for hours on her aching, swollen legs. *I* am the proletariat,' said Ellen, waving her ladle. 'When you throw a piece of bread across the room you are destroying what a man spent the night making, even though his back ached, even though his wife was ill. When you jostle and shove and spill the milk, you are belittling a man who gets up on a freezing morning and blows on his hands and goes into his shed to milk the cows while you are sleeping in your beds. And if you understand this, then I and all of us in the kitchen will do everything to serve good food, but if you can't then I swear it's back to fishbone risotto and mango shards because that's all you deserve!'

A stunned silence followed this. Then from the back of the room a deep voice called 'Bravo!' Marek's lead was one that was always followed. It was to an ovation that Ellen picked up her ladle and began to serve.

'You know, I almost wish I hadn't made it so clear that I didn't want her to get involved with the plays in any way,' said Bennet later that night. 'She seems to have a real flair for presentation.'

'That's true,' agreed Margaret Sinclair, who had come to his study with some letters for him to sign. 'But mind you, I don't know how much effect the speech would have had by itself. I think that it was the food she produced afterwards that did the trick. That sauce on the *Würstl* and that delicious *Kaiserschmarren*.'

'Well, you may be right. I'm just sorry I couldn't oblige her by letting Juan teach pottery. But Marek seems to have found work for him in the garden.' To have two people on his staff on whom he could rely so completely was a bonus, though Marek, he knew, would not stay.

Now Bennet remembered his first interview with Tarnowsky. He had rowed himself across the lake from Professor Steiner's house and asked for a job.

'It won't be long. A few months . . .'

'What can you teach?' Bennet had asked. It was not the way he engaged staff as a rule but he had no sooner seen the quiet, slow-moving man than he wanted him.

'I thought I might work in the grounds,' Marek had answered. 'The orchard is in poor shape and the trees behind the jousting ground want thinning.'

'Could you take fencing for the older boys?' asked Bennet, following his hunch.

'If you like. And carpentry, I suppose.'

Bennet had tried pottery – he had a much prized heap of clay in the cellar moistened periodically by trusted children awaiting someone worthy – but Marek disclaimed all knowledge of pottery.

'There's a book,' said Bennet, looking at the man's large, reassuringly 'unartistic' hands.

'I'll think about it.'

'I'm afraid I can't offer you much in the way of pay,' Bennet had said.

'I don't want any pay. But I tell you what I do want.'

He had wanted leave of absence to go with Professor Steiner on his folk-song-collecting expeditions whenever the Professor heard of a promising singer. As he reached the door, Bennet tried again. 'What about music? Could you take the choir?'

Marek turned, shook his head. 'Definitely not music,' he said.

Now it struck Bennet as singular that the three people on whom he could let his mind rest, certain that they would give of their best, were all of them uninterested in the ideas which for him empowered his school. Ellen, Marek and Margaret (who had come in at ten at night to help with his letters), did not seem to be concerned with freedom and self-expression – nor had they shown the slightest interest in the end of year play which everyone, though that was not its title, was calling *Abattoir*.

Ellen's friendship with Lieselotte grew day by day. Her promotion from kitchen maid to cook brought a glow to Lieselotte's eyes; her pride in her work, her skill, were a joy to behold. Within a week she had brought her Cousin Gretl to help out, and with Juan working in the gardens and Fräulein Waaltraut ensconced in the library to prepare a report on culinary herbs, the kitchen became a haven of cleanliness and skill.

Not only that, but in befriending Lieselotte, Ellen had acquired the goodwill of the Hallendorf tradesmen, who had hitherto held disapprovingly aloof from the school. The butcher was Lieselotte's uncle, the baker was her mother's brother-in-law, and a farmer at whose apricot orchards Ellen had cast longing glances, was married to her aunt. Assured that the castle no longer meant to import corned beef from deserving stockyards in Ecuador or brown rice with weevils from a distant cooperative, they promised to supply the Hallendorf kitchens with fresh meat and fruit – and at prices that were reasonable and fair.

All the same, when Ellen announced that she was accompanying Lieselotte to church the following Sunday, her remark was greeted with consternation. Swimming in a bathing costume was one thing, but this was courage taken to dangerous lengths.

'Can one?' asked Sophie, her eyes wide. 'Can one really do that?'

'Of course one can,' said Ellen. 'If one can worship Beethoven and Goya and Dostoevsky, why shouldn't one worship God? After all, who gave Beethoven and the others their vision? It might well have been God, don't you think?'

'It can't be, because God doesn't exist,' said Leon. 'And anyway religion is the opium of the people.'

'I used to go to church sometimes in Vienna,' said Sophie wistfully. 'The housekeeper took me. It was lovely – the incense and the music.'

Ellen, steeling herself, said nothing. She had taken no Sundays off since she came and had reached the stage, so familiar to those who work in schools, when she wanted to speak to no one under the age of twenty, and thirty would have been better.

'The steamer doesn't go till the afternoon on Sundays, does it?' she asked Lieselotte.

'No. There's a bus very early – but usually when he's here Marek takes us over in his boat: me and Frau Tauber and anyone else who wants to go. He has friends in the village. He's so kind and such a gentleman.'

And this of course was Ellen's undoing. Making her way down to the jetty soon after seven, she found Sophie sitting on the steps, her arms around her knees.

If she had begged to be taken Ellen would have been firm, promising to take her some other time with her friends. But of course Sophie did not beg. She knew she was not wanted, and sat quietly on the jetty, and looked.

'Would you like to come?' Ellen said, and saw the spectacular change that happiness made in the thin face.

'Am I tidy enough?' she asked – and of course she was; the only child in Hallendorf who could have got into a punt then and there and rowed to church.

Leon was another matter. He liked Sophie, Ellen

knew that even if Sophie didn't. Now he appeared and said he wanted to come too.

'We're going to church, Leon. As an atheist and a Marxist and a person to whom people have to be nice because he is a Jew, I don't think this is the place for you.'

'I don't mind.'

'They, however, will mind if you turn up with a dirty face and unbrushed hair. If you can clean yourself up in five minutes and behave yourself properly, you can come. And if you do, you will please leave Marek alone.'

'What do you mean?'

'You know exactly what I mean. Now hurry.'

Ellen had expected Marek to leave them at the door of the church, but to her surprise he followed them in and saw them bestowed in the pew behind Lieselotte's family before taking his place at the end of the row.

Their arrival caused a considerable stir. Marek was greeted by a surprising number of people, and Ellen's virtues had been proclaimed by Lieselotte, but no one had seen Hallendorf children in church before, and the old woman who had warned Ellen on the steamer could be seen whispering agitatedly to her friends.

Ellen's thoughts always wandered in church, but they wandered *well*. Now she allowed herself to admire the blond heads of Lieselotte's little brothers and sisters in the row in front, and to admit that Marek (who did not seem to need his spectacles to read the hymn book)

106

was looking extremely seigniorial in the loden jacket which had replaced his working clothes.

But mostly her thoughts wandered to Henny, for whose soul she prayed though she had no right to do so, not being a Catholic, and certainly no need, since Henny's soul, if any soul on earth, could look after itself in the hereafter.

When the service was over, Ellen said she would like to look round the church and this was approved of in every way but it was not apparently a thing that one did alone. Lieselotte's mother, Frau Becker, in particular expected to attend, as did her uncle and the old woman who had warned Ellen on the boat. Nor did Marek's suggestion that he wait for them on the terrace of the inn prove to be popular. Herr Tarnowsky, who had helped Lieselotte's mother mend her roof and chopped down the baker's diseased pear tree, was expected to be present at this treat.

But if there was a claque of villagers, it was Lieselotte who was allowed to be the spokesman, for in Hallendorf Church there was a star, a local celebrity; a saint to whom the church was consecrated but of whom they spoke as of any girl who had lived among them and in her own way done extremely well.

'Her name was Aniella,' said Lieselotte. 'And look; here are the pictures which show you her life.'

She pointed to a row of oil paintings hanging on the chancel wall.

'This is one of her with her family; she lived up on

the alp underneath the *Kugelspitze* quite close to here. You can see all the animals she cared for too.'

The painting contained all the loving detail with which eighteenth-century artists depicted simple things. Aniella's house had window boxes of petunias and French marigolds; a morning glory climbed the wall. She herself was sitting on a bench and bending down to an injured creature who had placed his head in her lap – not a lamb; there *were* lambs as in all holy paintings, but further away in the meadow. No, Aniella was tending the broken leg of a St Bernard dog – one could see the keg of brandy around his neck. He was holding his paw up trustingly and beside him, jostling for a place, was a goat with a broken horn. Surrounding the girl, with her calm face and long dark hair, was a host of other animals: some were wounded – a cat with a bandaged ear, a calf with a sore on its flank – but there were others who seemed to be there more for company: a salamander walking over her foot; a grass snake curled up around a stone. It was a place where Marek's tortoise would have been very much at home.

'She was a healer,' said Lieselotte. 'She healed everything; she didn't mind what it was. Cripples and grass snakes and people, and she never harmed a creature in her life.'

'Are those her children?' asked Sophie.

'No, she was very young, only eighteen. They're her brothers and sisters. They were orphans; their parents died and she looked after them even though she wasn't much older herself.'

The little peasant children in their dirndls and ker-chiefs might have been Lieselotte's own siblings, they looked so wholesome and so good. They were helping, trained to work as peasant children are: a small boy with yellow hair was tending goats higher up on the mountain; another, a girl, sat close to Aniella, stirring something in a wooden bowl; two more were forking hay into a barn and one – a frail child with long hair – leant adoringly over Aniella's shoulder.

'Look, there's her garden,' said Lieselotte. 'These are the herbs she grew and the flowers. She knew exactly what to use for healing.'

Aniella's garden, painted like a tea tray on the side of the mountain, was a miracle of husbandry. Rows of curly cabbages flecked in bright green paint, raspberry canes, small bushes which Lieselotte's mother named for them. 'Rosemary, fennel, St John's wort . . .'

'But she loved the wild flowers too,' Lieselotte went on. 'There's a picture of her over there in the triptych holding a bunch of gentians and marguerites and edel-weiss.'

But Sophie was already worried. No one became a saint for loving flowers and being good to their family. What dreadful fate lay in wait for this appealing girl? They had only to turn to the next painting to see. A vile knight on horseback, his face set in a conquering sneer, rode with his henchmen towards the mountain. You could almost hear the clattering of hoofs, the clash of lances.

'That's Count Alexei von Hohenstift,' said Lieselotte.

'He was a truly wicked knight and so were his followers, but when he saw Aniella he fell passionately in love with her and said she had to marry him. She wept and implored and begged him to leave her, but he said if she refused to be his bride he would kill every man and woman and child in the village and set it on fire.'

'Oh how awful,' said Sophie. 'What did she do?'

'Prayed, of course,' said Leon.

His irony was lost on these uncomplicated people.

'That's right,' said Lieselotte. 'She went into that little grotto there; you can see it in the inset. It's still there, halfway up the hill behind the castle. And an angel appeared to her and said she must prepare for her wedding and trust in God.'

In the next painting they could see that Aniella had obeyed. Helped by her brothers and sisters, down whose small faces there ran rows of perfectly painted tears, she was trying on her wedding dress while her friends put out trestle tables and food for the wedding feast – and even the salamander seemed to mourn.

'This is the one, I like best though,' said Lieselotte, moving down the row.

The picture showed a flotilla of boats crossing the lake towards the church. In one boat were the musicians with their instruments, in another the guilds, in a third the school children in the care of nuns. And in the centre of the flotilla, in a boat beautifully draped and swagged, sat Aniella in her wedding dress with her brothers and sisters, carrying a bouquet of the alpine flowers she loved so well and not looking at all as though she was going to her doom.

'Because she trusted in God, you see,' said Lieselotte.

Sophie, who could not bear unhappy endings, who was waiting for the dismemberment, the breaking on the wheel, was biting her lip. 'What happened?'

'You can see. Aniella reached the church and as she stood at the altar the vile count tried to ride into the church with his henchmen – but the horse reared, it wouldn't commit sacrilege – so he strode up the aisle and just as the priest started on the service Alexei stared at his bride and –' Lieselotte paused dramatically. 'Look!'

They leant over her shoulder. Aniella still stood there in her white dress with her bunch of flowers; but her face had become the hideous, wrinkled face of an old hag.

'God had made her into a dreadful old witch,' said Lieselotte. 'Just in an instant. And the count screamed and drew out his sword and thrust it into Aniella's heart – if you come closer you can see the blood.'

They could indeed see it. It streamed over Aniella's dress as she fell to the ground, and over the children bending in anguish over their sister; it dripped from the count's sword as he ran in terror from the church and spotted the carpet on the aisle.

'So she did die,' said Sophie. It was only what she had expected.

'No, it was all right. Because as soon as the count

had gone she became young and beautiful again and she rose up and up and God took her to him and flowers came down from everywhere.'

The last picture showed Aniella, floating over the roof of the Hallendorf church, radiant and lovely, and the angels leaning out of heaven to take her in.

'She went to God,' said Lieselotte, and such was her satisfaction that Sophie had to be content.

'It's a lovely story, Lieselotte,' said Ellen.

'It isn't a story,' said Lieselotte. 'It's true.'

'What was it like?' asked Ursula that night.

'It was nice,' said Sophie. 'We heard about this saint – she was very horticultural and good. Like a cross between Heidi and Saint Francis of Assisi. Or a bit like a chicken . . . you know, those hens that hold out their wings and protect their chicks?' Sitting up in bed, Sophie stretched out her skinny arms. 'She was a sheltering person.'

'Like Ellen,' said Janey.

'Yes,' said Sophie, 'exactly like Ellen.'

'What happened to her?' asked Ursula.

'She got killed.'

Ursula nodded. All the best people got killed: her mother and father, Geronimo . . . and Sitting Bull, who had been betrayed and assassinated at Standing Rock.

Two doors down Ellen leant out of her window, looking out at the soft, expectant night. Below her the half-heard, half-felt murmur of the lake came as a

112

counterpoint to her thoughts as she went back over the day.

After the service, Marek had taken them to the inn for coffee and cakes and then excused himself; he was going to meet Professor Steiner. Leaving the children to wander round the village, she had slipped back to the church. There was something she wanted to look at more carefully; the triptych in which Aniella was depicted holding a bunch of alpine flowers.

She was still examining the painting when she became aware of someone in a side chapel. A man who had put a coin in the offertory box and now lit a tall white candle which he placed with the other votive candles beneath the altar. For a moment he stood with bent head over the flame. Then he looked up, saw her – and came over, quite unembarrassed, to her side.

'Look,' she said, 'I think I've found them.'

Following her pointing finger, Marek saw the tiny black fists of the orchids among the brilliant colours of primulas and saxifrage and gentians.

'*Kohlröserl?*'

'Yes.' She was glad he had remembered. 'So they were there then, up on the alp.'

'Which means that they might be there now. And if they are, then we can find them.'

It was absurd how pleased she had been by that 'we'. But the happiness she had felt there in the church was shot through now with something else: puzzlement, anxiety . . .

For whom had this strong and self-sufficient man

needed to light a candle? For what person – or what enterprise – did he need to evoke the gods?

Meierwitz, had he been present in the church, might have been surprised, but pleased nonetheless. No more than Marek would he seriously imagine that a minor Austrian saint of uncertain provenance (for Aniella's sanctity had been disputed) would concern herself with one small Jew without a home or country . . . and one who didn't even attend his own synagogue let alone a church.

But candles are . . . candles. They are not confined to countries or religions; their living flame reaches upwards to places where disputation has long since ceased. Neither Krishna, nor Jehovah, nor Jesus Christ would claim to be the sole recipient of the hope and faith that goes into the act of candle-lighting, in the attics of unbelievers, in schools, on birthday cakes and trees . . .

Marek, lighting his candle, had uttered no specific prayer, yet it might be considered that the unuttered prayer was heard. For two days later, Isaac Meierwitz found the courage to leave the farm in which he had lain hidden for months and set off under cover of darkness for the place near the border where he was to meet his contacts. He had been too much afraid to leave the familiar shelter until then, and he was still afraid . . . but he had gone.

# 8

In the third week of term, FitzAllan arrived from England to direct the end of term play.

Owing to Hallendorf's emphasis on drama, the summer term was extended by nearly three weeks so that the play could not only be seen by parents and other visitors, but could serve as the opening of the Summer School which ran through August and the first part of September.

The play chosen was thus of a special importance, and differed from other performances throughout the year in that staff and pupils acted in it together, and the design, the music and the lighting were a joint effort between adults and children.

Bennet's decision to bring in an outsider to direct this year was a bold one. FitzAllan had demanded a substantial fee and fees – whether substantial or otherwise – came not out of the depleted coffers of the school but out of Bennet's own pocket. But Derek FitzAllan was not only a specialist in the Stanislavsky technique and a man who had studied under Meyerhold in Russia and Piscator in the Weimar Republic – he had produced a coup which Bennet could not afford to turn down.

He had apparently persuaded Bertolt Brecht, now in exile from Germany, to let the school put on a translation of his unperformed play, *Saint Johanna of the Stockyards*. Not only to put it on but to make the necessary alterations which would make it easy to perform in a school. Bennet, amazed that the playwright had shown himself so generous, accepted FitzAllan's offer, and reproached himself for a slight weariness, a faint longing for something with more colour and life affirmation than this Marxist drama seemed likely to provide.

So now, driving with Tamara to meet the director from the train, he did his best to feel encouraged. FitzAllan had long silver hair, a relatively young, tanned face and was dressed entirely in black. He was also, as he told Bennet immediately, a strict and undeviating vegan and asked that the information should be conveyed at once to the cook.

'My goodness, what is that?' asked Lieselotte when Ellen brought the news to the kitchen.

'It's someone who doesn't eat anything that comes from animals,' said Ellen. 'No meat, no eggs, no milk, no cheese . . .'

'But what does he eat then?' asked poor Lieselotte.

'Nuts,' said Ellen, curling her lip. The director had

116

already handed her his soiled underpants and socks to wash.

Ellen had made clear her determination not to go to meetings about plays. But the gathering that FitzAllan had convened in the Great Hall as soon as he arrived came at the end of a difficult day. Sophie had still not heard from her parents, Freya had had a rejective postcard from her Mats in Lapland, and Bruno had written SHRED THE LITTLE CABBAGE in red paint on an outhouse door. There was also the question of Hermine Ritter. It had not been Ellen's intention to get fond of Dr Ritter. Her flourishing moustache, her voice – with which one could have drilled a regiment of uhlans – and her complete inability to organise the life of her baby were not in themselves endearing.

But in her own way, Hermine cared deeply about her work. Unlike Tamara, whose apparent concern for the children was really directed at her own aggrandisement, Hermine spared herself no effort, and when she asked Ellen to come to the meeting, Ellen found herself weakening. She knew that it was Hermine who had directed the previous productions and realised that it would not be easy for her to submit to the authority of an outsider.

'I thought I might watch Andromeda for you,' she said.

But Hermine said she would take Andromeda and they could *share* her.

So Ellen was present when FitzAllan, introduced by

Bennet, leapt boyishly on to the platform and began to summarise the plot.

'As you may know, the play is set in the Chicago stockyards in the Twenties and follows the fate of a group of slaughterhouse workers threatened by a lock-out engineered by their capitalist bosses. The starving workers are visited by the band of the Salvation Army, led by the heroine, Johanna, who brings them soup and tries to convert them to Christianity, but though the workers eat the soup they reject the message of Christ.' He paused, raking his silver hair, and sighed. Some of the children looked small; others looked stupid. He had forgotten that the school accepted juniors. 'Johanna now begs the capitalists to relent, but though they pretend to listen, they do nothing; at which point she loses her faith, throws in her lot with the striking workers – and dies of starvation in the snow.'

Thus described, *Abattoir* could not be called a cheerful play, but its sentiments did everyone credit, and as FitzAllan pointed out, no one need be without a part since in addition to the capitalists, the Salvation Army and the proletariat, there were parts for stock breeders, labour leaders, speculators and newsboys, not to mention the possibility of a chorus of slaughtered cattle, pigs and sheep, though this was not in the original script.

Having summarised the play, the director invited suggestions as to how it should be treated.

'Clearly in a Marxist work of this sort the emphasis must be on the persecution of the workers,' said Jean-

Pierre. 'Their fate is paramount. We could show this by lighting them very strikingly – with military searchlights, for example – keeping the capitalists in the shadows.'

Rollo did not entirely agree. He felt that the core of the play lay in the three-tiered hierarchical structure of society and proposed a set built in layers of scaffolding: the workers at the bottom, the Salvation Army in the middle and the capitalists on top.

'But not metal . . .' said poor Chomsky under his breath. 'Not *metal* scaffolding' – and was ignored.

For Hermine, this was not the point at all: what she saw in *Abattoir* was a chance for the children to come into contact with their own physicality.

'I will make exercises for the hanging motion of the carcasses and the thrust of the knife. They can experience rictus . . . and spasms,' she said, handing her baby to Ellen so as to demonstrate the kind of thing she had in mind.

FitzAllan now put up his hand. 'That is all very interesting and true,' he said, and Bennet, watching him, recognised all the signs of a director who had not the slightest intention of doing anything that anyone suggested. 'But I have to remind you above all that Brecht invented the Alienation Theory. The *Verfremdungseffekt*,' he said, breaking into German for those of the children who were looking puzzled, 'is seminal to Brecht's thinking.'

A brave child, a small girl with red hair, now put up her hand and said: 'What *is* the Alienation Theory?'

and was rewarded by grateful looks from the other children.

'Alienation Theory demands that the audience is in no way emotionally involved with the action on the stage. Brecht believed that the lights should be left on during the performance so that people could walk about and smoke cigars . . . and so on.'

'What do you do if you don't smoke cigars?' asked a literal-minded boy with spectacles, and was quelled by a look from the director.

'Who's going to do the music?' asked Leon. 'What's going to happen about that?'

But here too *Abattoir* showed itself uniquely suited to the requirements of a school whose music teacher, swathed in unspeakable knitted balaclavas from his former pupils, was absent fighting in Spain. For as FitzAllan explained, the workers would sing the Internationale, the Salvation Army would bang tambourines and sing hymns, and the exploitative capitalists would listen to decadent jazz on the gramophone.

'But there must be a ballet,' declared Tamara – and a weary sigh ran round the room. 'A red ballet with a theme of . . . viscerality. It could come to the workers while they slept.'

FitzAllan opened his mouth, remembered she was the headmaster's wife and closed it again.

'We'll discuss it in private,' he said, treating her to one of his brilliantly boyish smiles.

'Who's going to be the heroine?' asked Janey. 'The

one who gives soup to the workers and dies in the snow?'

'I shall begin the auditions tomorrow,' said FitzAllen – and reminding them that the clue to the piece would lie in its truthful and monolithic drabness, he declared the meeting closed.

Although lessons continued in the mornings, the afternoons and evenings were now devoted to increasingly frenzied rehearsals for *Abattoir*. Not only rehearsals but workshops and seminars of every kind, many of which were conducted out of doors.

Predictably, the play was taking its toll. The director's determination to make the children call up their own experience of being cruel employers was particularly unfortunate.

'He said I oppressed Czernowitz because he came in on Sunday to feed the rats,' said Sophie, coming in from one such Method class in tears, 'but I didn't – honestly, Ellen; I *loved* Czernowitz. I still do. If it wasn't for him I'd never know where anyone was.'

Leon had fallen foul of FitzAllan by pointing out that the wicked stockyard owners shouldn't be playing jazz on the gramophone. 'Jazz comes from the Blues,' said Leon. 'It's the music the Negroes used to free themselves, so it isn't decadent at all,' he'd said and been thoroughly snubbed.

Worst of all was poor Flix. FitzAllan had had the sense to see that the talented and unassuming American girl was perfect casting as the heroine, Johanna, but he had insisted on giving her a lecture on the Judas sheep.

'It's a sheep that they set up to go into the slaughterhouse and lead all the others in. It never gets killed, it just goes round and round, but the others do. It seems so absolutely *awful* to make an animal do that,' said Flix, who had recently become a Jain and wore a muslin gauze over her mouth in the evenings so that she would not swallow, or damage, the gnats.

The staff were not immune either. Hermine's efforts to put the children in touch with their own physicality were affecting her milk and poor Chomsky's darkest fears had been realised. The three-tiered structure to represent the hierarchical nature of society *was* to be made of metal and the Hungarian, who had led a sheltered life getting the children to make bookends by bending a sheet of galvanised steel into a right angle, could be seen capering round the gigantic metal struts like a demented Rumpelstiltskin.

Under these circumstances, Ellen found herself more and more grateful for Marek's quiet world of trees and water and plants. For Sophie was right, Marek did show you things – and the showing *was* like getting presents. Marek found a stickleback nest in the reeds, he led her to a place where the emerging demozel dragonflies flew up into the light, and when a small barn owl was blown off course and sat like a bewildered powder puff under a fir tree, he fetched her from the kitchen so that she could help him feed it with strips of raw liver. After a short time with him out of doors, Ellen could return to her work and to the comforting of her children with renewed energy.

'Is it possible that someone like FitzAllan could after all produce something good?' she asked Marek as the director's strident voice came from the rehearsal room.

'Unlikely. But does it really matter?'

'I'd like it to work for Bennet. He's been writing "Toscanini's Aunt" letters all day – you know, letters to important people who he thinks might be interested in coming to the play. And Margaret says he's paying for FitzAllan out of his pocket.'

Marek leant for a moment on his spade.

'Yes, he's a good man. But –'

He was about to say to her what he had said at the well. That time was running out. Not only was there no money for the school, but the school was threatened from the outside. For how much longer could it exist, this confused Eden with its unfashionable belief in freedom, its multi-lingual staff? Austria was leaning more and more towards the Third Reich; the Brownshirts strutted unashamedly in Vienna's streets, and even here in Hallendorf . . .

But she knew, of course. He remembered what she had said when she'd asked him for storks. 'They'll still be here even if we are gone.' It was *because* time was short that she cared so much about the play.

'It may work out,' he said. 'I've seen men behave worse than FitzAllan and it was all right on the day.'

To Ellen, watching him as he went about his work, it seemed that Marek was not quite so relaxed as he had been; she sensed that some part of him was alert, was waiting for something which had nothing to do with his life in the school.

The impression was strengthened two days later when she saw him come out of the post office in the village. He was putting something into his pocket – a telegram, she thought – and for a moment he stared out across the sunlit square, unseeing. Then the blank gaze disappeared, his usual observant look returned, and he greeted her.

'I didn't know you were coming over. I'd have given you a lift. I've got the van.'

'I had some bills to pay and people to see.'

They began to stroll together towards the lake. The butcher, a little mild man, waved from his shop; the greengrocer sent his boy after her with a bunch of cornflowers, and the old lady who had hissed at her on the steamer rose from a bench and said Ellen must come to her house next time and try her raspberry wine.

'You've made a lot of friends in a month,' said Marek.

'It's mostly Lieselotte,' she said. 'But I love this village, don't you?'

They reached the fountain and she paused to take a stale roll from her basket and crumble it into the water for the carp. By the gate to the churchyard, they came to Aniella's shrine: a little wooden house on stilts like a bird table.

'Does she get fed too?' he asked as Ellen stopped once more.

She shook her head. 'Just on cornflowers.' She took a single flower from her bunch and laid it among the offerings the villagers had brought. 'She's such a sensible person – and her candles burn straight and true,' she said quietly.

Marek looked at her sharply, but she had turned away. 'I must go for the steamer,' she said.

'I'll take you back. I've finished with that old devil in the woodyard. But we'll have some coffee first at the *Krone*. The landlord's in a splendid mood because he's landed an entire conference of dentists for his new annexe. His wife thought he'd never fill it and lo, twenty-three dentists are descending in July!'

'Oh I am glad! They work so hard, those two.'

They found a table under the chestnuts, and Marek ordered coffee and *Streuselkuchen*. Ellen's coffee came with a glass of clear cold water, but Marek's, by courtesy of the landlord, was accompanied by a full measure of schnapps.

'Goodness, can you drink that so early in the morning?'

'Most certainly,' said Marek, raising his glass. 'Water is for the feet!'

She had collected a posse of sparrows and pigeons with whom she was sharing her cake.

'Everything isn't hungry, you know,' he pointed out. 'Those carp, for example.'

'No,' she said. 'Perhaps not. But everybody likes to eat.'

He watched her as she skilfully distributed the food

125

so that even the bluetits at the back were not upstaged by the pigeons, and remembered her each night in the dining room, assessing, portioning out the food fairly, keeping order without ever raising her voice.

'You remind me of my grandmother,' he said. 'She was English too.'

'Goodness! I didn't know any part of you was English. Is that why you speak it so well?'

'Perhaps. I spent a year in an English school. A horrible place, I must say.'

'Is she still alive – your grandmother?'

'Very much so.'

She waited, her head tilted so that a handful of curls fell over one shoulder. It was not a passive waiting and presently Marek conceded defeat and began.

'Her name was Nora Coutts,' he said, stirring his coffee. 'And when she was twenty years old she went to Russia to look after the three little daughters of a general in the army of the Tsar. Only of course being British she used to go for long walks by herself in the forest; even in the winter, even in the rain.'

'Naturally,' agreed Ellen.

'And one day she found a woodcutter sitting in front of his brazier under a clump of trees. Only he didn't seem to be an ordinary woodcutter. For one thing his brazier wasn't burning properly and for another he was reading a book.'

'What was the book?'

'*The Brothers Karamazov*. So my grandmother smelt a rat, and quite rightly, for it turned out that the young man was an anarchist who belonged to a freedom movement dedicated to the overthrow of the Tsar. He had been told to keep watch on the general and tell his superiors when it would be a good time to blow him up without blowing up his wife and children. They minded about blowing up women and children in those days,' said Marek, 'which shows you how old-fashioned they were.

'Needless to say, my grandmother thought this was not a good idea, and by this time the young man had fallen in love with her because she had red hair and freckles and was exceedingly nice. But of course by refusing to blow up the general, he was in danger from the anarchists, so he and my grandmother ran away together and when they got to Prague they stopped running and settled in a pink house so small you could heat it with matchsticks, and gave birth to a daughter who grew up to write poetry and be my mother . . . And who, if you met her, you would probably like a lot.'

She waited to make sure he had finished. Then: 'Thank you,' she said, 'that was a lovely story. I liked it a lot.'

Marek leant back in his chair, pierced by a sudden regret. His time here was almost over; he was going to miss this untroubling and selfless girl.

'Come,' he said, 'I've got something to show you.'

He led her back across the square and up a narrow street which sloped up towards the pastures. At the last house, with its lace curtains and pots of geraniums, he stopped and knocked.

A frail, elderly man with a limp came to the door and Marek said: 'I've brought Fräulein Ellen to see your animals. Is it convenient?'

The man nodded and led them through the front room into the kitchen with an extension built over the garden. On a large table were a number of wooden trays lined with layers of greaseproof paper.

'Herr Fischer makes them to sell in Klagenfurt but I thought you'd like to see them.'

But Ellen could scarcely speak; she was spellbound. The trays were full of rows and rows of little creatures made from marzipan. There were lions with wavy manes, and hedgehogs, each bristle as distinct as pins. There were squirrels crouching in the curve of their tails, and a dachshund, and piebald cows with tufts of grass held in their mouths. There was a frog with a golden chin and dark brown splodges, and a penguin, and a mouse with outsize whiskers . . .

'Oh!' Ellen turned to Herr Fischer. 'I can't *believe* it! The colours . . . the detail . . . You must be so proud. I would give anything to be able to make those.'

He flushed with pleasure, then shrugged. 'It's just a question of time, Fräulein; patience and time.'

'No it isn't. It's a skill. It's art.' She shook her head. 'Is it the usual recipe – almond paste and egg white?'

'Yes, but a softer mixture – and of course the colours are the difficulty. A good green dye . . .'

'Oh yes – green is so difficult!'

Marek listened, amused, as they became technical.

As Ellen turned back for a last look at the trays, he saw on her face an expression he had known in a number of women: a degree of longing that could only be described as lust. He had seen it on Brigitta Seefeld's face as she peered at a sable coat in a window in the Kärntnerstrasse, and on the face of the little Greek actress he had known in New York for a diamond brooch at Tiffany's. Now he saw it on Ellen's face as she gazed at Herr Fischer's handiwork.

'They're not for sale, I'm afraid,' said Marek. 'They all go to the patisserie in Klagenfurt.'

'That's true,' said the old man. 'But I can spare one for the Fräulein. Not to buy, of course; a gift.' He stepped aside to let Marek see clearly. 'If Herr Tarnowsky will pick one out.'

Marek moved forward. For a full minute he stood in silence. His hand hovered over a dementedly woolly lamb . . . rested momentarily above a blond snail with sky-blue eyes . . . and then came down with assured finality.

'This one, please,' he said, and Herr Fischer nodded, for even before he caught Ellen's intake of breath he had known that she would want the smallest, the most unassuming, yet somehow the brightest of all the little creatures on the tray.

'When are you going to eat it?' teased Marek as they came out into the street.

'Eat it! *Eat* it!' said Ellen, outraged. 'I'd rather die!'

Back in her room that evening she took her gift out

of its fluted twist of paper and stood holding it in her hand. She had always loved ladybirds especially: the guardians of roses, heroes of children's ditties and songs. If one flew up from your hand you could have a wish.

It had been a happy day. When she first came to Hallendorf she had been sure that Marek would help her and she had been right. He had helped her most truly and she was proud to have him for a friend.

These warming and uplifting sentiments ceased abruptly two days later when he threw one of her children into the lake.

It began with Leon's gramophone. Along with the other expensive presents with which Leon was showered, he had a blue portable gramophone which had arrived by special carrier at the beginning of term. New records packed in corrugated cardboard were added by his doting mother almost weekly. Half of them arrived broken, but enough of them survived to turn Leon into something of a hazard as he played them over and over again and was moved on from the steps of the terrace, the common room and the bedroom he shared with Bruno and a French boy called Daniel.

During the week in which FitzAllan came to direct *Abattoir* Leon received another batch of records, among which was a group of songs by a composer of whom Ursula instantly disapproved because he was still alive.

'People who are alive can never write tunes,' she said.

And it was true that the *Songs for Summer* were unusual and strange. If they depicted summer it was not the voluptuousness of droning bees and heavy scents, but rather the disembodied season of clarity and light. The tunes carried by the solo violin which rose above the orchestra, and the silvery soprano voice, seemed to Ellen to be 'almost tunes' – they appeared, stole into her ear and vanished before she could grasp them.

But after a few hearings, she began to follow the piece with interest and then slowly with a pleasure that was the greater for not having been instantaneous.

Leon, however, being Leon, could not leave well alone. He played the *Songs for Summer* inside the castle and outside it. He took his gramophone into the rowing boat, and he was winding up the gramophone yet again, sitting on the steps of the jetty, when Marek came past, carrying a hoe, and told him to stop.

Leon looked up, his thin face set in a look of obstinacy.

'I don't want to stop it. I like it. It's beautiful and the man who plays the violin obligato is fantastic. His name is Isaac Meierwitz and –'

Marek's hand came down and removed the needle.

In the ensuing silence, the boy got to his feet. 'You can't do that. You can't be horrid to me, because I'm Jewish. You may not care what happens to the Jews but –'

Watching Marek one would have seen only a slight tightening of the muscles round his mouth, but Janik and Stepan, the woodsmen whose job it had been to carry the infant Marek out into the fields until his devastating temper attacks had spent themselves, would have recognised the signs at once.

Then he put down his hoe, moved slowly forward and pitched Leon out into the lake.

Sophie and Ursula, running excitedly upstairs, brought the news to Ellen.

'It serves him right,' said Ursula. 'He was following Marek about again – and he was playing his beastly gramophone right by the jetty.'

'But Marek waited to see if he came up again. He wouldn't have let him drown.' Sophie was torn between pity for Leon and concern for her hero, Marek, who had certainly behaved oddly.

Leon himself, wrapped in a towel and shivering theatrically, now arrived escorted by Freya, who had been closest to the scene of the accident.

'He's had a shock, of course, but I don't think any harm's been done.' Her kind face was as puzzled and troubled as Sophie's. 'I don't know why . . .'

Ellen put her arms around Leon. 'Go and run a hot bath, Sophie,' she ordered. 'And Ursula, go and ask Lieselotte to bring up a hot-water bottle.'

'At least he didn't defenestrate me,' said Leon as she stripped off his wet clothes. 'That's what he usually does.'

'What do you mean, Leon?'

'Nothing.' Still sniffing and gulping down tears, Leon turned his head away. 'I don't mean anything.'

When she had dried him and put on clean pyjamas she found Lieselotte by his bed, plumping up his pillows.

'Could you stay with him a minute, Lieselotte? I won't be long.'

Ellen had no recollection of how she got to the door of Marek's room in the stable block. The rage she had suppressed while helping Leon now consumed her utterly.

'How *dare* you!' she shouted, before she was even across the threshold. 'How dare you use violence on any of my children?'

Marek looked up briefly from the drawer he was emptying into a battered pigskin case, then resumed his packing.

'No child here gets physically assaulted. It is the law of the school and it is my law.'

He took absolutely no notice. He had begun to take documents from a wooden chest – among them sheaves of manuscript paper.

His indifference incensed her to fever point. 'I have spent the whole term trying to calm Leon and now you have undone any good anyone might have done. If he gets pneumonia and dies –'

'Unlikely,' said Marek indifferently.

'You must be completely mad! It's all very well for you to amuse yourself here pretending to wear spectacles you don't need and parting your hair in a way that anyone can see it doesn't go. But when it causes you to brutalise the children –'

But she could not get him to react. She had the feeling that he was already somewhere where she and Hallendorf did not exist.

'I'm leaving,' he said. 'As you see.'

'Good!' Leon's pinched face, his running nose and shivering, scrawny limbs kept her anger at burning point. 'You can't go too soon for any of us.'

He did look at her then. For a moment she remembered what she had felt when she first saw him by the well: that she had been, for a moment, completely understood. This look was its opposite: she was obliterated; a nothing.

But her rage sustained her, and she turned and left him, slamming the door like a child.

When she got back she found Leon dozing, his colour restored. Lieselotte had remade his bed. Bending down to make sure he was tucked in properly, Ellen saw the corner of a white folder protruding from under the mattress and drew it out.

'I only borrowed it,' muttered Leon. 'I was going to give it back.'

'That's all right, Leon. Go to sleep.'

Examining what she held in her hand she found it was a concert programme – and pinned to it a number of sheets of paper covered in Kendrick's handwriting.

*

An hour later, Marek knocked at the door of Leon's room. The children and Ellen were in the dining room; the boy, as he'd expected, was alone.

'Now then, Leon,' he said, sitting down on the bed beside him, 'what exactly is it that you want?'

The tears started to flow again then; the twitchy face screwed itself into a grimace. 'I just want you to help me,' he sobbed. 'That's all I want. I want you to *help*.'

'How?'

'I don't know anything . . . I can't work out the fingering of my Beethoven sonata and I don't know if the quartet I've written is any good. My parents want me to be a musician – my mother's desperate for it, and my sisters too. They help me and help me, but I want someone to tell me if I've got any talent.'

'No one else can tell you that.'

'But how does one know if it's worth going on? I don't know whether I have any true creativity or –'

'Good God, Leon, why do you always turn back on yourself? If you feel the need to write music, or play it, then do so, but believe me your creativity is of no interest to anyone. Write something – then it's there. If it's what you wanted to write, if it *exists*, then leave it. If it doesn't, throw it away. Your beautiful state of mind is totally irrelevant.'

'But you –'

'What happened to me has nothing to do with it. As it happens I was not at all keen on my so-called creativity. I fought it hard and long because I saw that

135

it would take me away from the place I wanted to spend my life in, and the work I thought I had been born to do. If I wrote music it was because I didn't know how to stop. But you –'

'My mother loves music so much. And my sisters, and my father is a businessman but he'd have liked to be a pianist – he's very good. So I thought . . . I wanted. It's not that they force me, but –'

'Yes; I see.' For the first time, Marek felt pity and affection for the boy. 'Tell me, Leon, if I asked you what you wanted to do when you grow up, what would you say? Just answer quickly.'

'Make films,' said Leon in an instant.

Marek smiled. 'That has the ring of truth.' He sat in silence for a moment, then decided to give the boy what he had asked for – help. 'I said no one can judge another person's vocation and I meant that, but . . . I think that you are genuinely musical; you will make an excellent amateur – and remember please the meaning of the word. An amateur is a *lover* of music. You will be a fine facilitator, a person who can *make music happen*. It is because of people like you and your family that music is heard, that orchestras are formed, and paid for, and that's something to be proud of. But if you ask me whether you have the original spark, well then, I have to say I think probably not.'

He watched the boy carefully and saw the screwed-up look gradually vanish from his face. Then he leant back on the pillow and smiled – a slow smile of relief and happiness. Released from his burden, he looked like a child again, not a wizened old man.

'They'd believe me if you told them,' said Leon. 'I know you can't now but one day, if you go back.'

Marek got up and went to the window. 'Your romantic notions of me are mistaken. I am not at Heiligenstadt renouncing the world. Simply I need a few months in which I am not associated with my former life. But now you have –'

'I wouldn't say anything. Not *ever*. I've known you since you came because my mother was in Berlin when you defenestrated that Nazi and it was in all the papers and I saw your picture. But I can keep a secret.'

'If you cannot, the consequences would be very serious. I take it no one else knows?'

Leon hung his head. 'Ellen does. Now. Her fiancé sent her a programme of the concert where they played your songs. I sort of borrowed it and –'

'Her fiancé?' asked Marek, momentarily diverted.

'Well, she says she isn't going to marry him, but we think she will because he keeps on writing letters and she's sorry for him because he lives in a wet house and his mother delivered a camel on the way to church.'

His house would not stay wet long if she married him, thought Marek, and saw Ellen with a red-and-white-checked tea towel on a ladder, carefully drying the chimneys.

'His name is Kendrick Frobisher,' said Leon, 'and he was at school with you.'

'Really?' The name meant nothing to Marek. He

came back to the bed. 'You have a close and loving family, Leon,' he said. 'Not many children are as fortunate. Trust them. Tell them the truth.'

As he made his way to his room to pick up his case, a sudden image came to him of a small pale boy cowering beside a radiator. A much bullied boy always trying to hide in a corner with a book. Yes, he was almost sure that was Frobisher.

Well, that was ridiculous; there was no possible way that Ellen could be going to marry *him*?

Or was there? Could he turn out to be another creature that needed to be fed – not with breadcrumbs or kitchen scraps this time, but with her pity and her love? In which case she was going to be most seriously unhappy.

But Ellen's concerns had nothing to do with him. His life at Hallendorf was over. He had said goodbye to Bennet and given in his keys. By the time the children came out of the dining room, Marek was gone.

Ellen, hurrying upstairs, found Leon sitting up in bed – and totally transformed.

'Marek came!' he said in a voice resonant with hero worship. 'He came and it's all right, I don't have to be a great musician, I can just do ordinary things. I can do everything! Oh Ellen, isn't it marvellous? I think he must be the most marvellous person in the world.'

She stared at Leon. His face was glowing, his restored and golden future lay before him. It was in defence of this child that she had attacked Marek and sent him away with the memory of her senseless and infantile rage.

'I'm going to get my parents to send me a proper cine camera – you can get them quite cheaply – well, not very cheaply perhaps – and I'm going to write a script. Sophie can star in it and that will show her beastly mother –'

Ellen let him babble on. Then he stopped. 'Ellen, you always say we have to have handkerchiefs and it's you that's sniffing now.'

She tried to smile, wiping her eyes. 'It's all right. I quarrelled with Marek, that's all, and now he's gone.'

'Oh, he won't bother with that. A man like that wouldn't even notice. Ellen, when I'm grown up I'm going to write Marek's biography – if he'll let me. He's already had the most amazing life, what with throwing people out of windows and being a hero and having that opera singer in love with him. She's terribly famous too – Brigitta Seefeld – there was a lot about her in the sleeve notes to my record.'

Leon had collected almost as much information about his idol as Kendrick Frobisher. 'I'm going to be like Eckerman who wrote down everything that Goethe said, or that man Bennet told us about in English – Dr Johnson's friend Boswell. Do you think you could try and remember the things he said to you – because you were good friends, weren't you?'

'Yes, I think we were.'

*Never let the sun go down on your wrath.* But the sun had gone down; it was sinking spectacularly over the mountains, turning the rock face to crimson and amethyst and gold.

'Only where do you begin?' asked Leon, pondering his biography.

'At the beginning, I suppose, Leon,' she said wearily.

At the place in Bohemia where his mother had driven about with white doves in a washing basket . . .

At the place where there were storks . . .

# 9

The house had been a hunting lodge built of silvered aspen in the ancient forest preserved for their sport by the Hapsburg princes who ruled over the Bohemian lands. In the eighteenth century it was enlarged, became a manor, its windows shuttered, its stuccoed walls painted in the *Schönbrunn* yellow which Maria Theresa permitted to those who served her.

Marek's great-grandfather, the Freiherr Marcus von Altenburg, came there from Northern Germany, fell in love with the countryside – its ancient trees, its eagles and owls and unlimited game – and bought it. He cleared enough land round the house to make a small farm, dug a fish pond, and let the sun in on Pettelsdorf's roofs. It was then that the storks came.

For more than a hundred years the von Altenburgs were citizens of the Austro–Hungarian Empire. Then in 1918 Austria collapsed and Pettelsdorf – now Pettovice – found itself part of the new Republic of Czechoslovakia.

No one at Pettelsdorf greatly cared. Frontiers had marched back and forward in this part of Europe for generations, but the same wind still blew through the fields of oats and rye, the geese still made their way in single file towards the water, the high-cruppered dray horses still pulled their loads along the dusty, rutted roads.

Marek's father, though keeping his German nationality, was happy to throw in his lot with the new republic: Czechoslovakia, under Masaryk, was a model of democratic government. He had in any case married a wife brought up in Prague, a bluestocking reared in a little medieval house behind the castle. Milenka Tarnowsky's mother was English, her father Russian; she herself spoke five languages, had taken tea with Kafka and earned her living translating articles and poetry. To keep open house for all nationalities was as much a tradition of Marek's home as was the sheltering of wanderers by the monasteries that lined the pilgrim routes towards the east.

It was an unexpected marriage – that of Captain von Altenburg who lived for his hunting and his trees, and the intellectual girl whose spare, honed poems celebrated a unique and inner vision – but it became a byword for happiness.

No wonder then that the son who was born to them should regard the world as created for his personal delight. There were no divisions at Pettelsdorf between the manor and the farm, the farm and the forest. Geese patrolled his mother's hammock as she worked at her translations; his father's hunting dogs tumbled with Milenka's pop-eyed Tibetan terrier and the mongrels he rescued from the village. As soon as he could sit on a horse, Marek rode with his father on the never-ending work of the land, sometimes staying away for days.

He was a person much addicted to abundance.

'I don't like *either*, I like *and*,' said the five-year-old Marek when the cook asked which kind of filling he wanted baked into his birthday *beigli*. 'Apricots *and* poppy seed *and* walnuts,' he demanded – and got them.

But if the house servants spoilt him, the men in the fields did not. The woodcutters and charcoal burners and draymen who were his heroes knew better than to indulge the boy who would one day be the master, and thus the servant of their demesne. When he was overcome by one of his rare but devastating attacks of temper, it was in the hay barn or paddock that Marek took refuge, kicking and raging till old Stepan, the head forester, brought him back, tear-stained and purged.

That he would follow in his father's footsteps was something so obvious that Marek never consciously questioned it, so when a fuss was made about his music, he simply ignored it.

It had shown itself early, his talent, as it so often does. When he was three he had requested the bandmaster in the local town to make way for him so that he could conduct the band himself. Two years later he wrote a song in six-eight time for the birthday of a neighbouring landowner's daughter whom he passionately loved. He played the piano of course, and the violin, and had taught himself most of the instruments he found in the village band which played for funerals and weddings.

But what was so strange about that? Everybody in Bohemia was musical; half the horn players in the Vienna Philharmonic were Czech; their singers swarmed in the opera. Even when that cliche happened and the local music teacher said he could teach the boy no more, Marek refused to be deflected.

'I'm certainly not going to start roaming the world with little bits of my native earth in a pouch like poor Chopin,' he said.

Efforts to send him away to be educated had never been successful. He had discharged himself without fuss from an Academy for the Sons of Gentlemen in Brno, and from the British public school recommended by his grandmother, the redoubtable Nora Coutts, who lived in a wing of the house drinking Earl Grey tea from Harrods and bullying him about the syntax of the English language.

Even when at last he consented to go to the University of Vienna it was to read Forestry and Land Management. But Vienna is not a good place for a man fleeing from music. By the time he met Brigitta Seefeld, Marek's course in life was set.

He was twenty years old, sitting with his friends in the fourth gallery of the Opera, when the curtain went up on *Figaro*.

Seefeld was not singing Susanna, that life-affirming fixer; she sang the Countess, to whom in 'Dove Sono'

Mozart has given perhaps the most heart-rending lament for lost love in all opera.

Marek was overwhelmed. He heard her again as Violetta in *Traviata* and Pamina in *The Magic Flute*. The voice was ravishing; ethereal, silvery yet full and strong. That she was beautiful – fair-haired, blue-eyed, in the best tradition of the Viennese – was not a disadvantage.

Arriving at the door of her dressing room carrying a rather large arbutus in a pot, Marek had intended only to pay homage, but within a month the diva had led him firmly up the three steps that ascended to her bed: an absurd bed decorated with gilt swans – a present from an admirer after her first Elsa in *Lohengrin*.

It was not only the bed that was absurd: she herself was vain, self-regarding and extravagant, but when he held her in his arms (and there was plenty to hold) he felt as though he was embracing the great and glorious traditions of Viennese music. He wrote the *Songs for Summer* for her, and years afterwards his songs still came to him in Brigitta's voice.

It was a public liaison, much approved of by the gossipy Viennese. Brigitta lost no opportunity to parade her new admirer (now known as Marcus, the German version of his Christian name, for his descent as a *Freiherr* was very much to her taste). Marek would not have broken it up: Brigitta was more than ten years his senior and he had all the chivalry of the young. It was she who sent him away, 'Just for a little while.' She had dramatically overspent her salary and needed to audition a rich protector.

'If I go now I won't come back,' Marek had said.

She didn't believe him but he spoke the truth.

It was now, in the spring of 1929, that he went to Berlin, with its pompous architecture, its vile climate – and its superlative cultural life.

In Vienna he had been absorbed in his affair with Brigitta – now he made friends, and one friend in particular.

Isaac Meierwitz was a violinist, well known as a virtuoso soloist – but known too as something more: a true musician who continued to play chamber music, sat at the first desk of the Berlin Akademia and taught needy students without charge. Marek had met him at Professor Steiner's house. Outwardly he looked like everybody's idea of a Russian Jew: small, pop-eyed and splendidly neurotic. Meierwitz was allergic to egg white and sopranos, saw ghosts and kept his grandmother's pigtail in the case which held his Stradivarius, but he had the heart of a lion. He drank vodka like mother's milk, needed almost no sleep, was a first-class swimmer and a repository of unbelievably awful jokes.

Isaac was only a few years older than Marek but he know everybody. He introduced Marek to Schonberg and Stravinsky, took him to *Wozzeck* at the Kroll, and to hear Schnabel play Beethoven sonatas at the Volksbühne, wearing a lounge suit so that the workers would feel at home. He found cellars where the gypsies were not graduates of the Budapest Conservatoire but true *Zigeuners*, and cabarets where the chicanery of politicians was blisteringly exposed.

One day as they were walking through the Tiergarten after an all-night party, Isaac said he thought it was time he had his concerto.

'I have my immortality to think of, you know.'

'Good God, Isaac, surely your immortality doesn't depend on a violin concerto by somebody like me!'

But Meierwitz was serious. 'You're almost ready. And remember, if anyone but me gets to play the premiere, I'll haunt you to my dying day!'

Soon after this Marek was offered a two-year contract at the Curtis Institute in Philadelphia, the Mecca of all musicians and a true honour for a man still in his early twenties.

He had loved America, become completely absorbed in the music-making there. At the end of his stint he took six months off and went to live in a hut on the Hudson River. One day, walking by the water, he heard the theme for the slow movement.

Violin concertos have a distinguished provenance. Beethoven, Sibelius, Brahms, all wrote only one but they were written in blood. When he had finished it, Marek sent the score to Berlin.

Meierwitz cabled at once, full of superlatives. A premiere was arranged with the Berlin Akademia for the following spring, with Marek himself conducting. The year was 1933. Marek now took off for the Mato Grosso in Brazil to study the native music there. He was out of touch with civilisation for the whole winter

– even so, later, he was amazed at how naive he had been.

He sailed for Europe in the spring of 1934: the South American papers had made light of Hitler's doings and Meierwitz had written to say that he'd been promised permission to give the premiere and was staying on in Germany to do so. The *Bremen* ran into a storm. Marek arrived a day late and went straight to the concert hall to start rehearsals. He found the new music director waiting, full of smiles and affability. The premiere was attracting much attention, he said; to have Herr von Altenburg back in Germany was an honour.

Marek took little notice. He was waiting for the soloist. He had phoned Meierwitz's flat when the ship docked and left a message.

Then a young man, blond, friendly with innocent blue eyes walked on to the platform with his violin.

'I'm Anton Kessler, Herr von Altenburg,' he said, bowing. 'I have the honour to play your concerto. Believe me, this is a great day in my life.'

There was a dead silence in the concert hall.

Then: 'No, Herr Kessler, you do not have that honour. This concerto is dedicated to Isaac Meierwitz and he and he alone will play the premiere.'

The members of the orchestra shuffled their music; Anton Kessler flushed.

'Surely they told you . . . Meierwitz has been . . . Meierwitz is a Jew; there is no possibility that he should appear as a soloist.'

Marek turned to the director. 'I was told that Meierwitz would be playing. I had a letter to that effect before I sailed.'

The director smoothed his brilliantined hair. 'I think there must be some mistake. Meierwitz has been taken . . . Meierwitz has left. He refused the chance of emigration. He made difficulties and this is something that the Third Reich cannot allow. I assure you no harm will come to him, and Herr Kessler is an excellent musician. Please, Kessler, show Herr Altenburg.'

The blond young man moved to the front of the platform and the theme which had come to Marek out there by the Hudson River sang out over the hall. He played well.

'Stop,' said Marek.

Now he looked around the hall more carefully. Other faces were missing: the first horn, a man called Cohen, the second flautist . . .

'You will be kind enough to tell me where they have taken Meierwitz?' said Marek quietly.

'I'm afraid I haven't the slightest idea.' The director was becoming ruffled. 'You must agree yourself that German music needed purging from foreign influences and in particular from –'

Marek could never describe the onset of his rages; those first moments were out of time. When he came to himself, he was holding the portly, squealing little man out of the first-floor window by one pin-striped trouser leg.

'Where is he, you little toady? Where have they taken him?'

'Stop it, stop it! I'll be killed – pull me in, damn you. Help! Help!'

Marek lowered his grip so that he was holding only one ankle. Down in the street a crowd was gathering; a man hurried out of the house opposite with a camera . . .

'You heard what I said. Where is he? You've got exactly one minute.'

'He's in a camp . . . Weichenberg . . . near the Czech border. It is for resettlement.'

Overcome by disgust, Marek hauled him in and hung him over the sill. Then he turned to the orchestra.

'There will be no performance of this concerto, gentlemen. Nor of any of my music while the present regime is in power,' he said – and left the hall.

He went back to Pettelsdorf. His determination to find and rescue Meierwitz had been instantaneous and it seemed to him that he could do it better from somewhere familiar whose every hiding place he knew well.

But even his own country was not free from evil. Not all the Sudeten Germans were making trouble, not all of them wanted to belong to the German Reich, but there were enough hotheads, egged on by the Nazis in Berlin, to make life perilous for those who wished only to live in peace. Marek's father was insulted because he was content to be part of the Czech Republic; some of his workmen were beaten up when they went into the market town; and Marek's action in withdrawing his work from the Reich was seen by many as treachery. He found himself watched and visited by high-ranking Nazis trying to make him change his mind, and it soon became clear that he was making trouble for his family and that as Marcus Altenburg, the avowed friend of Jewish musicians and other 'Enemies of the Reich', he could not go unobserved.

It was then that he came to Hallendorf to find Professor Steiner, meaning only to borrow his van – and found a man as obstinately determined as he was himself to put right the wrongs that his homeland had perpetrated.

# 10

Kendrick Frobisher had his faults but he was a truthful young man. When he said that his mother had delivered a camel on the way to church he was reporting facts that were well known in the district, and when he said that Crowthorpe Hall was both wet and red, he did not exaggerate.

What he had perhaps not made clear to Ellen – for he was, in his own way, a modest person – was that it was also large. The house had fourteen bedrooms, only some of which were so mildewed and damp that they were virtually unusable. It had a drawing room, a billiard room, a library (some distant ancestor having gathered together the most unreadable collection of books ever assembled), a dining room lined in peeling Morocco leather and a gallery which ran round the vast and draughty hall.

The size of Crowthorpe was augmented by an eruption of turrets, gables and other protuberances, for the house had been extensively rebuilt in Victorian times, and stained-glass windows and heavily swathed curtains managed to reduce the light which came in from the melancholy, sheep-ridden countryside to the point where the lamps had to be lit by three o'clock in the afternoon, even in summer. Inside too the heavy, convoluted furniture, the claw-footed tables and blood-red Turkey carpets created an ambience in which Queen Victoria, not noted for her *joie de vivre*, would have been entirely at home.

The significance of Crowthorpe, however, lay not in the house, but in the land which surrounded it. The estate comprised nearly four thousand acres, and though much of it was in the same melancholy and largely useless vein that characterised the house – a lake full of ill-tempered pike, a bosom-shaped hill on which (despite its relatively low stature) two hikers had perished in a blizzard, a derelict gravel pit – there was also, in the fertile river valley which the mansion overlooked, a large and profitable farm, which had been managed frugally and effectively by the farm manager, a Cumbrian born and bred, for many years.

That the estate should go entire and unencumbered to the eldest son had been Mrs Kendrick's intention, as it was the intention of every landowner in this self-contained and rural district. Since her husband's death she had been in charge of Crowthorpe's affairs, and that Roland meant to leave the Indian Army and come home to Britain was a source of great satisfaction. Roland had been a pleasure to her from the moment of his birth; a handsome, outgoing, tough little boy who seldom cried, was good at sport, and went off to his prep school at seven with a brave smile. Roland would make a good master for Crowthorpe and as he had had the sense to marry out there, there might soon be a son.

And if anything happened to Roland there was William. William was not quite as steady as Roland – there had been a few debts during his young days and rumours of trouble with a girl who was undoubtedly common and had had to be paid off. But he had steadied down a lot; he was handsome and popular with the county, and no doubt would soon get himself engaged to someone suitable.

So the succession was secure and normally Mrs Frobisher would not have given a second thought to poor Kendrick, that unfortunate afterthought which had resulted from her permitting her husband what she had virtually ceased to permit after her elder sons were born. Kendrick had been a disaster from the first, embarrassing and distressing her with his inability to fit in; his asthma, his fear of horses, his shame-making crying fits when it was time to return to school . . . and, later, the way he buried himself in his room listening to obscure and depressing music and ruining his eyes with endless reading.

But that morning, in *The Times*, she had read that it was the intention of the Government to issue gas masks to the populace. Mrs Frobisher had not been very interested in the policies of Herr Hitler. She had no particular quarrel with him – indeed, with his attempts to clear away Jews, homosexuals, communists and gypsies she had a certain sympathy – but he was making a lot of noise about *Lebensraum* and colonies and that was a different matter. The art of colonisation was one that was only understood by the British, who knew how to deal with inferior races with justice and sternness. So it might after all be necessary to fight a war, and Mrs Frobisher, suppressing with an iron effort of will the panic that the memory of the last war and its hideous decimation of the nation's youth brought to her, had decided that Kendrick must be sent for and instructed to marry. Kendrick would survive whatever happened; with his asthma and his astigmatism, not to mention the slight curvature of his spine, there was no question of his being called up for military service. Horrible as it was to imagine him as master of Crowthorpe, it would be better than letting the estate go out of the family.

So Kendrick was sent for, and took Volume Three of *A la Recherche du Temps Perdu* for the train and a packet of Milk of Magnesia tablets, for a summons to Crowthorpe always gave him indigestion, and took the train north. At Carlisle, as always happened when he travelled home, it began to rain.

In the old Buick which his mother had sent for him, he watched the mist swirling round the hills, heard the forlorn bleating of the black-faced sheep, and the sinister rushing of the brown streams running almost at flood level, and wondered what he had done. Kendrick had his own income, inherited from a distant relative who had been sorry for the unwanted little boy, and owned his flat in Pimlico, so there was not really much that his mother could do to him, but logic played little part in Kendrick's perception of Patricia Frobisher.

It was not until after dinner, which he took alone with his mother in the freezing dining room, that he gathered why he had been summoned.

'I hope you can manage to have a sensible conversation about this, Kendrick,' she said, when the maid had delivered herself of the blancmange and retreated, her duty done. 'I don't want any hysteria or panic. But it seems possible that there is going to be a war.'

Kendrick put down his napkin, suddenly as pale as the pudding in front of him. In his head Zeppelins exploded into flame, planes zoomed, children ran screaming from their demolished houses.

'Do you really think so?' he managed to stammer.

'I don't know. Chamberlain is doing his best to avert it, but we must always look at possibilities unflinchingly.'

'Yes,' said Kendrick, and thought longingly of Marcel Proust, his hero, who had spent twelve years in a cork-lined room working on his masterpiece. Strictly speaking this could not be regarded as an unflinching way of carrying on, but of course he had been a genius.

'As you know, Roland is coming home, but if there's any trouble he's sure to join up and William is now an experienced pilot. If anything happens to them you will become the owner of Crowthorpe. Nothing can be done about this.'

Mother and son gazed at each other over the enormous dining table, both equally appalled by the prospect. Huge bulls pursued Kendrick in his mind as he tried to give orders to the farm manager; the wheels of threshing machines whirred, blowing chaff into his asthmatic lungs; girls on large horses rode up the drive and despised him . . .

'So it has become necessary for you to do your duty, Kendrick. You must marry.'

Kendrick blinked at his mother through his thick glasses. She wanted him to marry. And at the word 'marry' there came into his mind, erasing the terrifying prospects of war and agriculture, Ellen's lovely face, the soft mouth, the gentle eyes and floating hair.

'I should like to marry,' he said, 'but there is only one woman I am prepared to consider.'

Patricia stared at her son, who had spoken with unexpected certainty.

'Who is that?' she asked.

'Her name is Ellen Carr. She's working in Austria at the moment but her home is in London. She is a wonderful person.'

'What is she working at? What does anyone do in Austria?'

'She is a matron in a school. But she also cooks. She is highly trained.'

Patricia controlled herself with an effort of will.

'A cook! I take it you are joking. Even you would not imagine that a Frobisher could marry a cook?'

But the image of Ellen had given Kendrick unexpected courage.

'There is no one else I am prepared to marry,' he repeated. 'But she has refused me.'

'Refused you! Good heavens, what is a cook doing to refuse you? Does she know who you are?'

'Yes. But she is not in love with me. Of course a lot of people have proposed to her, but I shall never give up hope. Never.'

Making a heroic effort, Patricia tried to envisage a cook who had been much proposed to and did not want to espouse a Frobisher.

'What is her background?'

'Her mother is a doctor. She was a Norchester. There are three sisters who were all suffragettes. They are admirable women. Ellen's father was killed in the last war.'

'Good God, not the Norchester gals? Phyllis and Charlotte and what was the third one called?'

'Annie.'

'That's right. Well, well – Gussie Norchester's gals – mad as hatters, all of them, tying themselves to railings and God knows what. Gussie had a dreadful time with them – they wouldn't be presented or behave normally in any way.'

But the aberrant behaviour of the girls didn't seem to matter, Kendrick found, for Gussie Norchester had been the niece of Lord Avondale and entirely acceptable. If the cooking girl was her grand-daughter the whole thing was obviously another eccentricity and could be overlooked.

'Perhaps you have not been firm enough,' said Mrs

158

Frobisher. 'Girls like to be dominated. Why don't you go out there – to Austria – and press your suit. If she knows that I am not against the match it might make a difference.'

'I did wonder,' said Kendrick. He had indeed wondered very much, for the goings-on at Hallendorf as read out in Gowan Terrace had disturbed him increasingly. Ellen had written light-heartedly about Chomsky and the rest, but Kendrick was beginning to have nightmares in which his beloved was subjected to advances by naked metalwork professors or pinned to the wall by red-haired Welshmen. 'Perhaps I could ask her to meet me in Vienna?'

'A good idea,' said Mrs Frobisher. She did not care for waltzes, but was aware that they were considered beneficial for romance.

But Kendrick's plans for his visit to Vienna were cast in a much more serious vein. If he was to lure Ellen to the Austrian capital, it must be with a worthwhile programme of serious sightseeing as well as visits to concerts, art galleries and museums. Returning home, he was soon closeted in the London Library, where the delights of the Austrian capital could be carefully studied.

There was so much to see: the churches of Fischer d'Erlach (both the Elder and the Younger), at least a dozen equestrian statues of significance and a leprosy sanatorium in the suburbs which was said to represent the pinnacle of Secessionist architecture. There was the Hofburg, of course, and the vault of the Capuchin church containing the bodies of the Hapsburg Emperors, but not, apparently, their hearts and livers, for which it was necessary to go to the crypt of St Stephen's Cathedral. And of course there were all the places where the great composers had been born or died or simply resided. Schubert's spectacles could be visited in Nussdorf, and Beethoven's ear trumpet in the Stadtsmuseum, though the attribution of Mozart's billiard cue in a cafe in Grinzing was seriously disputed.

Best of all would be if he could take Ellen to the opera. After all, the Vienna Opera was the glory of Europe. Surely she would not refuse to come if he could offer her seats for a performance there?

Calling in at his favourite travel agency, one which specialised in Cultural Tours, he spoke to a helpful girl who showed him the programme for the Staatsoper and there, on 12 July, after the end of the official season, Kendrick found a cultural gem that no one could resist: Brigitta Seefeld, Vienna's reigning diva, was singing in *Rosenkavalier*.

'I'm not sure if I'll be able to get tickets,' said the girl. 'And if I can they'll be terribly expensive. It's a gala and they always put up the prices for them.'

But Kendrick, imagining himself beside his beloved as Seefeld renounced her young lover and sent him into the arms of a foolish young girl, said boldly that money was no object. She was to get tickets at any price and let him know. For the truth was that even if Ellen might prefer to investigate Demels Patisserie or the Nash Markt, he himself would do anything to hear Brigitta

Seefeld sing. And he would be able to tell Ellen more about the inspiring relationship between the diva and Marcus Altenburg, for he had done a lot of research on the composer's life since he realised that he had been at school with one of the most highly regarded musicians of the day.

He would not raise Ellen's hopes at once: he'd just say he hoped to get tickets for the opera. Or should he say nothing about it at all and give her a wonderful surprise?

Standing on the pavement, jostled by the passers-by, Kendrick sighed with anticipation, and blushed, for he had just remembered that the prelude of *Rosenkavalier* was supposed to depict, in music, the act of love.

Was this something he should explain – but very delicately of course – to Ellen? She listened so nicely when he told her things, her head on one side, her lids drooping a little over her gentle eyes. Sometimes he felt that that was what he had been born for – explaining things to the girl he loved so much.

# 11

The Viennese afternoon was warm and mellow. The sun shone down on the green and golden roofs of the churches, warmed the stone archdukes and marble composers in the parks; touched the courtyards of the Hofburg, which had once been the home of emperors and now housed government ministries, Lipizzaner horses and a few selected citizens who had been given grace-and-favour apartments by the state.

Among whom was Vienna's favourite diva, Brigitta Seefeld, who now woke in her famous Swan Bed, stretched her plump arms and demanded (but in a whisper for she never spoke on the day of a performance), 'Where are my eggs?'

Ufra shrugged. Her eggs were where they always were, in a bowl on the dressing table, fresh that morning from the market. An ugly black-haired Armenian in her fifties, she had worked for Brigitta for fifteen years and knew that today there would be trouble. Brigitta was singing Mimi in *La Bohème* and they had brought in a new Musetta from Hamburg who was said to be both excellent and young. And tonight too Benny Feldmann was due back from America, and if he hadn't found Marcus von Altenburg, thought Ufra, God help us all.

Brigitta rose, put on her peignoir and descended from her dais. On the walls of her bedroom, as on all the walls of her sumptuous apartment, with its inlaid floors and porcelain stoves, hung portraits of her in her most famous roles: as the Countess in *Figaro* . . . as Violetta in *La Traviata* . . . as a pig-tailed Marguerite in Gounod's *Faust*.

Reaching the dressing table, she broke the first egg and tipped it down her throat. A second egg followed; then came the exercises. 'Mi, mi, mi,' sang Brigitta, her hand on her diaphragm – and outside in the street, the porters looked up and grinned and the grooms leading the Lipizzaners to their stables nodded to each other, for Brigitta Seefeld's voice exercises were as much a part of Vienna as the bells of St Stephen's or the cooing of the pigeons on the roofs.

At four-thirty, Ufra admitted the masseuse and after her came Herr Köenig, the leader of Brigitta's claque.

Marcus had disapproved of claques. 'You don't need them,' he'd raged. 'It lowers you, paying for applause.'

How idealistic he'd been, that wild boy who'd come to her dressing room with an entire tree, and into her life. But what did he know about anything, with his tempestuous youth and his talent? It was all very well for him; he could afford to go slumming in the suburbs, conducting working men's choirs and writing pieces for tubercular schoolchildren to play. He wasn't dependent on an arbitrary collection of cords and tendons which could fail at any moment. A head cold, a chest infection, an impending nodule on her larynx would leave her defenceless, a prey to her rivals, her status threatened. No wonder she found it necessary to cultivate those who could help her.

Herr Köenig came forward to kiss her plump, soft hand – possibly the most kissed hand in Vienna – and was informed that Brigitta expected not less than twelve curtain calls, and for herself alone – not the beanpole from Hamburg who was singing Musetta.

Herr Köenig blanched. Twelve curtain calls, yes – but for her alone? The soprano from Hamburg was said to be very good. On the other hand, Seefeld was not singing again till her *Rosenkavalier* at the gala in four weeks' time. For the ordinary Viennese who could not afford gala prices, tonight was effectively her last appearance of the season. Looking into the diva's appealing blue eyes, he was driven to rashness.

'You shall have them,' he declared grandly – and could be seen, as he reached the street, striking his forehead and cursing his stupidity.

At five-thirty, Ufra prepared the dog. Combing the long, silky hair of the little Tibetan terrier, binding his topknot up in scarlet ribbon, took almost as long as dressing Brigitta's golden curls, but the public expected

Puppchen on his red lead, as they expected the sable stoles, the jewels, the famous smile.

'In Armenia we would have eaten you,' said Ufra as he wriggled and moaned.

At six-thirty the procession set off down the Augustinerstrasse watched by the shopkeepers, the man in the tobacco kiosk and those fortunate tourists who had been tipped off that Seefeld was en route to the evening's performance.

Arriving at the stage door, Brigitta was extremely gracious to the doorman, considerably less gracious to the tenor who was singing Rodolfo, and not gracious at all to the beanpole from Hamburg, who should have stayed where she was even if she did happen to be married to a Jew.

But the performance went well. The voice – that capricious Gestalt almost as external to herself as the tiresome little dog that Marcus had given her – had behaved itself, and Herr Köenig had kept his word. There *were* twelve curtain calls, and the other singers, relieved that Brigitta would be absent now for nearly a month, allowed her to take a substantial number of these alone.

Afterwards there was another smattering of applause as she crossed from the opera house to Sacher's, the hotel where she was accustomed to dine after a performance. There were roses on the table especially kept for her, and more hand-kissing, more bowing as she was greeted by the maître d'hôtel and her dinner companions rose to their feet.

'You were superb, *Liebchen*,' said Count Stallenbach, her current 'protector', a man sufficiently stricken in years to make few demands on her person.

Julius Staub, extinguishing his cigarette, added his congratulations. A pale playwright with an enormous forehead, who wandered about in a pall of cigarette ash like an extinct volcano, he had written the libretto of an opera about Helen of Troy which only lacked a composer to be a perfect vehicle for Seefeld.

But the man she most wanted to see had not yet arrived: Benny Feldmann, her agent and business manager, who had just returned from the United States.

'He phoned to say he'd be along in half an hour. The train was delayed and he's just gone home to change.'

Brigitta nodded, but as she chose her dishes and sipped her champagne, she could hardly conceal her impatience.

It had begun over a year ago, her desire to find Marcus von Altenburg again. She had been furious with him when he withdrew his violin concerto in that melodramatic way. To lose the chance of a Berlin premiere for a little Jew like Meierwitz was absurd, and she had written to tell him so. Music was above politics.

But if Marcus had been labelled as a person not welcome in the Third Reich, there were other countries, seemingly, which did want him. The French had just performed his First Symphony, the *Songs for Summer* had been recorded in London, and the Americans had invited him back on generous terms to conduct. He was rumoured to be over there now, negotiating.

'He hasn't been so stupid,' Benny Feldmann had told her before he left for the States. 'The future is over there, Brigitta. More and more people are going.'

Brigitta had no intention of leaving Vienna; she was Viennese through and through. But the news from Germany was bad: more and more Wagner operas staged for the Führer, more and more influence exerted by the Bayreuth clique. She was a lyric soprano: Wagner did not suit her voice. If Hitler's hand of friendship to Austria became a takeover, might it be wise to consider alternatives?

'Why don't you get Altenburg to write an opera for you? You'd be welcome anywhere in the world then,' Feldmann had said, as he was leaving. He was half joking. Men like Altenburg did not write operas *for* people – they wrote them or not.

But Brigitta had leapt at the idea. Altenburg understood her as no one had ever done. He had a devilish temper and had never quite lost his air of emerging from a forest in a bearskin, but the time she had spent with him had been like no other. It was he who had persuaded her to take on the role that had become her most famous one: that of the Marschallin in *Rosenkavalier* – the lovely, worldly aristocrat who gives up her young lover to an ingenue of his own age.

'I'm too young,' she'd said – and so she had been then: thirty-two to his twenty.

'But that's the point don't you see, to make the

sacrifice while you are at the height of your beauty – Strauss wrote it like that. It's not about some middle-aged woman making the best of a bad job; it's a supreme act of wisdom and renunciation.'

The boy had been right. She had been sensational in the role; her performance in what Richard Strauss called his 'Mozart Opera' had become legendary. It was because of Marcus that she was singing in four weeks' time before the President and the crowned heads of several European states.

And that was the trouble – that was why she was so desperate to find him *now*. The opera could wait, but not the gala. It was three years since she had sung the Marschallin: her fortieth birthday was behind her – rather more behind her than she admitted – and she felt suddenly terrified and stale. There were things badly wrong with the production, and Feuerbach, who was conducting, lacked the authority and presence to impose his will on the orchestra. Some of his tempi were absurd; she couldn't take the Act One monologue at that speed, and the girl who was singing Sophie lost no opportunity to put herself forward.

It had all been so different when she was with Marcus. He had been an amazing *répétiteur* and coach, and the orchestra listened to him. Even when he was twenty they had listened, and now . . . Marcus could make Feuerbach see sense, she was sure of it. There would be people at the gala longing to find fault with her – rival divas from Berlin and Paris; officials from the Met.

'Here he is!' said Staub as Benny came towards them, his black eyes lively in spite of the long journey.

Brigitta could only just give him time to sit down before she began: 'Well, what's the news? Did you find him?'

Benny shook his head. 'No I didn't. No one in Philadelphia had any idea where he was. The Director of the Sinfonia's been trying to get hold of him but he seems to have vanished off the face of the earth. They thought he was in that place of his in the forest but letters haven't been answered.'

'But that's absurd. He must be somewhere.'

Staub cleared his throat. His libretto was without doubt the best thing he had written. Seen from the point of view of a Greek soldier disgorged from the wooden horse who encounters the fabled Helen, huddled in a doorway of the burning city, it should interest Altenburg with his well-known concern for the common man. And Marcus might persuade Brigitta to *huddle* – a thing that he himself did not feel equal to.

Now he said: 'I think perhaps he may be here. In Austria, I mean. Brenner said he saw him down in Carinthia, driving with Professor Steiner. He didn't see him clearly but he's pretty sure it was Altenburg.'

'Steiner? That old folk-song collector?'

'Yes. I thought he must be mistaken because Marcus was in America but now I wonder. He and Steiner were friends, if you remember; Marcus stayed with him in Berlin.'

Brigitta frowned. The Professor belonged to that

group of musicians – Meierwitz was another one – who had allowed themselves to become entangled in politics.

'But what could he possibly be doing down there? And why hasn't he been in touch?'

Staub shrugged. 'Brenner may be wrong but he was quite close to him; the van stopped at a level crossing and he tried to wave but Altenburg just stared him down.'

What could it mean? thought Brigitta. Was he hiding himself away to work? And if so . . . if he was writing music for someone else? A *rival*? Oh, why did I send him away? she thought. I must have been mad. He'd said he wouldn't come back, and he hadn't, except as an acquaintance when their paths happened to cross. She'd only wanted a few months to sort out her affairs and really it was his fault, refusing to sell his wretched trees to pay for the sables she'd set her heart on.

'Where in Carinthia? Where did Brenner see him?'

'Hallendorf. They were driving away from the lake.'

'Hallendorf?' she repeated. 'Of course, that's the place with that dreadful school.' The headmaster had had the nerve to write to her asking her to attend some musical performance of the children's a couple of years ago. She hadn't even answered . . . but might it do as an excuse to make enquiries?

'Is there anywhere decent to stay down there?' she asked. 'Why don't we go and look for him?'

Staub agreed at once but Benny hesitated. He had not yet told Brigitta, but he had decided to emigrate

170

and was going to transfer his business to New York. If Brigitta did choose to follow him, there was little he could do for her: America was flooded with Lieder singers escaping Hitler, and the Met had their own stable of sopranos.

But Altenburg was a different matter; Benny had been surprised at the high value the Americans put on him. If Brigitta could really get Altenburg to write an opera with a part for her, the combination could be sensational. The old 'affaire' might be over, but a little carefully placed gossip could add savour, and where better to put that about – if Marcus could be persuaded to attend – than at the gala?

'Why don't you all come?' repeated Brigitta.

Benny made up his mind. 'All right,' he said, nodding. He hated the country but he could manage a few days.

'And you, *Liebchen*? asked Brigitta, a shade anxiously, turning to the count.

Stallenbach patted her hand. 'I think not,' he said, smiling. His role as Brigitta's 'protector' was a conventional one; his family for generations had supported singers or dancers, enjoying their favours and their company. But Stallenbach was in his sixties and had, moreover, a secret in the form of an abiding and deep enthusiasm for the company of his wife. A few quiet weeks without Brigitta were very welcome: nor was he worried about being usurped by Altenburg. The count knew rather better than Brigitta just how many women had thrown themselves at the composer.

'Actually,' he said, 'I have a cousin who has a villa near there. It's empty, I believe; I'm sure she'd lend it to you.' He was rewarded by Brigitta's famous, but genuinely lovely, smile.

# 12

'Of course he goes off suddenly like that. Of course he doesn't even bother to say goodbye. I could tell at once that he was no good,' said Tamara pettishly.

Bennet was silent. Marek had in fact said goodbye and told him why he was going and what had been his reason for coming to Hallendorf. He had explained that since Leon and Ellen now knew who he was, he could not risk any further involvement by anyone in the school. 'Knowing things can be a dangerous business nowadays,' he said.

Bennet had agreed. Ellen could make her own decisions, but Leon was a child for whom he was responsible.

'We shall miss you,' he said – and indeed it was extraordinary how much he minded losing this man whom he had trusted instinctively from the start.

'And Derek is making a complete mess of the play,' Tamara went on. She was the only person who used FitzAllan's Christian name. 'I've told him exactly where my ballet should go and he continues to misunderstand me.'

Bennet looked with reluctant pity at his wife. He knew exactly where Tamara's ballet would go in the end. FitzAllan had already shortened it and put it behind gauzes. The next stage – total exclusion – was only a matter of time. On occasions like these, the Russian ballerina vanished and Bennet found himself looking into the desperate, sallow face of Beryl Smith from Workington. And against his better judgement, he smiled at his wife and gave her arm an affectionate squeeze.

Too late he realised his mistake. Tamara swivelled round, seized him by the shoulders and kissed him hotly on the lips.

'I will wait for you upstairs,' she said hoarsely.

Oh God, thought Bennet, even as he gave a polite nod. Tamara claimed her rights so very rarely now – not more than a few times a year – and always after some blow to her pride. When she did expect him to make love to her the routine was one that never ceased to alarm him: the incense sticks which smoked out his bedroom, the record of the Polovtsian dances, to which Tamara undulated naked . . . and afterwards the floods of tears because Toussia Alexandrovna had found the sexual act so very, very sad.

But there was nothing for it. Bennet went to the cupboard where he kept his whisky and poured himself a large tumbler full. Then he took down the Shakespeare sonnets and turned to Number 116.

Number 18 was beneficial too in moments like this, and Number 66 . . . but after Number 116 it was impossible not to feel love for *someone*, and with luck it could be channelled in the direction of an avid wife. First, though, for no reason he could find, he went along to Margaret Sinclair's office. Though it was late, she was as usual working at her typewriter.

'There's a letter from Brigitta Seefeld – the opera singer. The one we invited for the play two years ago. She thinks she might come.'

'A bit late, I fear,' said Bennet. '*Abattoir* is hardly her style. Still, tell her she'll be welcome any time.'

He looked round Margaret's office: at the neatness, the quietness – and at Margaret herself, putting the cover on her Remington. A plain woman – plain as in bread, as in the hands of Rembrandt's mother, thought Bennet, who was a little fuzzy from the whisky.

The office looked out on to the courtyard. In the dusky light they could make out Ellen sitting on the rim of the well. She was holding something in both hands, seemingly talking to it.

'What is it?' Bennet asked.

'It's the tortoise,' said Margaret, coming to stand beside him.

'Ah yes.'

Ellen was spending rather a lot of time with the tortoise. I hope it's not too late, thought the headmaster, and made his way slowly upstairs towards his apartment. The Polovtsian dances had passed the languorous phase and reached the barbaric and shimmering middle

175

section during which Tamara usually paused to cover herself in Bessarabian Body Oil.

'*Love is not love which alters when it alteration finds . . .*' murmured Bennet, and opened the bedroom door.

It was not exactly too late. Marek's absence did not blot out the world for Ellen, though it took a little more concentration than formerly to become one with the skimming swallows, the stars crowding the night sky outside her window. It was not his absence that grieved her so much, for she had known he would not stay; it was the way that they had parted. Bennet had taken her into his confidence; she knew now just how dangerous was the work on which Marek was engaged, and that she had sent him away yelling like a fishwife was hard to bear. She had gone over the next day to apologise but Steiner's house was shuttered, the door locked and the van gone.

Fortunately there was so much to do that she had little time to brood. Both pupils and staff were throwing themselves into work for the play but the atmosphere was stormy. The director removed the tambourines from the girls in the Salvation Army on the grounds that they were too cheerful; children fell off the stage, dazzled by the searchlights that played on the capitalist oppressors; and the tiny, curly-haired Sabine from Zurich was forgotten in the darkened theatre, left hanging in a muslin bag to represent a side of pork after FitzAllan had tried out the disposition of the meat hooks.

The staff fared little better. Hermine had been reproached by the director for being too emotional.

'But for me it *is* emotional . . . to feel the pre-slaughtering fear . . . the twitching of the limbs . . . the flow of blood,' said poor Hermine, whose baby, while perfectly willing to bite into a ham sandwich, showed absolutely no inclination to be weaned.

It was Chomsky, however, about whom the greatest anxiety continued to be felt. With Marek gone there was no one to help him with the welding of the three-tiered struts and the first attempt to lift them on to the stage had been disastrous. From swimming three times a day, Chomsky now swam four and since the weather had turned cool and cloudy, Ellen became seriously concerned for his health.

Aware, perhaps that *Abbatoir* was not proceeding quite as smoothly as he had hoped, FitzAllan now came to Bennet to tell him that he thought it essential that those children taking part in the play should visit an actual slaughterhouse.

'There is a certain lack of authenticity in some of the performances which I'm sure could be put right by total immersion in the *mise en scène*,' said FitzAllan.

'I'm afraid that would be an expensive business – we'd have to hire a bus for a start,' said Bennet, 'and I have to point out that we already have an increase of thirty per cent in vegetarianism since rehearsals began.'

But FitzAllan was adamant. 'Time spent in research is never wasted,' he said, waving a slender hand.

From the uproar of *Abattoir*, Ellen escaped sometimes to Lieselotte's house on an alp above the village, where Lieselotte's family always welcomed her with open arms: Frau Becker was teaching her to make *Mandelschnitten* and *Zaunerstollen* and Lieselotte's brothers and sisters never tired of hearing stories about the school. Knowing how much Bennet wanted the villagers to be involved, Ellen had hoped that the Beckers would be able to come to *Abattoir* but it turned out that the play was due to open on the name day of Aniella.

'Of course I'm very sorry,' said Lieselotte with a mischievous smile. 'We would very much have liked to come, but it's a special day for us, you'll understand.'

'Of course. What happens on Aniella's name day?'

'Oh, we carry her picture round the church and sing some hymns. Her relics too. She has very nice relics: not toe bones or finger nails but a piece of veiling from her wedding dress, and a circlet of pearls. I don't think it's enough, but you know how people are: so lazy.'

It was when she was coming down the mountain after one such visit that Ellen met Sophie and Ursula running towards her.

'Guess what, Ellen – Chomsky's had a nervous breakdown! A proper one!' said Sophie, her eyes wide and alarmed.

'An ambulance came and took him away. He's gone

to a nursing home in Klagenfurt. I expect they'll put him in a straitjacket.' Ursula was gleeful.

'It was the scaffolding. FitzAllan yelled at him and he began to sob and wave his arms about and then he sort of dropped on the floor and shrieked.'

'Oh poor Chomsky!' Ellen was devastated.

'And Bennet wants to see you,' said Sophie. 'He said to come as soon as you got in.'

'This is a bad business, Ellen,' said the headmaster. He looked tired and strained, and the letter from his stock-broker lying on his desk seemed to be very long. 'I knew that Chomsky was highly strung; I should have been more careful.'

Ellen was indignant. 'How could you have been? How could anyone foresee what would happen?'

'Perhaps not. But the trouble is that Chomsky comes from a very wealthy and distinguished family – his father is a high-ranking diplomat who's served in the Hungarian government; he has connections every-where. Our Chomsky is the youngest of five brothers who are all powerful men. Laszlo wasn't quite up to those sort of pressures, which was why they sent him here. As a kind of refuge.'

'I see.' Marek's words came back to Ellen: 'His appendix was taken out in the most expensive clinic in Budapest.'

'I don't think they'll make trouble . . . sue us or any-thing like that. But if they did . . .' Bennet was silent for a moment, foreseeing yet another form of ruin for his beloved school. Then he came to the point. 'Chomsky asked for you when they took him away in the ambulance. He wanted you to bring some of his clothes and belongings, but mostly he just wanted to see you. I gather his mother and some other relatives are coming from Budapest to visit him in hospital. If you could go there, Ellen, and make contact – I think if anyone can turn away their wrath, it's you.'

But when, two days later, Ellen knocked on the door of Room 15 in the Sommerfeld Clinic for Nervous Conditions, she saw at once that there was no wrath to turn away.

The clinic was light, sunny and opulently furnished, with deep pile carpets and reproductions of modern art. Chomsky's room faced a courtyard with a Lebanon cedar and a fountain, and resembled a suite in an expensive hotel rather than a hospital.

But it was the gathered Chomskys, seeming to Ellen to be ranked tier upon tier like cherubim round Laszlo's bed, that gave the metalwork teacher the look of a potentate holding court. Beside his locker a woman in a superb embroidered jacket and silk shirt was arranging fruit in a crystal bowl: peaches and nectarines, figs and almonds and bunches of blue-black grapes. Her resemblance to her son was marked: the same fervent dark eyes, the same eager movements. Two handsome men, also unmistakable Chomskys, stood by the window: one was smoking a cigar, the other was just opening a bottle of champagne. A grey-haired woman, wearing a silver fox stole in spite of the heat, sat on a chair at the foot of the bed, her fingers clasped round an ebony cane.

'Ellen!' cried the invalid, sitting up in bed in yellow shantung pyjamas with his initials on the pocket. 'You have come!' His happy shout cut short the Hungarian babble. Madame Chomsky advanced towards Ellen and threw out her arms. Laszlo's brother Farkas and cousin Pali were introduced, as was his great aunt Eugenie who had been taking the waters at Baden when she received news of the accident.

'We've heard so much about you!' said Madame Chomsky in German, while cousin Pali, in English, offered champagne and brother Farkas took the suitcase Ellen had brought and found another chair.

Within minutes Ellen found herself in a huddle of approving Chomskys: Chomskys thanking her for her kindness to their Laszlo, Chomskys hoping that the suitcase had not been too heavy, Chomskys offering her a holiday in their villa on Lake Balaton, their mansion in Buda, their apartment in the Champs Elysées. Far from blaming anybody at the school for his accident, they seemed to feel only gratitude to Bennet for having found work for the baby of the family, whom they loved dearly but who had not shown himself to be quite in the ambitious, thrusting mode of his older siblings.

'Is she not like little Katya?' Chomsky wanted to know – and was reproved by his mother, who said that Ellen was much prettier than his nursemaid and how could he say such a thing?

An hour later, Ellen had still not been able to take her leave. She had the feeling that the Chomskys would have given her everything they possessed, including their youngest son in marriage. Every time she tried to go she was promised another treat – a new cousin arriving shortly from Transylvania, a slice of the special salami which Madame Chomsky had brought from Budapest because the Austrians could not be trusted where salamis were concerned; the ratio of donkeys to horses in the meat was never satisfactory west of the Hungarian border.

At six o'clock the nurse returned with the empty suitcase for Ellen to take back.

'We won't need the passport or the birth certificate,' she said. 'I've put them in the inside pocket; they don't like valuable documents lying round in the clinic.'

'But you must have dinner with us!' cried Farkas, as Ellen got to her feet. 'The food is not at all bad at the Imperial.'

Since the Imperial was a sensationally expensive hotel with its own park beside the lake, Ellen said she was sure this was so, but she had to get back to her children.

'Next time, then!' cried the Chomskys, kissing her fervently on both cheeks, and Madame Chomsky followed Ellen in the corridor to give her a last bulletin about her youngest son.

'It may be necessary to take him away to some spa to make a full recovery,' she said. 'But I think he just needs to rest quietly till this dreadful play is over. Please tell Mr Bennet he can be sure that Laszlo will not desert him; he will return.'

Ellen smiled, detecting behind the effusive warmth of Chomsky's mother, a flicker of anxiety lest her Laszlo might be returned permanently to the fold, and promised that she would set the headmaster's mind at rest.

'I have put a few little things in, also, for the children,' said Madame Chomsky as Ellen picked up the case, which certainly seemed to contain more than a passport and a few documents. 'You will not be offended?'

Ellen shook her head, kissed everybody yet again and was escorted to the bus station by Farkas, still complaining because she would not dine with them.

She had missed the bus which would have taken her past the castle and was compelled to walk from the village. On an impulse she decided to walk along the eastern shore of the lake, along the road which led her past Professor Steiner's house.

It was a foolish impulse, delaying her by nearly half an hour and pointlessly, for no light showed in the windows; the van was nowhere to be seen. It was time to face the fact that they had gone for good; that there would be no chance now to put things right between herself and Marek.

All the same, she paused for a moment by the path that led to the house – and as she did so she saw someone moving in the bushes. A man, furtive and silent in the dark. Not Marek – this man was smaller, and who could imagine Marek looking furtive?

She hesitated, then began to walk down the path.

'Is there anyone there?' she called. If it was a burglar maybe her voice would scare him off.

The man had vanished. Stupidly fearless, as she later realised, she made her way towards the door.

Then a hand come round behind her and she was pulled backwards on to the grass.

# 13

It began like all the other journeys they had made. Marek drove the van to the checkpoint and the guards examined their papers only perfunctorily.

'Got any good tunes?' Anton joked, and they played him a bit of the old lady singing 'Take a Pair of Sparkling Eyes' and he waved them through.

After twenty kilometres they turned north west towards the German border and presently Marek left the van and Steiner drove down a rutted lane and parked in a clearing. There was no hope of recording anything here; they had been here too often. He could only wait and pray while Marek plunged into the densest part of the forest to meet his contact and – if their luck held – the man for whom they had searched so long. And the waiting today was going to be harder than ever. The news that Meierwitz had broken cover and was on his way at last had come with another piece of news that they had been half expecting. The line of rescuers was breaking up: one man had been arrested and shot; the Sudeten Nazis had joined the Germans in patrolling the no man's land between the borders.

But when Marek had reached the meeting place, the man they knew only as Johann was there – and with him someone whom at first he did not recognise. Meierwitz had been a portly person, fond of his food, with an engaging tuft of reddish hair and bright black eyes. This man was thin and hunched and he shivered in the summer night.

Afraid to shine his torch or speak, Marek only put out his hand – but Isaac knew in an instant.

'You!' he whispered incredulously. 'My God, Marek – *you*!'

He managed to hold his emotion in check as they made their way towards the van but then, wrapped in a blanket, given coffee from a Thermos, the tears he had managed to control through his years of flight and danger and imprisonment could be held back no longer.

'You,' was all that he could say, over and over again. 'My God, Marek – you.'

Then Steiner came out of the driving seat and embraced his former colleague, and for Isaac there was another shock as he saw that this eminent and venerable scholar had involved himself in his rescue.

They set off then; Steiner drove and Marek sat in the back with his friend. There were several hours of relative safety before the next hazard, the crossing of the border into Poland. Marek took care to make light of his search, his obsessive determination to set

Meierwitz free, but Isaac guessed, and it was a while before he could speak calmly of what had happened in Berlin after the Nazis came to power.

'I was determined to play your concerto, and I told them so; I suppose I threw my weight about a bit; there was so much fear everywhere I didn't want to add to it, and I was damned if I was going to leave the country till I'd played your piece. Even so I was surprised when they agreed. It was a trick, of course; it was quite a shock to them when they turned round and found there was hardly a decent musician left in the country. Then when they were sure of you, they came to arrest me.'

He'd spent nearly a year in the concentration camp and then been transferred and managed to escape. 'A woman I'd never set eyes on hid me on her farm. She wasn't Jewish, she wasn't musical . . .' He shook his head. 'It's knowing you're endangering people that drives you mad.'

He wanted to know about the concerto. 'Who gave the premiere?'

'No one. You're giving the premiere and that's the end of the matter.'

'No, Marek. Don't be obstinate. I shan't play again professionally. It's been more than two years; that's too long to get my technique back, and in the camp my hands . . .' He broke off, biting his lip. 'You must get someone else.'

'Well I won't, so let's hear no more about it. What happened to your Stradivarius?'

'I left it with my landlady in Berlin. Do you

remember her – the one that went off into a faint whenever there was a thunderstorm?'

They spoke then of the unimportant things they remembered: the duck they had found wandering down the Kurfürstendamm and adopted; a girl called Millie who had stood on her head on the table at the Lord Mayor's banquet; the trombone player who'd got his girlfriend's shoe button stuck up his nostril before the first night of *Tristan*.

'And you're not married yet?' Isaac asked.

'No.'

'Your standards are probably too high,' said Isaac, 'with those parents of yours. What about Brigitta?'

Marek shrugged. 'I haven't seen her for ages. Stallenbach is looking after her, I believe.'

They had driven for three hours before Isaac, knowing that his respite in the warm dark van was nearly over, said: 'And what comes next?'

'Well firstly,' said Marek, 'I want you to dress up as a Jew. A proper one.'

Isaac stared at him. 'Are you mad?'

'No. There's a dark hat there, and a long coat.'

'We're going to try to get into Poland with me dressed as an orthodox Jew?'

'Exactly so.' Marek grinned; it had taken him months to fix up a suitable escape route for Meierwitz, who had no ambitions to join the Polish Air Force or become a partisan in the resistance, and he was a little proud of the route he had devised. 'Have you ever heard of the River Rats?'

Isaac frowned. 'Wait a minute . . . aren't they those Jews that make their living poling timber down the rivers? Weird people – very religious – who live on rafts and don't talk to anyone much?'

'That's right. People always think Jews are entirely urban, but these people are skilled woodsmen, amazingly so. I got to know them when I went round on business with my father. They take logs vast distances down the Niemen and the Vistula and along the waterways, sometimes as far as the Baltic. They're expecting you.'

'My God!'

'It's as safe as anything can be. They exist outside frontiers – no one bothers them; they're too poor. When you get to Königsberg they'll put you on a Swedish cargo boat; there'll be papers waiting for you. It's all fixed up.'

Isaac was silent, thinking of the long journey travelling through the dark, inhospitable waterways of Poland with these uncouth and pious strangers.

'Why?' he asked under his breath. 'Why will they take me?'

But he knew. He himself had scarcely set foot in a synagogue; his mother had been baptised, but Hitler had created a new kind of Jew – someone who existed to be hunted and killed – and these unknown men had accepted him as a brother.

Some ten kilometres inside the border they stopped. This was where they said goodbye to Steiner and continued on foot.

189

'I don't know what to say, Professor,' said Isaac. 'The words "Thank you" hardly seem to cover it.'

Steiner shook his hand. 'Nonsense. And remember you will always be welcome in Hallendorf. I'm on my way back now. My house is small as you know, but there will be room for you and you won't have to sleep on the verandah like you did when you came with the quartet. Austria is still free, so who knows?'

Isaac nodded. Austria was still free, that was true, but without a permit to stay he would be a fugitive once more, at best put into prison, at worst deported back into the Third Reich.

They had been driving through thick mist. Now it began to rain – steady grey sheets obscuring everything. Only Marek could have made any sense of the terrain in which they found themselves.

'Keep close,' he said.

He had given Isaac a compass, pepper to head off pursuing dogs, money – but in this Stygian world of dripping trees and cloud it would be a nightmare for him to try and find his way alone. They had just two hours of darkness still to find Franz and ford the river into Poland.

The barbed wire had been cut; everything seemed to be in order, but Marek could not shake off the feeling of unease that had been with him since the beginning of the journey.

They had reached the river. Nothing now except to wait for the cry of an owl repeated three times. The rain was relentless: the ground, the sky, the river merged in a sheet of greyness.

Then it came . . . once . . . twice . . . and they saw Franz's shadowy figure on the far bank.

But the third cry did not come. What came instead was the sound of a shot – and they saw Franz throw up his arms and fall.

'Go back, Isaac,' hissed Marek. 'Quickly. Run.'

'I won't go without you.'

'You'll do as I say. Try to get back to Steiner and warn him. I'll follow but I've got to see if there's anything I can do for Franz. He may not be dead.'

He disappeared in the direction of the river bank.

The sound of a second shot came minutes later.

# 14

Leon had made good his boast to direct a film and give Sophie a leading part. The leading part turned out to be the only part, because even his devoted parents had baulked at sending a new cine camera and the one they had found was turning out to be more complicated to handle than he had expected. There was moreover no sound equipment, so the role he had created for Sophie – that of Terrified Girl reacting to a Nameless Thing – was silent.

Sophie had written to both her parents begging them to come and see *Abattoir*. Even without her tambourine she felt that her role as a Salvation Army girl, largely hidden by a poke bonnet and surrounded by twelve others, would make it possible for her not to disgrace herself – and if they both came then perhaps – just *perhaps* – they would find that they still cared for each other and buy a house which would always be there and they would move into it, all together like a proper family.

For once the answers to her letters had come quite quickly; her mother was certain she couldn't come because she was still filming in Ireland, and the next day Czernowitz had written to say that her father was extremely sorry but he was delaying his return from America.

Her disappointment had brought the usual stricken look to her eyes. What if no one came ever again, what if the school emptied and she was forgotten? But Ellen had not been interested in this train of thought. 'If the school empties and you're forgotten I'll take you to Gowan Terrace and we'll go to the zoo and see lots of Charlie Chaplin films and make fudge.'

'I don't know why you want them to come,' said Leon. 'It's an awful play.'

But he too had responded to Sophie's distress, extending the role he had written for her so that in addition to being terrified in her hovel she was allowed to walk slowly into the lake, like Ludwig of Bavaria, and drown.

He was setting up this tricky shot during a gap in *Abattoir* rehearsals when Sophie, wading through the bulrushes, stopped suddenly and said: 'Goodness! Here comes Cleopatra in her barge!'

The children who had been resting in the grass sat up. The boat making its way in a stately manner towards them did indeed have something regal about it, though it was only a motor boat hired from the village. The woman who lay back against the cushions was amply built, dressed in a flowing, flowery garment with matching turban, and held a fringed parasol in a gloved hand. Behind her, wearing black, sat some kind of lesser person, probably a maid, hanging on to the collar of a small and excited dog.

'She doesn't look like a parent,' said Flix – and this was true.

Parents coming to see how their children were faring at the school seldom approached with that air of grandeur and self-assurance. They were usually thin people in corduroy or ethnic skirts and looked apprehensive.

As they drew close to the castle, Brigitta's hopes rose. Too vain to wear the spectacles she needed, she could make out only the beauty of the pink building and a number of children moving about in the grounds. Altenburg's devotion to children, his conviction that they could be taught to sing or play from infancy, had irritated her in Vienna, but made it more than likely that he should be lying low in a place like this. She had left Staub and Benny in the villa that Stallenbach had procured for them, wanting to be alone when she ran her old lover to ground. Now, as the boat slowed down by the landing stage, she promised herself that she would utter no word of reproach when she came face to face with Marcus. She would beg his help in the matter of the gala and he would not deny her, she was sure. Then when he was in Vienna and *Rosenkavalier* was safely over she would show him Staub's libretto and their true collaboration would begin. Cosima von

Bülow and Wagner . . . Alma Schindler and Gustav Mahler . . . George Sand and Chopin . . . there was nothing absurd in the comparison. Cosima had cut off her long, long hair and thrown it into Wagner's grave, thought Brigitta, fingering her short permed hair under the turban. If Marcus came back, if he set Staub's opera, she might even be prepared to *huddle*.

The children waiting on the landing stage were larger than she had expected and did not look salubrious, but that only made it more likely that Marcus was here.

'Can we help you?' said the only one that looked even remotely clean and decent, a girl with dark pigtails.

'I am Brigitta Seefeld,' the diva announced, not troubling to introduce her maid. 'And I am looking for Herr Altenburg, the composer, who I believe is working here.'

Sophie and the others, in all innocence, shook their heads. Only Leon stiffened and looked wary.

'There's no one here called that,' said Sophie.

'Definitely not,' agreed Flix, making her way towards the little dog.

But Brigitta was not so easily put off. 'Take me to your headmaster,' she ordered. 'Tell him that Brigitta Seefeld is here.'

As the children led her towards the steps, Leon took Sophie aside.

'Go in and find Ellen,' he whispered. 'Tell her

Brigitta Seefeld is here and looking for someone called Altenburg. Go on, quickly.'

Sophie, without question, turned and ran towards the kitchen. She did not pause to wonder why Ellen had to be told of this visit or its purpose: to fetch Ellen at all times was second nature now to the children in the school.

She found Ellen teaching the new kitchen hand how to slice angelica into interesting shapes. He was hoping to be a chef and had only been here a few days but everyone liked him: he was quick to learn and funny and would help with anything, indoors and out.

'Ellen, a great big blonde woman has just arrived; she's called Brigitta Seefeld and she's looking for someone called Altenburg. A musician. Leon said I should tell you.'

Ellen looked up, the egg whisk still in her hand. At the same time a small exclamation from the trainee chef made them both turn. Usually so neat and careful, he had cut his finger.

'Where is she now?' asked Ellen.

'Leon's taking her to see Bennet; we told her there wasn't anyone like that here but she didn't believe us.' But Sophie was staring at the new assistant, who had gone as white as his overalls. There were people who couldn't stand the sight of blood, she knew that. It was nothing to do with cowardice; it was just one of those things. 'Shall I go and get some sticking plaster from your box?' she offered.

Ellen shook her head. 'No, I'll see to it. Will you go

to Bennet and tell him I'll bring coffee and cakes to his study. I'll be there in ten minutes if he would just wait there. Would you tell him that?'

Sophie nodded and sped off, and Ellen went to shut the door of the scullery in which Frau Tauber was washing up.

'She knows you, of course.'

'Yes.' He was biting his lip. She could see the effort he was making to control himself.

'Well then, we must hide you,' she said, fetching a roll of plaster and some lint. She bound up the finger, thinking. Then: 'Didn't you offer to stand in for David Langley at the rehearsal?' And as he nodded: 'In that case, our troubles are over. You'll be as safe as houses there.'

Brigitta's route towards the headmaster's study, escorted by Leon and followed by Ursula and Janey, was unfortunate. Unaware that she had been spared Chomsky's appendix scar, she shuddered as the Biology teacher, virtually naked, ran past her with his net, searching for dragonfly larvae in the mud. An uncouth boy with dirty feet dropped from a tree, bumped into her, swore and disappeared.

'That's Frank,' explained Janey helpfully. 'His father's a famous philosopher and he's been through *five* psychoanalysts.'

'I'll wait outside,' said Ufra firmly, and led the dog away towards the kitchen garden.

As she passed the open doors of classrooms and

rehearsal rooms, Brigitta's certainty that she had found Marcus' hiding place began to evaporate. In one a sinewy female in a leotard was exhorting a group of sulky children to give vent to their viscerality; in another a mustachioed woman in flannels was demonstrating the Primal Scream. A child lay on the floor in the corridor, reading a book and eating a banana. Surely even Marcus with his passion for freedom and tolerance, would not be able to work in this kind of bedlam?

But when she reached Bennet's study she became more hopeful again. The headmaster was a cultivated and good-mannered man who spoke excellent German and was properly dressed. His walls were lined with books, and the bust of Shakespeare encouraged her; Marcus had set six of the sonnets for tenor, strings and percussion when he first came to Vienna, boring her with eulogies about the verse.

'I am Brigitta Seefeld –' she began – and frowned angrily as the boy who had put himself forward all along, had the impertinence to interrupt her.

'Madame Seefeld has come because she thinks Herr Altenburg has been here,' he said quickly. 'I've told her he hasn't, but –'

'Leon is right, Madame Seefeld. There has been no one here of that name,' said Bennet with perfect truthfulness, giving Leon a reassuring nod.

There was a brief knock at the door and Sophie entered with Ellen's message, 'She won't be more than ten minutes, she said.'

Bennet nodded and sent the children away. 'Ellen is our matron – and in charge of the kitchen too. An excellent woman.'

That Marek would want his stay in Hallendorf kept secret even now, Bennet was certain. Only three people knew his identity: Ellen, Leon and himself, and it was clear that the boy could be trusted.

Meanwhile he was in effect looking at a kind of Toscanini's Aunt. Brigitta Seefeld was known all over Europe as a brilliant singer, a doyenne of the operatic stage. Two years ago when Franz Lerner had produced an opera based on *The Pied Piper* he had written to invite her to Hallendorf and she had not even troubled to reply. Now she was here and all he had to show her was *Abbatoir*. But was it 'all'? Was he being unduly pessimistic? A premiere of a Brecht play directed by a man who had studied with Meyerhold and Stanislavsky . . .

Motioning her to his slightly disintegrating leather armchair, he set himself to be charming and flatter her.

'As you can imagine, this is a great honour for Hallendorf. If you'd given me a little warning we could have shown you some of the workshops in progress. Unfortunately our music is at present our weakest point. Our excellent music teacher has gone to fight in Spain and so far we've not found a replacement.'

'I understand Professor Steiner lives across the lake.' Brigitta was still suspicious. 'We called at his house but he seems to be away. Couldn't he help you?'

'I wouldn't trouble a man of such eminence,' said

Bennet truthfully. 'Or of his age. Some of the children here are a little . . . untutored.'

'Yes, I see that. But Altenburg has been seen with Professor Steiner. I find it hard to believe that he never came here. He is interested in working with children.'

Bennet gave a wistful smile. 'I assure you, we would have welcomed any help of that sort with open arms.'

A knock at the door interrupted them, and Ellen entered bearing a silver tray, a coffee pot and a plate of biscuits.

'Ah – *Vanilla Kipferl*! I think you won't do better than these even at Demels,' said Bennet.

Ellen set down the tray and smiled at the woman described so fulsomely in Kendrick's concert programme. Seefeld seemed middle-aged to her; there was a puffiness under the eyes and in Ellen's opinion she was not so much voluptuous as fat. But the eyes themselves were a bright periwinkle blue, the hair under the turban still golden – above all Seefeld had the assurance, the presence, that comes from years of fame. That the collaboration between her and Marek had been 'fruitful' in all senses of the word, seemed all too likely.

Brigitta in her turn examined Ellen with sudden interest. The girl was remarkably pretty; the careless curls, the big gold-brown eyes and soft mouth – and for an instant she thought that maybe she had found the reason for Marcus' sojourn in the neighbourhood. But that was absurd. She was a below stairs person, she worked in the kitchens. He might have flirted with such a girl but that she could seriously interest him, that he could write music for her was absurd. Even Marcus did not write music for cooks.

The coffee however was excellent, the *Vanilla Kipferl* delicious. When they were finished, Bennet invited her to the theatre, where a rehearsal for the play had just resumed.

'The theatre was built at the same time as the castle – in 1743. It's a remarkably pretty one; the work of Grunwald von Heilgen . . .'

He elaborated, and Brigitta suppressed a yawn. 'Very well. But I should like to look over the school first. I should like to see *everything*?'

That Marcus, for no reason she could imagine, was concealed in the building, was an idea that would not entirely go away.

But when they reached the theatre and found the *Abbatoir* rehearsal in full spate, Brigitta finally realised that wherever her former lover was it could not be here.

Chomsky's three-tiered structure was in place at last and FitzAllan was attempting to get everyone on stage together: the capitalists on top, the Salvation Army girls in the middle and the workers on the bottom.

Things were not going well. The Salvation Army girls came on too soon, were yelled at and vanished. The capitalists, rolling their dice, looked green, contemplating the distance to the ground – and there was trouble with the carcasses. There was always trouble with the carcasses. FitzAllan had insisted that the headless cadavers, completely swathed in muslin, were played by real people who could neither see nor be seen, and the opportunities for disaster were endless.

The arrival of the famous diva brought the director unctuously to her side.

'This is an honour indeed,' he said in excellent German, bowing over her hand, and led her towards the footlights. 'Carry on,' he shouted to the increasingly confused children, and a disorientated slaughterhouse worker crashed into a dimly lit side of beef, was sworn at and veered off at an angle. 'As you see, we are still feeling our way a little,' said FitzAllan.

Brigitta said she did indeed see this. She made however one last attempt before making her escape. 'Who does the music – presumably there is music?'

FitzAllan gave a modest smile. 'I have endeavoured to fill the gap left by the departure of Franz Lerner. Perhaps you'd like to hear one of the workers' songs? I've adapted it myself from one I found in a communist manifesto.'

He clapped his hands and those of the children who heard him came to the front of the stage. 'We're going straight into the Song of Starvation at the end of Act Two. I'll give you the note. Ready?'

Brigitta listened and the last of her doubts were laid to rest. Not in a hundred years could Marcus have countenanced a noise like that. Turning, she found the dark, intense boy who had met her at the landing stage standing beside her.

'If Herr von Altenburg could hear that, he'd turn in his grave, wouldn't you say?' he whispered.

Much as she wanted to snub the child, she could only agree.

'The premiere is at the end of July. If you happened to be in the district we should be most honoured,' said Bennet.

'Thank you, but my calendar for July is very full,' she said.

She found Ufra and Puppchen already in the launch. Puppchen was passionately chewing a large leather gardening glove. 'He found it in one of the sheds,' said Ufra. 'It belonged to the handyman. He's left now, so I thought he might as well have it.'

'It's disgusting,' said Brigitta, as the object became covered in the little dog's saliva. 'Take it away and throw it into the lake.'

But Puppchen wouldn't be parted from his treasure. He growled and showed his crooked teeth and he was still slobbering over it when the boat arrived in the village, and the local taxi bore Brigitta off to the villa so kindly provided by the count.

Ellen waited till the theatre was empty and dark before she made her way back stage.

'It's all right,' she said. 'You can come out now. She's been gone for ages.'

The ox carcass in its muslin wrapping swayed; the papier-mâché stump representing its severed neck was lifted.

'Goodness, you do look green! There's no need to be afraid; she's miles away.'

'It isn't fear, it's seasickness,' said Isaac Meierwitz, and climbed out of the bag.

By day Isaac could forget the terror in the forest; the moment when Marek had disappeared in the direction of the river, the second shot. He could forget the hours he had stumbled through the mist, trying to find Steiner's van, the baying of the guard dogs which had sent him crawling under barbed wire, to find himself in Austria . . . the long journey, footsore and starving, to Hallendorf, hoping against hope that Steiner and Marek were there.

But at night he played back the nightmare again and again, and then there was nothing to do except get up and go outside and sit on the steps of the little temple, looking out across the lake to Steiner's house, praying that a light would show in the windows . . . that the men who had risked their lives for him were safely back.

There Ellen found him the night after Brigitta's visit, wearing a coat over her nightdress, and bringing a blanket for him, for the night was cool.

'You should sleep, Ellen; you work so hard.'

'Flix woke me,' she said. 'She had a dream about the Judas sheep.'

She sat down beside him, wrapping the blanket round them both, and her closeness gave him a stab of something he did not recognise at first because it had become so unfamiliar. Happiness? thought Isaac – is that possible still? And answered himself: Where she is, it is possible.

The moment of panic by Steiner's door when he had tried to pull the intruder down on to the grass had not lasted long. The softness of her body, the way she crumpled in his arms and then stiffened, ready to fight, had overwhelmed him. He let her go, and then the dizziness he had been fighting overcame him, and he lost consciousness.

When he came round again his victim was kneeling beside him, opening a suitcase. 'I'm afraid I can't offer you a balanced diet,' she had said, shining a pocket torch on to a salami in a lattice of gold, a packet of Karlsbad plums, a cluster of grapes. 'You must eat very slowly,' she had instructed him in her gentle voice, with its very slight English accent, 'otherwise you'll be sick.'

He was famished, but he reached out not for the strange foods she was proffering from her magic suitcase but for her hair, touching it once where it clustered on the nape of her neck. She existed then; she was real.

'There seems to be a bottle of Tokay here also,' she said, lifting a flagon wrapped in straw out of its wooden box. 'But you mustn't drink that; not yet. There's a tap at the back of the house; I'll get you some water.'

Isaac had shaken himself out of his trance then. Ashamed of his weakness, he stretched out his hand for the bottle. 'Water is for the feet,' he said.

She'd looked up quickly as if what he had said was

a password. 'You're Marek's friend,' she'd stated, 'so I shall help you.'

He tried to argue. He had no papers; if he was questioned he would be transported back over the border or imprisoned. 'Anyone who helps me could be in trouble.'

'No one will question you. You're my new assistant. You were visiting Chomsky and I offered you a job for a while. Unpaid, of course!'

He had continued to protest but she took no notice; already then he was aware of her strange mixture of softness and steel. She'd returned with some of Chomsky's clothes, and so far she'd been right. In a school where Russian ballerinas came from Workington and Costa Rican revolutionaries were employed as groundsmen, no one questioned Isaac's presence as a trainee chef. Isaac slept in Chomsky's room, and did his best to make himself useful. It seemed to him that the great cathedrals of the Middle Ages which had given sanctuary to the hunted were as nothing compared to the Hallendorf kitchens: the warmth, the cleanliness, the rich and fragrant smells, the funny, kindly children – and Ellen, whom he could scarcely bear to let out of his sight.

But at night, Isaac kept watch. He had not told Ellen about that second shot but he knew that she too waited for the light in the window which never came.

Now, though, she wanted to know about Brigitta. 'Why did she come, Isaac, do you know? What did she want from Marek?'

He shrugged. 'I've been away for so long – but there was some rumour that she was commissioning an opera. Or it could be any crisis in her career. She's been trying to get him back ever since she sent him away.'

'But she must be quite old. Forty at least.'

'More. But music can build bridges between the most unlikely people. She's an awful woman but she sings Marek's music like no one else. I recorded the *Songs for Summer* with her in Berlin. She made scenes, she was impossible, but the finished result was superb. Mind you, women have been pursuing Marek ever since he was a boy in that forest of his.'

'Have you been there? To Pettelsdorf?'

Isaac shook his head, 'He only asks people who really matter to him. It's his sanctuary.'

'You matter to him. Surely he's shown that.'

'Perhaps. He did say that after the premiere he'd take me. I don't think he likes to mix his different lives. When he's at Pettelsdorf I think he somehow hopes his music will go away.'

'But it won't?'

'No, Ellen. Not ever. You can be sure of that.'

She nodded. She had understood in any case that no one who knew as little about music as she did could ever seriously matter to him, but she asked a feminine and foolish question.

'Has Brigitta been there?'

Isaac smiled. 'I don't think so. No, I'm sure. But it isn't for want of trying.'

A breeze was rising, ruffling the dark water. 'You should go in, Isaac, it's getting cold.'

But Isaac was in the grip of his devils.

'If anything's happened to him, Ellen . . .'

'It won't have. He'll be back. He'll bring Steiner and you'll get away to safety. I told you about the candle – it burnt straight and true.'

'Ah yes, the saint with the salamanders. You think she will concern herself with the rescue of one unimportant Jew?'

'If she can save salamanders she can save Jews – and you don't even have spots.'

Isaac shook his head. 'I said I'd haunt him till his dying day if he didn't let me play his concerto and sometimes I think I've done just that. He's wasted years trying to find me, getting people out . . . It's an amazing piece, the concerto . . . the slow movement . . . God! If I had known what he was going to do in Berlin – he practically killed the director. In Germany he's excoriated or worshipped – and he wants neither.'

'When you're safely away he'll go back to music, won't he?'

He turned to smile at her, thanking her for the 'when'. 'He must do. The Americans didn't want to let him go. He should go back there till all this blows over.'

'Yes.' Ellen bent her head. America was . . . far.

'He has this gift not only of writing fine music but making it happen. In Berlin, in Vienna too, wherever a dozen people came together, Marek had them doing something; he could get music out of three tram conductors and a road sweeper. He never saw it as something for professionals only, though he was so dedicated about his own work – his scores used to look like Egyptian palimpsests – he wrote and rewrote again. But when he was with ordinary people music was just something everyone could do.'

She nodded, silent and pensive, and he longed to reach out for her and hold her and never let her go.

'What about you, Ellen?' he asked. 'What does music mean to you?'

It was a while before she answered. 'When I was at school . . . quite little still . . . there was a girl there who had perfect pitch and a lovely voice and she played the piano. I used to hear people talking about her.' She paused, lacing her fingers together. '"She's musical," they used to say, "Deirdre's musical," and it was as if they'd said: "She's angelic." That's how it seemed to me to be musical: to be angelic.'

Isaac turned to her. 'My God, Ellen,' he said huskily, 'it is you who are angelic. If there's anyone in the world who is angelic it is you.'

# 15

The news for which Kendrick had been waiting so eagerly came through three days after his previous visit to the travel agency.

'We've got them, sir,' said the helpful girl. 'We've got the tickets for the gala! They were returns but they're wonderful seats – a box in the Grand Tier. They were reserved for an American diplomat and his wife, but he's been recalled to Washington.'

She seemed almost as pleased as Kendrick, but she was a conscientious girl and felt compelled to add: 'There have been rumours of a bit of trouble – Seefeld isn't pleased with the conductor, but I'm sure it'll be all right.'

For a moment, Kendrick blenched. What if he payed out so much money and then some inferior soprano took over the lead? How would Ellen react? Trying to assess this, he had to face the fact that he did not know exactly how deeply Ellen felt music. Once he had taken her to a Tchaikovsky concert at the Queen's Hall and

210

after the concert he had asked Ellen what she was thinking of and she had said, 'Sorrel Soup.'

She had explained that the slow movement of the *Pathétique* made her think of a green forest and this in turn had made her think of sorrel and made her wonder if she could get some to make into soup for one of the Gowan Terrace aunts who had a stomach complaint. All the same, it had been a shock.

But she would not think of Sorrel Soup after *Rosenkavalier*. After *Rosenkavalier* she would think – she would have to think – of love, and it was after the opera, in some spot that he had not yet finalised, that he intended to propose. This would not be a hasty declaration forced out of him in a kitchen like his previous one; it would be a brief but considered speech which would reach straight to her heart. He had made a short list of places that might be suitable: the Donner Fountain in the Neuer Markt (which personified the tributaries of the Danube), the Mozart Memorial in the Burg Garten, and the equestrian statue of the Archduke Albrecht on the steps of the Albertina – all of which were within a few minutes' walk of the opera house.

And this brought him to the delicate question of the hotel. They would need two rooms in a suitable establishment – but not adjoining rooms, which might frighten Ellen and give her a wrong idea of his intentions. Perhaps they should be on a different floor, thought Kendrick. He had heard his mother refer to men who could not control their instincts as 'animals'.

211

The idea that Ellen might think of him as in any way an animal was too dreadful to be borne.

Stammering slightly, Kendrick put the problem of accommodation to the nice girl in the agency, who recommended the Hotel Regina in the Graben, a historic street in the Inner City, and promised to make the booking straight away.

There was therefore nothing left to do except write a second letter to Ellen, begging her to come to Vienna, for she had not yet answered the first. But even in this letter he did not mention the gala and Seefeld. If anything did go wrong she would not be disappointed, and the idea of surprising her continued to excite him. She would think they were going to some ordinary ball with champagne and waltzes – and then he would spring on her a treat so far above the humdrum one of whirling round a dance floor as would completely overwhelm her.

That Ellen might not accept his invitation occurred to him but he fought it down. In a bookshop in the Tottenham Court Road, Kendrick had found a pamphlet called *Positive Thinking for Beginners*. He had not bought it – it was not the kind of book that a Frobisher bought – but he had read it in the shop and was determinedly putting its precepts into practice. He had even written cheerfully to his mother, announcing his plans – and writing cheerfully to Patricia Frobisher was not a thing he did often.

Fortunately he was expected that evening at Gowan Terrace to help with a lantern slide show in aid of

Basque refugees and could share his success with Ellen's mother and her aunts.

'She's sure to get leave just for a day or two, don't you think?' he asked, and they said they thought it more than likely.

Aunt Annie – the one who was a mycologist – continued to feel that it was unwise to encourage the poor young man, but Dr Carr was not sorry to think that her daughter might be having a break in that most beautiful of cities. In her last letter Ellen had sounded a little tired. It occurred to her that Ellen had not mentioned the groundsman recently – the one who had put the tortoise on wheels. She hoped he was still there; he had sounded sensible, and not many of the staff at Hallendorf sounded *that*.

As for Aunt Phyllis – she was having a thought which when it came to the surface of her mind upset her deeply, for it was a throwback to the days when she was Gussie Norchester's biddable daughter and leading a life of stifling conventionality. She had caught herself thinking that there were worse places than a large house in rural Cumberland, in the event of war, for her beloved niece.

# 16

As they drove down the winding road towards the first of the lakes, it began to rain. Marek wound down the window of his father's old Talbot and switched on the windscreen wipers, which fibrillated uncertainly and then stuck. The car was used only on the farm; an ancient pick-up. He had refused to borrow the Captain's Buick.

Beside him Steiner sat silent, his arm in its sling supported on the cushion that Marek's mother had arranged for him when they set off. He was angry with Marek.

'There's no need for you to do this,' he'd said. 'I can easily make my own way back by train.'

Marek had taken no notice, but now, as he drove through the prim, uncaring villages towards Steiner's house, there was little they could say to each other. Their long quest for Isaac had ended in tragedy; Steiner was hurt; the van had had to be left, hidden in a shed at Pettovice, to be dismantled and refitted as an ordinary lorry. Steiner's folk-song collecting days were over.

'You must get back to work, Marek,' the old man said eventually. 'You must book your passage to America. I shall stay and edit my papers and if you get in my way I shall be extremely cross. My house is too small for the two of us.'

Marek managed a smile. 'I won't stay long. Just long enough to see that your arm is healed.'

The bullet fired through the windscreen by the Nazi louts who had ambushed Steiner had only grazed the skin, but there were splinters of glass more deeply lodged.

'My arm *is* healed,' said the Professor angrily. 'Let me tell you, Marek, I will not endure being fussed over.' Dear God, he thought, what will make this obstinate man understand where his true destiny lies? 'There's nothing more you can do for Meierwitz.'

'I should like to have buried him,' said Marek grimly.

There had been no choice but to take the injured Steiner to Pettelsdorf. The van could only limp along at a snail's pace, the glass was shattered; there was no possibility of crossing the border and bringing him home. Remembering the fearless way his people had come forward, Marek could hardly bear to think that he had endangered them. He had scarcely brought the van to a standstill than it was removed, hidden. No one asked any questions – not Janik or Stepan, not Andras in the mill; everyone was instantly alert, everyone

215

understood. Lenitschka, usually so voluble, took Steiner upstairs in silence while the maids fetched bandages . . .

But with his mother he had quarrelled straight away. 'You had no right to keep your work a secret. We want to help, all of us. We want to fight this evil. We could have sheltered your fugitives and made everything easier.'

She had always been politically aware, reared among intellectuals. From the day Hitler burnt the books in front of the university, Milenka was implacably engaged against the Nazis. Nor was his grandmother an ally.

'Your mother is perfectly right,' said Nora Coutts, emerging from her room to interfere with Lenitschka as she dressed Steiner's wound. 'You have always been in danger of patronising women. I've told you before.'

He'd made no headway either in getting them to apply for emigration visas.

'You must see the way it's going,' he'd said. 'Please.'

And he had repeated what he had told them already: that it was a Czech voice, issuing from a thug in a Nazi uniform, that had boasted of Isaac's murder.

'You go ahead,' Milenka had said. 'Knowing you're safe is the only thing that matters. If you go, and prepare the way for us, we'll follow.'

He knew that she lied. His father would not leave, and while he stayed she would be with him. They were strung together on one bow, these two unlikely people;

their lives together made the melody that was Pettelsdorf.

For Steiner the week of pain and grief for Isaac had been shot through with a strange joy.

He'd been thirty years old when he first saw Milenka at a poetry reading in Berlin. She was nineteen, a bird-thin girl whose soul one could enter without subterfuge, for she hid nothing. He fell terribly in love . . . and lost her to someone who should have been utterly unsuitable and turned out to be her other half – this man who shot too many animals and read too few books.

Since then he had seen her in Berlin or Prague, had taken her to concerts; laboriously, grindingly, turning love to friendship – but he had never dared to come to her home. Now, nearing the end of his life, he was enormously thankful that his image of her was complete. That he had seen her at her desk, pushing aside the cat that sat on her papers . . . assuring herself that the goose they were to have for supper was not a goose she knew personally, but came from a neighbouring farm . . . That he had stood beside her in the moonlit garden listening to the orioles and heard her read once more, the poem he had heard first in her deep, slightly husky voice:

'Not vanished, but transfigured are the things that were,

To come again by, Oh, what bliss attended . . .'

Steiner played no games with himself. He did not pretend that Marek was the son they might have had;

there was far too much of the Freiherr von Altenburg in the boy. But when Marek had come to him to ask for his van, and Steiner realised he could share his adventure and his danger, he had been rewarded beyond his wildest dreams.

'We need some petrol,' said Marek now. 'And I'd like to check the oil.'

'There's a garage about ten kilometres away; on the other side of the village.'

Marek nodded and drove on.

The rain had stopped but the children in the bus had fallen silent. Sabine, her curls matted with sweat, was sitting beside Ellen; she had been sick three times and did not seem to be finished yet.

There was another hour at least to their destination. Sophie too felt sick. It was partly the motion of the bus, but mostly apprehension. Everything had gone wrong with this trip. If FitzAllan had been taking them Sophie wouldn't have minded what they were going to do so much, but it was Ellen. She'd had to step in at the last minute when FitzAllan developed a migraine, and the idea of getting Ellen into trouble was unbearable.

'I wish we hadn't come,' she said to Leon. 'I wish we could tell her and turn back.'

'Well we can't,' said Leon. 'We promised Flix we'd help.'

But Flix didn't look very good either. She too had had to stop once to be sick and Frank, whom she'd enlisted because he was supposed to be tough and fearless, was fidgeting and scowling, and now, in a throwback to his earlier schooling, he put up his hand and told Ellen that he needed to be excused.

Ellen nodded and asked Herr Tauber to stop at the next convenient place, but Frank's phraseology only confirmed her in the feeling that something strange was going on. Frank did not ask to be excused; he expressed the need to perform his bodily functions with Rabelaisian vigour. As she wiped Sabine's face with a damp flannel she looked down the bus, wondering what was wrong. Too many of the children had felt unwell. She'd been with them when they went by bus to the circus in Klagenfurt, and only Sabine and one other child had been sick.

Frank passed her and she saw that beneath his usual sullen expression there was something else; a kind of fear. He was sitting next to Flix and that was unexpected too; Flix usually had little use for him.

'There's no need for us to go on with this expedition,' she said, standing up to survey the children. 'Absolutely no need. We can go back without the slightest difficulty.'

For a moment the faces turned to her looked hopeful. Sophie half rose in her seat and was pulled down by Leon. Then Flix, still pale and puffy-eyed, said, 'No. We want to go on. We have to.'

Frank returned, they set off again. The road was steep now; they had left the lakes behind.

'I've got a headache,' said Janey miserably, laying her head against the window.

Ellen, comforting her, could have said the same. She also blamed herself very much for not having aborted this expedition from the start.

'It's a perfectly ridiculous idea,' she'd said to Bennet, when he told her of FitzAllan's determination to show the children a proper slaughterhouse. 'A man who eats nothing but nut cutlets wanting to expose them to all that.'

Bennet agreed. 'I told him in any case that hiring a bus would be far too expensive.'

But here he had been undermined by Herr Tauber, who was married to Lieselotte's aunt and had come to work in the grounds after Marek left. The beneficial mafia operated by Lieselotte's relatives was growing, and Herr Tauber now offered his bus for the price of the petrol only, if it would help the school.

Even so, the headmaster would not have given his consent, but to his amazement a number of the children – apparently led by the tender-hearted Flix – came to him and said they wanted to go.

'It would help us in understanding our parts in the play,' they said, echoing what had seemed to be Fitz-Allan's idiocy.

So it was agreed and then of course just before they were due to go, FitzAllan succumbed to a frightful migraine – or so he said.

Ellen had not intended to pull FitzAllan's irons out of the fire for him but for some reason the children had been very disappointed at the idea of cancelling the trip – and the truth was that she herself felt guilty about her reluctance to visit the Carinthian Municipal Abattoir. She was after all not a vegetarian – quite the contrary: her *Boeuf en Daube* had won first prize at the Lucy Hatton School of Household Management – yet she had never seen how the wretched beasts she cooked so readily were dispatched.

So she had agreed to go and now was bitterly regretting it.

They had passed Klagenfurt and the sanatorium where Chomsky still lay surrounded by devoted relatives. The last time Ellen had visited him they were debating whether to take Laszlo off to a spa to recuperate and had asked her if she would like to accompany him on the journey as his nurse.

If only she could trust Isaac to be sensible. She had left him with Lieselotte, determined to venture into *Kartoffelpuffer*, but he had begun to give up hope of Marek and was talking about getting away on his own.

Sophie, sitting in the row in front, turned around.

'Have you got a sick bag, Ellen?' she asked, and Ellen handed her the last one in her basket.

What was the *matter* with everyone?

As so often with Sophie, she was trying to reconcile her warring sides. In England she read school-girl stories in which sneaking and telling tales was the worst thing that could be done, but in Vienna with her father, it was breaking the law that was unforgivable. What if they caused Ellen to be put in prison? They didn't put children in prison but they put them in awful places – Borstal and worse. Should she tell Ellen what was hidden in Flix's basket beneath the picnic food and her rolled-up raincoat, or in Frank's? All of them had pliers and wire cutters but Flix and Frank had great files, and a handsaw.

Flix had planned it all. She was going to release the Judas sheep and shoo it away into the forest. 'Then the other sheep will follow,' she'd said, 'and while the men are chasing them the rest of you can free the animals in the trucks and in the pens.'

Sophie had wanted to help – one simply had to after FitzAllan had explained about the way the steers were stunned and had their throats cut while their hearts were still beating because that way the blood drained away better, as though animals were a kind of sewage. But she couldn't help wondering if it was going to be as simple as that: the stampeding beasts, the furious men, the blood . . . Oh God, what shall I do? thought Sophie, and was angry with Ursula, who had said from the start that it was silly and wouldn't work. She'd come along, but she wouldn't help in any way and she seemed to be the only person who wasn't feeling ill.

Another child put up his hand.

'Herr Tauber, I think we'd better have a break,' said Ellen. 'Do you know a suitable place to stop?'

He nodded. 'There's a garage at the bottom of the hill with a place to park. They have a fruit stall and toilets.'

'Then we'll pull in there if you'll be so kind.'

They drove into the forecourt.

'You can all get out and stretch your legs,' said

222

Ellen. 'But five minutes only – we have to get on. Anyone who wants to go to the toilets –'

But the children, for once, were not heeding her. Leon had given a shout and tumbled down the steps, Sophie followed and then all of them were rushing headlong towards the petrol pump in the far corner, where a tall man was standing talking to the attendant.

Marek was not pleased to see them come. He had finished with the school, and the events of last week had shown him how important it was that he involved no one in his concerns. But as more and more children ran towards him, he found himself smiling at their affection and enthusiasm.

'Where are you off to?' he asked, and they told him, excitedly, confusedly. Something fell from Frank's pocket and the boy picked it up quickly but not before Marek had seen what it was.

'Ellen's taking us,' said Sophie, and the worried look returned to her face. 'It was meant to be FitzAllan but now it's her.'

Marek looked across at the bus and saw Ellen standing on the steps. He had forgotten the way her hair fell asymetrically, more of it to the left side of her face. Remembering how she had yelled at him the last time he saw her, he waited – but she came down and walked towards him and said, 'Could I speak to you alone? Just for a moment?'

'Of course.'

He shooed away the children and together they walked to where they could not be overheard.

Then: 'I have him,' she said very quietly. 'I have your friend.'

Marek gave a half shake of the head. Her words made no sense to him.

'I have Meierwitz,' she repeated. 'He's with me, working in the kitchen.'

But the transition was too sudden. He had left Isaac in his mind, shot down in the forest; he could not believe her.

'I left him with Lieselotte. She's teaching him to make *Kartoffelpuffer*.'

The *Kartoffelpuffer* achieved what her assurance had been unable to do – no one invented that unnecessary way of dealing with potatoes – and now at last Marek heard her words and believed her, and understood that the impossible had happened and his friend was safe.

'Oh, Ellen,' he said.

Then he took a step towards her and, uncaring of the watching children, took her in his arms.

FitzAllan lay back on the pillows and covered his forehead with a languid hand. He had drawn the curtains, but enough light came through to hurt his eyes whenever he opened them. The purple zigzag stage of his migraine had passed but his head ached unbearably and he felt sick.

It was the strain, of course: the strain of pitting his

will against the staff and children who baulked him at every turn as he tried to put into practice his ideas. Strain always brought on one of his attacks, and Tamara's tantrum when he had felt compelled to shorten her ballet once again had made him worse.

But at least he had prevailed in the matter of the slaughter-house visit. Bennet had opposed him – everyone had opposed him, but he had won. Even now the children were being shown around the Carinthian Municipal Abattoir and perhaps that would get them to give some decent performances.

The castle was wonderfully quiet. They wouldn't be back till the evening and if he could get some sleep now he might be fit for work again tomorrow. He drifted off in a day dream of acclaim in which theatre producers congratulated him on what he had achieved with inferior material, and offered him work in Paris, London and New York. 'The risks you took were entirely justified,' they said.

He was woken by a door slamming; the sound of excitable voices. The corridors had filled once more with children. It must be the ones who had not gone on the trip – the bus couldn't possibly have returned yet. But he thought he heard Frank shouting, and then Bruno . . . and both of them had signed on to go.

Flinching as he turned on the bedside light, FitzAllan looked at his watch. Half past five. They must have run round the slaughterhouse in record time. There was a brief knock at the door, and Ellen entered.

Even in his feeble condition, FitzAllan noticed that

she looked cheerful. She looked, in point of fact, radiant, and the director, who did not like her, felt unaccountably nervous.

'I've brought you a present!' she announced. 'Shut your eyes and put out your hand.'

'I can hardly bear *not* to shut them,' said FitzAllan in a failing voice. But he put out his hand and felt a small, softish object placed in his palm.

'What is it?'

'It's a boa constrictor,' said Ellen tenderly.

In spite of himself he gave a scream and dropped it, and Ellen reproachfully put it back in his fingers. 'I'll open the curtains so you can see it properly. It's made of marzipan.'

'No!'

'Well, I'll describe it to you. I don't know if it's authentic – I think Herr Fischer hasn't seen a real one, but it's *better* than authentic. It's curled round on itself and has green zigzags and yellow diamonds and you can see its split tongue as clear as anything. All of us bought marzipan animals in Klagenfurt from Herr Fischer's shop. Marek gave every single child some money to do it and it's really interesting what they chose. Sophie has a crocodile and Leon chose a snail – not at all what I'd have expected, and –'

'Wait. Why did you go to the patisserie in Klagenfurt? I don't understand.'

'Well, after Marek told us that the slaughterhouse was closed because of foot and mouth disease –'

'What!' FitzAllan forgot his migraine, sat bolt

upright and groaned. 'But that's nonsense. I checked it yesterday.'

'Oh, it only happened this morning. Marek came from there – he brought Professor Steiner back and they went right past it and there were huge notices saying CLOSED. I assure you,' said Ellen sweetly, 'that it's true.'

'I don't believe it.'

'Well, you can ask Marek.'

And if I hadn't been going on your stupid trip I might have missed him, thought Ellen, and smiled at FitzAllan with ineffable joy. He would have dropped Steiner and gone away again and I wouldn't have seen him and he wouldn't have hugged me and thanked me for saving his friend and Isaac wouldn't be hopping up and down now in Chomsky's room. 'I must go and serve supper,' she said, 'though I doubt if anyone will eat very much. It was a sort of party we had after Marek told us we couldn't go, oh it was lovely – and so interesting! I think if I was Professor Freud I wouldn't waste so much time finding out what people had seen their parents do and about incest and all that – I'd take them to Herr Fischer's shop and see what they chose. You wouldn't believe it but Frank didn't pick an animal at all – he chose a *conker*. Just an ordinary brown marzipan chestnut – there was a tree in his mother's garden, he said, when he was small! And Sophie ate her crocodile then and there in two big bites; I was really encouraged – I think she may be getting just a little bit tough inside.'

At the door she paused and smiled once more at the patently uninterested invalid. 'If you want to know what animal I bought,' she said dreamily, 'I didn't buy anything. I already have one, you see. I have a lady-bird!'

The shutters were closed tight over the windows of Steiner's little house. The boat in which Ellen and Isaac had rowed across was hidden in the Professor's boathouse. The night was dark and moonless; hardly a ripple stirred the water.

Ellen had intended to let Isaac go alone; the reunion between him and Marek was something she thought should be conducted in privacy, but Isaac was not interested in privacy. He wanted her to come to Steiner's house; he wanted her to come everywhere with him always. So Ellen had busied herself checking the dressing on the Professor's wound and making coffee in the little kitchen while Isaac and Marek exchanged their memories of that frightful night. Now, over a glass of cognac, the map spread out on the table, they were discussing the next stage: Isaac's escape from Central Europe.

'The river line is still intact,' said Marek. 'Uri goes down once a week with the logs; he'll take you. But how to get you into Poland? We can't use the van any more, Franz is dead and they've doubled the guards. We'll have to go properly armed this time and –'

'Well I think that's completely silly,' said Ellen.

'Oh you do?' said Marek. 'You've a better idea, I suppose?'

'Yes. It's what I was going to do if you'd turned out to be dead,' she said.

'Well I'm not dead, so take that wistful note out of your voice.' And then reluctantly: 'All right then; how were you going to get Isaac into Poland?'

'In a train. In a first-class sleeper. A wagon-lit, preferably with Lalique panels and Art Nouveau lamps, because I'm interested in Secessionist architecture,' she said primly. 'He wouldn't be able to go to the dining car, because being a serious mental case he would have to stay in bed, but I would, because nurses are allowed to eat – and they do quail's eggs in aspic on the Warsaw Express, I've heard, and I've never tried them.'

They all stared at her. 'What are you talking about?'

'Chomsky,' said Ellen. 'That's what I'm talking about. They were thinking of taking him to a spa to recuperate. There's one there in Poland.' She pointed to a place near a bend on the Vistula river. 'They offered me the chance to accompany him as a sort of nurse and it so happens that I have his passport, so why shouldn't Isaac go instead? Could you get the photo changed?'

'Not in a hurry. The man who did the forgeries is the one they caught.'

'Well, it might not matter – Isaac's the same age as Chomsky, and it would be night time and he'd have his head bandaged.'

'It's still a risk,' said Marek. 'And not one that you will take. Get his passport and give it to me and –'

'No,' said Ellen. 'I won't. You can come along and start shooting people or hanging them out of windows if things go wrong but I'm going to be Isaac's nurse.'

'I would like her to be my nurse,' said Isaac – and Marek turned on him angrily.

'Be quiet, Isaac. This isn't a joking matter. I'm sorry, Ellen, but I absolutely will not allow you to become involved any further. I shall always be in your debt but –'

'Allow!' said Ellen, putting down her glass. '*Allow?* How dare you speak to me like that? I nearly turned Isaac over to the police because you didn't trust me enough to tell me what you're doing.'

'Ellen, this is no job for –'

'Don't!' She turned on him furiously. 'Just don't *dare* to say this is no job for a woman. My mother and my aunts didn't get kicked by police horses and thrown to the ground for you to go round treating me as an imbecile. Furthermore if war comes no one will bother to distinguish between men and women. Ask the women of Guernica whether anyone cared what sex they were when they bombed the market place. Getting Isaac out is part of fighting Hitler and I won't be left out of it.'

She broke off and they turned to look at Steiner. The old man was leaning back in his chair and laughing at some personal and highly amusing joke.

'Wonderful!' he said. 'Milenka would be delighted.

You should really take her to Pettovice, Marek. She and Ellen are sisters under the skin.'

Marek frowned, remembering his first sight of Ellen at the well and how he had thought that one day he might do just that.

'Don't you see how unbearable it is for me to put you into danger?' he said in a low voice.

But she gave no quarter. 'Don't you see how unbearable it is for me not to be allowed to help?' she answered. 'Isaac and I are *friends*.'

Friends? thought Marek, caught by the passion in her voice. Or something more? He had seen how Isaac followed her with his eyes.

He picked up his glass, drained it and smiled at her. Then: 'Since you seem to be an expert on Chomsky's passport, did you happen to see what he put under Distinguishing Characteristics?'

She beamed back at him. 'My Hungarian's not very good but I did look and he hasn't mentioned it. Which is just as well. Not that Isaac will be travelling in his swimming things, but all the same . . .'

# 17

Isaac turned over in his bunk and gazed, from under the huge bandage which covered his head, at Ellen. The soft light of the luxurious sleeping compartment shone on her fluted cap, her snowy apron. She looked like a nurse specially lowered from heaven for his benefit and he did not know how he could bear to leave her.

'You're being angelic, again,' he said.

'Hush. You're supposed to be asleep.'

Everything had gone smoothly. Marek had hired an ambulance and booked the sleeper. He himself had driven them to the station wearing a Red Cross arm-band, and they had settled Isaac into his quarantined compartment. Then Marek had driven the ambulance away, and returned dressed in his own clothes with his pigskin suitcase and his passport which stated truth-fully that he was Marcus Altenburg, a musician. If asked he would have said that he was travelling to a music festival in Warsaw, but he was not asked.

Ellen could see him now, standing in the corridor

unobtrusively keeping watch. He had booked a first-class compartment next to Isaac's and hers, and seemed to have it to himself. After they left the train, he and Isaac would go on on foot and she would return to Hallendorf.

Isaac, wearing a spare pair of Chomsky's pyjamas, lay back on the pillow. He was certain that he would be apprehended, either at the two checkpoints they faced on the train or as he reached the Baltic, and if they tried to send him back to Germany he had decided he would kill himself.

But meanwhile there was Ellen.

He put out a hand and she took it and held it. She could see his thoughts working across his face as clearly as if he had uttered them.

'Ellen, if I get out . . .'

'When.'

He managed a smile. 'When. Why don't we start a restaurant? I think I'd make quite a good chef.'

'Maybe. But you're a violinist.'

'I was. I'm not any more – I tried to make Marek see that it's over. In the camp, after they found out I was a violinist . . .' but he could never talk about what they had done to his hands. 'When I cut my finger the other day and it didn't *matter*, it was such a relief! I would work really hard. Think about it, Ellen. If I had something to look forward to . . . something we could do together, it might be worthwhile trying to stay alive. I've loved you from the moment I saw you kneeling there beside that extraordinary suitcase.'

'Oh Isaac, I love you too but –'

'Yes, I know. Not like that. But that might come. I think we'd make a splendid team. Perhaps Marek would put some money into it.'

'Marek is convinced that you're one of the best violinists in the world and that you'll play again.'

He shook his head. Pretending to close his eyes, he could still see her, her head bent over her book. He had hoped she would lie down on the bunk beside him; he wouldn't have laid a finger on her but it would have been something to remember while he sat huddled in the evil-smelling lean-tos in which the rivermen slept as they poled down towards the sea.

'It's an hour still till the border, Isaac. Get some rest.'

She looked up and saw Marek's silhouette against the window. He was still keeping watch and it was all she could do not to follow him into the corridor to draw comfort simply from his quiet presence, his size.

But they got through the first checkpoint without difficulty. The halt between Austria and Czechoslovakia was only a huddle of shacks and a road barrier. The two men who came along the corridor were friendly enough: Czechs with broad cheekbones; peasants without an axe to grind. Ellen gave them her passport and Chomsky's, putting her finger to her lips to show that her patient was asleep.

They scarcely looked at one of the passports, held the other long enough to make Ellen's heart thump almost unbearably in her chest.

'You're British,' said one of the soldiers, in heavily accented German, and Ellen saw that it was her passport he was holding.

'Yes.'

'Your government should help us,' he said. 'They should support us against Hitler,' and handed it back.

The first hurdle was over then.

She slipped out into the corridor and Marek, in his role as a well-to-do passenger starting a flirtation with a pretty nurse, turned to make way for her. They were travelling through wooded countryside towards Olomouc and Marek told her about the old woman who had sung the wrong songs to Steiner.

'Only they weren't the wrong songs, we were being absurd. They were the songs of her youth.'

People started going past them towards the dining car, among them a heavily painted woman in a fur cape who threw Marek a sultry glance from under clogged eyelashes.

'I'm sorry you can't come and try the quail's eggs in aspic.'

'I don't want to leave Isaac.'

'No.' He had seen how tenderly she leant over Isaac, held his hand. 'I'll bring him a bottle of champagne. He can drink it in his bed.'

'Like Chekhov,' she said. 'I was glad he died drinking champagne.'

'Yes. A good man.' He pointed out of the window

at a stream just visible in the gathering dusk. 'Do you see that river?'

'Yes.'

'My grandfather used to fish in there; it flows past our house about a hundred miles to the west.'

'The Russian anarchist? The one who wanted to blow up the general but your grandmother wouldn't let him?'

'That's the one. He loved fishing and he loved Chekhov. He was always quoting what Chekhov said about fishing.'

'*God won't subtract from man's appointed span the time spent fishing,*' she said. 'Is that the one?'

Marek nodded. 'One day about two years before I was born he was sitting by the bank with his rod and my mother came and told them what she'd just heard in town. That Chekhov was dead. My grandfather was absolutely shattered. "To think that I should outlive Chekhov," he kept saying – and he didn't go fishing once for the rest of the summer.'

'He was such a gentleman – Chekhov, I mean,' said Ellen. 'I always think of him coughing into little twists of sugar paper down in Yalta and writing to his wife in Moscow telling her not to worry; telling her to stay where she was and to do what she wanted. So he was an odd man for an anarchist to love so much.'

'Perhaps. But he was not a very good anarchist, if you remember. And Chekhov had been to the penal colony in Sakhalin and written about the fate of the prisoners there. My grandfather was very influenced by that.'

She was silent, thinking of the strange mix of ancestors that had gone to make the man beside her: Russian and English, German and Czech. No wonder he was at home in borderlands.

'Is this the sort of country Pettelsdorf is in?'

'Yes. The woods are denser perhaps.'

She thought of it, this tantalising demesne to which only the wounded were admitted. 'You'll miss it when you go to America.' He was planning to sail as soon as Isaac was on his way; this was almost the last time she would see him.

Marek shrugged. 'It's best not to get too attached to places in the kind of world we live in now.'

'Or to people, perhaps.'

She was silent, remembering her mother's latest letter. They were digging trenches in Hyde Park, she had said, and asked her daughter to come home at once if there was any sort of crisis.

'Or to people,' he agreed.

'Only I don't know how you would write music without attachment,' she went on. 'I suppose it would come out like Buddhist music; sort of prayer wheels tinkling in the wind and those sad horns. Not that I know anything about it,' she added, suddenly embarrassed.

'On the contrary, you clearly know a lot about it – and about most other things,' he said, and wondered why he wasn't simply kissing her instead of discussing

Chekhov and the Nature of Attachment. 'Even though you do look like a rather delectable ham with that ruffle on your head.'

'It's not a ruffle; it's a proper nurse's cap,' she said crossly. 'I thought if I got one that wasn't stodgy it would have a resale value. After all, I bought it with your money and I want to pay you back.'

More passengers came past, bound for the last sitting of dinner. 'Are you certain you won't come and join me? We'd be back long before we got to the border.'

It was hard to refuse; harder than she could have imagined, but she remembered the fear in Isaac's eyes and shook her head. 'Tell me what you ate, won't you? In detail?'

'I promise.'

But still he didn't go. Was he waiting for someone?

'Isaac is convinced he won't ever play the violin again because of something they did to his hands in the camp,' she said. 'But I watched him when he was helping me in the kitchen. I could swear his hands are all right now; he made piped eclairs and you can't do those without good coordination. I wish you'd make him see. He wants us to start a restaurant.'

He frowned. 'Us? You mean you and him?' Isaac must be seriously gone in love then, or mad. 'Do you want to do that?' he asked curtly.

She shook her head. She was about to make her way back to her compartment when a woman in a tight red satin skirt, a frilly gold lamé blouse and an outsize

238

feather boa came along the corridor – a blonde of unbelievable vulgarity who smiled unashamedly at Marek.

And whose smile was returned. Marek excused himself and to Ellen's chagrin followed the woman's waggling behind towards the dining car.

One hour, another. The passengers returned from dinner but Marek did not come in with the promised champagne. Then the train slowed down and stopped in the kind of place that was the same all over Europe: custom sheds, army huts in which men sat playing cards, road barriers – and a station at which no one who could help it ever got out.

Ellen opened her nurse's bag, took out a syringe partly filled with a red liquid, and stood by the door. Two border guards got on: a young private and a sergeant. The Poles had been fought over too often: there was nothing casual about these lean-faced, unsmiling men.

Ellen's door slid open. The sergeant went on up the train; the private entered.

'Passports, please.'

She handed him hers, then Chomsky's. The soldier motioned her aside. He wanted to see who was in the bed.

Ellen picked up her syringe. Instead of impeding him, she touched the soldier's arm, indicating that she needed more blood from her patient, soliciting his help.

For a moment it looked as though it would work. She had seen so many strong men keel over in a faint at first-aid classes, and the contents of the syringe, mixed in the art room at Hallendorf, were a good imitation of the real thing. But though the soldier made a gesture of distaste, he did not retreat.

'Turn him round,' he ordered.

Ellen touched Isaac's shoulder and he groaned.

'Hurry,' barked the Pole.

But before she could obey there was the sound of a dreadful and ear-splitting scream from the next compartment. A second scream followed, and the soldier elbowed Ellen aside and went out into the corridor. Seconds later the door was pushed open and a woman hurled herself into the soldier's arms. Her blonde hair was matted with sweat, her scarlet lipstick was a smear across her trembling mouth – and she was totally and spectacularly naked.

'Help me! Help me!' she yelled. 'Protect me! He tried to rape me, the brute!'

Her thin arms closed round the soldier's neck like a vice: the scent of her cheap perfume, her stale deodorant, pervaded the corridor.

The Pole was twenty-one years old and prepared for anything but this.

More doors opened; distressed passengers appeared; an old man and his wife . . . the sleeping car attendant. Then the door of the compartment from which the woman had erupted opened once more – to reveal Marek in a loosely knotted bathrobe, his hair on end. The sight of him caused the woman to become even more frenzied. 'You must take me with you!' she screamed at the soldier. 'You must look after me!' She began to cry, rubbing her face into his, pressing her body against the rough uniform. 'I'm afraid!'

Trying to free himself, he dropped the passports.

'She's lying,' said Marek. 'She said she'd do it for a hundred marks. She's a lying bitch.'

More passengers appeared, and the guard . . . then the sergeant who was in charge of the young Pole. Speaking furiously to the soldier, he tried to loosen the woman's hold, but she only clung tighter, babbling and weeping.

The sergeant spat, then pulled her free with a vicious gesture. 'Out,' he gestured to his underling. 'Out!' – and picked up the two passports and handed them to Ellen.

Five minutes later, the train was on its way.

Marek had chosen the town of Kalun for an overnight stop before the journey on foot to the River Rats.

Situated on a tributary of the Vistula some two hundred kilometres north of Warsaw, it was an austere and somewhat gloomy place which had survived the wars, sieges and other horrors of the past centuries with its buildings more or less intact.

In the guide books, Kalun advertised itself proudly as a spa, but it was some way from rivalling Baden-Baden with its clientele from the Almanac de Gotha and its Kurpark full of magnificent trees. No royal visitors had come to Kalun incognito and raced pretty girls through the woods in wheelbarrows; the Empress

Sissi had not taken the small grape cure there as she had done in Merano – and Goethe, who had spent thirteen summers in Karlsbad, had almost certainly never heard of Kalun, let alone set foot in it.

But the Poles, ever a hopeful race, had dug out a series of springs in the rocks above the little town and sent their sulphurous and evil-smelling water through into the bath houses of the spa hotels. Doctors had been persuaded to come and offer treatments for an impressive list of ailments; wheelchairs plied to and from the pump rooms, and a whole posse of attendants pummelled and immersed and weighed the sick and elderly for a quarter of the fee required in the spas of France and Germany.

Marek had booked three rooms in the Kalun Spa Hotel, an austere building with endless corridors and cavernous rooms permeated with the smell of hydrogen sulphide. The arrival of Isaac with his nurse in this sepulchral building passed without incident: the passport numbers were registered; the ambulance returned to the garage. Tomorrow a telegram would come necessitating Isaac's return for family reasons, but now he was requested to select the ailment for which he wished to be treated.

Consulting the impressive list on a kind of menu pinned to his door, Isaac unhesitatingly chose otorhinolaryngological disease, something which no one could prove he did not have, and was borne off in a sedan chair by two gleeful male nurses for a course of hydrotherapy and massive immersion in radioactive mud. The disease had been losing ground among clients and his choice had given great pleasure.

Marek had tried to persuade Millie to stay till the morning and travel back part of the way with Ellen; the girls seemed to get on well together. But Millie had an engagement in a Berlin cabaret; she was returning in a few hours on the sleeper. Ellen had suggested she come and rest in her room but though Millie came she was not exactly resting. She was in fact sprawling on Ellen's bed, chain-smoking de Reskes and reminiscing about the days in Berlin when she had known Marcus von Altenburg and his friend.

'They were such fun. You should have seen Isaac in his evening clothes all dolled up for a concert – he always had a white carnation; it had to be white, red wasn't any good – and handmade shoes. You'd think he was a proper little monkey but when he played – my God, it would make the hair stand up on the nape of your neck. That soulful music and then he'd be out on the town till the small hours, dancing and cracking jokes. It's awful to think what they've done to him.'

'Do you ever think of leaving Germany?'

'I think of it. But I've a mother and a brother – my father pushed off. Working in the cabaret helps . . . and sometimes . . . you know, I get other work. I can make good money like that.' She stretched out her arm and watched the gold bangle on her wrist with pleasure. 'He had no call to give me this; he paid me for what I did and I'd have done it for nothing. But Marcus is like that; he'd give anyone the skin off his back. People used

243

to think he was rich, but he wasn't, he just never seemed to count up what he had.'

'How long did you know them in Berlin?'

'Oh, most of the time Marcus was there – and I went on seeing Isaac till the Nazis came. They were such friends those two; it did you good to see them. So different . . . Isaac never stopped finding people to help Marcus; it was he that got him a break as a conductor. And they weren't ever jealous of each other like people so often are when they're in the same line of business. Even over women, though it must have been hard for Isaac.'

'What must?'

'Well, he'd pick up some girl in a nightclub maybe and bring her back to his table, and chat her up – he was always falling for women – and Marcus wouldn't say much; you could see him making himself quiet, sort of trying to be like one of his trees so that Isaac could have her, but by the end of the evening it was Marcus the girl wanted.'

'It doesn't seem fair.'

'No. But what's fair about life – turning a nice bloke like Isaac into an outcast because he's got a nip in his foreskin.' She broke off. 'Sorry, don't mind me. But I can tell you, when I met Marcus at the station and he asked me if I'd be willing to make a bit of a diversion if it was needed so as to help Isaac get through, I was as pleased as Punch. And I'll tell you though you haven't asked: no, I didn't do it with Marek, not on the train – not ever, in point of fact, though I'd have done it like a shot. It was strictly business.'

Ellen smiled at her, 'I wish you'd stay longer, Millie. You'll be so tired travelling back tonight.'

But Millie shook her head. 'I have to go, Ellen, but if ever you come to Berlin . . .'

'Or you to London.'

There was a knock at the door and an elderly maid announced the arrival of the taxi for the station.

The girls embraced.

'Take care,' said Millie. And at the door: 'Are you in love with Isaac?'

Ellen shook her head. 'No. I'm terribly fond of him, but –'

'Oh that!' Millie waved a dismissive arm. 'He's got it badly over you.'

'It's just because I found him and sheltered him. As soon as he's out in the world again he'll forget me.'

'Maybe.' Millie put on her scarlet beret, adjusted the angle. 'What's funny is that I don't see Marek trying to be a tree.'


The dining room of the Kalun Spa Hotel was a cavernous room whose heavy swagged curtains, dim chandeliers and dusty Turkish carpets gave off an air of sombre melancholy. It was as though here the authorities had finally given up hope of putting the town on the map of Great Spas of Europe, had accepted the fact that Queen Marie of Romania or Alfonso of Spain would never now drink the evil waters of the pump room. The few diners already assembled were in the last stages of disintegration, sitting in wheelchairs or precariously propped on cushions with their walking frames beside them; the smell of hydrogen sulphide blotted out the odour of frying onions from the kitchens and the waiters were as ancient and arthritic as the guests.

Entering the dining room, Ellen saw Marek at a table by the window scribbling something in the large menu, bound in maroon leather, provided by the management. As she reached him, and he got to his feet, she realised that what he had been writing, between the announcements of liver broth with dumplings, boiled beef with noodles and other delights – was music; and for a moment she felt as though a door had been opened on his other life; a life from which she must always be excluded, whatever he wrote on menus.

'Please don't let me disturb you,' she said.

He shook his head, put away his propelling pencil. 'It's of no importance. I'll finish later.'

'Like Mozart,' she said.

He grinned. 'Oh, exactly like Mozart.'

'I mean he was supposed to write anywhere and not mind being disturbed.'

He shrugged. 'It's not so mysterious, you know, composing. If you were writing a letter and I came in, you wouldn't fuss.' He pulled out a chair for her. 'You look charming. Where did you get that delightful dress?'

'I made it; the material comes from an old sari; it's a Gujarati design.'

Marek raised his eyebrows. The workmanship of the short blue silk jacket, the swirling skirt with its stylised design of roses and stars and tiny birds, was remarkable. 'I'm afraid you're unsettling the old gentlemen. I can hear the crunch of vertebrae as they try to turn their heads.'

'Perhaps it's you they're looking at because you're healthy and can get in and out of your dinner jacket by yourself. It makes one feel guilty, doesn't it?'

'Our turn will come,' said Marek. 'And Isaac? Is he on his way?'

She shook her head. 'He got ambushed by the masseuses. I think the excitement of having someone with an otorhinolaryngological complaint went to their heads. They're giving him a special supper in his room and weighing him and God knows what. I tried to persuade him to come down but he saw two people he thought were policemen in the corridor. I'm sure they were only fire engine inspectors, but I think the thought of tomorrow is making things hard. It must be so awful to start running again.'

'He'll be all right, you'll see. Let me pour you some champagne. The wine list was not encouraging but this is Dom Perignon, and it makes a very acceptable aperitif.'

They clinked glasses. 'Water is for the feet,' she said obediently. And then: 'Where does it come from, that toast?'

'I got it from Stravinsky. He always says he conducts best with a couple of glasses of cognac inside him. Mind you, I could show you a place where water isn't for the feet.'

'At Pettelsdorf.' It was not a question.

'Yes. There's a well in a field behind the orchard – it has the clearest and coldest water in Bohemia. The village girls go there after their wedding and draw a glass of it to take to their new husbands. It's supposed to ensure a long and faithful marriage.'

Not only the village girls, he thought. Lenitschka had told him of his mother, making her way between the apple trees, shielding her glass, when the Captain brought her as a newlywed from Prague.

But their waiter had now managed to reach their table. He seemed to be in his early eighties; his grey face suffused with anxiety as he set down their plates of soup. Beneath the circles of congealing grease, they could make out a posse of liver dumplings, like the drowned heads of ancient ghouls.

'At least one doesn't feel that Isaac is missing anything,' said Ellen. 'I promised I'd go up later and see that he's all right. A nurse shouldn't abscond to the dining room like this.'

'I'm glad she has. I shouldn't like to dine in this place alone.'

'I just want you to know that if Isaac can get himself to England my mother and my aunts will put him up till he finds his feet. Or sponsor him. I've written to them.'

'And they've agreed?'

'I haven't heard yet – I only wrote a few days ago. But you can rely on it.'

'A compliment – that you can speak for them so certainly.'

'Well, I can. It's not being in need that's the problem in Gowan Terrace. It's *not* being in need.' She bent her head, frowning momentarily. She had still not answered Kendrick's letter begging her to come to Vienna. And because Gowan Terrace made her think of her brave mother's insistence on facing facts, she said: 'Have you booked your passage yet?'

'There's a boat sailing from Genoa on the tenth. I'm trying to get a berth on that.' And then: 'I'm running away.'

'That isn't a thing you usually do, I imagine.'

'No. But the Americans were very good to me; there's an orchestra there that I shall enjoy licking into shape – and once I'm there I can put pressure on my parents to join me.'

They had been talking German throughout the journey on account of Isaac, and without thinking he had continued to do so though they were alone. Now he thought how sweet and funny it sounded, this intelligent girl speaking so softly and fluently but with a trace of an accent that seemed to come less from England than from some Austrian country province that he could not place.

'You know, your German is amazing. You can't have learnt it at college?'

'No. I learnt it from my grandfather's housekeeper. I wanted her to be my grandmother – she had to be. Talking to her was like entering another country, a country I needed.'

He nodded, remembering suddenly the words of a pedantic professor in Berlin. 'Love is a matter of linguistics,' the old man had said. 'It is completely different in French or German or Spanish . . . even in the dark, even when no words are spoken.'

She had been struggling valiantly with the soup, not wanting to hurt the feelings of the waiter, but now she laid down her spoon. 'It makes one wonder if Fräulein Waaltraut has a sister working in the kitchens.'

The waiter, sad but unsurprised, removed their plates and tottered back with two helpings of gristly grey beef surrounded by a mass of self-adhesive noodles.

'Perhaps we should have had your piece?' said Ellen, looking down at the staves of music Marek had written between the mythical alternatives to their entrée.

'I think perhaps the answer is another bottle of champagne.'

He was right, thought Ellen, as he so often was. Champagne might not be the natural choice to go with what they were eating, but it was beginning to put a barrier between her and the knowledge that this was the last time she would see Marek. When they parted now she would be casual – she would be British – and that was what all along she had been aiming for.

'Perhaps we'd better skip the dessert,' said Marek. 'Just have coffee?'

But the waiter, when they suggested this, was desperate. He had, he announced, a special treat for Mademoiselle, his own speciality, perfected when he spent a year in France as a young man. He wished – indeed he implored her – to let him make a crêpe suzette.

'I don't know if he should be doing that,' said Ellen worriedly. 'It's quite tricky.'

But they could not resist his entreaties, and when at last he reappeared pushing the trolley with its copper pan of folded crêpes, its spirit lamp, its small bottle of orange liqueur and large bottle of brandy, his look of pride was such that they could only be glad they had relented.

With a shaking hand, he poured a measure of orange liqueur on to the crêpes and then a measure – indeed a very large measure – of brandy.

Then, with what he clearly intended as a flourish, he lit a match and put it to the contents of the pan. There was a whooshing noise of surprising loudness – a sheet of flame shot upwards – and Ellen lifted her head with a small and startled cry.

Marek's response was so instantaneous that those watching could have sworn that there was no gap between the moment when the girl's hair caught fire and the moment when he picked up the champagne bottle and hurled its contents at her head. Then he pulled the tablecloth away, and as the glasses and lamps and cutlery crashed to the floor, he wrapped the damask tightly round her head, pulling her towards him to pat out the last possible smouldering embers.

They were surrounded now by people: the panic-stricken waiter, flapping his napkin; a maid trying to pull the fire extinguisher from the wall; one of the diners hobbling towards them on crutches.

'Go away!' commanded Marek. 'Everyone. Now.'

'But –'

'*Go!*'

He bent over her, unwrapped her . . . and saw a drenched girl missing a number of curls . . . a girl with startled eyes – but without the burns he had dreaded.

'Thank God! Come on – let's get out of here. You need some air.'

He put his arm round her and led her out through the hall and into the deserted garden. It was growing dark, but he found a bench under an acacia tree lit by a single lantern and made her sit down while he examined her face more carefully, pushing the hair back off her forehead. There was only the smallest of red marks, but as he searched, one imperilled curl came off in his hand, and he put it in his pocket.

'You're soaked,' he said, and took off his jacket and wrapped it round her shoulders.

'I'm all right, honestly. It's the waiter I'm worried about. I don't want to get him into trouble.'

'Interceding for that old fool comes later,' said Marek, sitting down beside her. 'Quite a lot later.'

She put up a hand to her hair, let it fall. 'It's best not to think how I look.'

'I'll tell you how you look,' he said gently. 'Flambéed . . . asymmetrical . . . and like Madame Malmaison in the rain.'

'Madame Malmaison?'

'My mother's favourite rose. Very tousled, very fragrant. She sheds petals as you shed curls but there are always plenty more.'

He had spoken in a voice she had not heard him use before and it seemed to her that she must now be as silent and unmoving as she had ever been. That she must accept obediently what the next moments brought and that this uncomplaining acceptance was the most important thing she had ever had to do.

But it was not necessary. He did not move away or make a brisk remark. What she had to accept was different: it was the touch of his hands as he turned her face towards his . . . and then the homecoming, the moment that was out of time, yet contained the whole of time. What she had to accept was his kiss.

# 18

They had walked for a day and part of a night and now were on their way again: two Jews in long dark coats wearing wide-brimmed hats, with pedlars' packs on their backs.

No one stopped them or asked their business; they were too poor. The Polish forest had seen wanderers and fugitives and pilgrims since the dawn of time. This was the *Urwald* with the bisons that Marek had craved as a boy, angry that they were not to be found as far west as Pettelsdorf. Once some children in a village threw stones at them, but when the taller of the 'Jews' turned round they stopped and ran away.

'It's not Jews they are stoning,' Marek had said quietly, seeing Isaac's face. 'It's strangers.'

In their packs they had bread, pepper to turn away dogs, trinkets and prayer shawls. Marek's staff was sharpened to a lethal point but he carried no gun. They had spent the night in a brushwood shelter. Scooping up dry leaves and ferns to make a bed, they found something metallic and round which glinted in the moonlight: the greatcoat button of a Russian soldier from the Battle of Tannenberg. It could as easily have belonged to one of Napoleon's fusiliers or a marauding Turk. The whole history of Eastern Europe could be unearthed here beneath the leaf mould and pine needles of these woods.

On the afternoon of the second day they came to the river. It was already wide here; a silent silver highway which would join the tributaries of the Vistula and the great lakes, on its journey to the sea. Here and there swathes had been cut in the dark phalanx of the trees and the logs trundled down the ramps. They were not far now from the men they had come to find.

Marek was looking with pleasure at the herons fishing in the shallows, the trout jumping for flies, but Isaac saw only the dreaded journey in appalling conditions with men of whose skills and traditions he knew nothing – and at the end uncertainty again, and danger.

'Listen, Marek . . . my violin is in Berlin with my landlady. The Stradivarius, I mean – the others I gave to the Institute.'

'With your grandmother's pigtail still safe inside, I hope?'

'Yes.' But Isaac was in a serious mood. 'If anything happens to me and you can get it out, I want Ellen to have it.'

'Ellen? But she doesn't play, does she?'

'She doesn't need to; she *is* music,' said Isaac, and Marek frowned at the uncharacteristically high-flown language. It was serious, then, Isaac's passion; in Ellen lay this tormented man's hope for the future.

'Very well, I'll see to it. But you will get out. You'll get to Königsberg; you'll get on to the boat; you'll get your papers and in no time at all you'll be parading about in your tails on a concert platform.'

Isaac shook his head. 'It's over, Marek, I've told you. I shan't play again. But if I could have her . . . If she would . . .' He stopped and turned to look up at his friend. 'I've never minded in the past, not really. I always understood why they preferred you. But this time, Marek, please . . .'

He broke off, ashamed. They walked on for another hour and came to a clearing. Piles of felled timber were being pushed down a wooden chute towards the water, steadied by men in dark hats and sideburns wielding their long spiked poles. More men, calling to each other in Yiddish, were balancing on the logs already in the river, getting ready to surround the floating island with a ring of chains. A raft with an open-sided lean-to on the deck was moored by the pontoon bridge; inside they could see piles of sacking and a crate of chickens.

'That's where you'll sleep,' said Marek, grinning. 'But don't worry – the chickens won't trouble you for long; they're the larder.'

On a slight rise, commanding a view of the river in both directions was a neat wooden hut surrounded by a fence, the only permanent structure in this floating world. Uri, the overseer, was old and had laid claim to a piece of Polish earth. There were sunflowers in the tiny garden and a plot of vegetables. He had been married once and came here between journeys.

He was waiting, sitting on a wooden bench.

Marek's greeting was in Polish – neither he nor Isaac spoke more than a few words of Yiddish.

'I thought you wouldn't come,' said Uri.

'There were troubles,' said Marek.

'Yes. There are always troubles. So this is the man.'

'Yes.'

Uri nodded. He had blue eyes, unexpected in the dark bearded face. Isaac stood before him with bowed head. Alienated, grateful and apprehensive, he said: 'I have only the ordinary words. Thank you.'

He spoke in German but Uri understood. 'It is enough.' He pointed down to the bustle of the river. 'We leave in the morning; there's another load coming down, still.'

'You've a fine team,' said Marek, looking with admiration at the men freeing a log jam that had built up round the end of the raft. To make the journey which so appalled Isaac had been Marek's dream since childhood.

'Yes. They'll be knocking off soon; the light's going.'

He led them into the hut; there was a table spread with newspaper, a few chairs, a bunk bed. On the walls were hooks for coats, lanterns; on a shelf lay something wrapped in a shawl from which Isaac averted his eyes.

Uri went to a ramshackle cupboard and took out a grimy vodka bottle and three glasses which he filled almost to the brim.

'*Lechaim!*' he said, and they raised their glasses and repeated the age-old Hebrew toast: 'To Life!'

The men came up later when they had washed and said their prayers. Marek had brought what he could carry: smoked sausage, tobacco, a few small gifts . . . Another bottle of vodka was produced; they drank it neat with pepper. When they talked it was in Yiddish with a smattering of Polish, a few words of German, but they did not talk much; they ate and drank and watched their protégé and the man who had brought him.

But when the level in the bottle had sunk almost to nothing, Uri rose and went to the shelf at the back and fetched something wrapped in a piece of coloured cloth.

'Do you play?' he asked Isaac, carefully unwrapping the violin.

Marek watched with narrowed eyes. He had told the old man nothing about Isaac; only that he was a Jew and a fugitive.

Isaac pushed back his chair, trying to distance himself from the object on the table.

'No,' he said violently. 'No, I do not play.'

There was a murmur of disappointment. Uri spread out his fingers, bent with rheumatism, to show why he could no longer make music.

And suddenly Marek was filled with rage.

He got up, towering over Isaac, and the words he spoke were spat at him as to an enemy.

'How dare you!' he said to the man who was his

dearest friend. 'How dare you be so arrogant – so mean and ungiving. They're risking their lives for you and you're too small-minded to play for them.'

Isaac was dumbfounded, cringing in his chair.

'I told you . . . I can't . . . my hands . . .'

'I'm not interested in your hands. No one is interested in them. Dear God, I'm not asking you to give a concert performance. These people are tired – they want a fiddler. A fiddler on the roof as your people have always had – but I suppose you're too grand for that.'

Isaac had grown white with shock. Marek's contempt had never been turned against him before. The men were silent, not understanding.

'Oh go to hell,' said Marek, turning away.

But Isaac had picked up the violin . . . the bow . . . he was testing the strings. An old country fiddle, but lovingly cared for. He put it to his chin; began to tune it.

Then again he lost heart, put it down. But now it was too late; the men were watching him; he saw the hunger in their eyes. He could not speak to them, he knew nothing of their religion.

But he knew their music.

He did not even know that he knew it till he began. What grandmother, what ancient retainer in some *shetl* had hummed the lullaby he played now? Where did it come from, the lilting wedding song that followed? Isaac's fingers found the old dances, the old serenades . . . they found the music that the *Zigeuners* had

259

borrowed from the Jews, and altered, and given back
again . . . and the melodies crooned beside the wagons
that made their way west across the steppes, fleeing
from pogroms . . .

His fingers were stiff but it didn't matter; the vodka
had helped, and Marek's rage.

When he stopped at last they didn't thank him or
clap. They blinked themselves back into the world and
sighed – and one man, toothless and scarred, leant forward and touched him for a moment on the arm.

'Wait,' said Isaac. 'I'll play you one more tune. A
new one.'

Uri translated; the men settled themselves again. But
after he had retuned the fiddle, Isaac didn't start at
once. He went to the door and opened it wide to the
starry night.

The men were puzzled. They had enough fresh air in
their lives; the whine of the mosquitoes, the cry of a
forest animal in pain filled the room.

But Isaac wanted the river. He wanted to look out
on it as Marek had looked out at the Hudson all that
time ago.

Then he began to play.


The villa which Count Stallenbach's cousin had put
at Brigitta's disposal was sufficiently comfortable for
the diva and her party to spend another week by the
Wörthersee even after the search for Marcus had ended
in failure.

Now however their return to Vienna could not be

put off any longer. Leaning back on the cushions of the first-class compartment, Brigitta surveyed the rehearsals which awaited her with deep foreboding. They had given her the Hamburg beanpole for her Octavian, the *répétiteur* was new and inexperienced, and her deadly rival was already spreading slanders about the state of Brigitta's voice.

But the real disaster was Feuerbach. Attempts to get the regular conductor of the Philharmonic to return from his summer engagements abroad had failed, and she was supposed to work with an opinionated upstart who wasn't fit to have charge of a band of superannuated dustmen.

Staub, sitting beside her, was regretting the failure of their quest. He had worked on his libretto solidly . . . had framed the story of burning Troy in the words of the soldier in the wooden horse returning home and trying to get someone to listen to him. A sort of Ancient Mariner whom no one heeded, except one small boy. Altenburg would have loved it, he was sure.

Benny as usual was doing his sums. He would stay for the gala and then leave for the States. Brigitta on her own was no use to him; maybe he could get her a short tour as a Lieder singer next year but that was the extent of it.

'All change next stop. All change at St Polzen,' said the guard, coming down the corridor. Why this obscure town had been chosen as an important railway junction, no one had ever discovered; certainly it wasn't for the facilities it offered to travellers.

'You'd think they could run a direct service to Vienna,' grumbled Brigitta, and stood by while the men took down her hat boxes, her make-up case, her furs and portmanteau. Ufra, who travelled third class with the dog, put on her coat.

The train slowed down . . . stopped. Ufra opened the carriage door and Puppchen leapt down, gave vent to a frenzy of barking, tugged the lead out of her hand and raced across the platform.

'For goodness sake – can't you control the wretched animal,' scolded Brigitta, descending in her turn.

Her maid stood looking after the dog, now leaping up and down in front of a man sitting alone on a wooden bench.

'No,' said Ufra. 'As a matter of fact, I can't.'

Marek had travelled overnight from Warsaw. He had seen Isaac off down river and now had broken the journey at this junction where he had left his father's car when he'd picked up the ambulance. He only had to go across the road, fetch the car and drive to Pettelsdorf to pick up his things and say goodbye to his family. He had already taken his leave of Steiner – and of Hallendorf.

But he was tired now that the adventure was over, and for a moment he sat down on a bench in the sun. There was a train to Hallendorf in twenty minutes – he could get on it and in three hours be there. Would she be serving supper at the hatch, her burnt curls hidden under her hygienic hat . . . or leading her modest girls into the lake? Closing his eyes, he let the memories come: Ellen garnering gym shoes that first morning . . . feeding Aniella on cornflowers . . . taking a splinter out of Sabine's foot.

And then he was back in the sulphur-smelling garden at Kalun as she lifted her face for his kiss – and this now was not remembering, it was 'being there'. During those moments as he held her in his arms he had wondered if at last he need no longer envy his parents; if he too had found the supreme simplicity of a total and committed love. Leading her back to her room afterwards, putting the key in the lock for her, he had begun to speak – and then the neighbouring door had opened and Isaac had appeared, tied up in some ridiculous medical corset, and as Ellen went forward to help him, the moment had passed.

Marek had not answered Isaac's appeal by the river. He did not believe that self-sacrifice was a sound principle on which to base one's life. And yet . . . As they had washed in the stream that first morning, Marek had seen the concentration camp mark branded on Isaac's arm. Was something special owed perhaps to such a man?

Ten minutes before the train came back . . . he could still go. There was nearly a fortnight before he sailed; much could be sorted out in that time.

But now, on the other platform, a train was drawing in – not the one to Hallendorf, but the one from there. How absurd that everyone had to change always in this uninteresting little town.

A carriage door opened. Marek heard the fierce yapping of a little dog and then the creature was upon him, leaping up, rolling over, wagging his tail in a paroxysm of welcome.

And after him, of course, came Brigitta, her arms thrown out.

'Marcus! Darling! But this is incredible! We've been looking for you everywhere!'

Staub came forward to shake hands, then Benny, much hampered by the antics of Puppchen, whose sole achievement seemed to be to remember Marcus for remarkable periods of time.

'It's a miracle!' said Briggita. 'It's destiny, finding you. A portent. Now I know you'll come to Vienna and –'

'I'm sorry, Brigitta, but you're mistaken. I'm going home and then to America.'

'But you can't! You can't! You tell him about the gala, Benny. Tell him about Feuerbach.'

'It certainly seems to be bedlam there,' said Benny. 'If you could come even for a few days . . .'

'I'm sorry,' Marek repeated. Of the group surrounding him, he was the most pleased to see the little dog he had bestowed on Brigitta all those years ago: the dog and Ufra, for whom he had always felt respect.

'Well, at least, darling, come and have some coffee. Please. We've an hour to kill,' begged Brigitta, who was convinced that no man could remain even a few minutes in her presence and not be persuaded to do what she wanted.

'All right, Brigitta.' There were limits to churlishness. 'We'll have a coffee for old times' sake.'

As they made their way across the square, he heard the little train for Hallendorf come chugging in.

Fate had spoken and it had spoken rightly. For after all, what bound him was not just loyalty to a friend who had suffered. It was not the mark branded on Isaac's arm; it was the moment when Isaac had turned to him in the hut, his face alight for the first time in weeks, and said: 'I told you, didn't I? I told you I'd play the premiere!'

He had played only the theme of the slow movement, but it was enough.

From this man, whose musicality and dedication had somehow survived through so much hardship, one did not snatch what he believed was his fulfilment and his future.

Two days after Ellen returned from Kalun, Bennet gave an assembly which she found a little disquieting.

It was about a Greek warrier called Philoctetes who was bitten in the foot by a serpent and abandoned by his friends on a lonely island because they couldn't stand the stench from his wound. True, the story ended happily: finding they needed him to fight the Trojan War, his companions returned and after much grovelling persuaded him to sail with them to Troy, where he dispatched Paris with his bow and arrow, thus bringing the whole sorry business to an end.

But the somewhat lachrymose way in which the

headmaster dwelt on the abandoned hero's wounds and his friends' ingratitude was not at all in Bennet's usual style and Ellen was not surprised, when she spoke to Margaret, to hear that the secretary was getting very worried.

'It's that wretched FitzAllan and his play,' she said. 'He carries on as though there's nothing else in the world and asks for more and more. Everyone's told him the money just isn't there. And Tamara's chasing after him in the most blatant manner, trying to save her stupid ballet.'

'Surely he wouldn't –'

'Oh no, not him. He's far too selfish to notice anyone else, but really her sunbathing is getting perfectly ridiculous. She went and laid herself down right in the middle of David Langley's frit fly experiment, even though he labelled it quite clearly.'

'I tell you one thing, Margaret, if I ever catch her sunbathing on *Kohlröserl* I won't answer for the consequences,' said Ellen.

'I wish Bennet wouldn't worry about the play so much. His own workshop on *The Winter's Tale* is what they'll come for anyway in the Summer School.' She looked admiringly at Ellen. 'I must say, your fringe is quite enchanting. What a strange boy Bruno is.'

'Yes, indeed.'

Coming into her room on the night she got back, Bruno had found Ellen trying to repair the damage done by the crêpe suzette. He had watched for a moment as she tried to level out the mangled curls and then shaken his head.

'You want to cut more off. A lot more.' 'What do you mean?'

Words were not Bruno's coinage. He took the scissors from her and told her to shut her eyes. It was not easy sitting still while this badly behaved boy cut off what felt like large chunks of her hair but she did it, while the other children watched in silence.

But when he had finished and Ellen went to the mirror, she found herself smiling with surprise and pleasure. He had reduced her damaged curls to little half-moons and brought more hair in to make a tousled, tentative fringe which lapped her brows and echoed the gold-brown of her eyes. If she looked like a courtesan who had just got out of bed, she looked like a very expensive one.

Marek would like it, thought Ellen, while the children exclaimed. Except that Marek will never see it, she told herself – but the smile persisted, as though the memory of that kiss in the garden could not be set aside. She could not hear from him till he was back from Poland but after that . . . Surely before he sailed he would write to her once, or even come, if only to give her news of Isaac. It seemed impossible that the whispered pre-dawn farewell for the three of them could be the last goodbye.

Meanwhile, as always, there was work and the need to console others. Bruno, her hair sorted, retreated into his usual uncooperative state, denying the slightest artistic ability and refusing to help poor Rollo, who had been informed by FitzAllan that the masks he had made for the animals were not suitably monolithic and drab.

'If you've ever seen a monolithic and drab piglet I'd like to see it,' said Rollo angrily.

Hermine had been told by the director not to feed her baby in the theatre. 'I think he does not like my bosom,' said Hermine, coming tearfully to Ellen. 'And this I understand. I do not like it myself,' she said mournfully, looking down at her cleavage, 'but I cannot leave Andromeda so far away. Of course I should not have let the Professor overcome me –' But at this point Ellen changed the subject, for she could not bear Hermine's remorse over her seduction by the Vocal Rehabilitation expert who had drunk too much gentian brandy at the conference in Hinterbruhl.

'I could put ground glass into his nut cutlet?' suggested Lieselotte, who had taken against the director from the start. She was particularly incensed when she compared the demands FitzAllan was making with the cheeseparing that went on in the village about Aniella's name day celebrations. 'Every year we say we will do something really nice for her and every year people are too lazy or too tired or too poor.'

FitzAllan had of course rung the slaughterhouse to check about the foot and mouth disease and found out the truth, and what he regarded as Ellen's collusion with Marek in tricking him, and had scarcely spoken to her since.

Fortunately Chomsky, when she visited him, was improving. Not to the extent of returning to school but to the point where there was no longer any question of anyone taking him to a foreign place and asking her for his passport.

It was when she had been back for a week that Ellen realised that her ability to cope and comfort others had had an underlying cause. That somehow, against all reason and sense, she believed that she would see Marek again. That the time she had spent with him in the garden at Kalun had meant to him, perhaps not what it had meant to her – he was after all an experienced man with many affairs to his credit – but something. It was as though she was unable to conceive that this sense of total belonging, this mingling of utter peace and overwhelming excitement, was something she had felt all by herself.

As the days passed and she realised he must have returned from Poland she found herself waiting in the morning for the post bus – not now to console Freya if there was no news from Mats, or Sophie vainly awaiting a letter from her parents, but on her own account, and beneath the longing – a longing the depth of which she could not have imagined – there was anger. For she remembered very well what she had said to Bennet during her first interview when he asked her what she was afraid of. 'Not seeing,' she had said. 'Being obsessed by something that blots out the world. That awful kind of love that makes leaves and birds and cherry blossom invisible because it's not the face of some man.'

Now, when she had a rare moment to herself, it was Marek's face that she saw again and again as he paused in front of her door in the hotel corridor and said: 'Ellen, if I were to ask you –'

And then the door of Isaac's room had burst open and poor Isaac came out trussed up in bandages and by the time she had helped him, Marek was gone.

What had he been going to say? Sometimes, deliriously, she thought it was 'If I were to ask you, would you come to America?' or 'If I asked you, would you stay with me tonight?', and to both those questions she would have answered 'Yes' with every cell and fibre in her body.

But as the days went by and she heard nothing, she knew it could have been neither of those things. At the most perhaps he wanted her to look after the tortoise or see to Steiner's bandages.

She did in fact go and see Steiner whenever she could; she had become extremely fond of the old man, but he too had heard nothing.

Then, about ten days after her return, she was coming off the steamer with a basket full of shopping, when Sophie ran towards her, waving a letter.

'It's just come for you! It's Express and Special Delivery and everything!'

Ellen put down her basket. For a moment she experienced a joy so pervasive and complete that she was surprised she had not been borne aloft by angels. Then she took the letter.

The joy died more gradually than she expected.

Though she saw almost at once that the letter was from Kendrick, the message reached her brain only slowly. She was still smiling when she opened it, though the tears already stung her eyes.

'I'm awfully sorry to bother you again, Ellen,' Kendrick had written, 'but it would be so lovely if you could come to Vienna and I still haven't heard. Even if you'd just come for the weekend – I've got a surprise for you on Saturday night as I told you; something at which you could wear the amazing dress you made for your graduation. It would make me so happy and there is so much to see.'

'Is it from the man in the wet house?' asked Sophie, who seemed to be developing second sight.

Ellen nodded and handed her the letter. She still couldn't trust herself to speak. Sophie obediently read through Kendrick's hopes and his expectations of the cultural life in Vienna, but when she lifted her head again she had to draw a deep and unexpected breath. Ellen had always looked after them; now, suddenly, she had an intimation of a different state; a state in which she and her friends might have to look after Ellen.

And growing up a little, she said briskly: 'Lieselotte's waiting for the icing sugar,' – and saw Ellen bend to pick up her basket – and her life.

The letter Ellen had been waiting for came the next day – not to her but to Professor Steiner.

'He wrote it from Pettelsdorf,' said the old man gently and put it in her hand.

This time she was forewarned. There was no hope, no expectation of angels bearing her aloft.

'Isaac got away safely down river,' Marek had scrawled. 'I've confirmed my passage and am sailing on the tenth from Genoa. Please say goodbye to Ellen for me once again and thank her for me. I shall always be in her debt and in yours. Marek.'

The following morning Bennet sent for her.

'The children tell me you've been invited to Vienna.'

'Yes.'

Damn, thought the headmaster. Damn, damn, damn. He had seen it happening but he had hoped somehow that she would be spared. She will get over it; she will light her lamp again, he told himself – but it had been the brightest, loveliest lamp he had seen in years.

'I think you should go,' he said. 'It's only a weekend, and you'd be back for the play.'

'I've just been away.'

'But you still have time off owing to you. Freya will look after your children.'

'Very well,' she said listlessly.

'Sophie tells me that you have a dress?'

She managed a smile then. 'Yes,' she said. 'Sophie is right.' She lifted her head, and the smile became a proper one. 'I definitely have a dress.'

# 19

Brigitta's persuasions in the cafe at St Polzen had been ineffectual. The intrigues of the gala interested Marek not at all and he felt no obligation to involve himself in her affairs.

Yet less than a week after their encounter, he found himself in Vienna, having decided to break his journey there on the way to Genoa. The person who had effected this change of plan was not the diva but a quiet, grey-haired, bespectacled man; the head of Universal Editions, who had been Marek's music publishers for the past ten years. Herr Jaeger ran the firm from a dusty office in the Kohlmarkt; a place of hallowed associations for all those who cared for music, and it was his letter to Pettovice which had brought Marek to town.

Marek booked in at the Imperial, feeling in the mood for luxury after his week in the forest, telephoned Herr Jaeger, and went to have his hair cut in the Graben, where the barber was displeased with the way his client's thick, springy hair formed itself into unexpected whorls.

'I don't know what you've been doing to it, sir,' he grumbled. 'It looks as though you've been sleeping in a hedge.'

Marek did not enlighten him and the conversation turned inevitably to the gala. 'You'll have seen the paper,' said the barber. 'She's threatening to cancel.'

'She?' asked Marek, but already he knew.

'Seefeld,' said the barber. 'She's fallen out with the conductor: chap called Feuerbach. He's a stopgap because Weingartner's abroad.'

'She's got no business to carry on like that,' said a burly man in working clothes, the driver of a petrol tanker, having a trim in the neighbouring chair. 'Tantrums the whole time. They ought to give the role to Baumberger.'

'No, they oughtn't,' said a fat man with a shiny red face, waiting his turn. He spoke in the thickest of dialects and wore the blue overalls of a meat porter. 'Tantrums or not, she's the best. My mother's seen every *Rosenkavalier* they've done since 1911 and she swears there's no one to touch Seefeld.'

'I didn't say she wasn't good,' said the lorry driver. 'I didn't say she wasn't great. But she's got the whole cast at sixes and sevens, and once you get on the wrong side of the Vienna Philharmonic, God help you.'

'It's not the orchestra she's got the wrong side of; it's Feuerbach, and she's quite right. I heard him conduct Bruckner's Seventh in Linz and he was crap,' said the meat porter, wiping his face with a spotted handker-chief.

Marek took the newspaper the barber handed him. That day there had been a massacre in Peking, the city of Bilbao fell to Franco and Moscow had executed another thirty intellectuals on the grounds of 'spying', but the headline of the *Wiener Tageblatt* said 'Seefeld Threatens Cancellation. Gala in Jeopardy.'

Coming out into the street, Marek thought with exasperation of the Viennese, to whom nothing mattered except what was going on at their opera house. And yet . . . perhaps it was because he knew this was goodbye, because he foresaw much suffering for this absurd city, that he felt himself able to surrender to the sheer beauty of the Biedermeier houses, the compact and companionable streets, the domes of green and gold. If the Viennese fiddled while Rome burnt perhaps there were worse occupations, and when it was over – the catastrophe he saw so clearly – they would still quarrel at the barbers about the high C of some soprano not yet born, or argue over the tessitura of a newly imported tenor.

Herr Jaeger was waiting in his dark little office.

'Herr Altenburg!' he said, rising to shake hands. 'This is a pleasure. It was good of you to come in person.'

'Not at all,' said Marek, dropping his hat and gloves on to a bust of Mahler. 'I see you share my view of what is to come.'

'I'm afraid I do. We're transferring our business to

London as I told you. We're hoping to be able to forge some transatlantic links too from there. It was a hard decision – as you know, our traditions go back three hundred years.'

Marek nodded. He had dealt with Universal Editions since his student days; they had proved competent and fair, but it was more than that: under glass in a corner of the office was the facsimile of the Schubert *Quartetsatz*. The first edition of Berg's *Wozzeck*, heavily annotated, lay in another case.

'We were hoping of course that you would stay with us, but –'

'I have decided to do so. I'm leaving for America very soon, but if you're setting up links with the United States, London could be a convenient halfway house.'

'I'm very pleased to hear it and my partner will be too. He's going ahead; he's Jewish and we feel . . .'

'Yes, you may feel that.'

'You don't have anything ready now? To arrive in London with a piece by Altenburg would be a certain triumph.'

'Soon,' said Marek. 'I've been doing other things.'

'But you'll be staying for the gala?'

'I doubt it. I gather there have been ructions.'

Herr Jaeger smiled. 'Yes, you could say that. You could certainly say that. Now, as to the contracts; I wonder if you could glance at these . . .'

Leaving the office, making his way towards the Hofburg, Marek saw a group of tourists outside the Stallburg waiting for the Lipizzaners to be led from the Spanish Riding School back to their princely stable. This was how they had waited – and probably waited still – for Brigitta to come out of her apartment and make her way to the Opera, and that was reasonable enough. She was after all a kind of human Lipizzaner, richly caparisoned, adored and nobly housed, and knowing perhaps at some level that he had meant to do this all along, he made his way past the Augustiner Kirche and the Albertina, and found himself by the small unobtrusive door which said simply: 'Zur Bühne.'

Outside, on an upright chair sat an old man, still wearing the uniform of the stage doorkeeper though he had been retired for many years. His son was the doorkeeper now but Josef was an institution, allowed to watch the great and the good come through that small entrance into the opera.

'Good afternoon, Josef.'

The old man looked up, blinked – and recognised him. 'Herr Altenburg,' he said. 'You're back in Vienna. Well, well – wait till I tell my son.'

Nothing could stop him getting to his feet and leading Marek into the cluttered office. 'Here's Herr Altenburg, Wenzel; you'll remember him.'

His son nodded. 'There's a bit of a to-do in there, sir. It's the gala – they're doing Act One and well . . . I expect you've heard. No one's to be admitted, but as it's you . . .'

Both father and son could remember the time when Herr Altenburg had accompanied the diva to rehearsals.

A golden age, he'd heard it referred to, when she'd behaved herself and sung like an angel.

'They're in the auditorium, sir. It's the first rehearsal with the full orchestra.'

Marek nodded, made his way down the familiar corridors, pushed open the heavy door – and stood quietly at the back.

'I shall cancel!' cried Brigitta. 'I tell you, I shall cancel. You can go now, you can tell the papers, you can tell anyone! I cannot sing at this tempo, it is an insult to me and an impossibility for my voice. Either you fetch Weingartner or I cancel.'

'Now Brigitta, please . . .' The voice coach came out of the wings and tried to mollify her. The music director, sitting in the front row, groaned. Nothing but tantrums and tempers from the wretched woman. There was a week to go to the gala and he was sick of it. He didn't just want her to cancel, he wanted her to be run over by a tram or eaten by rats or both. But who could they get at the last minute? The gala had been set up with her in mind.

'Perhaps we could try again, Herr Feuerbach,' said the director. He detested Brigitta, but it had to be admitted that Feuerbach was a disappointment: an arrogant little man who had got on the wrong side of the orchestra. Once that venerable body of men despised a conductor they were implacable. If the Vienna Philharmonic could ever be said to play badly they were doing it now.

'I gather you want it played like a funeral march,' sneered Feuerbach.

'No. Just a little more andante. It is after all a lament for the passing of time,' said the director, wondering why it was necessary to explain the score of Richard Strauss's most famous opera to the man who was conducting it.

Feuerbach curled his lip and raised his baton. Brigitta moved forward.

They were rehearsing the first of the famous monologues on the mystery of time and its inexplicable passing. The Marschallin is alone on the stage; so far she has been presented as a *grande dame* voluptuously loved, or as the centre of a melee of courtiers. Now the mood changes: the orchestra is reduced to solo strings and clarinets as she goes to the mirror and evokes the young girl she has once been, coming fresh from the convent – and then, in a moment of terror, the old woman she will one day be, mocked and pointed out, her beauty gone. Yet it has to be endured, she muses – and the oboe (now coming in magnificently in spite of Feuerbach) echoes her bewildered question: 'Only *how? Wie?* . . . *How* does one endure it?'

And as he listened to her, Marek was suddenly overwhelmed. He was back in the fourth gallery, shaken by the sheer beauty of the voice that God had placed so capriciously inside the body of this tiresome woman. Brigitta was trying, in spite of Feuerbach's dragging beat. She did not want to cancel; this was her role.

And all at once there came into Marek's head with

the force of an explosion, a vision of the whole glorious masterpiece that was *Rosenkavalier*, with its riotous waltzes, its soaring invocation of young love and the sense of sublimity and honour that was at its heart. *Rosenkavalier* as it should sound and could sound even now.

For it could still be done. Brigitta would have to be coaxed and bullied, forbidden to scoop and sentimentalise. Feuerbach, though one longed to throttle him, would have to be appeased, the orchestra schooled to heed him. It would take every moment of the day and night, every ounce of energy, but it could still be done.

Only not by me, thought Marek. Absolutely not by me. I'm sailing on the *Risorgimento*. This is goodbye.

'Very well,' said the director. 'We'll break there.'

The conductor left the rostrum but the musicians did not follow him. Marek, without realising it, had moved closer as Brigitta sang. Now one of the double bass players leant forward and whispered something to a cellist, who passed on the word and spread it back to the woodwind, the brass, and forward to the violas, till it reached the violins . . .

The leader turned his head.

'Are you sure?' he said quietly.

'Positive,' said his neighbour. 'I played for him in Berlin.'

The leader nodded. Then he rose to his feet and as he did so the orchestra, to a man, rose with him. And as the violins tapped their bows against the music stands, he said: 'Welcome back to Vienna, Herr Altenburg.'

The homage was not for his political stance, Marek knew that. It was not for him personally at all: it was for what he and these men shared and served. It was for music.

But now Brigitta had moved towards the footlights, shading her eyes. Then she gave a theatrical shriek, disappeared into the wings, and reappeared again in the stalls to hurl herself into his arms.

'Marcus!' she cried. 'I knew you would come! I knew you would help me. Now everything's going to be all right.'

'If you want me to help you, you can start by not sentimentalising "Where are the Snows of Yesteryear". You held that B flat far too long. I've told you, you must not be maudlin. Pity and self-pity are mutually exclusive.'

'It's not my fault. It's Feuerbach's. I have no help from –'

'I take it you're not complaining about the way the oboe followed you?' said Marek icily.

'No, but –'

'Good. I suggest you look to your own performance and the rest will sort itself out. I'll be back in an hour. We'll start with Baron Ochs' exit and go on to the rest of the act.'

# 20

'You're limping, Kendrick,' said Ellen. 'Would you like to sit down for a while? We could have a cup of coffee over there.' She pointed to a beguiling cafe with pavement tables across the square, but Kendrick shook his head.

'I'll be all right. We've still got the Hofburg to see, and the cathedral. We can't afford to waste a minute.'

But actually his foot was hurting quite badly. He had a big blister on the heel and a corn developing on the left toe and this was because he had already spent three days in Vienna sightseeing before Ellen arrived. Kendrick had visited the Central Cemetery to see the graves of Beethoven, Schubert and Brahms, paying particular attention to Beethoven's grave because it was said to contain the pince-nez of Anton Bruckner, who had dropped them into the open coffin by mistake when the composer's relics were transferred from the cemetery in Wahring. He had taken a tram to St Marc's, which turned out to be a long way away, to look at the place where Mozart had possibly been interred, and another to another suburb to pay homage to the tomb of Gustav Mahler.

And that was only the graves: there were still all the places where composers had been born or died or simply *done* things: hammered pianos to death or quarrelled with their landladies or thrown chamber pots out of the windows, often in houses which were surprisingly far apart.

All this had made his feet very sore, and then there had been the Art: the Secessionist building, which was near a rather messy food market and the Kunsthistorisches Museum, which was deeply inspiring, but the marble floors were surprisingly hard and the lavatories difficult to find.

But he had kept the best-known sights for Ellen, who had arrived that morning and was standing patiently beside him, looking cool in her cream linen dress, as they waited to go into the crypt of the Capuchin church where the Hapsburg Emperors were buried. Or rather their bodies were buried – their hearts and organs were elsewhere, as he had explained to Ellen, and fitting them in was going to be a problem. Peering at his Baedeker, worrying, Kendrick felt Ellen's cool touch on his arm and realised that the guide had come and they were moving down into the vaults with their heavy, ornate marble sarcophagi.

The Emperor Franz Joseph . . . his unfortunate wife, the lovely Sissi, assassinated by an anarchist on Lake

Geneva . . . their son, the Crown Prince Rudolf, dead by his own hand at Mayerling . . .

Moving past the gloomy opulence of the tombs, Ellen found one she liked.

'Look, Kendrick! This one isn't an emperor or an empress! It's a governess – Maria Theresa's governess. The Empress loved her so much she was allowed to be buried here even though she wasn't royal. So if a governess, why not a cook? Perhaps I shall end up in the vaults at Windsor!'

Ellen had not wanted to come to Vienna, but now she was here she was determined to enjoy herself. The weather was glorious, the city was beautiful – there could be no better place to forget Marek, who would be sailing away now to a new life. She had been foolish, attaching so much importance to a flirtation and the courtesy of a kiss, but she did not intend to become a victim. 'One has a choice,' she had told herself – and she had chosen healing and happiness, if not immediately, then *soon*.

Their next tour, that of the Private Apartments in the Hofburg, revealed the Royal Treasure Chest containing a number of priceless objects of surprising ugliness and a suite of claustrophobic apartments characterised by a total lack of bathrooms. As they came out into the Michaeler Platz, Kendrick, peering at his guide book, said that they just had time to make their way to the house where Hugo Wolf had written the *Mörike Lieder*.

'Look – it's in this little street here – we take the first left and then the first right –'

'Kendrick, *you* go and see the house where Hugo Wolf wrote the *Mörike Lieder*, but I'm going to Demels to have a large coffee and eat *Indianerkrapfen* and study their patisserie.'

A terrible conflict raged in Kendrick's breast. To leave Ellen whom he loved so much even for half an hour was hard – but to miss Hugo Wolf's house, which the guide book particularly recommended was hard too.

'Remember you've got a whole day after I've gone. I have to go back tomorrow.'

'Very well, I'll come with you,' said Kendrick and limped with her towards Demels, where he was rewarded by Ellen's face as she gazed at the counter, her eyes moving from the intricate lattice of the *Linzertorte*, to the baroque magnificence of the layered chocolate cakes, and back to the *Schaumrollen*, fat and soft as puppies. And even Kendrick took pleasure in seeing the eclairs they had chosen wheeled away by attendents, as if to a select nursing home, to be injected with fresh whipped cream.

It was as she poured a second cup of the marvellous coffee that Ellen said: 'Don't you think we ought to call at a chemist's and see if we can get a proper dressing for your foot? It's going to be really painful for you trying to dance with that blister.'

She was looking forward to the ball – the orchestra was sure to be good and even if she and Kendrick danced very little she would enjoy watching the other people.

But to her surprise, Kendrick coloured up and put

285

down his cup. He had not meant to reveal his delightful surprise till they were back in the hotel, but this was as good a moment as any.

'Ellen, we're not going to a ball,' he said, leaning across to her. 'We're going somewhere much more exciting. Somewhere absolutely special.'

'And where is that?' A slight foreboding touched Ellen.

'The opera!' said Kendrick happily. 'The Vienna State Opera! We're going to see *Rosenkavalier* – and guess who is singing the leading role.'

'Who?' asked Ellen obediently – but the foreboding had, so to speak, settled in.

'Brigitta Seefeld! Her interpretation is absolutely legendary. She's marvellous; remember I wrote to you about her, about the songs Altenburg wrote for her. I can't tell you what a miracle it was getting the tickets. Everyone in Vienna will be there.' And suddenly seeing something in her face: 'You're pleased, aren't you? You wouldn't rather have gone to a ball?'

She lifted her head. 'No, no, Kendrick. Of course I'm pleased. It'll be lovely.' There was no point in spoiling his pleasure, and if she wanted to watch that overweight cow sing about as much as she wanted to spend the night in a sewage farm, she would keep it to herself. With Marek on the ocean and Isaac safely out of the country, Seefeld posed no threat. All the same she felt entitled to some consolation, and: 'I'm going to have another *Indianerkrapfen*,' she said.

'*Another* one?' asked Kendrick, shocked.

'Yes.' I need cheering up, she could have said, but didn't because of the wet house and the camel and the fact that Kendrick looked so very pleased.

'Oh, Ellen!' said Kendrick as she floated down the stairs dressed for the opera. 'You look –'

But what *did* she look like? The *Primavera* certainly – that Botticelli – like floating as if she was weightless – though the way her lustrous hair curved and coiled around her brow was more like Venus rising from the waves . . . except that Venus wasn't wearing anything at all, whereas Ellen was dressed in a marvellous white concoction that frothed and foamed and swirled like sea spray, like gossamer, like flakes of snow. Stumbling from painter to painter, from woodland nymphs and enchanted swans and back again, Kendrick tried to bring his erudition to bear on Ellen, *en grande tenue*, and failed.

But if he was confounded he had a right to be, for Ellen and the Gorgon needlework professor at the Lucy Hatton School of Household Management had wrought a masterpiece.

'You can't use tulle, like that,' Miss Ellis had said sniffily. 'Not if you want the finest denier. You'll be up all night setting the ruffles.'

'Then I'll be up all night,' Ellen had said, and almost was for several nights, by which time Miss Ellis had caught the infection. The dress had won first prize at the graduation ceremony, but it had done considerably more than that.

As the taxi dropped them on the steps of the opera house and Ellen got out, a little girl held aloft on her father's shoulder said, 'Is she a princess?' and was as instantly put right by someone in the watching crowd who said dismissively, 'Not her – she's far too pretty.'

For they knew all about the aristocracy, the bystanders that had come to watch, and they thirsted for them. Having deposed the last Hapsburg some twenty years ago, they had become specialists in those kings and queens who had hung on to their thrones. The Austrian President was greeted by the smallest of cheers, but King Carol of Romania, with his dubious personal life, got an ovation.

Inside the foyer, the excitement of a gala seemed to Ellen to be augmented by something else. The dowagers in ropes of pearls, the men with their decorations, the clusters of beautiful women, appeared to be buzzing with news of some kind of scandal or calamity. Their faces as they repeated, 'Are you sure?' or 'I can't *believe* it,' reflected the kind of salacious glee, masking as concern, that is devoted to disasters which do not affect one personally.

From the general hum of words, Ellen repeatedly caught one name.

'Who's Feuerbach?' she asked Kendrick as they made their way up the magnificent staircase.

'The conductor.' He had noticed nothing; his German was poor and he was busy bringing out his pocket score, his magnifying glass and the notes on the opera he had copied in the London Library.

'Kendrick, what marvellous seats!'

'They are, aren't they,' said Kendrick, and couldn't resist telling her what they cost.

In the box on their right, two men were talking, their voices perfectly audible to Ellen.

'It's all right!' said a small dark man who had just joined his friend. 'They've talked him round, but it was a struggle. He chased Feuerbach all over town trying to get him to change his mind, but it was no good.'

'What did he do to make Feuerbach walk out – defenestrate him or something?'

'Not a bit of it. He kept his temper all the way through. It was the orchestra. They made life impossible for Feuerbach. But this is it, Staub – there can't be any doubt about it now – she's got him back and Stallenbach's away. Your opera's in the bag.'

Staub nodded. 'I showed him the libretto and he was definitely interested.'

The last of the kings and queens had arrived; tired-looking persons weighed down by their jewels – and then a lone elderly man who attracted rather more attention as he appeared in the stage box. Richard Strauss, the opera's composer, the most famous musician in the world, who had travelled up from Garmisch.

The lights were going down now, but the whispers of rumour and speculation had not yet died away.

Then the curtains parted and the manager appeared.

'Your Majesties, your Royal Highnesses, Herr President, Ladies and Gentlemen – I have an announcement to make. Owing to the indisposition of Herr Feuerbach, tonight's performance of *Rosenkavalier* will be conducted by Marcus Altenburg.'

The audience behaved badly. They clapped, they cheered, they hugged each other. The gossip had been known for days – that Brigitta Seefeld's lover had returned to coach her, that their famous *affaire* had been resumed, that the unpopular Feuerbach had made scene after scene . . .

And now here was Altenburg, riding to the rescue!

'Are you all right, Ellen?' whispered Kendrick, for she had given a sudden sharp intake of breath. 'Oh Ellen, isn't this exciting, isn't this amazing! I didn't even know he was in Vienna! I wonder if I dare make myself known to him – he wouldn't remember me, of course, though –'

But the house lights were fully dimmed now. Only the lamps on the rostrum and the musicians' desks shone through the auditorium.

The conductor appeared and received an ovation which, waiting for silence, he ignored. Then he turned to bow – not to the crowned heads in their boxes or to the audience but to the old gentleman sitting alone in his box. To Richard Strauss.

Then he raised his stick and unleashed the prelude that Kendrick had worried about, and rightly – for it did indeed depict in music, and unmistakably, the act of love.

*

The shock, for Ellen, was overwhelming. This was his real life, this was his world. She had had an intimation in the dining room at Kalun but nothing had prepared her for this. Why did she think he belonged with lame tortoises and trees and storks? Even his bravery in the woods was only a small part of his life. Here where a band of the world's most highly trained musicians were welded by his movements into one whole – here in front of this glittering audience with the composer sitting in his box, was where he belonged. Here with Brigitta Seefeld, who had stopped, the moment she opened her mouth, being a foolish, vain, over-painted woman and become the great artist that she was.

Only why did he lie to me? she thought wretchedly – for that hurt the most, that he had lied. I asked nothing from him so why did he pretend that he was sailing for America, that he had finished with Vienna, and with her?

It was some time before she really heard the music. She did not know the opera; at first she missed the obvious 'tunes', the dramatic ensembles. But then Baron Ochs entered, accompanied by his glorious, absurd waltzes, and the bustling courtiers . . . so that by the time Seefeld came to the famous monologue in which she mourns, with touching bewilderment, the passage of time, Ellen, who wanted to hate her, was strung out on the liquid notes, as hurt and puzzled as the singer wondering what God meant by it all.

'*One day you will leave me,*' Seefeld sang to her young lover. '*Today or tomorrow or the next day . . .*'

But Marek was not leaving. He was returning, thought Ellen. As the curtain fell on the first act, the applause was frenetic. Everyone recognised a triumph, a performance that would become an operatic legend.

'Isn't she amazing?' said Kendrick. 'Her interpretation has never been surpassed. But the conductor! I knew she was his muse, of course, but I had no idea he was in Vienna. Imagine, I used to sing in the same choir as him!'

Ellen said nothing, and a man staring at her admiringly as they made their way towards the refreshment room, dropped his eyes as she came closer, wondering why a young girl should look like that.

If only it was over, thought Ellen. If only I could go home . . . not to Hallendorf with its memories but right away from Austria. Back to grey and rainy London where they were digging trenches in the parks.

'I've been to see her,' said Benny, returning to his box. 'She's over the moon. I tell you, no one can resist what happens to Brigitta when she gives that kind of performance. She'll have him in that Swan Bed of hers before the night is out if she hasn't done it already. I'll give her a few days – and then sign them both up. She'll have to work out her contract here but she can follow him.'

Seefeld did not appear in the second act, which is devoted to the instant and joyous love of Octavian, the faithless *Rosenkavalier*, for the young Sophie von Faninal. But if Seefeld was missed, the orchestra under Altenburg played the Presentation of the Rose, the ecstatic duet for the young lovers and Baron Ochs' sentimental, irresistible waltz as if for the first time. Women mopped their eyes; Benny shook his head. How had he coaxed playing like that even out of this famous orchestra?

Only one voice of dissent was heard in the second interval, from a sallow man wearing an Iron Cross in his lapel.

'I grant you he's a fine conductor but it doesn't do to antagonise the Germans. He's hated in Berlin; we shouldn't seem to condone the stance he takes against Hitler, not with what may happen.'

But he was the only one and the others moved away from him. They might not be so brave tomorrow but tonight they were willing to snap their fingers at the Third Reich and Hitler's offer of union and brotherhood.

The last act now. Comedy, bustle, misunderstandings . . . Baron Ochs discredited . . . And the entrance of the Marschallin, perhaps the most heart-stopping moment in opera. She stands in the doorway of the inn, knowing that her young lover has deserted her: not 'someday', not 'soon', but *now*. Yet Octavian is no knave, the girl he has fallen for no scheming minx. The lovers are caught by the one thing she cannot ever again reach out for – their youth. Bewildered, ashamed yet ecstatic, they look to her . . .

And she puts it right. The trio that follows is of a beauty that stills all turmoil. The Marschallin sings – not grandly, not histrionically – of the need for self-sacrifice. She sings, in fact, of something unbelievably simple and unbelievably difficult: the *need to behave well*. And the lovers reproach themselves, tremble and – blessed by her understanding – claim each other.

But when she leaves them, though they sing on, the opera is over. Not one person in the audience, or any audience anywhere, but weeps for the Marschallin. Everyone is on her side.

The curtain fell. Kendrick, looking at Ellen, was proud to see that she was crying. After the incident of the Sorrel Soup, he sometimes wondered how deeply she *felt* music.

Did she feel it almost too much? She was a girl who always had a handkerchief, but now he gave her his, for she was not doing anything to stem her tears.

Renunciation. Letting go. Brigitta who had nothing to renounce had sung of it. But I, who do not sing, I have to do it, thought Ellen. Only I wish I had something to renounce. I do so very much wish that.

The endless clapping, the cries of 'Bravo' and 'Bis', the flowers raining down, passed before her like a dream. But when at last Marek allowed himself to be dragged on to the stage, and brought his orchestra to their feet, when Brigitta came towards him with outstretched arms and he kissed her, to the delight and noisy approval of the Viennese, she saw that. She saw that quite clearly.

# 21

'Well, we shall have something to tell our grandchildren after tonight,' said Benny triumphantly. He was not married and had no intention of becoming so, but tonight he felt dynastic. Mahler's *Fidelio* . . . Karajan's *Tristan* . . . and now Seefeld's *Rosenkavalier*. Or would it go down as Altenburg's *Rosenkavalier?* But what did it matter? It was the combination that had made this evening into an operatic legend.

Everyone knew it; they came past their table at Sacher's – acerbic critics, carping musicologists – and gushed like schoolchildren. The management had presented two bottles of champagne, Brigitta glowed and sparkled, and every so often she put a hand with loving ownership on Marek's arm.

He's mine again, she thought exultantly. I've got him back. Her mind went forward to the end of the meal . . . to the moment when they reached her apartment. Ufra would have done everything: the candles would be lit, the bed sprayed with Nuit d'Eté – but only a little, for Marcus had never liked strong scents – and the little dog safely shut up, for nothing could shatter the mood more than the boisterous welcome the creature would give him. And afterwards she would make the first of the many sacrifices she was going to make to inspire him for his art.

Marek was only partly aware of the babble around him and her coy possessiveness. He was still with the orchestra as they followed him through the extraordinary richness and intricacy of the score. The performance had not been perfect: the *più tranquillo* before the Presentation of the Rose had been too drawn out – Feuerbach's sentimentality could not be eradicated in an instant – but they had played like . . . well, like the Vienna Philharmonic.

But I'll make my Americans just as good, he swore to himself; they can do it. He had missed the boat from Genoa but there was a faster one leaving from Marseilles; he would hardly be late.

Brigitta leant even closer against him; she had decided to make her sacrifice now, rather than in the privacy of her rooms, knowing how much it would please Staub, who was sitting on her other side. Hitherto she had been firm in her refusal to portray Helen of Troy crouching in a state of terror in a doorway, but now . . .

'Darling,' she said confidingly to Marek. 'I've decided. If you set the opera I'm prepared to do it. I'm prepared to huddle.'

Marek looked at her, trying to focus on her words.

Benny had refilled his glass and he had not resisted, needing to unwind. The last time he had drunk champagne had been in the dining room at Kalun.

And at that moment, as if conjured up from that sulphurous place, he saw a girl in a white dress standing under a street lamp and staring at him through the glass.

'Excuse me,' he said and got to his feet. But when he reached the street she was nowhere. He must have been drunker than he realised.

'I'm sorry, Brigitta,' he said, sitting down again. 'I thought I saw someone I knew.' And making an effort: 'What was it you were telling me?'

'That I was prepared to huddle,' said Brigitta crossly – but this time it did not sound the same.

Some two hours after the end of the opera, Kendrick was still pursuing suitable locales for his proposal of marriage. They had had supper in a restaurant on the Albertinaplatz, but as they came out and he saw, commanding a flight of steps, the equestrian statue of the Archduke Albrecht, his courage failed him. Close to, the horse reminded him too much of the horses his brothers had ridden at Crowthorpe. Their taunts at Kendrick as he repeatedly fell off a small Welsh pony, their efforts to make him less cowardly by tying him to a tree and galloping at him with home-made lances, came back to him as if it were yesterday, and now he suggested to Ellen that they take a stroll in the Burg

Garten, where he had selected the Mozart Memorial as another suitable venue in which to declare himself.

'All right, Kendrick. But I'd like to get back soon – I'm rather tired.'

She was in fact having the greatest difficulty in connecting with what Kendrick was saying, or even hearing his voice, but she walked with him into the cool dark garden, where the sight of Austria's best loved composer greatly cheered Kendrick, erasing the memory of his brothers, for in this man's music there was a purity and goodness which must surely reach out and bless his enterprise.

But when they got closer Kendrick saw that the spirit of the composer was already blessing someone else – a youth in a loden jacket passionately embracing a plump and acquiescent girl – and there was nothing for it except to circle the gardens and come out again into the street.

The third of Kendrick's chosen sites was the Donner Fountain in the Neuer Markt. It was on the way back to the hotel and the guide book spoke highly of it, but when he suggested to Ellen that they walk back to the Graben she turned to him and said: 'Kendrick, I've got rather a headache. Do you think you could try and get a taxi? There are some in the Philharmonikergasse.'

'Yes . . . yes, of course.' Kendrick hid his consternation. People did propose in taxis, but not Frobishers; the possibility of being overheard by the driver put that entirely out of court.

They walked down the narrow street, approaching

Sacher's, where (as he was able to inform Ellen) Billroth had frequently breakfasted on oysters with Johannes Brahms. But Ellen, who had hitherto been so receptive to the information he offered her, seemed scarcely to take it in, and only asked him again to get a taxi. 'Look, there's one just coming in – I'll wait while you run and get it.'

He had done as she asked and when he came back for her, he found her standing on the pavement outside the lighted windows of the famous restaurant looking so shaken and weary that all he could do was help her quickly into the car.

But the image of Patricia Frobisher, like a matrimonial Boadicea, was still with him, urging him on. He had to propose and he had to do it tonight in the balmy romantic ambience of a summer night in Vienna. Tomorrow morning would not do. He was going to try and see the leprosy sanatorium by Otto Wagner and the place where Wilibald Gluek had breathed his last, as well as the cathedral, and at midday Ellen was going back.

The taxi stopped in the Graben and Kendrick saw his chance. Opposite the hotel was a tall marble pillar decorated with convoluted statuary and topped with gold: the Trinity Column, which he had not had time yet to study in detail. With unusual firmness he walked Ellen over to examine it and found, as he had hoped, that at this late hour there was no one else there.

'Ellen,' he began. 'You know how much I love you and now it is not only I who want to make you my wife, it is also my mother.' He broke off, aware of problems with his syntax, and tried again. 'I mean, my mother has begged me to marry and I have told her that there is no one I could consider except you.' He paused to examine Ellen's face, hopeful that the approval of Patricia Frobisher had effected a change in Ellen's sentiments, and found that she had closed her eyes. 'So please, darling Ellen, won't you –'

He rambled on, expressing devotion and a stammering hope. To Ellen it was a fitting end to this nightmare evening and as soon as she could, she said: 'Kendrick, I wrote to you quite clearly when I accepted your invitation that I was coming as a friend. You have no right to put me through this again.'

But Kendrick had reached that state of obstinate exaltation so common to those who believe that a passion as great as theirs must somehow find an echo in the recipient. It was only gradually that her continuing refusal reached him, and exaltation was turned to misery and the familiar fear of his mother's wrath.

'Of course I shouldn't have hoped,' he said wretchedly. 'If it had been Roland or William, but –'

'*No*, Kendrick, *no*!' said Ellen – and made a last effort before this horrendous evening could end in solitude and her bed. 'It's not that at all. You sound much nicer than your brothers – you're the nicest possible person but –' and then with an impulse to comfort which was stronger than discretion and her inmost desire for privacy, she said: 'It's just that . . . I'm in love with someone else. He's not in love with me; he doesn't

300

care about me at all but I can't help –' And found to her horror that she had burst into tears.

But her chivalry achieved its aim. That Ellen was wretched made Kendrick's own misery bearable. Since his dreadful childhood, Kendrick had known that the world was a dark and threatening place; sadness was a country in which he felt entirely at home. That Ellen, so beautiful, so desirable, should also be unhappily in love was a profound consolation. To be allowed to put his arms round her in brotherly love, to let her cry on his shoulder, eased his own distress immeasurably. He murmured condolences, he promised always to be her friend, and of course to be there if ever she should change her mind. He even managed to make a kind of joke, for he had remembered now what the Viennese called the statue they were standing under: the *Pestseule*. 'It's a monument to the Great Plague – about a hundred thousand people died in it, pretty horribly,' he said, 'so perhaps I didn't choose too well!' – and was rewarded by Ellen's smile, and her arm in his as they walked back to the hotel.

Marek was extraordinarily tired. The Feuerbach crisis had meant a day of incessant rehearsals and then four hours on the rostrum for the opera. Nothing had seemed quite real to him since the curtain went down, and now he realised how foolish he had been. It had seemed polite to escort Brigitta to her apartment, and now here it all was: the double doors open to reveal the ridiculous Swan Bed, the plumped-up cushions, the

301

clinging smell of her scent. Brigitta had disappeared and reappeared in a cream lace peignoir, and was trying to snuggle up to him on the sofa.

He moved away.

'Brigitta, that's over, you know it is. I came to help with the opera. We're colleagues, that's all.'

She lifted her face to his. The periwinkle-blue eyes filled with tears. 'Darling, how can you say that? When you know I love you.'

'But I don't love you, Brigitta.' God, how hard it was to say that to a woman. He pushed a hand through his hair, angry that she had put him in this position. 'I respect you enormously as a musician; you gave a marvellous performance tonight, but our affair is *over*. I'm going to America and you have Stallenbach.'

'Oh him!' She edged closer. The peignoir was wide open now; clearly he was supposed to be dazzled by her breasts, her stomach – and indeed if quantity were all this would have been no problem.

'Don't you remember, my darling, how marvellous it was?'

Marek sighed. It had been good at times, but even then it was that she had always stood for something. It was Mozart's lovelorn Countess or Violetta – doomed and dying with perfect breath control – that he had felt he was holding in his arms.

She had begun to cry now, but carefully, for she still wore make-up. 'It's because I'm getting old. It's because I'm nearly forty.'

She was forty-three and she was using blackmail.

302

She was still playing the role she had played in the opera. 'You're like Octavian,' she stormed. 'The first young thing you see and you're away.'

'No, Brigitta, it isn't that; you're still a very beautiful woman.'

It wasn't because she was young that he had wanted Ellen.

Brigitta was crying in earnest now. 'I worked so hard for you. And now because my youth has gone . . .'

She *had* worked hard. She had been as obedient as a child, this bullying, autocratic woman.

'Come, Brigitta; you'll be stopping all the clocks next.'

She had played that scene superbly; the scene where the Marschallin describes the 'unrelenting flow of time' and how sometimes she gets up in the night and stops the clocks in the palace. He could hear their soft chiming, evoked by the harps and the celeste, and her voice soaring above them. Did he have the right to deride her fear of ageing even if she was using it to get her way?

*Never sleep with anyone out of pity.* The maxim was engraved on his heart, as on the heart of everyone who wished to take and receive pleasure in the act of love.

'I'm leaving, Brigitta. I'm going to America, you know that.'

'Then stay with me just one more time. Stay with me because of what we made tonight.'

'All right, Brigitta. I'll stay for that.'

At three a.m. he woke in the opulent bed, hot and oppressed, and sat up suddenly.

'What's the matter?' she asked sleepily.

He turned a blank face to her. 'What?'

'You said something. Did you have a nightmare?'

He pushed the hair out of his eyes, longing to leap out of bed, to go and walk and walk, away from this stifling place.

'What did I say?'

'You said "I've forgotten the wheel!"'

He stared at her, suddenly wide awake. 'Did I say that? That's right. It's true.'

# 22

As the train slowed down at Hallendorf station, Ellen saw that the platform was full of children. They were piled on to the benches, draped round the wrought-iron pillars with their hanging baskets of geraniums or just hopping excitedly up and down. Sophie was there, of course, and Leon and Ursula . . . Janey and Flix and Bruno too, but also Frank, swishing a stick through the air, and a handful of village children.

She had expected to have the journey across the lake still to gather herself together, but when they surged towards her she was unexpectedly pleased to be among them again.

'We got permission to come and meet you,' shouted Leon.

'There's been a disaster,' said Sophie.

'No, it isn't a disaster,' contradicted Ursula.

'Yes it is. It is for Bennet. It's awful for him when he's written to all the Toscanini Aunts. And it's a disgrace for the school.' Flix's lovely face was creased with concern.

Ellen put down her suitcase. 'Could you please tell me what's *happened*?'

'It's *Abattoir*!' Sophie had come very close, trying to convey the bad news in a suitably serious voice, but overjoyed to see Ellen again. 'It's finished. Kaput. We're not doing it!'

'*What*? But what about FitzAllan?'

'Some men came.' To Ellen's surprise, Frank came and picked up her suitcase.

'They were solicitors. Lawyers anyway,' said Janey.

All the children were talking at once, clustered round Ellen. Even the village children, though everyone was speaking English, seemed to be involved in breaking the extraordinary news.

'And they said they represented . . . they worked for Bertolt Brecht and he'd never given permission for the play to be done at all!'

'They were absolutely furious. They told Bennet he was breaking the law of copyright and if one single scene was acted they'd sue him!'

'So Margaret got furious. She said it wasn't Bennet, it was FitzAllan who said he'd got permission, and they all trooped off to the theatre –'

'We were just rehearsing the bit where all the workers go on strike and start to die in the snow,' said Flix, 'and they marched up to the front – the men in the dark suits – and said: "*Stop this at once!*"'

'They were as red as Turkey cocks. Absolutely gobbling. And Bennet said: "I assure you that Mr FitzAllan has permission from Bertolt Brecht to perform this play; you will hear it from him." He was very *dignified*,' said Sophie.

'And then everyone looked at FitzAllan and he just turned a sort of yellow and started stammering and saying there must have been a misunderstanding.'

'But there wasn't!' Leon's thin face was contorted with contempt. 'He'd made the whole thing up! He'd never been near Brecht, he just thought he could get away with it. The men went away threatening all sorts of things . . . libel actions and stuff like that. And the next morning Lieselotte put out his horrible nut cutlet and he never came down for breakfast!'

'He did a bunk in the night!'

'So now we haven't got anything to show the parents, not a thing,' said Leon. 'It's the first time the school hasn't had a proper play for the end of term, and with the music being hopeless too . . .'

Ellen, walking with the excited, hopping children towards the landing stage, was as indignant as they were. So much work wasted, so much money too . . . the masks for the animals over which Rollo had laboured, often far into the night . . . Jean-Pierre's military searchlights . . . yards and yards of muslin . . . And poor Chomsky, felled by the three-tiered structure, all to no purpose.

In the staffroom that evening she heard the details. 'One of the parents was at a party in Zurich and boasted about the coup the school had pulled off,' said Freya, 'and someone who knew Brecht was there.'

'But why?' Ellen couldn't understand it. 'Why should he go to such lengths to cheat? It's only a school play.'

Jean-Pierre put down his newspaper. 'Not so "only" perhaps – after all, some of the parents here are very distinguished: Frank's father, and Bruno's . . . the parents of the little Sabine who own half of Locarno Chemicals. And the director of the Festspielhaus in Bonn had promised to come: he's almost a Toscanini's Uncle, one could say. If FitzAllan had pulled it off it could have been quite a coup for him.'

'Do you suppose everything else was a lie too?' asked Ellen. 'I mean that he worked with Meyerhold and Stanislavsky?'

'Probably.' David Langley, who had wasted weeks of good summer weather, which could have been spent collecting frit fly, being a bloated stockyard owner or a carcass, was especially bitter. 'Still, he wasn't so stupid; he got paid in advance.'

Like the children, the staff were particularly upset for Bennet, who blamed himself for being taken in and made it clear that the whole responsibility for the disaster was his and his alone.

'But that is not so,' said Hermine. 'If I had not permitted the Professor to overcome me in Hinterbruhl I could have produced a play as in the years before. It was to save me work that this *Schweinkopf* was engaged.'

'What about Tamara? How has she taken it?' asked Ellen.

Glances were exchanged, heads shaken. 'Badly, as you can imagine. Very badly,' said David. 'I think she thought he fancied her. She's been storming about like a tragedy queen ever since he went.'

But it was worse than that. Going down after she had put her children to bed to comfort Margaret, Ellen found the secretary standing at the open window of her office. She looked weary and wretched, but when Ellen came she managed to smile, for she had no secrets from her.

'Listen!' she said.

Ellen went to stand beside her. From the floor above, faint but unmistakable, came the sound of the Polovtsian dances played on Tamara's gramophone.

'As though he hasn't enough to put up with,' said Margaret bitterly. 'The stockbrokers have written again; there's real doubt about whether we can go on even for another term – and he's so *tired*.'

Ellen put her arm round the secretary's shoulders, 'You love him, don't you?' she said quietly. 'I mean, really?'

Margaret shrugged. 'Yes, I think it probably is . . . *really*.' She shook her head. 'Never mind; I'll get over it. And you? Did you have a nice time in Vienna?'

'Not very,' said Ellen.

And then, because they were both Englishwomen and their hearts were somewhat broken, they turned back into the room and put on the kettle and made themselves a cup of tea.

The newspapers from Vienna arrived the following day. All of them carried the story of the gala and Marek's heroic rescue, and though the pictures of him which they had been able to get hold of were years out of date, there was no mistaking him. Both the *Tageblatt* and the *Neue Zeitung* concentrated on the musical aspects of the performance, but *Wiener Leben* carried the full gossip of Altenburg's relationship with Seefeld as well as a picture of the composer embracing the diva under the benevolent eyes of Richard Strauss.

'And yet one is not absolutely surprised,' said Hermine as these revelations were discussed in the staffroom. 'That he was *someone* one always felt . . .'

'And from the way he ran from Tamara's balalaika one should have guessed that he was a musician,' said Jean-Pierre.

'Did you hear anything about this in Vienna?' they asked Ellen, and she shook her head. She could not bear to speak about the opera.

The children, like the staff, reacted with mixed feelings to the news. That it was an eminent composer who had healed their tortoise and hoed their garden paths was as exciting as anything in a film – but that he was going to America with Brigitta Seefeld, as the papers unequivocally stated, was sad. During her short tour of the school, the diva had not endeared herself to those whose path she had crossed.

Bennet, in order to allay speculation, made a short announcement in Assembly in which he said that Marek had wanted to spend some time incognito in order to rest and refresh himself, and implied that he had been gestating a composition of some importance in his room above the stables. If this contented most people, it did nothing to soothe Tamara's rage. That she had let an eminent musician slip through her fingers was almost more than she could bear.

'He could have created a ballet on me,' she said peevishly. 'I would not have prevented him. He is an idiot to have missed such a chance.'

It was the only child who was not surprised by the news who was the most affected.

Looking for Leon at bed time, Ellen found him standing forlornly in Marek's old room. A spider had made a web across the window; Lieselotte had put some early windfalls to ripen on the sill and the tangy, wholesome smell seemed strangely to conjure up Marek in his blue work shirt.

'I keep thinking of what he wrote here, maybe,' said Leon. 'I looked in the chest to see if there were any fragments but there aren't.'

Ellen was silent, coming to stand beside him. She remembered Marek packing up his papers the day she had shouted at him for throwing Leon into the lake.

'It's going to be awfully difficult writing his biography if he's in America,' the boy said bleakly.

'I don't see why,' said Ellen. 'You may have to postpone it for a while but you're not so far from being grown-up. Why don't you simply decide to go there when you're old enough?'

Leon looked at her gratefully. 'Yes, I could do that.' He sighed. 'He's the best, you know, Ellen. Honestly. I mean not just his music. He's absolutely the best.'

'Yes, I know, Leon. But come to bed.'

The excitement of discovering Marek's true identity lasted a day or two but then the children became listless and depressed. They had complained about *Abattoir*, but the play had been the centre of their lives. Hermine was organising Movement workshops for the end of term, Freya intended to put on a demonstration of PE for the parents and Bennet was preparing extracts from *The Winter's Tale*, but for visitors who had expected to see an original play by Brecht this would hardly make exciting theatre.

The demise *of Abattoir* had one immediate consequence. Chomsky returned! The news that FitzAllan was disgraced had effected an instant cure. Curiously enough, everyone was pleased to see him: they attended his classes more enthusiastically than before, bent sheets of metal into bookends and looked at his appendix scar with a sense of familiarity and relief. Ellen waited daily for him to discover the loss of his passport, but the Hungarian's room was so untidy that he was lucky to find his bed, let alone examine the state of his documents, and having met his family she felt no anxiety about Laszlo's ability to get home when the time was ripe.

Then, two days after Chomsky's return, the deputation came.

They came not by steamer but by road in two cars: the Mayor of Hallendorf, the butcher who was Lieselotte's uncle, the head of the Farmers' Cooperative and several other dignitaries, wearing stiff collars and looking important, embarrassed and hot.

Instinctively, both Ellen and Margaret, who were in the headmaster's office, came to stand on either side of him.

'Now what, I wonder,' said Bennet wearily. 'It can't be Chomsky caught in their fishing nets already – he hasn't been back long enough. Perhaps Frank has been lighting fires?'

'No,' said Ellen. 'I'm sure not.'

The men approached. Their expressions could be seen to be serious. That would be the last straw – a complaint from the village when at last relations between the school and Hallendorf itself had so much improved.

But Bennet was not one to shirk his duties. 'I think we shall need some beer, Ellen,' he said – and went forward to greet the Mayor and shake hands with everyone and lead them to his study.

It had seemed simple enough. He would call on the old farmer who had promised him the wheel off a derelict hay cart, pay him, leave instructions and a gratuity for the farmer's boy who would put it up – and return to Vienna.

In the event it was not simple at all. While old Schneider admitted that Herr Tarnowsky had enquired about a wheel some weeks ago, the farmer did not recollect having given a firm promise to let him have it.

'I can't go giving farm equipment away,' he said, leaning against the door of his filthy shed.

'I didn't ask you to let me have it. I offered you a fair price for it. However, if that isn't enough I'll increase it – on condition you and your boy put it up for me.'

Herr Schneider, though interested in the price Marek now mentioned, said there was no question of them putting it up. He had haemorrhoids and was not allowed on a ladder and his son was up on the high pasture dealing with the cows.

'It's a tricky job, putting up wheels.'

'Rubbish. It's going on the gable end of the coach house. Any able-bodied man can do it in ten minutes.'

But this gambit was a mistake, leading back to Herr Schneider's haemorrhoids and the fact that the doctors in Klagenfurt knew nothing and cared less. 'I'll sell you the wheel but you must put it up yourself,' said Herr Schneider, adding grudgingly that Herr Tarnowsky could use the tools in the outhouse.

Marek swore and handed over a sheaf of notes. Seemingly he had hit on the one man in the district who was not related to Lieselotte. 'I'll have to borrow your van,' he said.

An hour later, the wheel lashed to the back, he was on his way to Hallendorf.

If it hadn't been for Lieselotte, Ellen wouldn't have come – her dislike of meetings was growing worse rather than better – but this one mattered terribly to her helper, so she had found her usual place on the windowsill and now, with Sophie on one side and Lieselotte on the other, she listened to Bennet's summing up.

'I explained to the Mayor that we were greatly honoured to be asked – as you know, a closer union of the school and the village is something I have always wanted. On the other hand, I had to tell him that I didn't feel that the school as a whole could be involved in the project. Of course any individuals – staff or pupils – who want to help in their own time are entirely free to do so, but –'

'Why?'

The interruption came from Sophie, whose shyness was proverbial, and who now blushed crimson at her own daring.

Bennet looked across at her with his charming smile.

'You mean why can't the school be involved in a pageant to celebrate the life of St Aniella?'

'Yes.' Sophie nodded, still crimson.

'Because we would be taking part in a religious ritual,' explained Bennet. 'It would be outside our brief as an educational establishment.'

'She's nice though, Aniella is.' The tiny Sabine spoke with unexpected resolution.

'Yes, she is,' said Sophie. 'She's ordinary but she's special too. She's a chicken saint – you know, the kind that shelters people.' She stuck out her thin arms, turning them into sheltering wings. 'She looks after children and old people –'

'And after animals,' put in Flix. 'Every kind of animal. Even salamanders and hedgehogs and grass snakes. The pictures are in the church.'

'Do you all know the story then?' Bennet was surprised.

'No, we don't,' said some children at the back.

'Perhaps you'd better tell us then, Sophie,' said the headmaster.

'Oh no, I couldn't!'

'Go on, Sophie,' said Ellen gently.

So Sophie took a deep breath and began. Her mother had told her she couldn't project her voice and her father had said one must never put oneself forward but now she forgot both of them. As she spoke, the children could see Aniella moving among the sick and wounded animals in her flower-filled meadow ... could hear the clatter of hoofs as the evil knights rode towards her house. They were with her as she prayed in the grotto ('It's the one above the larch plantation, the one full of bicycle tyres,' said Sophie) and hear the wing beats of the angel who consoled her. They followed the saint across the lake in a flotilla of boats, and felt the horror as she was stabbed and blood flowed over her wedding dress. 'But it was all right,' said Sophie, using the words that Lieselotte had used in the church. 'Because she became beautiful again and floated up and up and flowers came down and lovely music played.'

'It could be a promenade performance,' said Leon when she had finished.

'What's a promenade performance?' asked Janey.

'It's where people follow the action round. You'd start in Aniella's house and go on to the grotto and so on. Not that I could have anything to do with it,' Leon went on hastily, 'because religion is the opium of the people.'

'Well that's really stupid,' said Ursula hotly. 'You might as well say you can't do a play about the Arctic because you're not a penguin.'

'Leon is perfectly correct, however,' said Jean-Pierre. 'It is out of the question that we should have anything to do with a piece of Catholic superstition. Still, the lighting in the cave could be interesting: by using mirrors and back projection . . .' His gaze became inward as he gave vent to a farrago of technicalities.

'We've got all those animal masks spare from *Abattoir*. I don't see why we couldn't let them have those,' said Rollo.

'You could use some of the muslin that's left over and dye it and use it to swag the boats, each one a different colour,' said Bruno – and Rollo stared at him open-mouthed, for the boy had seized a piece of paper and begun to draw.

Bennet, letting the discussion move freely, found himself totally amazed. His agnostic – not to say atheistic – children, his Marxist staff with their detestation of any kind of superstition, were seriously discussing a religious pageant celebrating the life of a minor

Austrian saint whose authenticity was much disputed. He imagined Frank's father hearing of it, or the other parents who had entrusted their children to him on the understanding that they would grow up free of the spurious consolations of an afterlife. And why was Jean-Pierre, who slept with a poster of Lenin above his head, holding forth on the merits of the lighting technique known as Pepper's Ghost?

'I wouldn't mind being a salamander,' said Sabine firmly. 'I'd rather be a salamander than a carcass.'

Bennet called the meeting to order. 'I shall not prevent anyone from helping,' he said, 'but it must be made clear that it is done on an individual basis.'

The children, however, were concerned with a more important point.

'Who's going to be Aniella?' they asked each other. 'Who's going to be the saint?'

It would have to be a grown-up – Aniella wasn't a child – and someone whom everybody liked, both the village and the school.

But really the question was already answered. Bennet saw them nod to each other, heard Ellen's name go through the room like wind through corn . . . saw them looking to where she sat, leaning her head against the window.

They were right, of course. She would be wonderful as Aniella. She would pull this amateurish escapade together with her warmth, her gravitas. Surely this time she would not refuse to be singled out, to be in the limelight?

Yes, she was going to do it! She had risen to her feet and shaken out her hair – and she looked as happy as she had done when he first saw her. Happy and honoured, perhaps, at the obvious wishes, now being expressed, that she should be the pageant's centre and its star.

Except that she wasn't looking at the people now surging towards her; she had turned back to the window and was looking out at the coach house roof, on to the gable of which a man on a tall ladder was fixing a wooden wheel.

# 23

For three days Marek shut himself up in his old room in the stable block. People who came to knock on his door did not do so twice, and even Tamara respected his wishes and stayed away.

His intention at first was simply to adapt some of the well-known folk songs and hymns of the district, orchestrating them for such instruments as were to hand and teaching the smaller children a simple accompaniment.

Then on the first day Ellen had come in with a tray, for he had made it clear that he would not come in for meals. The tray contained a plate with a pork chop, a helping of mashed potatoes and some garden peas. For dessert she had given him fresh fruit: a bunch of black grapes, a peach. A pot of coffee was keeping warm under a cosy.

She put the tray down and for a moment he saw her: the asymmetrical hair, the concerned eyes and strongly marked brows.

'How's it going?' he asked her.

'It's amazing. The exact opposite of *Abattoir*. People are coming from everywhere to help. We've even found a fierce horse for Count Alexei – it used to pull the dustcart and it's a stinker. And believe it or not, they all want Frank to be the angel: a huge, ferocious angel like Raphael with enormous wings and –'

But Marek had stopped listening. She saw the sudden withdrawal into his own thoughts and left him. As soon as she was gone, he dropped the manuscript paper on to the floor. Two hours later, he had written what came to be called the Aniella theme.

My God, this is worse than Hollywood, he thought. A girl comes in with a pork chop and I write a song for her. It wasn't quite like that, of course, but it was true that he had wanted suddenly to express the sense of joy in simple things which characterised her. But now he was done for. The growling march for the evil knights was already in his head, and now the interaction of Aniella's theme with that of the angel in the grotto.

'Idiot!' he told himself, facing days without sleep and an amount of work out of all proportion to the occasion – but nothing now could have stopped him.

In the evening she came again with the fresh supply of manuscript paper he had sent out for, and a supper tray.

'I need a large Thermos of coffee,' he said. 'Black. Nothing else.'

When she had gone he went to the window and

stretched. It occurred to him to wonder if he would have written this music if Ellen had agreed to be Aniella; if she had given in to the clamour of those who wanted her to be the pageant's star. But she had not considered it even for a moment.

'It would be completely wrong for me to do it; I'm not Austrian and I'm not a Catholic. I'll help in any way I can but there's only one person who can do it – you must see that.'

And they *had* seen it. Lieselotte would not have to act – she *was* Aniella – and by insisting on this uncomplicated and well-loved girl, Ellen had brought the village round behind the enterprise to a man. But it had touched Marek, as it had touched Bennet, that she had meant what she said when she'd insisted that she herself did not want to act or sing or be singled out in any way.

'What if it rains?' asked Frau Tischlein. She was the old woman who had warned Ellen of the wild children at Hallendorf. Now suddenly the wild children were everywhere; in the village, in Lieselotte's house . . . suggesting, rehearsing . . . They were even in the church, where hammering and sawing could be heard all day, for Lieselotte, at her own insistence, was to be flown upwards to the tower.

'It won't rain,' said Frau Becker. 'God would not permit it when we are working so hard in his name.'

They were certainly working hard. The scheme for the pageant seemed to grow spontaneously like a river gathering tributaries. Lieselotte's own house was too high up the mountain to be used, but a similar wooden house not far from the grotto was commandeered. To this house the villagers brought flowers for the window boxes and tubs of ornamental shrubs, and when Rollo fixed an imitation morning glory up one wall, it became the house in the painting.

'I want to be a salamander too,' said the six-year-old son of the shoemaker and was sent to Bruno to be fitted out with yellow spots.

What had happened to Bruno was as great a miracle to Ellen as anything that had happened to the saint. Coming to look for him late one night, she found him in the art room.

'Don't tell me to go to bed,' he said angrily – and she didn't, for she had seen what he was making: the mask that would turn Aniella into an old crone, an uncanny masterpiece fashioned from rice paper and silk in which Lieselotte's pretty features were still discernible beneath the wrinkles.

'They have taken my baby!' cried Hermine, finding the herring box empty and coming distraught to Ellen.

'It's all right, she's with Frau Becker and the others in the sewing room.'

'But they will give her bad things to eat – sweet things, and in the book it says –'

But when Andromeda was returned, with icing sugar on her cheeks, she smiled and cooed and slept the night through for the first time since she was born.

Problems arose continuously. How would the

followers get from the house to the church? Not everyone could go in the flotilla of boats. No one expected the tight-fisted Captain Harrar to offer his paddle steamer, but he did; it would follow at a distance and there would be room for everyone.

When it became clear that even with all the village women sewing, the dresses would not be done, six nuns appeared from the convent, asked for Ellen, and were led to the hall which had been taken over as a workshop. One of these, Sister Felicity, turned out to be an expert botanist and supervised the making of Alpenrosen petals for Aniella to strew over the lake, and head-dresses of saxifrage and gentians and cornflowers for the guests. But it was Ellen who made Aniella's wedding gown, fighting Bruno for the last of the muslin and creating a dream dress which had Lieselotte in tears.

Only Ursula still stood aside.

'I wish you'd be one of the bridesmaids like us,' said Sophie. 'We'll be sailing over the lake with Aniella; it'll be fun. Ellen's got a dirndl for you, she told me.'

'Don't be silly,' said Ursula. 'No one wore braces on their teeth in those days. People would jeer at me.'

'No they wouldn't,' began Sophie – but Ursula had already marched off with her red exercise book.

There was to be as little 'acting' as possible, everyone agreed on that. Enacting yes, acting no, but it had been decided that there should be a brief commentary to link the scenes together and to his utter amazement, Bennet himself had agreed to write it.

What am I doing? he asked himself. I'm an atheist; I've been one all my life. Yet now he wrote words for an Austrian saint who lived by God, for an angel lit from behind (if the generator worked) by a Marxist teacher of Mathematics. He wrote words to proclaim the treachery of the greengrocer, who had been cast as Count Alexei – and told himself he was an idiot and did not stop.

By now no one remembered any more who belonged to the village and who to the school. Bennet cancelled all afternoon lessons, did not even open the letter from his stockbroker and told Margaret to abandon all correspondence with Toscanini Aunts. Convinced that he faced ruin and derision from such parents as would make their way to Hallendorf, Bennet found he did not greatly care. If this was the end of his beloved school, it was a good one.

Into this creative chaos, there now burst Marek's music.

On the morning of the fourth day he showered, shaved and went to find Ellen.

'I want Leon – tell him to copy these parts; I need three copies at least. And find me Flix and those Italian twins and the red-haired boy with a scar behind his ear.'

'Oliver?' she said. 'You want him?'

'Yes; he can sing. I heard him when he was carving. And Sophie; she can hold a tune. I'll teach them first and they can help the others. Three o'clock this afternoon in the music room.'

He then commandeered Bennet's car and drove to the village where he asked to see the leader of the Hallendorf Brass Band and said he expected him and his players next morning at the castle.

'But we're competing in the finals at Klagenfurt in a month,' said the leader. 'We –'

Marek said this was a pity, but he expected them at ten, and disappeared into the kitchens of the *Goldene Krone*, summoned the assistant chef and told him to fetch his brother and his accordion. Two hours later he was in Klagenfurt, in the School of Music, and said he needed a fiddler, a cellist and a viola player for the coming week.

'But that is out of the question. No one will come for a country pageant. They have exams.'

'Ask them,' said Marek briefly – and handed over his card.

The principal backed away. They were true, then, the rumours he had heard.

'Yes, sir; of course. I'll send the best players I've got.'

'They'll need strong shoes,' said Marek. 'Ten o'clock at the castle.'

In the days that followed, Bennet, watching Marek's rehearsals, saw every one of his educational beliefs thrown over.

'I can't sing;' said Sophie, 'my mother says I have a voice like a corncrake,' – and was treated to a blistering attack on people who at the age of twelve were still under their mother's thumb. 'If you were an Arab you'd be married by now,' said Marek. '*I* decide who can't, and no one else. Now open your mouth and sing.'

Leon, after three hours of copying music, said he was tired and was treated to a stare of such contempt that he changed his mind, and reached for another pile of manuscript paper.

'You're late,' said Marek to the students of the Klagenfurt Academy, emerging from their car.

'I'm sorry, Herr Altenburg. We had a puncture.'

'Don't let it happen again. Here's your music. I want it by heart tonight. You represent continuity; you'll go from venue to venue accompanying the narrator. In the last scene you'll be playing in the tower of the church.'

'Herr Altenburg, I can't; I have vertigo.' And as Marek looked at him: 'All right – I'll get the chemist to fix me something.'

But with the youngest children from the village and the school Marek was gentle. He played the tune for Aniella once, and again and for the third time. He played the tune for the wicked knights (to be enacted, unexpectedly, by the greengrocer, the butcher – and Chomsky) and the music for the wedding feast. And he told them that they must be strong and trust him while they learnt to play their triangles and shake their tambourines and bang their drums in the right way, because while this happened the tunes would go away.

'But they'll come back,' he said, 'all the tunes will

come back and you'll see how important you are,' and they nodded and let themselves be led away by Freya to practise.

Odd things happened. A boatload of dentists from the conference booked into the annexe of the *Krone* overheard a rehearsal.

'You're short on the woodwind,' said one of them. 'I play the clarinet – I can go and get it.'

And he got it, and cut a symposium on Geriatric Orthodontics and said he could stay till the pageant. A girl on a walking tour turned out to be a singing student from Paris and stayed also – perhaps because of the music, more probably because of the dentist, who looked like Cary Grant.

Odder still perhaps was a plaintive letter from Sophie's mother to complain that her daughter hadn't written.

'I *forgot*,' Sophie told Leon, half appalled, half excited. 'I forgot to write to her!'

'About time too,' said Leon. He had graduated to being Professor Steiner's assistant in transcribing parts and had begun to see what hard work really meant.

Then came the day when Marek led the youngest children to Aniella's house for a rehearsal, and told them to beat their drums and shake their tambourines and their triangles in the way that they had learnt – and as Lieselotte came out of the door, the assembled musicians began to play, and they saw, these obedient, small musicians, where they fitted in – that by themselves they were nothing, but now, with everybody joining in, they were part of something glorious.

And it was then that the little fat boy who loved mathematics put down his triangle and sighed and said: 'Oh gosh! It's better than the calculus.'

# 24

It did not rain.

At seven in the morning, the dentist who played the clarinet was woken by the chambermaid at the inn and went downstairs to find a small, fierce-looking child standing in the hall.

'I want you to take out my brace,' said Ursula.

The dentist, scarcely awake, blinked and rubbed his eyes.

'What?' he said stupidly.

'My brace. They didn't have them when Aniella was alive.'

'My dear, I can't do that. I don't have the right equipment; it would hurt, and in any case –'

Ursula stood unmoving. She had woken at dawn and trudged on foot round the lake. Now she dredged up a word she scarcely ever used. 'Please,' she said.

In the house on the alp, Lieselotte woke and stretched and was suddenly terrified.

'I can't, Mama. All those people . . . I can't. You must tell –'

But at that moment Ellen came up the path, carrying the basket of pins and needles, of scissors and glue, that had become a symbol of all that went into the making of Aniella's name day, and kissed her friend, and looked so pleased and happy, and so calm, that Lieselotte's panic abated and she decided she could after all swallow a cup of coffee and eat a roll.

A charabanc drove into the village square and disgorged a busload of tourists, but no one had time to bother with them. Everyone was gathered outside the little wooden house, the rows of waiting animals in their place, and the sun shining out of a clear blue sky. Then the head boy of the village school stepped forward to speak Bennet's words: 'We have come together to celebrate the name day of Saint Aniella who was born here at Hallendorf on a morning such as this . . .'

And as Lieselotte stepped out of the door, Marek brought in his musicians – and the pageant began.

No one who was present ever forgot it. They had rehearsed it separately in every combination, but now, coming together, it took on a life of its own. An amazed recognition, a kind of wonder at what they had made, lifted them out of themselves. Propelled by Marek's music through the familiar story, they constantly found new meanings, new gestures, which were yet always part of the whole.

And those who had come to watch were drawn in

also. When a small hedgehog stumbled, a woman on the edge of the crowd came forward to help her, blurring the separation between watchers and participants, which was so much a characteristic of the day. Frank's father, who had threatened to withdraw his son from school, could be seen elbowing his way to the front as they reached the grotto – the only example of bad manners to be seen all day.

Even the unexpected things, the mishaps, turned into marvels.

'Are we sinking?' asked Ursula, sitting in Aniella's boat, forgetting her sore mouth.

'No.' But it was true that the rim of the brocaded canopy (the best bedspread of Frau Becker's aunt) had dropped into the water and was slowing the boat . . . slowing it more and more, so that it echoed uncannily Aniella's reluctance to go to her wedding.

Outside the church, the dustcart horse, who had a dozen times walked up the church steps in rehearsals, reared and refused – and the peace-loving greengrocer became a red-faced, furious seducer, kicking his mount with his heels as if he really was Count Alexei of Hohenstift.

The trick with the mask worked – even those who had been warned hissed with distress as Lieselotte became a wrinkled crone – and Rollo had been more than generous with the blood.

And then, like a hand reaching down from heaven (or from the bell tower, where the brave dentist was perched on a joist and the vertiginous violinist played gallantly on) came Marek's music, a high, pure skein of sound in which all the themes reached resolution, drawing the girl up and up for her apotheosis.

And as Sister Felicity's flowers drifted down from the heights, caught in a moment of enchantment in the spotlights, there came from those who packed the body of the church – not clapping, not cheering – but a sigh that seemed to be one sigh . . . and then it was done.

# 25

'We'll do it again, won't we?' they promised each other – Frau Becker and Jean-Pierre, the butcher and Freya, everyone hugging everyone else . . . forgetting the troops mustered on the border, forgetting the final letter from Bennet's stockbroker. The old woman who'd said it would rain was kissing Sabine, Chomsky and the greengrocer wandered arm in arm, and the reporters from the local newspapers clustered round Lieselotte, photographing her with her bridesmaids, her animals . . . 'This won't be the last time,' they told each other. 'We'll do it every single year.'

There was a party, of course; the kind of party that just happens but happens rather better if there is someone in the background, putting butter on rolls, opening bottles of wine, of lemonade . . . fetching hoarded delicacies out of the fridge.

Ellen had excused herself from the proceedings and for an hour or more had been sending plates of food up to the terrace with its strings of fairy lights, and the music was playing on the gramophone now so that everyone could dance. The dentist was dancing with Ursula; Chomsky with Frau Becker's aunt – and Leon's father with Sophie.

'And if her mother and father had come it would have been a miracle, I suppose,' Ellen had said to the headmaster, watching Sophie's vivid face, 'and there aren't a lot of those.'

'No. But it might work out best like this. Leon's parents have invited her to stay in London; they're good people. She may be someone who has to get her warmth from outside the family.'

Later Bennet had taken her aside and said: 'We owe this to you, Ellen. If you hadn't befriended Lieselotte and made the links with the village, none of this would have happened.'

She had shaken her head – yet it was true that some of what she had imagined that morning by the well and spoken of to Marek had materialised this day. People *had* come from everywhere . . . *had* received with hospitality what was offered . . . the lion, just a little, had lain down with the lamb.

Children came to the kitchen, offering to help, but she only loaded them with food and sent them upstairs again. She was content to be alone and glad to be out of the way, for she knew all too well what was happening – not on the noisy terrace, but in the hastily erected marquee in the jousting ground, where Bennet, with the assistance of the landlord and chef of the

*Krone*, was entertaining the most extraordinary collection of Toscanini Aunts ever assembled in Hallendorf.

It had been the most amazing and unexpected thing: now, when Bennet had abandoned all hope of interesting anyone in the significance of the school, Aunts – and indeed Uncles – of the highest stature had appeared from everywhere. The director of the Festspielhaus in Geneva had been seen lumbering over the muddy boards at the lake's edge, scrambling for a place in the lighter which would take him to the boat. The manager of the Bruckner Theatre in Linz, to whom Bennet had written vainly two years before, had puffed his way up to the grotto, writing in his notebook – and Madame Racelli, of the Academy of the Performing Arts in Paris, had cantered in her high heels and silver fox stole across the meadows, so as to miss no moment of what was going on.

The kitchen door opened and Lieselotte came in. She had changed into her dirndl, but the flush of happiness was still on her cheeks.

'I've come to help,' she said, reaching for her apron and tying it round her waist.

'No, you haven't. You're going straight back up to dance with all your suitors and be the belle of the ball. This is your night, Lieselotte, and I don't want you down here.'

Lieselotte took not the slightest notice. She had taken up a knife and begun to slice the rolls. 'We need more of the salami ones – Chomsky's eaten three already.'

'Lieselotte, I am your supervisor and I *order* you to go back and dance,' said Ellen.

Lieselotte put down her knife. 'Yes, you are my supervisor, but also, I think . . . you are my friend? And I want to be with you tonight.'

But this was a mistake. Ellen's defences crumbled; tears gathered in her eyes – and nothing could be sillier, for she had known – everybody knew – that Marek was leaving the following day, that his boat sailed in a week – and that Brigitta Seefeld, the mightiest and most redoubtable of the uninvited 'Aunts', had come to fetch him.

Marek's abrupt departure from Vienna had infuriated Benny and Staub, puzzled the musical establishment, and caused Brigitta to erupt into a series of violent scenes.

'How dare he treat me like that?' she raged. 'He *begs* to spend the night with me and then goes off as if I was a plaything!'

Then, about a week after his disappearance and shortly before he was due to sail, Benny called at Brigitta's apartment in an obvious state of excitement.

'Do you know where he is?' he asked her, shooing away the masseuse.

'Where?'

'In Hallendorf. Where they all swore they'd never heard of him. And do you know what he's doing?'

'What?'

'Writing music for a local pageant. For some obscure saint called Anabella or something.'

'I don't believe it.'

'It's true. I had it from Ferdie Notar at the Central who heard it from the clarinettist of the Philharmonic who heard it from the director of the Klagenfurt Academy.'

'But that's ridiculous. Marcus hates all that sort of thing – villagers with fat legs and mud and everything going wrong.' Brigitta's mind was racing. Was he writing *her* music for some female yokel with blonde plaits and cow's eyes?

'I checked with the Klagenfurt tourist board.'

'I'm going back, Benny,' said Brigitta imperiously.

'Me too,' said Benny. 'I smell gold.'

Unfortunately he was not the only one. There were too many rivals brought by rumours of Altenburg's involvement in the proceedings. The director of the Festspielhaus, sitting across the table, had a nasty glitter in his eyes.

But with Brigitta to help him, with her influence over Marcus, he was bound to succeed. Staub wasn't much use – he'd insisted on coming but he thought of nothing except his libretto. It was Brigitta who would carry the day.

'I tell you, Marcus, the piece is made for the States,' he said now. 'They'd gobble it up. A music theatre piece with a message . . . You might think they'd object to God and peasants and so on, but I promise it's not so. People always turn to religion when they think there might be a war.'

Marek smiled at him lazily. 'That's very kind of them – but I'm afraid what they think about God or peasants has nothing to do with anything. The music for the pageant stays here. It was written for these people at this moment of time. They can use it again or not, but it's theirs.'

Benny put down his glass. 'For heaven's sake, Marcus, be reasonable. Don't you see how you'd be helping them here if your piece became known all over the world? Think of Oberammergau. You've only got to score that theme you wrote for the saint for Brigitta and it would be a sensation.'

'Possibly,' Marek agreed, but he did not seem disposed to continue the conversation, and the director of the Festspielhaus now leant across the table to put in his own bid.

'I'd be prepared to put it on with all the actors – everyone from here who took part in it. That way it would stay in Europe.'

Brigitta glared at him and put her hand on Marek's arm. It was time to assert her personal dominion over the composer.

'Darling, you can't just keep your work hidden away, you know that really. It belongs to the world. You've no right to keep it to yourself.'

'I shan't be doing that. The population of Hallendorf is considerable.'

'Well then, at least rescore that incredible theme – it would work marvellously on its own.'

'I've done that already,' said Marek. 'But that too stays here.'

Brigitta's eyes narrowed. For whom had he written that amazing tune? Who was behind the whole escapade? She had seen Lieselotte come out of her house at the beginning of the pageant with a certain relief – the girl was hardly more than a child, a peasant through and through. Brigitta had watched her like a hawk afterwards, but she'd made no attempt to come up to Marek – it was her own family she sought out.

But if not Lieselotte, then who? Not that ridiculous Russian woman drifting about in a shroud, not the pretty Norwegian, she was sure of it. No, there could be no one; not in that crazy school, nor in the village. She was silly even to think of it.

'You wrote that melody for me, didn't you? I know you did. It falls exactly for my voice.'

She sang a few bars of the slow, ascending phrase to which the girl emerges into the sunlit morning, and she was right. The silvery, ethereal notes rose in the evening air and the people sitting close by fell silent.

Marek's face was closed; a mask; he hated what he had to do.

'No, Brigitta, I didn't write it for you. If I wrote it for anyone – if that's how it works and I'm still not sure – I wrote it for a girl who had no part in the pageant, whom nobody saw, who did not act or sing or play an instrument . . . and who is not here now at the party but in the kitchen, making the food we are eating.'

Brigitta's cry of fury and revelation rent the air.

'The cook!' she cried. 'You wrote that music for the cook!'

'Yes.'

It could have gone either way. Marek, certainly, was braced for pathos and tears – and they would have been justified, for she would have made a lovely thing of Aniella's music. But the fates who had smiled on Hallendorf all day still looked benignly on the inhabitants. Brigitta did not weep or beseech as she had done after the opera. She rose, expanded her well-documented ribcage – and exploded into righteousness and rage.

'How *dare* you insult me like that? How dare you beg for a place in my bed and then go and sport with domestics? I offered you my art and my love and you go off to roll in the gutter. Well, do it then – make *Knödel* with your cook, but don't come running back to me. When I think what I was prepared to do for you!' She turned majestically to Staub. 'Go on. Remind him of what I was prepared to do!'

'She was prepared to huddle,' said Staub weakly.

'I was prepared to huddle,' repeated Brigitta, to the interest of those in earshot. 'But not now. Not ever again. Get the driver, Benny – we're leaving.'

But this was not so simple. Infected by the day's proceedings, the taxi driver had pinned Hermine against the wall of the Greek temple, where he was outlining

the plot of a possible music drama based on his grandmother's experience with her husband's ghost, and
made it clear that he was in no way ready to depart.

It was after midnight when Ellen was finished. Now she
sat on the rim of the well where she had sat at the
beginning, garnering gym shoes. Fireflies danced in
the catalpa tree; an owl hooted – perhaps the same
one which Marek had shown her how to feed. The
music still came faintly from the terrace, but the younger
children were in bed; the party had moved on to the
village and would continue until dawn. Enough light
came from the upstairs window to show her the outline
of the wheel on the coach house roof. Would they come
next year, the storks – and would there be anyone left
to welcome them?

He came upon her quietly, but she knew his step and
braced herself. This was where one let love go lightly –
bade it goodbye with an open hand in the way the
detestable Brigitta had sung about. And seeking help,
she called up her pantheon of people who had behaved
well as she now had to do: Mozart's sister, as talented
as he was, who had disappeared uncomplainingly into
oblivion and domesticity; Van Gogh's brother Theo,
always helping, sending money, asking nothing for
himself.

But there are times for thinking about Mozart's sister, and a night full of fireflies and stars did not seem to
be one of them. Marek had sat down beside her and the
memory of Kalun, his arms round her, the place on his

shoulder made specially to fit her head, made her close her eyes.

'I've brought you some news,' he said. 'Isaac is safe.'

She looked up then. 'Oh, that's wonderful. I'm so glad!'

'They hope to get him across to England, so your family may be hearing from him soon.'

'They'll help him, I promise you.'

'You know that Isaac is in love with you,' he said abruptly.

She sighed. 'He was afraid; I helped him – he was bound to feel that. I explained it all to Millie. But now that he's safe –'

'I'm not so sure.' He was silent for a moment. Then: 'If he asked you to marry him would you accept? Could you be persuaded to?'

'What?' she asked stupidly. The question made no sense to her.

'Your friend Kendrick came to see me in Vienna. He told me you were in love with someone else. I thought it might be Isaac.'

But even as he spoke he realised that her answer did not matter. Whatever she might say about Isaac was irrelevant; the time for chivalry was past. When he had first seen her by the well he'd thought of her as a girl in a genre painting: as *Seamstress* or *Lacemaker* – but he'd been wrong. She was a Lifemaker; he'd seen that watching her ceaseless, selfless work for the pageant. Had his friend still been in danger Marek might have continued to stand aside, but not now. Isaac must take his chance.

Ellen had shrunk away from him. 'I don't know why you're putting me through all this,' she said, her voice full of bewilderment. 'When you know –' she broke off, reaching for the tatters of her pride. 'I've never asked you for anything. I've always known that you were going to America with Brigitta . . . and that no one who doesn't understand about . . . enharmonic intervals and tritones . . . and species counterpoint can matter seriously to you. But –'

'You're so right,' interrupted Marek earnestly. 'So absolutely right! The idea of sharing my bed and board with someone who doesn't understand tritones and enharmonic intervals is absolutely abhorrent to me. I can conceive of nothing more dreadful. I am particularly attached to conversations about enharmonic intervals before breakfast – and species counterpoint too, though in general I prefer to discuss that in my bath.'

She looked up, trying to read his voice. He had bent down to pick up a tin punched with holes, which he handed her.

'I've brought you a present.'

'Not a frog? Because I don't kiss them, if you remember, so it would be a waste.'

'No, not a frog. Open it.'

She could not clearly see the flowers lying on the damp moss, but she could smell them – and Henny had been right. Only in heaven could one find such a scent.

'Sister Felicity told me where to look for them. I only brought a few; they're getting rare.'

She couldn't speak. Any other farewell present she could have taken lightly, but not this.

Marek had risen and now stood looking down at her.

'I'm leaving in the morning,' he said.

'Yes, I know.'

'But not for America.'

'Oh? Why not?'

He shrugged. 'I don't really know. I suppose you could say that I have decided to stay and share the fate of my countrymen.'

She took a steadying breath. 'Where to, then?'

'To Pettelsdorf,' he said, using the old name for his home. 'And I want you to come.'

Mozart's sister vanished into the shadows; Van Gogh's brother dematerialised. Joy exploded and the night stars sang.

'To see the storks?' she asked.

'That also,' said Marek – and pulled her to her feet.

Tamara, alone of those at Hallendorf, had had a frustrating and unpleasant day. Not one of the Toscanini Aunts had noticed her or asked about her career. She had been presented simply as the headmaster's wife and then ignored.

Well, now Bennet should make it up to her; he should make her feel special and wanted again. In the bedroom, with its windows over the courtyard, she took

345

the record of the Polovtsian dances out of the sleeve, sharpened the fibre needle of the gramophone, took off her dress.

Bennet turned from the window to find the proceedings well under way. But this time he did not view them with his usual mixture of dread and resignation. Instead he smiled pleasantly at his wife and said: 'Not tonight, dear. I'm rather tired.'

He did not, however, show any particular signs of fatigue. Instead he walked past Tamara, who was in the act of unstoppering the Bessarabian Body Oil, and made his way downstairs.

It seemed to him to be his duty as well as his pleasure to be the first to congratulate the two people he had seen embracing so closely and passionately by the well.

'*A consummation devoutly to be wished,*' he murmured, thinking of Marek and Ellen sharing a life.

There could have been no better ending to this happy day.

# 26

It was as lovely as she had expected, the famous Forest of Bohemia. Pools of light between ancient trees, new-minted streams tumbling over glistening stones . . . Squirrels ran along the branches of great limes; woodpeckers hammered at the trunks of oaks that had stood 'from everlasting to everlasting'.

Bennet had insisted on lending them his car for the few days he could spare Ellen. It was an open Morris Minor; they drove along the lanes as if in a beneficent perambulator, at one with the birdsong and the sky.

'Are you hungry?' Marek said. 'Would you like to stop somewhere for lunch?', and she wondered how soon it would be before just seeing him turn his head would no longer send her heart leaping. It *would* stop, this joy, she told herself; she had watched married couples on the Underground, in tea shops, and it was clear they didn't feel like this, but at the moment it was impossible to imagine.

She shook her head. 'I'm fine.'

But he decided to stop the car just the same. 'It seems I need to kiss you,' he explained. 'If you have no objection.'

They drove on, past a tiny chapel with silvered aspen tiles on the roof and water wheels which seemed as much a part of the forest as the trees. No wonder, she thought, that Marek growing up in this had such assurance, such strength – and the gift of silence which came from it.

The assurance, too, to state his plans without embarrassment.

'I am going to take Ellen home to meet my parents,' he had said to the children and the staff. 'And when term is over, I'm going to marry her.'

'Can we come to the wedding?' the children asked: Flix and Janey, Bruno and Ursula . . . and Sophie, trying to be happy for Ellen, trying to fight down her fear of loss.

'Of course.'

Later he had asked her if she wanted to be married from Gowan Terrace. 'Your mother would like it, I imagine?'

Ellen did not mind 'where' or even 'whether'. She lived in a Blake-ian world of *now*; if God had arrived she would have asked him to dinner, unsurprised.

Marek too had shrugged off his restless concern for his country's future and his own. He would stay at Pettelsdorf, write the symphony that for some time now had declared its intention to be composed, and fetch Ellen when the term was done.

They had been so kind at Hallendorf, so happy for her, thought Ellen gratefully: Freya and Lieselotte offering to do her work, Hermine hugging her . . . Chomsky had been surprised, understandably, that anyone could be preferred to him, but if he had to lose he was content to lose to Marek. Now she remembered Leon's face as Marek handed him two sheets of music – a serenade he had written as a boy and found in Steiner's trunk.

'For my biographer,' Marek had said, teasing him, and the boy had flushed with pleasure and for once been silent.

Only Tamara had not been there to see them off.

'She's got a migraine,' Margaret had whispered. 'It's a good one – Toussia Alexandrovna was an expert!'

But it was Steiner Ellen thought of now, fingering the silver filigree cross she wore round her neck. He had come across the lake to say goodbye and taken her aside.

'I bought this for Marek's mother many years ago . . . before she was engaged. I'd like you to have it,' he'd said.

She'd made no attempt to refuse. There were no games to be played with this old man. She only kissed him and wiped her eyes and asked no more questions, for his lifelong love for Milenka was obvious in the way he opened the box and took out the beautiful thing he had chosen with such care, and never proffered.

*

In the early afternoon they stopped at an inn and sat outside at a wooden table beside a stone trough where the dray horses came to drink. They ate rye bread and cheese and drank the famous beer of Marek's country – and she asked again those questions which are the best of all because the answers are waited for, and known. Will Nora Coutts still be in her room drinking Earl Grey from Harrods? Will Lenitschka have baked a *beigli* for you and will it contain apricots *and* hazelnuts? Will the geese be patrolling your mother's hammock and is it honestly true that your father goes hunting with Albanian Indigestion Pills? She found she knew the name of Marek's wolfhound but not of his mother's Tibetan terrier, and now too she wanted to know what the old man was called, the one who kept bees and said: 'Pity; pity about the music,' whenever Marek went away.

'Tell it again,' she begged, asking about the spare doves that had to be driven away in washing baskets, and the grandfather who had outlived Chekhov and was buried with his fishing flies – and he would begin to do so and then decide it was more urgent to hold her and kiss her and learn the exact disposition of the freckles on her nose.

'The light will be right,' he said as they got back into the car. 'The house faces west.' She would see it with the ochre walls bathed in the sleepy gold of early evening. 'It's just a house,' he said, trying to rein back, but it was useless. Her love for Pettelsdorf, before she had ever set foot in it, was ineradicable.

Oh Henny, if only you were here, she thought; if only you knew. But Henny did know. It was Henny who had taught her not to fear happiness. 'It takes courage to be happy,' Henny had said. But I have it, thought Ellen, and looked at Marek's hands on the steering wheel and vowed she would give him space to work and time to be alone, but not perhaps at this second when it was necessary to touch one of his knuckles carefully with her fingertips in case it went away.

'I'd like to go to the well first,' she said, 'the one you told me about in Kalun . . . where the girls go after their betrothal and draw a glass of water and bring it to their lovers.' She looked at him a shade anxiously. 'You will drink it, won't you – even though water is for the feet?'

'Yes, Ellen,' he said, his voice suddenly husky. 'I will drink it.'

They drove on for another hour. Then the trees seemed to grow more luxuriant, more spacious and the verges of the road were tended. They were coming to a demesne.

Marek had been right about the light. The sun was beginning to drop behind the trees, to send rays across the trunks, illumining the willow herb and foxglove in the grass. The time of day that means home-coming, the end of labour, the welcoming hearth.

She leant out, filling her lungs with the scents of the forest: resin, mushrooms, the peppery scent of the birches – and something else.

'A bonfire?' she said. 'Or are they burning stubble?'

She did not realise anything was wrong till she saw Marek's face and then, suddenly, she was terribly afraid. And at the same time, the smell grew stronger and there was a sound like the wind, which grew louder, became a roar. Even then she thought only of forest fires. That anything else could be burning was out of her power to imagine.

Marek had put his foot down on the accelerator. The little car lurched forward, rounded a bend . . . and she found that she had whimpered like a stricken animal.

It was the house that was burning. Flames licked the ochre walls; tongues of fire shot through the blackened window frames . . . had reached the roof – and all the time, worse than the smoke, the heat, was that terrifying, monstrous roar.

She should have stopped him. In her nightmares, for the rest of her life, she struggled with him, but he was too quick. He didn't open the car door; he vaulted over it, and ran.

At the gates the men, pathetic firemen in toy helmets with buckets, tried to hold him back, but he pushed them away as if they were flies and raced towards the house and vanished.

'No!' they shouted after him. 'No! Come back!'

She followed. Knowing it was madness, she ran after him, but the men were ready for her. They pinned her down as she struggled; held her fast. 'No,' they repeated in Czech. 'No' – hurting her in their grasp, forcing her on to the ground.

As she gasped for breath, lying pinioned, she saw high above the burning house, the storks circling and flapping for a last time above their ravaged nests. Then they became black streaks in the polluted, hellish sky, and were gone.

# PART 2

# 27

Kendrick Frobisher's house, in the summer of 1940, was not wet.

It was a heavenly summer, the summer in which France fell and the British Expeditionary Force was evacuated from Dunkirk. Leaves were never such an intense and iridescent green; sunlight glinted on flower-studded meadows as the Germans encircled the Maginot Line and overran not only France but Belgium and Holland. Birdsong filled the air in the lull between bursts of gunfire and accompanied the fleeing refugees who blocked the roads. It was as though the weather was preparing a glorious requiem for the death of Europe.

In London, where Ellen was making sandwiches in the basement of the National Gallery, the barrage balloons swayed and glinted in the milky skies; nurses and air-raid wardens and office workers lay in the grass in their snatched lunch hours. Anxious relatives, scouring the bulletin boards to see who was safely returned across the Channel, found it easier to hope because of the warmth.

There are a lot of sandwiches to be made in a war. Ellen made them in the National Gallery at lunch time, where the exhausted Londoners could hear the best music in the land for a shilling. She made them in a canteen for soldiers on leave in Shaftesbury Avenue, and she made them, along with basic meals of mince and mashed turnips, in one of the British restaurants set up by the government to help with the rations. She also went fire watching twice a week on the roof of the Methodist Chapel near Gowan Terrace because she liked, even now, three years after she had last seen Marek, to go to bed extremely tired, and acted as model for the St John's Ambulance classes on Thursday afternoons, being bandaged by zealous housewives and carried about on gates.

She would have done rather more than that – would have joined the Auxiliary Territorial Service, in fact – if it hadn't been for a visit she paid, in late June, to Kendrick's house in Cumberland.

As Patricia Frobisher had expected, Kendrick had been declared unfit for military service. He had been directed into the offices of the Ministry of Food, where he had been instrumental in issuing the first ration books and writing the edict forbidding the use of icing sugar in wedding cakes.

Ellen had seen him occasionally but it was not till he came to a lunch-time concert in a state of great distress that she allowed him to resume anything like their former friendship.

Kendrick's eyes were rimmed with red and he had come to take his leave of her. For the thing that Patricia had dreaded most of all had come to pass. Kendrick's brother William had been killed in a flying accident at the beginning of the war and now it turned out that Roland, his elder brother, had been lost during the retreat from France.

'I'm so sorry,' said Ellen, trying to comfort him – but it seemed that Kendrick's grief was not for his brothers, who had behaved to him with unrelenting cruelty, but for his mother.

'If only it had been me,' Kendrick said, 'I'm no use to anyone – but it had to be Roland.'

This had annoyed Ellen very much – to the point where she had agreed to come and visit Kendrick, who had been perfectly happy in the Ministry of Food and was now the sole owner of Crowthorpe: the house, the farm, the derelict quarry and two thousand acres of woodland.

Ellen had gone with her raincoat and sou'wester, her Wellington boots and three sweaters, prepared for the glowering house beneath its grey scree of fells and rock.

But something had gone wrong. She got out at the station to find a landscape of brilliant sun and dramatic purple cloud shadows; of luminous cushions of moss and laundered lambs. The air was full of the scent of may blossom; walking up the drive she came on clumps of brilliant pink and golden azaleas. Crowthorpe itself was certainly an unattractive house: mottled brick, mock Tudor arches, narrow ecclesiastical windows, but there was a kitchen garden whose greenhouses, untended since the call-up of the gardener, still produced tomatoes and cucumbers, and nothing could stop the roses climbing up the liver-coloured walls.

If only it had rained, she thought afterwards . . . but all that weekend the Lake District preened itself, the air was as soft as wine, a silken sheen lay on the waters of Crowthorpe Tarn and when she climbed the hill where the hikers had perished she saw a view to make her catch her breath. In Kendrick's woods the bluebells lay like a lake; there were kingfishers in the stream . . .

If only Patricia Frobisher had been there to lay her dead, authoritarian hand over the house and spoil Ellen's image of Crowthorpe as a kind of jolie laide which could be brought back to life . . . But Patricia had overestimated her own strength: stricken by her double loss, appalled at the thought of Kendrick as sole owner of her home, she had allowed her brothers to take her away with them to Kenya.

Perhaps it was the blond Jersey calf, the youngest in the herd, which the farm manager made her feed from a bucket . . . Or the two old servants, the only ones who had not left to do war work, who invited her into the kitchen and fed her on shortcake . . . Or the sight of the sunshine streaming into a small summer house, where her Aunt Annie, facing a gall bladder operation, could so suitably recuperate. But most probably it was the sight of three small, pale faces – Elsie and Joanie and Doris – the Cockney evacuees banished by Mrs Frobisher before her departure to the gun room on account of ringworm, who threw themselves on Ellen and said they wanted their mam.

Travelling back to London, Ellen thought of Sophie, needing somewhere quiet to study for her University Entrance, and Ursula, whose appalling grandparents tried to keep her captive in their hospitalised house among spittoons and bedpans. Margaret Sinclair was working in the dungeons of the Ministry of Information and seldom saw the daylight; she would benefit from weekends in the country. Bennet was incommunicado doing something unbelievably secret in Bletchley Park, but her mother was working far too hard in her hospital. And if the bombing started, as everyone thought it must do any day, there could be no safer place in England than Kendrick's home.

Even so Ellen held off until the day she met two men in uniform wearing the badge of the Czechoslovak Air Force – and realised that her heart had not leapt into her mouth. That she no longer expected Marek to appear, or claim her. That dead or alive she knew him to be lost for ever.

Kendrick would not have dared to propose to her again. No one proposed to Ellen in those years since Marek vanished. Isaac was sheltering in Gowan Terrace, waiting for his visa to the States, when Ellen came back from Hallendorf. He had seen in an instant that his case was lost, and shown his quality by leaving her alone. And the procession of young men who came to the house after he left for America, though they fell in love as they had always done (she was perhaps more beautiful than ever) knew better than to declare themselves. Perfectly friendly as Ellen was, there was something in her manner that put that out of court.

It was Ellen who informed Kendrick that if he was willing to consider a marriage of the old-fashioned kind, for the management of land and the care of children, she was prepared to become his wife.

Sophie and Leon met during their lunch break in Hyde Park to discuss the news of the engagement. Sophie's father, complete with experimental rats and Czernowitz, was now installed in a big house in Surrey and her mother was in Scotland, so she spent the week boarding in Gowan Terrace.

The bedding plants had been removed and the ground divided into allotments so that Londoners could dig for victory; the gas masks abandoned during the phony war now hung again from people's shoulders – but Sophie, who had been so terrified of rejection and abandonment, found herself less frightened than she had expected at the prospect of invasion and total war.

'Why is she doing this?' Leon asked. He was working as tea boy in a film studio, but still enjoyed the comforts of his parents' mansion near Marble Arch.

'She's sorry for Kendrick and the evacuees, and Aunt Annie has to have a gall bladder operation, and she wants us all to go there when the bombing starts – or even if it doesn't.'

They were both silent, remembering Ellen driving off with Marek; the joy on her face – the absolute happiness that transformed everything about her – and her return after the fire.

'Do you think he's dead?'

Sophie shrugged. 'I almost wish he was; she wouldn't be so hurt that way. Anyway, whether he's dead or not doesn't make any difference.'

'No.'

Ellen had explained to them carefully what had happened at Pettelsdorf and why she would not be seeing Marek again. She had stayed on for the autumn term, the last term at Hallendorf, and packed up the children's trunks and helped to clear the building. She had taken the tortoise to Lieselotte's house and then everyone left. Two months later, Hitler had marched into Vienna and been greeted by jubilant and cheering crowds. Finis Austria . . .

'No storks have come yet,' Lieselotte had written that spring and the following spring – and then she became 'the enemy' and could write no more.

'I suppose I'd better go and congratulate her,' said Leon now. 'I'll come round on Sunday.'

But on Sunday the inhabitants of Gowan Terrace, having baked an egg-free cake in his honour, waited in vain, and when they phoned him, the telephone rang in an empty house.


The wedding was planned for December, but long before then the poor British, waiting for invasion, standing alone against Hitler, succumbed not to panic, for that was not in their nature, but to paranoia. Nazis disguised as parachuting nuns were reported daily; old ladies with a chink in their blackout curtains were taken away for questioning – and now, in an act of madness, they began to round up and imprison just those 'enemy aliens' who had the most to fear from Hitler and Mussolini, and who had been engaged in the fight against Fascism while high-ranking British diplomats were still taking tea with the Führer and admiring the fact that the trains ran on time.

Austrian and German professors were hauled out of lecture rooms, doctors out of hospitals, students out of libraries, told they could pack one suitcase and taken away by the police. Italian shopkeepers, German bakers who had spent years in Britain, disappeared within an hour, weeping and bewildered. Spy mania was everywhere; even one traitor among the thousands of innocent refugees could not be tolerated. The camps they were taken to were not in fact concentration camps, the Tommies who guarded them were no Storm Troopers, but the bewilderment and anguish, particularly among older refugees, was appalling.

Leon happened to be at home when two policemen came for his father. He lied about his age, packed his current film scenario – and was taken to an internment camp consisting of a large number of seaside boarding houses on the Isle of Man.

The views of the landladies evicted from their villas – from Bay View and Sunnydene and Resthaven – are not recorded. Forced to leave behind their garden gnomes, their monkey puzzles and brass plates offering Bed and Breakfast, they were replaced by rolls of barbed wire, observation towers and iron gates. Facing the sea but unable to reach it, cut off from all news of the outside world, the inmates wandered about, guarded by soldiers with fixed bayonets, trying to understand the nightmare that had enveloped them. Housed in villas stripped of everything except camp beds and a few cooking utensils, the men assembled each morning for roll call and the rations which they had no idea how to cook. And each day more confused 'enemy aliens' arrived – Nobel Laureates, old men with diabetes, social democrats who had been tortured in the prisons of the Reich and had come to Britain as to Mecca or Shangri La.

Although it was obvious to even the thickest British Tommy that Hitler, if he had been relying on these men for spies, would have little hope of winning the war, the net which produced such a strange catch did just occasionally dredge up a genuine Nazi. When this happened, the results were unfortunate. Immolated in boarding houses with at least a dozen Jews whose suffering at the hands of the Nazis had been unspeakable, a man polishing his boots and saying that Hitler would soon overrun Britain did not have a happy life. He was refused his rations, ostracised, the blankets stolen from his bed. Most of them capitulated and learnt to hold their tongues, but one of them, a handsome blond young man called Erich Unterhausen, continued each morning to polish his boots, give the Nazi salute and say, 'Heil Hitler!'

At least he did until a rainy morning in late July when he flew suddenly out of the first-floor window of Mon Repos, bounced off a privet bush, and landed on a flower bed planted with crimson salvias and purple aubretia.

He was not hurt, only bruised, which was a pity, but the news, spreading quickly·through the camp, was regarded by the inmates as the first glimmer of light since the fall of France.

Needless to say, the perpetrator of this brutality was immediately marched off to the camp commandant in his office, where he admitted his guilt and was entirely unrepentant.

'If you don't get rid of people like Unterhausen you'll have a murder on your hands,' he said, confusing the commandant with his flawless English. 'Rounding up accredited Nazis with these people is madness. You know perfectly well who the real Nazis are in this camp – I've only been here a day but I can tell you: Schweger in Sunnydene, Pischinger in that place with the blue pottery cat – and the chap I threw out of the window. He's the only one who could possibly be a spy, and the sooner he's in a proper prison the better – anyone worth their salt could signal from here. As for Schweger, he's in with some hotheads from the Jewish Freedom Movement and they're starving him to death.'

'Thank you for telling me my business,' said the

commandant, and was disconcerted by an entirely friendly smile from the tall, broad-shouldered man with the scar on his forehead. He looked down at the papers that had come with the prisoner.

'You say you're a Czech.'

'I don't say I am; I am,' said the prisoner unruffledly.

'So what are you doing here? The Czechs are our allies.'

Marek was silent. The Czechs might be allies now, but before, at Munich, they had been betrayed.

'Your name is German.'

'Yes. I came over in a fishing boat; we were strafed and capsized outside Dover. I got concussion. Apparently I spoke German to the dogs.'

'The dogs?'

'There was a whole compound of stray dogs which the Tommies had smuggled out of France when they were taken off at Dunkirk – you've never heard such a racket. They put my stretcher down beside a big black and tan pointer. My father's hunting dogs were always trained in German and when I came round –' He shook his head. 'It doesn't matter about me; they'll sort it out. I'm quite glad to be out of the way till the Czechoslovak Air Force reassembles. But Unterhausen must go, and the other Nazis – and old Professor Cohen must go to hospital – the one who stands by the barbed wire and gets his beard caught. He's very eminent and very ill – if he dies there'll be questions asked. They're being asked already in Parliament and elsewhere.'

'Is there anything else you'd like to tell us?' sneered the second in command, a brash young lieutenant, but the commandant frowned him down. A humane man, he knew full well that he was caught up in one of those administrative muddles that happens in war and can claim lives.

It was to him that Marek spoke. 'Most of the people in here understand what has happened – that there was bound to be confusion after the French surrendered, that we've got mixed up with the parachuting nuns and that it won't go on for ever. But not all of them. There have been two suicides in one of the other camps, as you no doubt know. This whole business – interning the people who have most of all to fear from Hitler – is going to be a pretty discreditable episode in retrospect. What's more, if Hitler does invade, you've made it nice and easy for him, corralling all the Jews and the anti-Nazis together so he doesn't have to go looking.'

'So what is it you want?' asked the commandant.

'A piano,' said Marek.

As he came out he found a knot of excited people standing in the street.

'I told you,' cried a young man, scarcely more than a boy, who rushed up and threw his arms round Marek. 'I told them it had to be you! I said if someone had defenestrated Unterhausen it would be you! But you aren't German, are you? How did you get here?'

'How did *you* get here?' said Marek, suddenly

368

angry. 'You can't even be seventeen.' Were they interning children now?

'I told them I was older,' said Leon. 'When they
came to take my father, I wanted to come too. My
mother and sisters are in a camp on the other side of
the island.'

Leon's father, Herr Rosenheimer, now came forward
to shake Marek's hand. Though he had filed natural-
isation papers the week before his arrest and his export-
import business employed more than four hundred
British workers, he seemed to be without bitterness, and
had persuaded the internees (from whom all news of the
outside world was forbidden) to save the newspapers
that came wrapped round their ration of kippers, so
that he could keep in touch with the stock exchange.

Other familiar faces now appeared in the throng:
the erst-while flautist of the Berlin Philharmonic; a
copying clerk from the office of Universal Editions;
Marek's old tailor from the Kärntnerstrasse . . . and all
the time more people appeared, overjoyed by the news
of Unterhausen's fate.

But Marek did not intend to waste too much time
on swapping stories – and Leon, whose reminiscences
would lead to Hallendorf and thus to Ellen, had
straight away to understand that there would be no discussion of the past.

'There's a piano locked in the basement of the Palm
Court Hotel,' he said. 'We can have it. It'll have to be
moved into some kind of hall or shed – anything. We're
going to give a concert.'

'Of your music?' asked Leon eagerly.

'No. Not now.'

'Of what then?'

Marek looked round at the weary men, the drab streets, the barbed wire.

'There's only one answer to that, don't you think?'

'Johann Sebastian Bach,' said the flautist.

Marek nodded. 'Exactly so.' For a moment he raised his eyes to heaven, seeking guidance not so much from God (whose musicality was not well documented) as from his erstwhile representative on earth, the *Kapellmeister* of Leipzig. Would it seem sacrilege to the old man to put on his masterpiece with an exhausted chorus of amateurs and an orchestra which, if it could be found at all, would be a travesty of what Bach had demanded? Yet it was this monumental work, which embraced the whole of the human condition, from the painful pleading of the *Kyrie* to the blaze of jubilant ecstasy of the *Resurrexit*, that these bewildered exiles needed and deserved.

Marek made up his mind. 'We're going to perform the Mass in B minor,' he said. 'And no one had better release us till we've got it right!'

After the fire Marek had spent several weeks in hospital in Prague. He'd been moved there from the local nursing home when it became clear that although his apparent injuries had cleared up quickly – a burn on his temple where a beam had glanced his forehead, the smoke inhalation which had saved his life by rendering

370

him unconscious before he could go far into the building – there was something else most seriously wrong.

At first the doctors and psychiatrists who examined him, the nuns who nursed him, put down the patient's other symptoms to grief for his parents' death, but as time passed and he became wilder and more distressed, the possibility of brain fever or dementia was seriously discussed.

Marek had not resisted the move, for the contacts he needed to carry out what he now saw as his life's work could be assembled best in Prague, where the headquarters of resistance to the Germans had recently been established.

It did not take him long to prepare a dossier on the man who had set his home alight and killed his parents, Oskar Schwachek, who had also killed Franz by the river and tried to murder Meierwitz, was a Sudeten German who since the age of fourteen had been a member of the Nazi party – a fire raiser as a child, a disturbed and vicious adolescent and now, at the age of twenty-five, a killer who put his evil talents at the disposal of those who wanted to hand Czechoslovakia over to the Nazis.

Stepan and Janik had seen him near the house on the day before the fire; old Lenitschka, who had perished with the Captain and his wife, had warned them. Every servant at Pettelsdorf was looking out for him and every member of the resistance.

'But I want him alive,' Marek said. 'I want him to

know who kills him. And he is not to be shot. It will happen slowly . . . very slowly.'

During those days of convalescence when the specialists conferred and the nuns prayed over his bed, there were only two visitors Marek did not want to see.

The first was his grandmother, Nora Coutts. She had been going for one of her famous walks when the fire began and had survived unscathed. Nora had lost her only daughter, whom she adored, and her son-in-law. She looked ten years older and something had happened to her mouth, which had been set in a firm line and now, on occasion, had to be covered with her hand. But Marek's obsession with his vendetta, which grew with his returning strength, shocked her deeply.

'Your parents died together and almost instantly, I understand. What do you think they'd feel if they knew you were going to poison the rest of your life with this hatred? What do you think they would feel if they knew what you were doing to Ellen?'

But Marek was deaf and blind. Ellen was a danger. Ellen, who came every day and sat quietly and patiently by his bed, waiting for him to become sane again . . . Ellen, who was so beautiful and whole and true, would weaken him. Even less than his grandmother did she understand that nothing but hatred must now rule his life. To track down Schwachek, to kill him very slowly and carefully, explaining at each stage what was happening to him and why – nothing else existed. And when this was done, to face prison or hanging on his own account without regret, knowing that Ellen was out of it and safe.

'There will be no more love and no more weddings,' he had said when she first came.

But she had not believed him. She thought as the nuns thought that the shock had temporarily unhinged him. That he should wish to avenge his parents' murder was understandable perhaps, but to make this vendetta his only reason for existing seemed impossible. Surely somewhere the man who cared for every living thing could not be wholly and permanently dead?

But the weeks passed and Marek became steadily more hostile, more obsessed, more angry. Even so, it was not till the doctors who were treating him told her that she was making him worse and delaying his recovery, that she gave up.

He was standing by the window of his hospital room when she told him she was leaving. A tortoise-shell butterfly was beating its way against the window, and as he caught it in his hand she held her breath, for she expected him to crush it between his fingers, so mad had he become.

But he opened the window and released it carefully into the summer afternoon. That was her last memory of him: the killer with the scar on his forehead, gently freeing the butterfly – and then his bleak, toneless and unadorned: 'Goodbye.'

The betrayal of the Czechs at Munich came soon afterwards. Marek joined the Czech Air Force, flew his plane to Poland when the Germans overran his country, went on fighting with the Poles – and when they were beaten, with the French.

When the Germans advanced through Northern France, he was flying Potez 63s with a reconnaissance squadron of the French Air Force, never sure whether the airfield from which he took off would still be there when he returned, attacked both in the air and on the ground.

The occupation of Paris in mid-June put an end to these adventures. The crews were summoned, given rations and their pay, and told they were on their own. Marek was caught up in the demoralisation of the retreating troops, the fleeing refugees. Separated from his crew, he reached Brittany at last, found a fishing boat willing to take him across to Dover, and opened his eyes to the extraordinary sight of dozens of baying, quarantined dogs.

The slobbering, excited animals had given him his first glimmer of hope – for it struck him as possible that a nation mad enough to carry stray dogs on to the boats that took them off the beaches might – just might – be mad enough not to surrender simply because all hope was lost.

Closest to his stretcher was a pointer bitch with anguished eyes. Marek soothed her, was overheard by an exhausted sergeant who was trying to sort out the flotsam that still came over the Channel in the wake of the debacle – and presently found himself on the Isle of Man, watching Erich Unterhausen polish his boots and give the Nazi salute.

# 28

It had been Ellen's intention to get married quietly in the Bloomsbury Registry Office, invite a few friends back to Gowan Terrace, and go up to Crowthorpe the next day.

But in September the Blitz began. Broken glass was swept from the streets along with the autumn leaves; the scent of smoke was seldom out of people's nostrils; nights spent in shelters or the basements of their houses left everyone exhausted – and a new band of heroes emerged: the pilots who went up each night to give battle to the bombers that came across to devastate the cities. Doris and Elsie and Joanie, who had crept back to their parents in London, were sent back to Cumberland, the cook general who had struggled on at Gowan Terrace left to make munitions and at the end of October, the Registry Office received a direct hit.

Under these circumstances it seemed sensible to have the wedding at Crowthorpe, and if the villagers were not to be upset, to make it a wedding in the local church – and this in turn meant Sophie and Ursula as bridesmaids and inviting the guests to stay the night before, since travel on the blacked-out trains was far too unreliable to make a day trip possible.

Announcing her engagement to the ladies with whom she made sandwiches, her fellow fire watchers and the women who bandaged her on Thursday afternoons, Ellen now became lucky. She knew she was lucky because everybody told her so.

'Lucky you, going to live in the country, away from it all,' or 'Lucky you, not having to worry about the rations; they say you can get butter and eggs and everything up there,' or 'I wish I was you, getting a good night's sleep.'

Ellen's response to her great good fortune was unvarying; she instantly invited whoever had congratulated her to Crowthorpe: the milkman's sister who had taken over his round when he was called up, an old man who came to lick envelopes at Gowan Terrace and an orderly at her mother's hospital. It was as though the provision of fresh air, birdsong and undisturbed nights was what made being so very lucky endurable.

But it was her family – her mother working too hard at the hospital, her Aunt Annie whose operation had been postponed as the wards filled up with the casualties of the Blitz, the aunt who ran a bookshop, and, of course, the Hallendorf children – for whom she particularly wanted to provide sanctuary.

'You will come, won't you?' she begged them. 'Not

just for the wedding – you'll stay, won't you? There'll be log fires, it'll be really comfortable, you'll see,' – and they said, yes of course they would come, though Dr Carr pointed out that she could not leave her patients for long, and Aunt Phyllis and Aunt Annie, who were helping to organise petitions demanding the release of the interned 'enemy aliens' as well as their other work, were not sure that they could take too much time off in the north.

'She *is* happy, isn't she?' asked Dr Carr of her sisters, who said they were sure she was, and anyway it was probably a mistake to start a marriage with too many expectations. 'Better to build it up slowly,' Phyllis said, a view which Ellen shared and propounded to Margaret Sinclair over pilchards on toast in Lyon's Corner House.

'People always used to get married for sensible reasons,' she said – and Margaret, whose heart smote her, had perforce to remain silent, for her own existence was hardly a blueprint for a successful love life. Immured in his secret hide-out in Surrey, reputedly breaking codes, Bennet had been compelled, when the air raids began, to send Tamara for safekeeping to her mother in the north, and Margaret, deprived of the hope that a bomb would instantly and painlessly destroy the Russian ballerina, spent her free time in her bedsitting room in case Bennet could get to London and needed a cup of tea.

Sophie and Ursula (for whom Ellen was making dresses out of parachute silk which scratched her hands) tried to cheer each other up, but without success.

'She reminds me of Sydney Carton,' said Sophie. 'You know, the man who said "It is a far, far better thing that I do now than I have ever done before" and then went off to be executed.' She sighed. 'I wish they'd let Leon out; he could help with the music at least.'

'You really miss him, don't you?' said Ursula.

'Yes, I do. And his family. They've been incredibly good to me.'

Kendrick was now officially released from the Ministry of Food, since farming – which he was believed to be about to do – was regarded as work of national importance, and went north to Cumberland, but could not be relied upon for practical arrangements. He was in a state of profound exaltation but slightly apprehensive. The Facts of Life had been told to Kendrick not by his mother, who had better things to do, or even by a kindly nursemaid, as is so often the case with the English upper classes – the maids engaged by Mrs Frobisher were seldom kindly – but by a boy called Preston Minor at his prep school.

Although the horrific information conveyed by this unpleasant child had been modified later by the reading of Great Literature, there was still a considerable gap between Kendrick's conception of Ellen as the *Primavera* or Rembrandt's Saskia crowned with flowers, and what was supposed to happen in his father's four-poster bed after the nuptials were complete.

The wedding was planned for the eighteenth of

December, and now the submarine menace came to the rescue of the bridegroom and the bride. Patricia Frobisher was unable to secure a place on any of the convoys sailing from Africa and would not be able to attend.

Ellen, navigating with meticulous concentration the route to the day which would make her so happy and so fortunate, saw in this the hand of Providence. Her plans for Crowthorpe could now go ahead without battles: the proper housing of the evacuees, the installation of land girls (a move opposed by Patricia) and the removal of the green lines which Mrs Frobisher, glorying in the restrictions of wartime, had painted round the bath to show the limits of hot water which might be used.

Both the recent bereavement in the Frobisher family and the bride's own inclinations made a small wedding desirable. In addition to the immediate families, they invited only a few university friends, those of the Hallendorf children who could get away, Margaret Sinclair – and Bennet, whose kindness to her after her return from Prague Ellen had never forgotten. Since it was unlikely that Bennet would get leave, Ellen had hoped to be spared Tamara, but fate decreed otherwise.

On a visit to Carlisle not long before the wedding, Ellen saw a sight which no one could have beheld unmoved. Two women were plodding wearily along the rain-washed pavement. Both carried string bags of heavy groceries, both wore raincoats and unbecoming sou'westers, both had noses reddened by the cold. One was considerably older than the other, but their resemblance was marked: mother and daughter, clearly bored with each other's company, on the weekly and wearisome shopping trip.

It was only when the younger woman stopped and greeted her that Ellen realised she was in the presence of the Russian ballerina who had been Diaghilev's inspiration and the confidante of Toussia Alexandrovna, now returned for wartime safekeeping to her mother, and demoted most pitiably to Mrs Smith's daughter Beryl.

'Ellen – how lovely to see you!'

Tamara's pleasure in the meeting was unfeigned. Her mother's colliery village on the bleak coastal plain was only thirty miles from Crowthorpe; she knew of the Frobishers' importance and Crowthorpe's size. She wanted an invitation to the wedding, and she got it. Appalled by the reduction of the sinewy sun worshipper and maker of icon corners to Mrs Smith's Beryl, Ellen invited her not only to the wedding but – since there were no buses from Tamara's village – to the house party on the night before.

On a morning in late November a number of men were pulled out of the routine roll call in the camp and told to report to the commandant. From Sunnydene, an elderly lawyer named Koblitzer who walked with a stick, and a journalist named Klaus Fischer; from Resthaven, Herr Rosenheimer and his son Leon; and from Mon Repos (from which the defenestrated Unterhausen had been taken to Brixton Jail), Marcus von Altenburg.

Wondering what they had done, they made their way down the grey rain-washed streets towards the hotel by the gates which housed Captain Henley's office.

'We'll need a chair for Koblitzer,' said Marek when they were assembled, and a chair was brought.

In spite of this request, an air of cheerfulness prevailed. The commandant had shown himself a good friend to the inmates; conditions in the camp had improved considerably in the last two months. Even the disagreeable lieutenant looked relaxed.

'I have good news for you,' said the commandant. 'The order has come through for your release. You're to collect your belongings and be ready for the transport at seven in the morning. The ferry for Liverpool sails at ten, and tickets will be issued for your chosen destination.'

The men looked at each other, hardly taking it in at first.

'On what grounds, as a matter of curiosity?' asked Leon's father. 'To whom do we owe our freedom?'

Captain Henley looked down at his papers. 'You, Rosenheimer, on the grounds that you are employing nearly five hundred British workers in your business, and your son on the grounds that he is under age. Klaus Fischer has been spoken for by the Society of Authors, who say he's been writing anti-Nazi books since 1933, and Koblitzer on grounds of ill health.'

Not one of them pointed out that all this information was available at the time they were arrested. Yet their joy was not unalloyed; they had made friendships of great intensity, had started enterprises which must be left undone. Fischer ran a poetry class, Rosenheimer had started a business school – and all of them sang in Marek's choir.

One by one the men stepped forward, signed a paper to say they had not been ill treated, were given their documents. Then it was Marek's turn.

'You've been requested by the commander of the Royal Air Force depot, Cosford. The Czechs have formed a squadron there to fly with the RAF.' Henley looked at Marek with a certain reproach. 'You could have told us you flew with the Poles and the French.'

Marek, who had in fact explained this several times to the interrogators at Dover and elsewhere, only smiled – and then produced his bombshell.

'I shall be very happy to be released,' he said, 'but not before the end of next week.'

'*What?*' The second lieutenant couldn't believe his ears.

'We're performing the B Minor Mass on Sunday week. The men have been rehearsing for months; there's absolutely no question of my walking out on them at this stage. They'll understand at Cosford.'

The commandant was an easy-going man, but this was mutiny. 'Men in this eamp are released as and when the orders come through. I'm not running a holiday camp.'

Nobody made the obvious comment. They were all staring at Marek.

'If you want me to go before the concert you'll have to take me by force. I shall resist and Klaus here can make a scandal when he gets to London; he's an excellent journalist. "Czech Pilot Manhandled by Brutal Soldiery" – that kind of thing. I'm entirely serious about this.'

No one knew what to say. They thought of the work of the last weeks, the slow growth of confidence, the obstacles overcome – and then the excitement as the sublime music grew under Marek's tutelage. No one who had sung *Dona Nobis Pacem* in this miserable place would ever forget it.

'They're coming from the other camps,' Marek reminded him.

The commandant did not need to be told this. He himself had authorised a hundred men to come and had borrowed spare copies of the score from the cathedral choir in Douglas; news of the performance had attracted interest all over the island. If morale had improved, if there had been no suicides, no serious breakdowns in his camp, the Mass in B Minor had played a part.

'Someone else can take your place, I'm sure,' said the lieutenant!

'No, they can't. They can't!' Leon spoke for the first time. 'Only Marek can do it.' He stepped forward, leaning towards the commandant. 'And I want to stay too! I don't want to be released till Marek is; I want to –'

'*No*,' said Marek, at the same time as Herr

Rosenheimer turned in fury on his son: 'You will please to stop talking nonsense, Leon. You will come with me. Do you want to kill your mother with worry?'

Frau Rosenheimer had been released three weeks earlier and it was likely that her lamentations, petitions and bribery had hurried her husband's release.

Leon might have argued with his father, but Marek's face made it clear that he would give no quarter.

'I'll get in touch with the depot and see what they say,' said the commandant.

It was a defeat, but as the men returned to their houses, Captain Henley was not altogether sorry. He had rejoined the army hoping to be sent on active service, but they had told him he was too old and sent him here to do this uncongenial job. Yet sometimes there were rewards. He was not a musical man but now, without knowing that he knew it, he hummed the opening bars of the *Sanctus* with its soaring, ever ascending solo on the flute.

Then he picked up the telephone and asked for Cosford.

Outside a number of men were gathered, for rumours of a new batch of releases had come through.

'Is it true you're going tomorrow, Marek?' said a thin, white-faced man with his collar turned up. He had dragged himself to rehearsals of the Mass day in day out, in spite of a weakness of the lungs.

'No.'

Marek said no more but Leon, in a white heat of hero worship, spoke for him. 'They wanted to release him straight away but he won't go till after the concert.'

'Is it true?'

The news spread among the men, faces lightened, someone came and shook him by the hand.

'All right, that will do,' said Marek, getting irritated. 'I'll see you at two o'clock in the hall.'

Knocking on the door of Mon Repos that night, Leon shivered with apprehension and the cold wind from the sea. He had come to a resolution which took all his courage. Ever since Marek had appeared in the camp, he had made it clear that Hallendorf and Ellen were taboo subjects – but now Leon was leaving and he was going to speak.

'I've come to say goodbye and to give you my father's address in London. He says you'll be welcome at any time for as long as you like – but you know that. We've got a splendid air-raid shelter!'

'Thank you.'

Leon took a deep breath and plunged.

'I've heard from Sophie,' he said.

Marek was silent, his eyes wary.

'She's going to be a bridesmaid at Ellen's wedding.'

He did not expect Marek to reply, but he said: 'To Kendrick Frobisher, I take it?'

'Not exactly,' said Leon. 'More to his kitchen garden and his cows and his evacuees. It's supposed to be a sanctuary for us all, the wet house. She hasn't asked us if we want to be there.'

Marek had reverted to silence, his eyes fixed on a sampler saying *East West, Home's Best*, which the departing landlady of Mon Repos had forgotten to take down.

'She's getting married on the eighteenth of December, just a week before Christmas. The wedding is at Crowthorpe in the village church at two o'clock in the afternoon. Crowthorpe is where Kendrick lives, it's between Keswick and Carlisle . . .'

He babbled on, repeating the time and place, the nearest railway station, till Marek turned his head.

'Shut up, Leon.' There was no feeling in: his voice, only a great weariness.

'I could tell her you're here. I could tell her you're free. She doesn't know you're in England – Sophie didn't know whether we should –'

Now though Marek did show emotion. The onset of one of his instant and famous rages.

'You will say nothing about me to Ellen. You will not mention my name. I put you on your honour,' said Marek, reverting unexpectedly to his year at an English public school. 'You will only hurt her,' he said presently.

Leon's hero worship subsided momentarily. 'I could hardly hurt her more than you have done,' he said.

'Oh darling, you look *beautiful*,' said Dr Carr, stepping back and smiling at her daughter. 'You look quite lovely!'

This is always said to brides by their doting mothers – but as she turned from the mirror in her white dress, it had to be admitted that Ellen's beauty was of an unexpected kind. Perhaps it was the sepulchral light of Crowthorpe in the mist and rain of December as it came through the stained-glass windows, but Ellen looked submerged, muted, like a bride found under the sea.

She had altered the dress she had worn to the opera in Vienna and covered it with a short jacket, and her curls were held in place by a circlet of pearls left to her by her august grandmother, Gussie Norchester. She wore no veil, and Sophie had gone to fetch the bouquet of Christmas roses which Ellen had made that morning. The Christmas roses had been a bonus; they had helped Ellen very much when she found them unexpectedly growing behind a potting shed in the dank and freezing garden, for it was not easy to remember her vision of Crowthorpe as she had first seen it on that summer day. But she would be faithful; she would do it all; everyone who came here should be fed and warm and comfortable – and the farm manager had suggested they keep goats, whose milk was not rationed.

Thinking of goats, of whom she was extremely fond, Ellen began to make her way downstairs.

Sophie and Ursula, shawls over their bridesmaid's dresses, were on the landing, talking to Leon. The lights had had to be turned on by midday, but only a faint glow, cast by a lamp in the shape of a Pre-

Raphaelite maiden, illumined the stairs and they were too absorbed to notice her.

'Janey's absolutely sure,' Leon was saying. 'He wasn't on the train. She waited till every single person had got off, and there isn't another one today.'

'He doesn't *have* to come by train. Pilots get petrol, I'll bet. He could come up by car even now.' Sophie, usually so inclined to fear the worst, had all along been convinced that Marek would come – that he would stride in at the last minute and carry Ellen off.

'Can't we do something to slow her up?'

They thought of Aniella in her swagged boat, the draperies trailing in the water. Crowthorpe was wet enough, God knew, but Ellen was doing the short drive to the church in the estate's old Morris.

'We could put sugar in the carburettor,' suggested Ursula, who had become addicted to gangster films.

But sugar was rationed, and the wedding was in half an hour.

'He might still come,' said Sophie obstinately. 'Marek's just the sort of person to burst into the church and if he does I'll tug at Ellen's dress or tell her to faint or something.'

From upstairs they heard the rustle of silk, a sharp intake of breath – then Ellen came down the stairs towards them.

'Marek is here?' she said very quietly. 'He's in England?'

All three turned to her, consternation in their faces.

'Yes,' said Leon, 'I was with him in the internment camp.'

'And he knows that I'm getting married today?'

Silently they nodded.

'I see.'

Anguished, waiting, they looked at her.

But she did not crumple up, nor weep. She straightened her shoulders and they saw pride cover her face like a film of ice.

'I'll have my flowers, please, Sophie.' And then: 'It's time to go –'

Kendrick was waiting at the altar beside his best man, a Cambridge acquaintance whom no one had met before. Pausing inside the church, Ellen surveyed the guests as they turned their heads. The Crowthorpe retainers in their dark heavy overcoats fared best, accustomed as they were to the hardship of the Frobisher regime and the freezing church. Margaret Sinclair was there, giving her a heartening smile, but not Bennet, who was still breaking his codes . . . Janey beside Frank, in the uniform of a private . . . a whole bevy of gallant aunts, real ones and honorary ones, in hats they had dusted out specially – and, sitting a little apart and looking not at all like Beryl Smith but entirely like Tamara Tatriatova (and wearing – Ellen had time to notice – a pilfered geranium from the conservatory in her turban), the Russian ballerina. Yet it was the detestable Tamara who had made the previous night endurable, taking Kendrick into his study to listen to Stravinsky and leaving Ellen free to help the maids with preparations for the wedding lunch.

But now it was beginning. Leon was sitting beside the old lady who played the organ; he had insisted on helping her turn the pages, ignoring her plea that she knew the music by heart. He was shuffling the music, still playing for time. She saw him look directly at Sophie, who half shook her head.

There was nothing more to be done. The first strains of Widor's Toccata rang out over the church, Sophie and Ursula arranged the folds of Ellen's dress, and she began to walk slowly towards her bridegroom.

She was halfway up the aisle when they heard it – Sophie and Ursula, Leon with his keen hearing . . . and Ellen too, even above the sound of the music. The creaking of the heavy oaken door on its rusty hinges; and the gust of wind as it blew open. Sophie tugged once at Ellen's dress and Leon's hand came down on the organist's arm so that she faltered . . .

What they saw then was a strange reversal of what had happened to Aniella in the pageant. For Ellen turned, and as she saw the tall, broad-shouldered figure outlined in the lintel of the door, her face became transfigured. The pride and endurance which had made her look almost old, vanished in an instant, and she became so beautiful, so radiant, that those who watched her held their breath in wonder.

Then the latecomer, a neighbouring landowner who

was Kendrick's godfather, removed his hat and hurried, embarrassed, to his pew.

And the wedding went on.

In allowing the two ancient maids to prepare the master bedroom for their use, Ellen realised she had made a mistake. But she had not wanted to stop them having the chimney swept and doing what they could to air the bedclothes. Shut for years in their basement kitchen, chilblained and deprived of light, the Frobisher maids did not often use their initiative, and Ellen had no wish to deprive them of their traditional expectations.

But she had not examined the room in detail, having expected little from her wedding night except to endure it, and she had not realised that there was quite so much furniture: tables both round and square, brass pots, palms and fenders, bellows and tallboys and a stuffed osprey in a case. A picture of the *The Released Garrison of Lucknow Crossing the Ganges* hung above the bed, which was high and, considering its nuptial purpose, surprisingly narrow, and on the opposite wall was a painting of a pale, dead shepherd in the snow, guarded by two collies who did not seem to have gathered that he was no longer in a position to tell them what to do.

The farm manager had sent up a basket of logs, but the vast size of the chimneypiece made the small fire seem even smaller, and Kendrick, in an unexpected attack of masculinity, had earlier hit the logs with a poker and almost destroyed it. On the chest in the dressing room were photographs of Roland and William in various manly situations – playing cricket, decimating tigers or passing out on parade at Sandhurst – and none as usual of Kendrick – who now came nervously into the bedroom in his striped pyjamas, fell over a padded stool and said: 'Oh Ellen!'

His tone was reverent rather than passionate and he looked cold.

'Come and get warm,' said Ellen, who was already in bed, her hair brushed out, looking, as Kendrick stammeringly began to tell her, like Danaë or Cleopatra, or perhaps Goya's Maya on her satin couch.

But even he realised that the time for conversation was past, and with a gulp he got into bed beside her where, considering how thin he was, he seemed to take up a surprising amount of room, especially his feet, which were icy and very large.

Once in bed, he found himself staring straight at the dead shepherd being guarded by dogs and Ellen saw a flicker of alarm pass over his face.

'What is it, Kendrick?'

'I always used to look at that picture when Mummy was telling me what I'd done wrong. She used to send for me while she answered letters at that desk. That was where she read me my school reports too.' His gaze turned inwards to the terrors of the past.

'We'll change the pictures tomorrow,' promised Ellen – but the idea that anything connected with his mother could be changed seemed to frighten Kendrick even more.

She lay back on the pillow, stifling a yawn, and waited to see if Kendrick had any idea of how to proceed – he might after all have read a book. When this did not seem to be the case, she stretched out her arms and drew her trembling husband towards her, letting his head rest on her breast, where he continued, though short of air, to proclaim his worship and to liken her to various people whose names she did not catch.

'I think we should get undressed properly,' said Ellen, trying to repress the school-mistressy note in her voice.

She slipped off her nightdress, but the sight of her naked, fire-lit body affected him so strongly that he became hopelessly entangled in his pyjama cord.

Ellen freed him, glad that her time at Cambridge had given her some experience. 'Don't worry, darling,' she said. 'We've lots of time.' And: 'Everything's all right,' she said at intervals during the long night, wondering what exactly she meant by this, while Kendrick shivered and stuttered out his admiration and said he was no good to anyone and never had been but he loved her more than anyone had ever loved before.

'Do you think you would be better in another room, Kendrick?' she asked towards dawn. 'Somewhere that doesn't have these associations?'

For a moment, Kendrick brightened. 'There's the old nursery at the top of the house. I slept there when I was little with my nanny.' Kendrick's face had relaxed; clearly he was remembering a golden age. 'It's quite a big room and it clears the trees so you can see the river.'

'Good. We'll try that as soon as I can make some blackout curtains. Now don't worry any more, darling. We'll be fine up there. Just go to sleep.'

But Kendrick had sat up, in the grip of a terrible panic: 'You won't leave me, Ellen, will you? You won't go away and leave me alone? I've always been alone and I couldn't –'

He began to weep and Ellen, fighting a weariness so profound that she thought it must pull her down to the centre of the earth, managed to take him into her arms.

'No, Kendrick, I won't leave you alone, I promise. I'll never leave you alone.'

He became calm then, and slept, and snored (but not unpleasantly), while Ellen lay awake till the image of the dead shepherd in the snow became visible and she had achieved the dawn.

'That's extraordinary,' said Jan Chopek, looking at Marek stretched out on his iron bed in the Air Force barrack at Cosford. 'I've never seen him drunk. Not like this. Not incapable. God knows he drank all right with the Poles, and with those idiots from the Foreign Legion in France – but I've never known him pass out.'

'Well, he's passed out now. Thank God he's not on duty for the next forty-eight hours.'

'If he had been he wouldn't have done it,' said Jan, and the British Pilot Officer shrugged. He'd already noticed that Marek was hero-worshipped by his fellow Czechs.

Marek had approached his blackout systematically, retiring to his room, loosening his tunic, and tilting the vodka bottle into his mouth so that no one would have to drag him to his bed. He had not even been sick, but all efforts to rouse him were unavailing.

Between his locker and Jan's was a picture of a pneumatic blonde left behind by the previous occupant who had not returned from a night raid on Bremen, and a calendar. Under the date – December the eighteenth – was the motto: *No Man Can Bathe Twice In The Same River.*

'Something went wrong,' said Jan. 'He tried to get leave for the weekend – he was going up north to the Lake District for something. He got it, too – and then Phillips pranged his car and he had to go up instead of him. He didn't say much, but he was very upset, I think.'

Marek, when things went wrong, became extremely silent, but he had not often resorted to the standard panacea for disappointment.

'Well, there's nothing we can do except wait till he comes round,' said the Pilot Officer.

This Marek did some six hours later, about the time that Ellen was rising from her nuptial bed. He had a shower, changed and decided that Fate had spoken. He was not certain now if he would have gone north and interrupted the wedding like someone in an opera. Certainly he had intended to. But the war had intervened – while Ellen was being married he was turning back over the Channel – and it was for the best. For Oskar Schwachek, now *Gruppenführer* Schwachek, still lived, and while he did so, Ellen must be protected from whatever was to come.

# 29

It wasn't only Goethe who said beware of what you wish for in youth in case in later years it is granted to you.

He *did* say it – in the course of his long life Goethe said almost everything – but others said it too, among them Nora Coutts, Marek's formidable grandmother, who now sat by his bed and said: 'Did you expect to be pleased then, when you heard?'

Eighteen months had passed since Ellen's marriage. In the summer of 1941 Hitler's madness had caused him to attack Russia, but even if the danger of invasion had ceased, the British, their cities ceaselessly bombed, their Air Force stretched beyond its limits, were experiencing total war as never before.

Marek had flown Wellingtons with the Czech Squadron of Bomber Command since his release from the Isle of Man and always returned safely, but the previous week a hit to his port engine had forced him to bail out with his crew before he could land. His leg was in plaster and in traction, and now, to his fury, he was being taken out of active service and sent to Canada as an instructor.

'I'll be fit in another month,' he'd raged, but without avail.

'We need first-class people to train the younger men,' the Station Commander had said, not liking to point out that two years of solid flying were enough for a man well into his thirties and one who had been through hell before he ever reached Great Britain.

But it was not this news to which Nora Coutts was referring. As next of kin she had been summoned when Marek was injured, and now she sat at the head of his bed, knitting comforts for the troops. The balaclavas and mittens she made bore no resemblance to the misshapen artefacts which Ellen had garnered from the gardens at Hallendorf: Nora was a champion knitter as she was a champion roller of bandages and provider of meals-on-wheels, and since her return to her native land just before the outbreak of war had been the mainstay of the WVS.

'What did you expect?' she repeated.

'To be pleased. To be relieved . . . to feel that a weight had dropped from my mind,' said Marek, and wondered why he had been so stupid as to share with his grandmother the news he had received three days before from Europe. If he hadn't been feeling so groggy and confused after they set his leg he would have had more sense.

'You ordered a man to be killed and to know who

398

was responsible. Your orders have been carried out, Schwachek is dead – and you expect to be pleased? *You?*'

'Yes.'

But looking into her face, whose implacable sanity reminded him somehow of Ellen, he began to realise how mad he had been. 'I should have done it myself. I wanted them to find him but it was for me to do.'

'It's done now; there was no choice.'

But she said no more, for the fracture in his leg was a multiple one and he had a dislocated shoulder – and now he was to be separated from his comrades and the work he loved.

Lying back on the pillows, weary and in pain, Marek reached out once more for the triumph that should have been his – and once again it eluded him. Schwachek had been bound for Russia. That horrific campaign in which the Germans were dying like flies might well have done Marek's work for him. His grandmother was right; he had been mad.

'Do you ever think of Ellen?' she asked suddenly.

Marek turned his head on the pillow and smiled.

'What do you think?' he said.

After she left Marek, Nora Coutts did something she did very seldom; she hesitated.

She had not hesitated when she told the Russian anarchist not to be silly, and she had not hesitated when she left all her possessions behind and walked to the Czech border, arriving there an hour before the Germans invaded, but she hesitated now.

'Do you ever think of Ellen?' she had asked Marek, and got her answer.

But Ellen was married. In the world into which Nora had been born that would have been the end of the matter. But in the world as it was now, where human beings were shot out of the sky, or torpedoed or gunned down, was it perhaps important that people should part without misunderstanding, with the air clear between them? She did not for a moment consider that Ellen would leave her husband, and would have been shocked if anyone had suggested it – but would it comfort Ellen to know that Marek was aware now of his madness? That it would console Marek to see her before he sailed, she was certain.

In the end she decided to do nothing, but a month after her visit to the hospital, a troop ship en route from Canada was torpedoed.

Two days later, she set off for the north.

Nora walked from the station; at eighty-two she would have scorned to take a taxi for a distance of two miles. Marek had been discharged from hospital and was waiting for his orders to sail. Glad though she was that he was no longer flying, she would miss him badly when he went overseas. He talked of her joining him in Canada, but she would stay now and die here.

Once again the Lake District failed to live up to expectations. It was not raining; the late summer afternoon was golden and serene; after the devastation of the cities, this piece of untouched countryside with its dark, leafy trees, its running brooks, its silence, was Paradise indeed. Nor did the first sight of Crowthorpe dismay her; she had after all been born when Queen Victoria was on the throne; the gables and turrets and pointless timbering did not trouble her. She herself in Folkestone had been brought up in a villa not unlike Kendrick's house.

But at the gate she hesitated. She had not told anyone she was coming; only Ellen knew her – to anyone else she would be just an old lady in stout shoes going for a walk. Her case was still at the station – she had wanted to leave her options open – and now she decided to take a path that led towards the back of the house and seemed to slope upwards towards the hill. In this country of ramblers it was probably a right of way, and she wanted above all to get the feel of the place, and of Ellen's life.

She had not told Marek what she was going to do, for the simple reason that she did not know herself. To see if Ellen was happy? Nothing as simple as that – yet there was some question that she expected this visit to answer.

In a small meadow by the house she saw a flock of Angora goats; beautiful animals, their bells reminding her of the cowbells in the Bohemian hills and bringing a sudden stab of homesickness for Pettelsdorf. Down by the stream in the valley, children were paddling and calling to each other in Cockney accents.

Evacuees. Yes, there would be evacuees; Ellen would welcome them with open arms.

She had come to the kitchen garden; looking through the gate in the wall she saw tomatoes ripening in the greenhouses and well-kept vegetable beds. As she gazed, a land girl came by trundling a barrow, but Nora was not ready yet and turned away. What had been a lawn had been ploughed up and planted with potatoes. As she might have expected, Ellen was presiding over a house and grounds most excellently and patriotically kept, and in a countryside of unsurpassed loveliness, and to her own dismay she found herself experiencing a pang of disappointment. Yes, there was no other word for it, and she was shocked. Had she wanted to find that Ellen was unhappy, full of regrets . . . even ill-treated or misunderstood? Had she wanted to take the girl in her arms and comfort her and tell her that Marek still loved her, and marriages could be annulled?

Surely not, thought Nora, shocked at her own thoughts. Her father had been a clergyman; she had the strongest views on the sanctity of marriage.

She walked on, making a loop behind the house. She passed a flock of bantam hens, their feathers brilliant in the sunlight, a little copse of foxgloves and meadowsweet – and found herself by the edge of the orchard.

The plums had been picked, and the cherries, but the apples were ripening: red and gold and green. Between the trees two washing lines were strung and a girl was hanging out the washing. Household washing: tea towels and pillow cases, shirts . . . and nappies; a lot of nappies. She moved gracefully, bending down to the basket, shaking out the garment, fastening it to the line, and because she had known at once who it was, Nora stepped back into the shelter of the copse so that she could watch unseen.

Ellen looked well. She was sunburnt, her faded cotton dress and sandals were the acme of comfort and ease; she was absorbed completely in her task; Nora could sense her satisfaction in seeing the clean clothes, caught by the breeze, billowing gently. There were three baskets: Ellen had emptied two of them, but now she turned, for from the third had come a small whimpering sound and she dropped the shirt she was holding back into the basket and went over and very gently picked up the baby that had just woken and put it over her shoulder, and began to rub its back. It was the essence of love, of motherhood, that gesture: the baby's soft head nestling into Ellen's throat, her bent head as she spoke to it, its sudden pleasurable wriggle of response . . . Nora could feel it as if it was her own shoulder that the baby leant against – so had she held Milenka, and so Marek, and the thought that this child could have been Marek's child, flesh of her flesh, went through her, bringing an atavistic pang of loss.

But her question was answered and she could only give thanks that she had not made her presence known. A marriage could be annulled – an adult could take his chance and Kendrick must have known of the love

Ellen bore Marek. But not a child; a child could not be set aside.

Long after she had made her way back and sat in the train as it crawled southwards, Nora still saw this idyllic vision: the red apples, the blue sky, Ellen with her windblown curls stroking softly, rhythmically the back of the child that lay against her shoulder, and somewhere in the orchard, a blackbird singing.

A man leaving wartime London, perhaps for ever, will say goodbye to a number of places. To St Martin-in-the-Fields to hear the Blind Choir sing Evensong; to Joe's All Night Stall near Westminster Bridge where Wordsworth's famous view can be combined with the best jellied eels in London; to the grill room of the Cafe Royal . . .

And to the Lunchtime Concerts at the National Gallery, possibly the best loved institution to come out of the war. If the British had heroines during these gruelling years – the Queen, tottering in her high heels through the rubble to bring comfort to those bombed from their homes, the Red Cross nurses accompanying the soldiers to the front – there was no one they loved more than Dame Myra Hess with her frumpish clothes, her grey hair rolled in a hausfrau bun, her musicality and her smile.

For it was this indomitable woman who had coaxed the best musicians in the land to play in the emptied gallery for a pittance and bullied the authorities again and again to repair the bomb-damaged building, making these lunch hours into an oasis for all those who cared for music. Marek, who knew her and loved her, had come early, knowing that on the days that she herself played the piano, the queue stretched round Trafalgar Square. He had every reason to be grateful to her; a protégé of hers had played his violin sonata here, and he had heard the finest quartets in the country here on his leaves, but today, probably his last time here, he wanted to sit quietly as a member of the audience, for he knew that the sight of the tired housewives, the sailors and office workers listening rapt to her playing would be one of the memories he would take with him overseas.

He was in London for a few days, waiting to hear the time and place of his departure, which was always a secret till the last minute. He wore uniform and his stick was on the floor under his chair. He walked with a limp still but his leg was almost healed.

The dark-haired girl next to him had come in late and moved in deliberately beside the distinguished-looking Flight Lieutenant. She was a dedicated intellectual and tended to pick up men in places where their intelligence was guaranteed – art galleries, concerts, serious plays. Marek, well aware of her intentions, was disinclined to take the encounter further than the remarks they exchanged in the interval . . . and yet it was a long time since he had had a woman.

But Myra Hess was returning; she had begun to play the Mozart A Minor Sonata and Marek closed his eyes, savouring the directness and simplicity of her playing. Then in the middle of the slow movement, the sirens went.

Attempts by performers and audiences alike to carry on during air raids as though nothing had happened had long since been frustrated. Gallery curators appeared from all sides, shepherding the audience down into the basement shelter – and Marek, who had hoped to escape from the building, found himself leaning against a wall, the dark-haired girl still pinned to his side.

'Shall I get you a sandwich?' she asked. 'They seem to have opened the canteen.'

Marek looked up and found himself staring straight at Ellen.

She had come down the day before for her mother's fiftieth birthday, bringing butter and eggs from the farm and dahlias and chrysanthemums from the garden. Two of the windows of Gowan Terrace were boarded up, leaking sandbags surrounded the house, but the sisters saw nothing wrong; Holloway Prison had been far more uncomfortable

Ellen had provided the kind of instant party she was famous for, and assured her mother, as she invariably did, that she was blissfully happy and leading exactly the life she would have chosen.

Then on the following day she went to the National Gallery to visit her sandwich ladies. It was meant to be a purely social visit, after which it was Ellen's intention to go upstairs and hear the concert properly and not in the occasional snatches she had been permitted as a canteen worker when somebody opened a door.

But she was unlucky. The ladies who ran the canteen were members of the aristocracy and famous alike for the excellence of their sandwiches and the ferocity of their discipline. Ellen chanced to arrive on the day that the Honourable Mrs Framlington had been delayed by a time bomb on the District Line, and presently found herself behind the counter, slicing tomatoes and piling them on to wholemeal bread. But even the canteen ladies had to take shelter when the sirens went, moving across to the reinforced basement and setting up their trestle tables among the audience.

It was then that Ellen, finding herself opposite Marek, did something unexpected. She put down the plate of sandwiches, walked over to him and grasped his sleeve in a gesture in which desperation and possession were so strangely intermingled that the dark-haired girl vanished into the crowd. Only then, still grasping the cloth as though to let go would be to risk drowning, did she respond to his greeting, and speak his name.

An hour later they sat on a bench in St James's Park, looking not at each other but at the ducks, waddling complacently up and down in front of them. The meat ration was down to eight ounces a week but the British would have eaten each other rather than the wildfowl in their parks. Ellen did not look at Marek because what she had experienced when she saw him had frightened her so badly that she had to search out neutral things to look at: the withered grass, the empty deck chairs and in the distance the gold railings of Buckingham Palace. Marek looked away because he was summoning up his last ounce of strength for what was to come and sensed already that it might not be enough.

The things they would normally have done to compose themselves were denied to them. Since his leg was still stiff and painful, they could not walk the streets, or find, later, somewhere to dance where they could hold each other with perfect propriety. They could not, in the middle of the afternoon, have dinner and sit in intimacy at a shaded table.

'I must get back to Gowan Terrace,' said Ellen presently, her voice hardly audible. 'They'll be expecting me.'

'So you've said,' said Marek. 'Several times.' But when he turned he saw that her eyes were full of tears.

'We shall have tea,' decided Marek. 'Tea at the Dorchester. Tea is not threatening; we will drink it calmly.'

'Yes,' she said.

They found a taxi and it *was* calming to drink Lapsang Souchong and eat petits fours overlooking Hyde Park as though four years were not between them and there was no war. He had told her about Schwachek's death. Now he told her that he was going to Canada; that this was the last time they would meet, and at once the intimacy of the tea room, the soupy music vanished and Ellen found herself trembling, plunged into a sudden hell.

'I have to go,' she said pitifully.

He nodded and limped to the reception desk.

'Have you got one?' she asked when he returned.

'Got what?'

'A taxi.'

He shook his head. 'No. What I've got is a room for the night.'

She shrank back in her chair. 'You can't have done that. You can't.' She was unable to believe that he could be so cruel.

'You don't have to sleep with me. You don't have to remove a single stitch of clothing. But before I go we must talk properly. I must know if you're happy and if you can forgive me for what I did to us both.'

She was silent for long enough to make him very frightened. Then she lifted her head and said that sad thing that girls say when all is lost. She said: 'I haven't got a toothbrush.'

But for a long time no talking was done. There was a moment when she first lay in his arms, both of them perfectly still like children about to sleep, when she thought that maybe she could hold back what was to happen – when she thought that perhaps she did not have to know what was to be denied her for the rest of her life. Perhaps Marek also was afraid of the pain that knowledge would bring, for he too made himself very quiet as though to rest like this was enough to assuage his longing.

But of course it was not to be, and later, when it was over, she realised that it was as bad as she had feared – that it was worse . . . That to try and live without the love of this one man was going to destroy her – and yet that somehow it had to be done.

'All right,' said Marek. 'Now talk. I want to know everything about your life. Everything.'

Darkness had fallen; the sky was clear and full of stars; being able to see them, undazzled by the neon lights, had been one of the benisons of the war. Marek had gone to the window. Now he came back to bed, and kissed her chastely on the forehead to show her she could converse uninterrupted, and like a child she folded her hands and began.

'I have goats,' she said. 'Nearly twenty of them. Angoras. They're very beautiful animals. Kendrick doesn't like the milk – no one likes the milk – but we make cheese, and they don't smell at all, they're very –'

'Thank you,' said Marek. 'I am acquainted with goats.'

'Yes.' She admitted this, her head bent. 'And bantams; I have a flock of Silkies, they're beautiful birds, white feathers and black legs. Of course the eggs they lay aren't very large – you wouldn't expect it – but they have a very good flavour. And we won first prize in the Village Show for our onions, and –'

She babbled on, producing her strange agricultural

410

litany, and Marek, afraid he would be given the milk yield per Jersey cow, gently turned her head towards him. 'You were going to make Crowthorpe into a sanctuary,' he prompted, remembering Leon's words in the internment camp.

'Yes.' She was silent, remembering her vow. 'And I have. It's just that when you have a sanctuary you can't exactly choose. I mean, when people came and knocked at the door of a cathedral in the olden days, the priest couldn't say "I'll have you and you and the rest must go away"; he had to have everyone.' She paused, surveying in her mind the current population of Crowthorpe. 'The land girls are all right, and so are the evacuees that came first, the little Cockney ones, but then we had two more lots from Coventry and Birmingham and they hate each other and their children make Molotov cocktails in lemonade bottles and throw them out of the window, and the people I wanted like my mother and Sophie can't get away; Sophie's in Cambridge and Leon's joined the pioneers, so I'm left with people like Tamara –'

'Tamara! You're not serious? The Little Cabbage?'

She nodded. 'She's not there all the time but she doesn't get on with her mother and I don't mind her too much because she plays the gramophone with Kendrick and he tells her about Dostoevsky. Of course it would be nice if she brought her ration book and stopped stealing the flowers from the conservatory, but it's not easy for Kendrick, me being so busy . . . and none of it matters because it's wartime and compared to people all over the world –' She broke off and he saw her pass a finger along her lower eyelid, in the gesture he had seen her use at Hallendorf to stem the tears of a child.

'Ellen, I don't understand this,' he said, gathering her into his arms. 'I don't understand what you're saying. Nora said . . . that's why I didn't come . . . Not because of Kendrick – he can go to the devil – but because of you.'

'Nora,' said Ellen, bewildered. 'How does Nora know?'

'She came up to see you.' But he could not go on. Nora's description of Ellen in her fruit-filled orchard still had the power to sear him. 'She was like that girl in the Mille Fleurs tapestry,' she had said. 'The one with the unicorn. You must let her be, Marek. You must promise me to let her be.' Forcing himself, he tried to put into words what Nora had told him. 'That's why I didn't come; because of the child.'

Ellen stared at him; a searchlight fingering the sky passed over her face and he saw the huge, bewildered eyes.

'Oh God!'

The bleakness in her voice made him overcome his own misery. Somehow he must enter into what now seemed her reason for living.

'What is it, the baby? A boy or a girl?'

She lay back against the pillows. 'I don't know,' she said wearily. 'It might have been Tyrone or Errol or

Gary . . . there are so many of them and they're all named after film stars.'

He pulled her up, grasping her shoulders. 'Explain,' he said urgently. 'Don't play games with me.'

She tried to smile. 'I told you about sanctuaries; you can't choose. The billeting people asked me if I'd take unmarried mothers – the idea is they help with light housework in exchange for their keep and then when they've had their babies, after a month, they go away and put their babies in a crèche and find work. The first part works all right – they're nice enough girls; they've mostly been made pregnant by some soldier who's posted overseas. It's when they're supposed to go away that it's not so good.'

But he was scarcely listening. 'You mean you haven't got a child; you're not even expecting one?'

She gave a forlorn shake of the, head. 'Nor likely to,' she could have said, but did not, for it seemed important to protect Kendrick. The move from the master bedroom to the old nursery had not made much difference. Kendrick continued to stammer out his adoration and to beg her night after night not to leave him alone, but that was as far as it went. At first the knowledge that his talentless fumblings were unlikely to produce a child had devastated Ellen, but the endless infants produced by her unmarried mothers had calmed her distress. There would be plenty of children after the war in need of homes. She would adopt one then.

But Marek was transfigured. He would not have

taken her from her child, or deprived a man of his flesh and blood, but now there was no obstacle.

'Thank God,' he said. 'You're mine then' – and reached for her again.

The second time is better than the first; more certainty and already that touch of recognition that is one of the most precious elements of love. Marek now was a conqueror; the relief, the joy he felt transmitted in every gesture, and Ellen followed him movement for movement . . . remembering as if her life depended on it the feel of his skin, the muscles of his shoulder, the touch of his hair.

So that when morning came and she said she must go back, he did not believe it.

'You're mad. You're absolutely mad. Do you think you're making that poor devil happy with your pity? Surely he deserves better than that?'

But he was not frightened yet. He was still certain of victory.

'I promised,' she kept repeating. 'I promised I wouldn't leave him alone. Night after night, I promised. He's always been alone. His brothers bullied him and his mother despises him. The whole house is full of photos of Roland and William and not one of Kendrick –'

'For God's sake, Ellen, do you suppose I care about any of that? I remember him from school – he was always by a radiator. You can't help people like that.'

She shook her head. 'I promised,' she kept

repeating. 'He's so afraid; he follows me about all day and tells me how much he loves me. You can't take your happiness by trampling on other people.' And then, very quietly, 'What will happen to the world, Marek, if people don't keep their promises?'

She saw his jaw tighten and waited almost with relief for him to give way to one of his rages. A man who defenestrated Nazis and threw children into the lake would surely lose his temper and make it easier for her.

But at the last minute he understood, and held her very quietly and very closely, and that was almost more than she could bear.

'If you change your mind I'll be at the Czech Club in Bedford Place till I sail.'

But she only shook her head, and opened one of his hands and held the palm for a moment against her cheek, and then she said: 'It's time to go.'

The train was exactly what she needed; it was freezing cold, the toilet did not flush, someone had been sick in the corridor. In such a train one could let the tears come, and opposite her in the evil-smelling frowsty compartment, an old woman leant forward and touched her knee and said: 'Aye, there's always something to cry about these days.'

Kendrick would not be expecting her; she had intended to stay away three days. She left the taxi at the gates and walked to the house on foot; the night air might undo some of the ravages of her tears. For a moment she halted, tipping her head back at the moon just freeing itself from the scudding clouds.

'I'm trying to do what's right, Henny,' she said. 'I'm trying to be good. You said that mattered, so help me, please!'

But Henny had never been a nocturnal person; she flourished in sunlight among pats of yellow butter and golden buttercups, and there was no rift in the wild and stormy sky.

By the back door she put down her case and let herself in silently. Everything was dark; Kendrick would be in bed on the top floor.

She crept upstairs, careful not to wake the other occupants of the house. On the second-floor landing she paused. Surely that was music coming from the master bedroom which she and Kendrick had vacated – music both so unexpected and yet so familiar that she could not at first think what it was.

Puzzled, she made her way along the corridor; and silently she opened the door . . .

Marek's orders to report for embarkation at Liverpool came a day later. He spent his last afternoon in London alone in his room in the Czech Club, trying to overcome his wretchedness sufficiently to join his friends drinking down below – and watching through the window the procession of girls who were not Ellen which had haunted him since he left her. Girls with her way of walking, except that no one walked with her lightness and grace; girls whose burnished heads turned as they passed to show him a completely different face.

There was one crossing the garden square now, a girl with raindrops in her hair, carrying a suitcase . . .

Only she did not go past as the others had done; she did not show him a completely different face as she came closer. She made her way up the steps and when she saw him at the window she collapsed, helpless, against the rails.

'What is it, my darling?' he said, running down and gathering her in his arms. For God's sake, Ellen, what's happened?'

She turned her face to his; and he saw her tears.

'The Polovtsian dances is what's happened! Oh Marek, you won't believe it,' she gasped, and he saw that she was helpless with laughter. 'The Polovtsian dances and the Bessarabian Body Oil and the undulating – all of it. Only I can't tell you here, it's too indelicate.'

But even when they retreated to the privacy of his room, she was too convulsed to speak.

'I promised I wouldn't leave him *alone* – but he wasn't alone! You see, he couldn't . . . with me . . . because I was a goddess to him . . . But Tamara is not a goddess; she is an elemental, she is a dark Life Force . . .' Laughter overcame her once more. 'They tried to explain it to me . . . Oh, if you could have seen her growling at him and calling him *galubchick* – and then she pulled him on to the bed and the osprey fell on top of them!'

But later, when Marek had finished kissing her and showering her with instructions about what she had to do – go to Canada House, get permits, set the annulment in train – she grew suddenly silent and pensive and for a moment his heart contracted.

'What are you thinking, Ellen? Tell me, for God's sake.'

She turned to him and because she knew that what she was about to say might hurt him, she laid her hands in a gesture of reassurance against his chest.

'I was thinking,' she said very seriously, 'that I was really going to miss the goats.'

# EPILOGUE

'We'll do it again, won't we?' they'd promised each other after the pageant: Frau Becker and Jean-Pierre, the butcher and Freya and the old woman who said it would rain. 'This won't be the last time,' they'd said; Chomsky arm in arm with the greengrocer, the reporters photographing Lieselotte, and everywhere the happiness, the triumph.

And they did do it again, but many things had to happen first. The end of the war, defeat for Austria and years of occupation and hardship when the country was policed by the Allied Powers.

But in May 1955 the State Treaty was signed, giving Austria full independence once again, and soon afterwards the bombed opera house, sumptuously rebuilt, opened with a gala performance of *Fidelio*. For those who could not get tickets, the music was relayed by a public address system, and as they stood outside, many of them in tears, Brigitta Seefeld in the auditorium was obliging enough to cause the kind of scandal so necessary to this kind of occasion by flouncing out before curtain rise because she was expected to share a box with a rival she detested.

And in that year too the people of Hallendorf once more celebrated the name day of Aniella. Lieselotte, now a matron with children of her own, had coached her niece Steffi to play the saint but the greengrocer and the butcher still portrayed the wicked knights, though Chomsky, now a paterfamilias in Budapest and somewhat henpecked, was only allowed to be part of the audience.

There were heartbreaking absences: Bruno, who had been killed on the Russian front, and Jean-Pierre, betrayed and shot while working in the resistance. But Isaac was there with the young wife he had found when he came to give a concert in liberated Belsen – a cellist who had survived by playing in the camp orchestra and who even now could scarcely bear to let him out of her sight. Bennet and Margaret were there, their obvious contentment in each other's company a joy to behold, and Sophie and Leon, returned from their kibbutz in Israel. Leon's attack of Jewishness had not lasted long: it was Sophie who had enjoyed the companionship and friendliness of communal life. They were back in London now, and married, and planning to join Ursula in Wounded Knee to make a film about her Indians.

Even more people came than had come the first time, and when it was over – when Steffi had soared up to her apotheosis and Marek had once again made it clear to the agents and impresarios who had flocked to attend that his music was a gift to the people of

Hallendorf, and would remain so – there was the kind of joy in the village that they had forgotten in those grim years of war.

'And it's because of you,' they said, surrounding Marek and Ellen and their nine-year-old son, Lucas. 'We know how busy and important you are,' they said to Marek, 'but you came all the way from Canada to help us.'

It was not till the next morning that Ellen could slip away with Lieselotte and row across the lake. The castle had been a convalescent home during the war and now stood empty once again. As they tied the boat to the jetty and made their way up the steps, Ellen's memories of her first day were as vivid as if it were yesterday. The scent of verbena and jasmine, the sight of the skimming swallows, all were as she had remembered them. Here was the patch of reeds from which the dripping Chomsky had risen, here was the door from which Sophie, the first of the 'wild' children, had come running towards her – and here was the patch of grass which the sunbathing Tamara had flattened, ruining poor Langley's frit fly experiment. But thoughts of the Little Cabbage, who had seen off Patricia Frobisher (the camel notwithstanding) within a month of her return from Kenya, now brought nothing but amusement.

'Here he is,' said Lieselotte, pointing to a wooden cross beneath the cypress tree. 'He died in our house but the children thought he'd like to be buried in the castle.'

Ellen bent down to read the inscription, carefully painted in gothic script by Lieselotte's eldest daughter.

HERE LIES ACHILLES
A TORTOISE WHO LIVED LONG AND WELL
R.I.P.

Oh God, how right I was, she thought; how unbelievably and absolutely right. As soon as I saw what he did for the tortoise I knew that he would help me – and she felt such gratitude and joy that she leant for a moment against the sun-warmed balustrade and closed her eyes.

But it was not to see a grave that Lieselotte had brought her friend. She forged ahead, across the courtyard with the well and the catalpa tree.

'Oh, I hope they're there,' she said. Then she nodded with relief and stepped aside to let Ellen see.

And there indeed they were – the strange medieval birds standing sentinel on the monstrously overbuilt nest they had made on Marek's wheel.

'They came the very week we decided to do the pageant again! You said they blessed a place, didn't you? I think things are going to be good for us once more.'

'I know they are,' said Ellen quietly.

As she stood looking up at the birds, so outré yet so universally loved, she heard footsteps and turned to find Marek, his hand on the shoulder of their son, coming over the cobbles towards them.

'Well, you did it,' said Marek as Lieselotte tactfully melted away.

She shook her head. 'It was your wheel.'

'But your vision.'

They stood with the boy between them to pay their respects to the birds, which, for a while at least, would have to be the sole keepers of the castle. Perhaps they're your storks, Ellen wanted to say, perhaps they're the ones from Pettelsdorf, but did not. The peace and freedom which the Czechs had so richly earned had been theirs for only three years before the communists, under Moscow's direction, had once again turned the country into a police state. Pettelsdorf had been confiscated as being the property of a capitalist oppressor; Marek had not been back since the war. He had tried to explain to his son that there had been a demesne, now lost, which should have been his, but Lucas had not been interested.

'I didn't think anyone owned trees,' he said, looking at the miles of virgin forest behind their house.

Now – though continuing to gaze respectfully at the storks – he said: 'Do you think we could go home soon?'

Ellen and Marek exchanged glances. Both of them had been so lost in the past that they were for a moment at a loss. Did he mean home to the little house which Steiner, dying peacefully a year after the war, had left to them and where they were staying? Or had he picked up their thoughts about Pettelsdorf . . . or was he referring to Gowan Terrace, where he had been ludicrously spoilt on the way over?

But of course he meant none of those things. He

meant home to the light-filled house on Vancouver Island with its big windows overlooking the Pacific. He meant home to his Newfoundland puppy and his sailing dinghy and his young sister, who was frequently a nuisance but had many uses. For to Lucas, the castle and its storks, the lost domain in the Forest of Bohemia, the palace they had shown him in London where lived a king and queen, belonged to the stuff of fairy tales. He liked the stories but what he yearned for now was his real and proper life.

'Maybe even tomorrow?' he suggested, his head on one side.

Marek and Ellen looked at each other. Then: 'I don't see why not,' said Marek, and the three of them linked hands and went to find the boat.

Read the opening of
*The Morning Gift*, a sweeping story of love,
independence and belonging

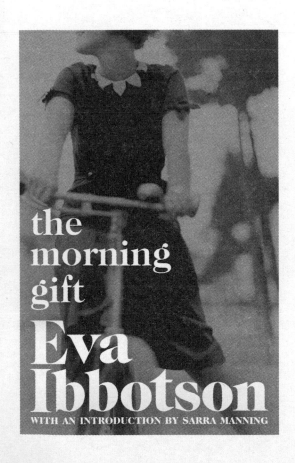

the
morning
gift
Eva
Ibbotson
WITH AN INTRODUCTION BY SARRA MANNING

# 1

On the day that Hitler marched into Vienna, Professor
Somerville was leading his not noticeably grateful expedition down a defile so narrow that overshadowing
precipices blocked out all but a strip of the clear blue
sky of Central Asia.

'You can't possibly get the animals down this way,'
a Belgian geologist he had been compelled to take along
had complained.

But Quin had just said vaguely that he thought it
might be all right, by which he meant that if everyone
nearly killed themselves and did exactly what he told
them, there was a chance – and now, sure enough, the
chasm widened, they passed the first trees growing
wherever roots could take hold, and made their way
through forests of pine and cedar to reach, at last, the
bottom of the valley.

'We'll camp here,' said Quin, pointing to a place
where the untroubled river, idling past, dragged at the

overhanging willows, and drifts of orchids and asphodels studded the grass.

Later, when the mules were grazing and the smoke from the fire curled upwards in the still air, he leant back against a tree and took out the battered pipe which many women had tried to replace. He was thirty years old now, lines were etched into the crumpled-looking forehead and the sides of the mouth, and the dark eyes could look hard, but at this moment he was entirely happy. For he had been right. In spite of the gloomy prognostications of the Belgian whose spectacles had been stepped on by a yak; in spite of the assurances of his porters that it was impossible to reach the remoter valleys of the Siwalik Range in the spring, he had found as rich a collection of Miocene fossils as anyone could hope for. Wrapped now in woodwool and canvas, more valuable than any golden treasure from a tomb, was the unmistakable evidence of *Ramapithecus*, one of the earliest ancestors of man.

There were three weeks of travelling still along the river valley before they could load their specimens onto lorries for the drive down to Simla, but the problems now would be social: the drinking of terrible tea with the villagers, bedbugs, hospitality . . .

A lammergeier hung like a nail in the sky. The bells of browsing cattle came from a distant meadow, and the wail of a flute.

Quin closed his eyes.

News of the outside world when it came at last was brought by an Indian army officer in the rest house above Simla and was delivered in the order of importance. Oxford had won the Boat Race, an outsider named Battleship had romped home at Aintree.

'Oh, and Hitler's annexed Austria. Marched into Vienna without a shot being fired.'

'Will you still go?' asked Milner, his research assistant and a trusted friend.

'I don't know.'

'I suppose it's a terrific honour. I mean, they don't give away degrees in a place like that.'

Quin shrugged. It was not the first honorary degree he had been awarded. Persuaded three years ago to take up a professorship in London, he still managed to pursue his investigations in the more exotic corners of the world, and he had been lucky with his finds.

'Berger arranged it. He's Dean of the Science Faculty now. If it wasn't for him I doubt if I'd go; I've no desire to go anywhere near the Nazis. But I owe him a lot and his family were very good to me. I stayed with them one summer.'

He smiled, remembering the excitable, affectionate Bergers, the massive meals in the Viennese apartment, and the wooden house on the Grundlsee. There'd been an accident-prone anthropologist whose monograph on the Mi-Mi had fallen out of a rowing boat, and a pig-tailed little girl with a biblical name he couldn't now recall. Rachel . . .? Hannah . . .?

'I'll go,' he decided. 'If I jump ship at Izmir I can connect with the Orient Express. It won't delay me more than a couple of days. I know I can trust you to see the stuff through the customs, but if there's any trouble I'll sort it out when I come.'

The pigeons were still there, wheeling as if to music in this absurdly music-minded city; the cobbles, the spire of St Stephan's glimpsed continually from the narrow streets as his taxi took him from the station. The smell of vanilla too, as he pulled down the windows, and the lilacs and laburnums in the park.

But the swastika banners now hung from the windows, relics of the city's welcome to the Führer, groups of soldiers with the insignia of the SS stood together on street corners – and when the taxi turned into a narrow lane, he saw the hideous daubings on the doors of Jewish shops, the broken windows.

In Sacher's Hotel he found that his booking had been honoured. The welcome was friendly, Kaiser Franz Joseph in his mutton chop whiskers still hung in the foyer, not yet replaced by the Führer's banal face. But in the bar three German officers with their peroxided girlfriends were talking loudly in Berlin accents. Even if there had been time to have a drink, Quin would not have joined them. In fact there was no time at all for the unthinkable had happened and the fabled Orient Express had developed engine trouble. Changing quickly into a dark suit, he hurried to the university. Berger's secretary had written to him before he left England, explaining that robes would be hired for him, and all degree ceremonies were much the same. It was only necessary to follow the person in front in the manner of penguins.

All the same, it was even later than he had realized. Groups of men in scarlet and gold, in black and purple, with hoods bound in ermine or tasselled caps, stood on the steps; streams of proud relatives in their best clothes moved through the imposing doors.

'Ah, Professor Somerville, you are expected, everything is ready.' The Registrar's secretary greeted him with relief. 'I'll take you straight to the robing room. The Dean was hoping to welcome you before the ceremony, but he's already in the hall so he'll meet you at the reception.'

'I'm looking forward to seeing him.'

Quin's gown of scarlet silk, lined with palatine purple, was laid out on a table beside a card bearing his name. The velvet hat was too big, but he pushed it onto the back of his head and went out to join the other candidates waiting in the anteroom.

The organist launched into a Bach passacaglia, and between a fat lady professor from the Argentine and what seemed to be the oldest entomologist in the world, Quin marched down the aisle of the Great Hall towards the Chancellor's throne.

As he'd expected in this city, where even the cab horses were caparisoned, the ceremony proceeded with the maximum of pomp. Men rose, doffed their caps, bowed to each other, sat down again. The organ pealed. Long-dead alumni in golden frames stared down from the wall.

Seated to the right of the dais, Quin, looking for Berger in the row of academics opposite, was impeded by the hat of the lady professor from the Argentine who seemed to be wearing an outsize academic soup tureen.

One by one, the graduates to be honoured were called out to have their achievements proclaimed in Latin, to be hit on the shoulder by a silver sausage containing the charter bestowed on the university by the Emperor Maximilian, and receive a parchment scroll. Quin, helping the entomologist from his chair, wondered whether the old gentleman would survive being hit by anything at all, but he did. The fat lady professor went next. His view now unimpeded, Quin searched the gaudily robed row of senior university members but could see no sign of Berger. It was eight years since they had met, but surely he would recognize that wise, dark face?

His turn now.

'It has been decided to confer the degree of Doctor of Science, Honoris Causa on Quinton Alexander St John Somerville. The public orator will now introduce Professor Somerville to you.'

Quin rose and went to stand facing the Chancellor, one of whose weak blue eyes was partly obscured by the golden tassel hanging from his cap. While the fulsome platitudes in praise of his achievements rolled out, Quin grew increasingly uneasy – and suddenly what had seemed to be an archaic but not undignified attempt to maintain the traditions of the past, became a travesty, an absurd charade mouthed by puppets.

The oration ceased, leaving him the youngest professor in the University of Thameside, Fellow of the Royal Society, Gold Medallist of the Geographical Association and the Sherlock Holmes of pre-history whose inspired investigations had unlocked the secrets of the past.

Quin scowled and climbed the dais. The Chancellor raised his sausage – and recoiled.

'The chap looked as though he wanted to kill me,' he complained afterwards.

Quin mastered himself, took the scroll, returned to his place.

And now at last it was over and he could ask the question that had haunted him throughout the tedious ceremony.

'Where is Professor Berger?'

He had spoken to the Registrar whose pale eyes slid away from him.

'Professor Berger is no longer with us. But the new Dean, Professor Schlesinger, is waiting to greet you.'

'I, however, am not waiting to greet him. Where is Professor Berger? Please answer my question.'

The Registrar shuffled his feet. 'He has been relieved of his post.'

'Why?'

'The Nuremberg Laws were implemented immediately after the Anschluss. Nobody who is not racially pure can hold high office.' He took a step backwards. 'It's not my fault, I'm only –'

'Where is Berger? Is he still in Vienna?'

The Registrar shook his head. 'I don't know. Many Jews have been trying to emigrate.'

'Find me his last address.'

'Yes, Professor, certainly, after the reception.'

'No, not after the reception,' said Quin. '*Now.*'

He remembered the street but not, at first, the house. Then a particularly well-nourished pair of caryatids sent him through an archway and into the courtyard. The concierge was not in her box; no one impeded him as he made his way up the wide marble staircase to the first floor.

Professor Berger's brass plate was still screwed onto the door, but the door itself, surprisingly, was ajar. He pushed it open. Here in the old days he had been met by a maid in a black apron, but there was no one there. The Professor's umbrella and walking sticks were still in the stand, his hat hung on its hook. Making his way down the passage with its thick Turkey carpet, he knocked on the door of the study and opened it. He had spent many hours here working on the symposium, awed by Berger's scholarship and the generosity with which he shared his ideas. The Professor's books lined the wall, the Remington, under its black cover, stood on the desk.

Yet the silence was eerie. He thought of the *Mary Celeste*, the boat found abandoned in mid-ocean with the cups still on the table, the uneaten food. A double door led from the study into the dining room with its massive table and tall leather-backed chairs. The Meissen plates were still on the dresser; a cup the Professor had won for fencing stood on the sideboard. Increasingly puzzled, he moved on into the drawing room. The paintings of alpine landscapes hung undisturbed on the walls; the Professor's war medals lay in their cases under glass. A palm tree in a brass pot had been watered – yet he had never sensed such desolation, such emptiness.

No, not emptiness after all. In a distant room some-one was playing the piano. Hardly playing, though, for one phrase was repeated again and again: an incongru-ous, chirruping phrase like the song of a bird.

He was in the rooms facing the courtyard now, open-ing more doors. And now a last door, and the source of the sound. A girl, her head cradled in the curve of her arm as it lay on the piano, the other hand touching the keys. In the moment before she noticed him, he saw how weary she was, how bereft of hope. Then she lifted her head and as she looked at him he remembered, suddenly, her name.

'You must be Professor Berger's daughter. You must be Ruth.'

# ABOUT THE AUTHOR

**Eva Ibbotson** was born in Vienna in 1925 and fled to England with her family when the Nazis came to power. She became a writer while bringing up her four children in Newcastle. Her bestselling novels have been published and loved by readers around the world.

In 2001, her novel *Journey to the River Sea* won the Nestlé Gold Award and was shortlisted for the Carnegie Medal, the Whitbread Children's Book of the Year (now the Costa Children's Book Award) and the *Guardian* Children's Fiction Prize.

Her novels for adults, all rich historical romances, convey her deep love of the arts, the Austrian countryside, and the importance of belonging.

Eva passed away peacefully in October 2010 at the age of eighty-five.